LOVE'S WAKING DREAM

Celia finally found him asleep on a beach near the crater of Diamond Head, a jewel-like span of sand protected on either side by outcroppings of lava rock that gave it privacy.

How beautiful Roman was, she thought with indrawn breath. How strong he looked, with his muscled arms and wide chest that tapered to a flat waist. His long thighs revealed the lithe, total maleness that drew her eyes irresistibly.

"Ah, God . . ." The sudden, drowsy exclamation startled her. Then, like a god coming to life, Roman sat up, his hands reaching for her, grasping hold of her, pulling her into his arms . . . into his overwhelming power. . . .

ENCHANTED NIGHTS

Passionate Scarlet Ribbons Romances from SIGNET

(0451)

- [ ] ENCHANTED NIGHTS by Julia Grice. (128974—$2.95)*
- [ ] DRAGON FLOWER by Alyssa Welks. (128044—$2.95)*
- [ ] PASSIONATE EXILE by Helene Thornton. (127560—$2.95)*
- [ ] CHANDRA by Catherine Coulter. (126726—$2.95)*
- [ ] RAGE TO LOVE by Maggie Osborne. (126033—$2.95)*
- [ ] SEASON OF DESIRE by Julia Grice. (125495—$2.95)*
- [ ] KIMBERLEY FLAME by Julia Grice. (124375—$3.50)*
- [ ] PASSION'S REBEL by Kay Cameron. (125037—$2.95)*
- [ ] THE DEVIL'S HEART by Kathleen Maxwell. (124723—$2.95)*

*Price is slightly higher in Canada

ENCHANTED NIGHTS

JULIA GRICE

A SIGNET BOOK

NEW AMERICAN LIBRARY

NAL BOOKS ARE AVAILABLE AT QUANTITY DISCOUNTS WHEN USED
TO PROMOTE PRODUCTS OR SERVICES. FOR INFORMATION PLEASE
WRITE TO PREMIUM MARKETING DIVISION, NEW AMERICAN LIBRARY,
1633 BROADWAY, NEW YORK, NEW YORK 10019.

SIGNET TRADEMARK REG. U.S. PAT. OFF. AND FOREIGN COUNTRIES
REGISTERED TRADEMARK—MARCA REGISTRADA
HECHO EN CHICAGO, U.S.A.

SIGNET, SIGNET CLASSIC, MENTOR, PLUME, MERIDIAN and NAL BOOKS
are published by New American Library,
1633 Broadway, New York, New York 10019

First Printing, April, 1984

1 2 3 4 5 6 7 8 9

PRINTED IN THE UNITED STATES OF AMERICA

For all those I love,
for my friends new and old,
and for those who read
and treasured my books,
I thank you.

The days dawn in rose colour and die in gold, and through their long hours a sea of delicious blue shimmers beneath the sun, so soft, so blue, so dreamlike, an ocean worthy of its name, the enchanted region of perpetual calm, and an endless summer.

—Isabella L. Bird, after a
visit to the Sandwich Islands
in 1873

Author's Note

I lived on Maui for eight months, and grew to know many aspects of this intriguing island well. But in writing this book, I also owe a debt to the authors of many books who helped "old" Hawaii to come alive for me. *Grove Farm Plantation, the Biography of a Hawaiian Sugar Plantation,* by Bob Krauss with W. P. Alexander, is a lively and interesting account of a sugar plantation on Kauai. A fascinating contemporary traveler's account is Isabella L. Bird's book *Six Months in the Sandwich Islands.* For those who want a broader picture of Hawaii's history, I recommend W. Storrs Lee's book *The Islands*, a book that is not only informative but also witty and easy to read.

I would like to thank my agent, Al Zuckerman, for his generous help, and my fine editor, Hilary Ross, for her suggestions and encouragement. Also my close friends Margaret Duda, Elizabeth Buzzelli, and Carolyn Hall, for moral support, and the Detroit Women Writers, for *all* they have done.

Of course, all characters in this book are fictional, and come strictly from my imagination.

1

The wind had whipped up the waves into great, choppy swells that crashed and pounded against the barnacle-covered sides of the *Fair Wind*. Droplets of spray flew into Celia Griffin's face. She could hear the snaps and groans of stays.

She leaned against the ship's rail, staring upward at the great sweep of tropical night. The sky was as soft as black velvet, lit by a curved moon. She could see the Pleiades, the Belt of Orion, so many millions of stars that they merged together, forming glowing clouds. Never in Boston had there been so many stars.

And never had she imagined she'd be on a ship to the Sandwich Islands, which some called Hawaii. She was being punished, sent as far away as her family could think to banish her. . . .

Celia forced away the thought, looking down at the foaming silver lace that topped the waves. The passage had been rough, and most of the forty passengers were seasick, including Cousin Rebecca, who had been appointed as Celia's chaperon. Otherwise, garrulous Becky would have been by Celia's side, chattering ship's gossip and speculating on the other passengers.

It was a relief to be alone, Celia thought. Not to have to apply cool compresses to Rebecca's forehead, to read aloud to her cousin, or to fan her perspiring body. She didn't mind being of help, but still, passage across thousands of miles of open Pacific ought to be an adventure, not a project in nursing.

The sea wind buffeted her, snapping at the hem of her long cambric skirt. Celia shifted restlessly, wiping droplets of salt water from her upper lip. She wished it would storm. It would be exciting to be in the midst of a hurricane or to see the water spouts that she'd heard the crew talking about.

"Deep thoughts?" There was a movement in the shadows to Celia's left near the forecastle. She turned to see a man materialize out of the blackness, striding toward the rail with an easy, confident walk.

"I was just looking at the waves," she admitted. "And wishing it would storm."

"Ah, you'd wish discomfort upon us? Water washing through the skylights and into the dining salon, noise and confusion, and the harried stewards not bothering to bring us our meals?"

Celia peered into the darkness, wondering just which of the male passengers this could be. There was Mr. Parnell Forbes, a banker of about fifty. And Mr. Ivory, an elderly pastor going to live with a daughter in Honolulu. And dozens of other men, some young, some old, but all of them attentive to Celia, who was indisputably the prettiest woman of the eight aboard the *Fair Wind*.

"Roman Burnside," he introduced himself, stepping into the pale beam of moonlight that splashed down on the deck.

Some impulse made Celia pretend she didn't know who he was. "Were we introduced?"

Gray eyes met hers. "I'm the doctor, the man responsible for attending a shipful of seasick passengers, and thoroughly tired of it. How is it that you aren't ill, Miss Griffin? Do you have a constitution of cast iron, or do you possess some secret you could share with me?"

He grinned, revealing even white teeth, and then, not waiting for her answer, turned to look out at the night sea. Celia stole a look at him. The statement that *all* the men aboard ship were attentive had not been entirely correct. There was one who had barely noticed her, and she gazed at him now, seeing the large, almost massive physique, the wide shoulders and bold stance. -

"I don't have any secrets," she told him, dimpling.

His smile teased, playing her game. "Ah? You're a woman, aren't you? All women have secrets."

He had kept to himself for most of the voyage, appearing at the second sitting for dinner, which was sparsely populated because of the number of passengers indisposed. All the women had eyed him, for his dark good looks carried a hint of reserve and mystery. But he had showed no interest in any of them, not even Celia, whose table had been only a few feet away.

Now Celia took another look at her companion. Boldly she studied him. The sea wind ruffled his black hair back from a wide forehead. In the moonlight his profile was handsome and chiseled. His chin was strong, firm, beautifully carved, with a slight cleft that tantalized, that made her long to touch it with her fingertips.

She shook herself, feeling a little flutter inside. Oh, he *was* handsome. . . .

Beginning to enjoy herself, she gave him one of the brilliant, glowing smiles that Cousin Rebecca called "wanton." To her excitement, he smiled back. His smile reached his eyes and made them alive with interest—in her.

Celia felt a curious, glad thump of her heart. She'd seen that interested look many times before in the drawing rooms of Boston. Men responded to her. They always had; it was something she seemed to have been born with.

Now she drew herself taller and held her smile, knowing full well what he saw. The sea wind pushing the fabric of her long dress against her, molding the cloth to her thighs, her breasts.

Very full breasts, they were. There had never been the slightest need for Celia to sew ruffles in the front of her camisole, as her three older sisters had had to do. She owned what Cousin Rebecca called a "scandalous shape." By that Becky meant a figure that appealed to men. Although a woman in 1873 was supposed to be pretty, and could even be referred to as "a beauty," there was not supposed to be anything carnal about her looks.

Nor was she supposed to be quite so . . . vivid. Yes, that was the word. Celia had heard it dozens of times as she grew up, always spoken disapprovingly. Her mane of black hair was too thick, too full, too glossy. Her eyes were a rich, expressive brown, fringed with extravagantly thick lashes. But they were too flashing, Mama said, too full of spirit and mischief. Her skin, though, Mama approved of. It was translucent porcelain, milk-creamy, and could flush to an enchanting shade of pink.

Dozens of men had called her beautiful. Had paid her elaborate compliments. Had fought to sit near her, teased and flirted, sent flowers, toyed with the idea of fighting duels over her. One had even rejected a fiancée in a quarrel over her. All the attention had quite turned Celia's head, Mama insisted. She was an incorrigible flirt and ought to be punished for her behavior.

Well, she was being punished, wasn't she? The *Fair Wind* was punishment, and the crashing ocean, and the gorgeous display of stars. Celia smiled to herself, thinking what a joke life was sometimes.

"I amuse you?" Roman Burnside wanted to know.

The directness of his look made Celia redden. "I was just smiling . . . At fate, really. My family sent me off halfway around the world thinking that I would hate it. And I don't. I've loved every minute of this voyage, and I can't wait to see what Honolulu is like."

"Oh?" He was silent a moment, and she thought she saw a look of sadness cross his face. "Do you mean you didn't want to come?"

"No."

"Then why did you?"

"I . . . They made me." Blushing even brighter, she subsided into silence.

"I see. Well, I don't want to pry into your personal business, Miss Griffin, and anyway, that isn't the reason I approached you. Your cousin dropped her book on deck this morning, and I happened to find it. I hoped to see her at dinner to return it, but apparently the *mal de mer* kept her from her meal. So I am taking the liberty of returning it to you."

Disappointment crashed through her, surprising her with its intensity. So he hadn't sought her out for any particular reason, only to return a book.

"I'll give this book to Rebecca. And thank you for thinking of her," she said stiffly.

"You're welcome." He gave her a polite bow. Seldom had Celia been treated so coolly by a man, and it was disconcerting, even irritating.

"Are you always so *courteous?*"

His eyes gleamed at her. "Yes, I am, Miss Griffin. Did you wish me to be rude?"

"No! I . . . Oh, never mind!" The sea wind teased her skirts, blowing them into a froth of petticoats as, her back straight, salvaging her dignity, Celia marched toward the companionway.

She stepped down the dark ship's staircase, holding tight to the support rope that had been strung along the paneling. Four months ago, a disastrous family conference had changed her life. Mama and Papa, Celia's sisters and their husbands, everyone had had something to say. Words like "wanton" and "incorrigible" and "betrayer" had flown about the Griffin library like firecrackers.

Celia had been engaged twice, and had jilted both fiancés, one within hours of the wedding. There had been a flirtation with a handsome second cousin, ending when Celia and Bobby had been discovered on the back lawn near the day lilies, locked in passionate embrace. To Celia, it had been a moment's impulsive pleasure, and she'd meant to curb matters before they went too far.

But to the family, it was disgrace. One brother-in-law even questioned her virginity, an insult that Celia bore with a lift of her chin and a defiant flash of her eyes. She *was* a virgin. Accuse her as they would, she'd done nothing wrong.

But still the jiltings and the flirting, upsetting as these were, were not the real cause of her banishment. No, the articles in *Scribner's* were. All her life, Celia had loved to read, and she'd been the top student at Miss Tanny's Day School, avidly interested in everything they had to teach. Since the age of fifteen she had kept a journal, outlining her thoughts and conjectures about the world around her.

One day, she sent some edited pages of her journal to *Scribner's* magazine, to which her father subscribed. The essay was about the Griffin Wool Manufactory, which Hale Griffin owned, and several other wool companies. All had made money weaving fabric for Union Army uniforms. Each sent the effluvia from their waste pipes into a nearby millpond.

Writing under a male pseudonym, Celia accused the companies of profiting unduly from the war, and of contaminating the water near them. She wrote well, with sharp, biting wit, and her father stormed at the dinner table about the ''upstart'' who had dared to write such lies.

Two days later, Lydia Griffin, checking to see if the upstairs maid had done a good job of dusting, found the rough draft of Celia's essay.

Celia had ''betrayed'' her family. Not only had she shamed everyone by jilting, not one, but *two* fiancés, she had done the unthinkable, entering a male arena under a male name. Something had to be done about her.

So that was how she found herself with Rebecca, garrulous straitlaced Becky, on her way to the Sandwich Islands. Celia hadn't wanted a chaperon, had begged to go by herself. But of course Mama and Papa refused to listen. No Boston girl of good family traveled alone. Besides, when would such an opportunity ever present itself again? It was sheer luck. Rebecca Salsner, a childless widow, was traveling to the islands to marry a well-to-do minister with whom she had been in correspondence for two years. Celia could travel with her.

A Griffin aunt resided in Honolulu with her husband, running the Hawaii Nei school, a preparatory school for white boys. Both Aunt Hatteras and Uncle Jud were pillars of island society. Celia would teach in the school for a year or two. Then, after a suitable time, she would be married off.

In the long letter that she had given to Rebecca, Celia's mother had been specific on this point. The gentleman should be over forty, settled, established. He should have firm ideas on how he wished his wife to behave.

It is to be hoped that Celia's rebellious instincts can thus be curbed, Mama had written in her beautiful copperplate hand. *To that end I am enclosing a sizable bank draft to be put to her use. It will pay for her keep and provide a dowry when she marries. I am also sending a large trousseau for her, as I understand fashionable wear is in short supply in the islands. You will see to her marriage, won't you, dear Hatteras?*

The plan seemed tailor-made. Hard work to drive some sense into Celia, then a respectable marriage.

And the worst of it was: her family loved her. Celia knew that they did, she had been her father's favorite, her mother's baby, her sisters' pet. They all thought they were doing the best for her. In their minds it was unthinkable that a young woman should cause controversy or scandal. She had to be protected from herself. . . .

Celia entered the cabin, her face still pink from her encounter with Dr. Roman Burnside. Rebecca, who was lying on the lower bunk, looked up. She was thirty-one years old, plump and full-figured, with mousy brown hair. Ordinarily her complexion held a ruddy color, but repeated bouts of seasickness had left her sallow.

"What have you there in your hand, Celia?"

Celia looked down, startled. She had forgotten all about the novel.

"My book!" Rebecca reached out a hand to claim it. "Where on earth did you find it? I've been looking all night."

"I believe you left it on deck, Becky, this morning when you took your stroll."

"I suppose. Who turned it over to you?"

"Why, Dr. Roman Burnside." And Celia could not help the bright flush that rose to her face.

"Him?" Becky tossed the book onto the bunk. "It's amazing he deigned to notice anything, he's so standoffish, he wouldn't speak to a fish."

"But don't you think he's handsome?" Celia dared to say.

"Handsome is as handsome does. There is something about the cut of his mouth—he looks as if he could be cruel."

Celia lifted her chin. She went to her trunk and got out a long, frilly nightgown, elaborately woven with silk ribbons at the yoke and sleeves, part of her large trousseau. She pulled it over her head and began pulling off her garments from underneath, as she had been taught.

"I like him," some devil impulse made her say.

"What?"

"I said, I like him . . . or, rather, I find him intriguing. He looks as if he has been desperately unhappy, don't you think, Becky? As if he has been through some great sorrow.''

Rebecca sat up noisily in her bunk, sniffing with disapproval. "I see. Oh, I see, all right. You plan to have a flirtation with him, don't you, Celia? Right here on shipboard, underneath my very eyes!"

Celia struggled with the nightgown, feeling at a disadvantage. "I—"

"You *are* a flirt, you know. You are notorious for it. It's as if you tease men and toy with them, utterly unaware of what you do. Oh, I wish you were married, Celia, so we could talk!"

Celia did not know whether to be irritated or amused. "Aren't we talking now?"

"Not the way we ought. Celia, do you realize how dangerous your behavior is? You could end up bringing deep shame on yourself.''

Celia decided that she was irritated. "No, Becky," she remarked, "I don't think I will be shamed—not with you to guard me and put Mama's plans into action." She finished with the nightgown and reached out to douse the little oil lamp. Instantly darkness descended on them, thick and warm. "And now," she added crossly, "I think I'll try to sleep."

"No more tossing and turning," Rebecca warned. "That top bunk moves and sways with every motion of the ship—it makes me queasy just to hear it."

"Yes, Becky."

Celia climbed into her bunk and lay on top of the sheets, fidgeting in the dark.

"This is your own fault, you know, Celia," Rebecca remarked. "You brought it all on yourself. If you had just quietly gotten married, as your sisters did, you could have had a baby or two by now, and been peaceful and contented with your lot.''

Her *lot*. A horrid word, with its connotations of duty, and liking your fate, whatever was handed out to you. Celia lay staring into warm tropical blackness, listening to the noises of the ship.

The following day, Celia felt restless, like a caged lioness pacing the interior of a too-small cell. She walked endlessly

up and down the deck, wondering if she would like teaching
in a boys' schol. She felt sure that Aunt Hatteras (named after
Cape Hatteras by a seafaring father) would turn out to be a
strict old martinet. How could she not be, with a name like
that? Anyway, if Hatteras and Jud weren't severe and dull,
Mama would never have sent her to them.

Worse, what if Aunt Hatteras didn't even want her? Because of the slow passage of the mails by ship, there hadn't
been time to write a letter in advance. Celia would arrive on
her aunt's doorstep unannounced.

Her thoughts worried on, jabbing at her. A husband? She
could imagine some formidable gentleman with white hair, or
balding, probably a widower who had already gone through
two or more wives. . . . She shuddered at the very thought.
Maybe she would defy her aunt. Refuse to marry anyone at
all.

Some flying fish came flopping on deck, their scales gleaming in the hot sunlight, and a crewman chased after them.
Celia tried to absorb herself in this small shipboard event.
Soon, all too soon, the voyage would be over. Real life
would begin. . . .

Roman Burnside did not appear at the second sitting for
dinner. Captain Burns announced that he had been forced to
amputate the leg of a crewman injured in an accident. All the
passengers were abuzz with the news, speculating on how
such a trauma might feel. But Celia thought, instead, of
Roman. Could it be easy to inflict such pain? Had he waited
until the last possible moment, praying that he would still be
able to save the leg?

That night after dinner, Becky complained again of a queasy
stomach, and Celia bathed her cousin's forehead with a cool
cloth. Finally she was able to escape the stuffy cabin and go
on deck.

She breathed deeply of the salty, tangy air, deciding that
she would stop worrying. Who knew what the future would
hold? Honolulu, the Sandwich Islands . . . almost no one had
ever been to such an exotic place. Why, some of Celia's
friends thought that the natives were all cannibals.

It was going to be an adventure. She'd make it one.

Suddenly she spotted Roman Burnside standing at the rail,

in the exact place where she had seen him last night. She felt her heart give a little twist and realized that she'd come here in the hope of seeing him again.

But tonight he did not even glance in her direction. He stared out at the vista of rolling silver-capped surf and velvet sky, the moon a glowing half-coin. She saw that his hands were clenched tightly on the brass trim of the rail. His chiseled profile looked grim.

"How did the operation go?" she dared to ask him.

His response was almost a growl. "The patient lived, if that's what you mean."

"Did it hurt him much?"

Savagely Roman turned, and she saw that his eyes were gray, the color of the Pacific on a stormy morning.

"Why do you ask? Did you wish to enjoy his suffering vicariously, like the rest of the passengers? Well, for your information, I used ether and opium and the poor man is now resting comfortably. I also washed the wound with carbolic, and there is even a chance that infection will not set in, that my patient will live."

So it had been hard, Celia thought. But she forced herself to remain silent, turning to gaze, like Roman, at the star-dusted sky. Silence filled the air between them, and she became aware of the physical presence of him. How big he was, she thought, how male. His shoulders were massive, dwarfing her. And he was suffering. She felt it.

"I love the stars, the night sky," she ventured. "Don't you? They seem almost . . . magic."

For an instant she thought he was going to turn on his heel and walk away from her. But then he did not.

"Yes. Did you know that the ancient Polynesians used the stars to guide them? Using no more than the stars, wind patterns, ocean current, and patterns of bird flight, they managed to go in their canoes from Bora Bora and Tahiti to Hawaii. It was nothing short of a miracle."

They talked then of the stars, of the islands. Oahu, Maui, Kahoolawe, Molokai, Lanai, Kauai, Niihau . . . Roman's voice softened, and Celia sensed in his tone his great love for the islands, where, he told her, he had been born.

"Before Captain Cook discovered the Hawaiian islands, the

people were ruled by a system of *tabus* so strict that if a person broke one, he risked death. Women, especially, were under the power of the *tabus*. They couldn't eat at the same table with men, and there were many foods they couldn't touch, under pain of death.''

Celia was fascinated. This was exotic, far removed from prosaic Boston, with its tea parties and galas and embroidery parties. "What kind of foods?"

"Oh, pork, bananas, many kinds of fish. However, some women sneaked away and ate forbidden things, and many died for it."

Celia shivered at such rebellion. "Oh, that's terrible—to kill a woman for eating food!"

"Indeed it was, but the *tabus* are gone now. The zealous missionaries have converted the Hawaiians and brought them schooling. Things are civilized enough now, perhaps too much so."

They continued to talk of the islands, while Celia eyed Roman, wondering why he had that look of sadness. Surely it had been caused by more than just a patient, an amputation, which must be commonplace enough for doctors. Finally she gave him a long look from under her curved lashes, and another dazzling smile.

"You have a look of mystery, Roman, all the ladies agree. Tell me, why are you coming back to the islands?"

His expression grew suddenly cold. "Why do you ask? Idle curiosity?"

"No. That is, I wanted to know because—"

"Because you're a young, lovely, inquisitive little witch and think all men will respond to your wiles. Am I not right?"

The words stung, especially since they held an element of truth. Celia drew herself up. "I heard talk among the passengers. They say you are a widower, you have a medical practice on the island of Maui, that you—"

"Enough." He gave her a black look. "I don't want to discuss it."

She felt like a child being rebuked, and it wasn't fair—she didn't deserve it.

"Well, I'd like to discuss your *rudeness*," she snapped.

"I've never encountered anyone as curt and bitter as you are. I was merely trying to make polite conversation, and you've no cause to bite my head off. I'm sorry you had to amputate that poor man's leg. I'm sorry for . . . for whatever makes you as nasty as you are."

She turned, flouncing her skirts, and was about to head below, when he stopped her.

He spoke in a low voice. "I'm sorry, Miss Griffin, that I was rude. I am heading back to Maui, yes. I was married while I was in the United States. My wife was Hope Biddle, only nineteen, with eyes the deep blue of a summer pansy. We were as happy as any young couple ever could expect to be, but three months after our wedding, Hope was dead of miscarriage. Puerperal fever, childbed infection, killed her. Our unborn son died with her. I believe that I took out my pain on you—most inexcusable."

A wave of sympathy swept over Celia, and impulsively she reached out her hand to cover Roman's. His hand was large and very warm, the touch of his skin sending an electric tingle through her.

"How tragic!" she began. "I'm sorry to hear—"

But before she could finish, she was interrupted by the sound of the companionway door and Rebecca's strident voice. "Celia! Whatever are you doing on deck at this hour? I've been looking high and low for you." Celia's cousin marched on deck, a plump, officious figure in black taffeta.

"Why, I was merely talking to . . ."

But Roman had already turned, melting into the tropical darkness. Disappointed, Celia followed her cousin belowdecks.

"I'm shocked at you, Celia," Rebecca rebuked her when they reached their cabin. "What could you have been thinking of, strolling alone on deck with that man?"

"He isn't 'that man.' And I didn't know he was going to be there, I met him by accident." Celia was tired of being treated like a prisoner, her every footstep dogged by her vigilant chaperon. "I'm *glad* I encountered him, Becky, do you hear me? I'm not a girl anymore, I'm a woman, and as soon as I get to the Sandwich Islands, I'm going to make some decisions of my own."

Rebecca's mouth dropped open, then clamped shut again.

"In Honolulu you'll be under the strict control of your aunt and uncle. As for Dr. Roman Burnside, you're not to speak to him again for the remainder of the voyage. Is that clear? You're forbidden even to glance at him."

Rebellion flared in Celia like a brushfire. She leveled her eyes at her cousin. "I'm going to look at anyone I choose, Becky. And you can't stop me. No one can."

2

But the following day there was no opportunity for Celia to rebel, even if she wished to. The sea had roughened, and huge, rolling combers tossed the ship about as if it were a scrap of wood. Celia was stuck in their small cabin ministering to Rebecca's seasickness.

"Oh . . ." groaned Rebecca. She clung to the metal slop pail with which each cabin was equipped. Her hair was matted and tangled, her face perspiring. "Oh, I can't believe this. . . . Why am I always the only one who gets sick? And why, *why* did I consent to sail halfway around the world?"

Celia had fetched and carried all morning, cleaning up after her cousin and enduring her scolding during the periods when Rebecca felt more like herself.

"To get a husband, of course," she retorted.

Rebecca roused herself from her misery long enough to prop herself on one elbow and fix Celia with a sharp stare. "Are you mocking me?"

"Of course not, Becky."

"Well, you'd better not be. Every woman needs a husband —in our society she is a misfit without one. Everyone knows that."

"But to wed a man she doesn't even want? Or, like you, hasn't even met face-to-face, but only corresponded with?" Celia dared to say. "A marriage without love?"

"Oh, dear girl, love is only a dream. Something we read of in romantic novels but which has little to do with real life.

I certainly don't expect it. No, I have made my own plans very carefully. Mr. Fielding is a man of high rectitude and moral character, and a hard worker." Rebecca stirred, coughing. "But why must you torment me with such arguments now? My stomach is clenching so. Is there anything you can get for me?"

Celia looked at her cousin and decided that for all her crossness, Rebecca was indeed in need of medical help. Droplets of perspiration stood on her cousin's brow, and her skin seemed more sallow than an hour previously.

"Do you mean in the luggage, Becky?"

"No," Rebecca groaned. "I've tried all the remedies I brought with me. They only make me sicker. I'm afraid I'm going to have to ask you to consult Dr. Burnside. Perhaps he has something in his pharmacy." Then Becky recovered some of her old fire. "But *no* lingering, Celia. This is a medical call, *not* a personal one!"

Celia practically skipped on deck, feeling like a child let out of school for a holiday. The *Fair Wind,* as if in mockery of her name, labored under the heavy seas, her deck pitching up and down. Sprays of water struck her sides with explosive force, splashing on board. There were few passengers in sight, but Celia saw crewmen scurrying about the rigging. She heard deafening bangs, roars, and snaps as the vessel strained under the heavy weather.

It was glorious. Almost a storm, if not quite, disastrous to the systems of those prone to *mal de mer.* And it was Celia's opportunity to approach Roman Burnside again, legitimately.

But she did not find him on deck, and finally she managed to locate the steward, who told her Roman's cabin number.

"The passengers are all complaining, the doctor has been in constant demand, and we can barely serve meals. Further, the saloon has sprung a leak in the skylight," the man added.

But Celia didn't care about leaks. She hurried back down the companionway and made her way along the long, dark passage to cabin eight. Firmly she rapped on the door.

"Yes, yes?" Roman's voice was impatient.

"It's me, Celia Griffin. I wanted . . . that is, my cousin needs to consult you."

He pulled the door open. "Is she seasick again? There isn't anything I can do for her, Miss Griffin, nor can I help the other three dozen people who have all begged my help today. If she would climb on deck and remain there, rather than staying sequestered in her cabin, she'd feel less ill. A hot, smelly cabin is the worst thing for seasickness. And I've told her that before."

As the vessel gave a sudden toss, it flung Celia forward, and she caught herself on the framing of the door. Roman was so close to her that she could actually smell the starch used on his shirt and the fragrant odor of his shaving soap.

He loomed in the doorway, a handsome man in his early thirties wearing a fresh white shirt and silk cravat. His nearness rattled her. He was *so* good-looking. And she'd never seen eyes of that particular shade of gray, almost colorless, yet shot through with darker flecks. For the first time, too, she noticed how high his cheekbones were. They gave him a rugged, fierce look.

"But my cousin is miserable," she managed to say.

"All the passengers are. Except for you, and you seem as feisty as a pretty little kitten. Why is that, Miss Griffin?" His grin transformed his face. "But I suppose I can mix up something to serve as a placebo that will satisfy her." He turned. "Come on into the cabin and I'll think of something."

She followed him into the cabin, which was a single, smaller than the one she shared with Rebecca, and scrupulously neat. A metal sea trunk served as a table, and Roman went to it, lifting the lid. Inside she saw a large collection of bottles and vials and sacks of herbs, all meticulously labeled.

"What's a placebo?"

"Mostly black magic and abracadabra." He rummaged in the collection of medicaments. "Many patients tend to believe in the effectiveness of the medicine they're given, whether or not there's any basis in reality. They think it helps them, and who's to say whether or not they are wrong? Here." He pulled out a small vial and handed it to Celia. "Give your cousin some of this. It's an elixir I distilled myself. It is mostly alcohol and will probably put her to sleep. Since she won't go on deck, that's the next best thing for her."

Celia took the vial and stood holding it.

Roman closed the trunk lid and looked at her. "Well?" He said it impatiently. "Was there something more you wanted?"

"No. I . . . that is . . ."

"I'm very busy, Miss Griffin. I have dozens of seasick passengers, and an amputation patient. In fact, I was just on my way to visit him now."

"Oh." He was dismissing her, and suddenly she didn't feel ready to be dismissed. Last night they had talked for nearly an hour, and he'd apologized to her with a rough tenderness in his voice. She felt sure he would have said more if Rebecca hadn't interrupted them.

Now she gave him the long, level look with flashing eyes that had been wildly successful with men in Boston. "Do you think I'm pretty?"

He raised an eyebrow. "You know what you look like, Miss Griffin, I'm sure, better than anyone."

She pouted. "But what do *you* think of me? Do you think I'm attractive?"

"I think you're beautiful," he said quietly.

His eyes locked with hers. They scoured her, seeming to see every vestige of her; never had she felt so exposed to another. Quivers of feeling ran up and down her arms and legs, shivering into her groin. Celia had the wild feeling that she was calling up something powerful, something which—if it were allowed to get loose—could go out of control.

Then the ship pitched again, and Celia yielded to impulse and to the strange, quaking weakness in her knees.

She allowed herself to stumble forward. As if they were born to be there, her arms reached up and slid themselves around Roman's neck. Daringly she lifted her face to his.

It all happened in a split second. Roman's momentary hesitation, then his groan. Suddenly he pulled her to him and kissed her fiercely.

Celia's heart pounded in her throat like a wild animal, and her breath caught and threatened to stop. She'd been kissed before, of course. By Bostonian heirs to fortunes, by aspiring young senators and West Point cadets. But never had it been like this, so demanding, so *total*.

Roman's lips searched hers, forcing her lips apart, demanding everything from her. His sweet breath, his insistent tongue . . . His arms crushed her to him, bending her backward to meet his urgent passion. And passion it was, surging between them as powerfully as the waves that pounded at the ship.

Celia was the first to pull away. She was almost frightened, she had to come up for air, she was trembling all over. What had *happened*?

She took a step backward, breathing heavily. Had Roman felt it too, the sheer violent power of the feelings unleashed between the two of them?

"My God." Roman's eyes had darkened to slate, and a muscle flickered in his jawline. "What are you, a witch?"

"No. Of course not!"

He took her hand, pressed her fingers around the little vial of medication. She shivered like a filly under his touch. "Take this and give it to your cousin."

"But . . ."

He seemed to withdraw from her, his face closing. "Wasn't that your excuse for coming here? Apparently you've had great success with men in the past, Miss Griffin, and hoped to make me another conquest. A charming seduction in a ship's cabin, an amusement on a stormy day. Well, I'm sorry to disappoint you."

She couldn't believe he'd really said it, spoiling everything. Tears of shame and chagrin stung her eyes. "I wasn't trying to seduce you!" She glared at him, her heart slamming furiously. "If I wanted amusement, I'm sure any good book would be a lot better than *you*. As for our kiss, you participated in it too. And further . . ."

But his smoky eyes rested on her—was it anger she saw in them? Amusement? Derision? She could not finish what she had been going to say. Humiliated, her face flaming, Celia fled the cabin.

A day later, the rough weather was gone. The sea stretched out again before them, a deep, soft, ineffable blue that extended to the horizon. Sun glittered on the waves, radiating tropic heat.

As she had done before, Celia hung on the rail, a hat brim pulled over her forehead to protect her complexion from the worst of the glare. She watched for an occasional porpoise or flying fish, those sudden scraps of magic that came leaping over the waves when you least expected them.

But her heart wasn't in it. All she could think of was Roman Burnside.

True, she saw him every evening in the dining saloon. But

he was as standoffish as before, and several times left the meal early to attend to patients. He gave her polite, cool nods as if nothing at all had happened between them. As if she were just anyone, a stranger who happened to be sharing the same ship with him.

It was infuriating. He had kissed her! Not just casually, but with such force and passion that the memory still left her weak. And then he'd accused her of seduction, his eyes as cold as the Arctic. She went over and over the whole incident in her mind, trying to make sense of it. Surely he'd been attracted to her; she couldn't have imagined that.

One sultry afternoon, she was on an errand to fetch Rebecca's crochet work, which her cousin had left in the dining saloon. On her way out, she nearly crashed into Roman as he strode along the deck, his medical bag swinging from his hand. He looked preoccupied and in a hurry, his black hair tumbled across his forehead.

At the sight of him, Celia felt her heartbeat change to an erratic flutter. She stopped in her tracks, clutching the wool yarn to her breast. "Why . . . hello, Dr. Burnside."

"Hello!" He paused. "And where are you off to on this fine, humid day, Miss Griffin?"

"Oh, to fetch Becky's yarn." She held it up for his inspection. "She is making a bedcover for her new husband . . . that is, for herself and her husband—"

"A woolen comforter? For Hawaii?" He laughed. "I'm afraid your cousin has much to learn about the islands."

And so did she, his chuckle implied. Celia flushed, aware of his scrutiny, the eyes that seemed to see every detail of the fine pink silk she wore today, the tight lines of the bodice clinging to her full figure.

"Rebecca and *I*," she emphasized, "might not know much about the islands yet, but we'll learn."

His eyes glinted. "Undoubtedly. Although I think, Celia Griffin, that you already know a great deal. Perhaps entirely too much."

"What do you mean by that?"

He inclined his head in a slight bow. "I inquired about you from the captain, who, by the way, seems quite taken with your looks. I'm informed that you are quite a girl. You have been engaged to be married twice, and jilted each fiancé. Couldn't you find one to please you?''

Why must her face flush such a vivid red? Why did Roman Burnside have to gaze at her with such amused contempt, as if she were only a pretty, willful toy?

''No, I couldn't,'' she told him coldly, turning to go below. She swept away from him, holding her spine as straight as she could.

Two days later, the *Fair Wind* docked at Honolulu harbor. As they neared the island of Oahu, Celia saw mountain peaks cleft by deep chasms and ravines, painted in hues of green and smoky blue. Finally the coastline itself came into view, white beaches fringed by a long, feathery-white line of surf. Rearing above the surf line was the grand promontory of Diamond Head.

''Honolulu!'' Celia was giddy with excitement as she pointed.

''Yes, I suppose so.'' Rebecca sighed, pushing fretfully at the high neck of her black dress, which did not make any concessions to the tropical heat. All of the passengers were crowded along the rail, eagerly gawking at their destination. All except Roman Burnside. Celia had craned her neck, searching for Roman among them, but it seemed he was not interested in gazing at a tiny settlement built on the fringe of a volcanic island.

''It seems . . . small.'' Celia stared at the scraps of habitation visible over treetops: two church spires and a few gray roofs.

''But at least there are churches.''

Celia nodded, thinking that churches didn't seem very exciting. ''And natives, Becky! With brown skins and tattoos and—''

''I don't want to hear about that. Heathens. That's what I'll be living among! Even if they have converted to Christianity, they will still be savage at heart.'' Rebecca pressed her hands together nervously. The closer they had neared the Sandwich Islands, the quieter Celia's cousin had grown. She had begun taking out the dog-eared letters she had received from her fiancé, Bertrand Fielding, reading them over and over, as if to extract some hidden information from them.

But Celia was in no mood to listen to Rebecca's trepidations.

They were here, their long voyage over! Even the prospect of working hard in a boys' school, of marrying some unknown stern gentleman, did not seem quite so horrid today. It hadn't happened yet. Maybe it wouldn't. Anything could happen here.

She listened to the deep thunder of the surf as the ship neared the coral reef that guarded Honolulu harbor. The water was a deep indigo. There were canoes with outriggers, and brown-bodied men who dived into the waves, as agile as fish. Then they were inside the reef, in calm water. Crowds of vessels were moored in this safe area: the American ironclads *California* and *Benicia*, a British corvette, and dozens of smaller schooners. Among these ships threaded countless canoes filled with natives.

Celia leaned over the rail and waved joyfully to one canoe full of brown men, delighted when they waved back to her.

"Celia, you mustn't!" Rebecca roused out of her gloom to scold her.

But Celia kept on waving, enjoying every minute of their arrival. She was here, in the Sandwich Islands, and in a few hours she'd find out for herself if the natives were cannibals, and what tropical fruits tasted like. And no one, especially Rebecca, was going to spoil that pleasure for her.

By noon they were moored at the wharf, looking down from the deck at a crowd of two or three thousand people who had swarmed to the docks, apparently in a sightseeing mood. And the sightseers themselves were the sight, Celia realized with amusement.

Hundreds of natives streamed on board the *Fair Wind*, laughing and chattering in a language that sounded as soft as wind in the trees. Such handsome people, the Hawaiians were, Celia thought. The women wore bright, long garments. The men sported white trousers and Garibaldi shirts, or the briefest of loincloths, worn with utter ease. Everyone wore jaunty straw hats or bandanna handkerchiefs knotted around the neck, and all flaunted necklaces of flowers. Carmine, orange, white, lustrous purples, pinks, and lavender. And the scents! The entire ship smelled of perfume and of the coconut oil the Hawaiians rubbed on their skin.

An hour later, their luggage had finally been unloaded and piled in a huge stack on the wharf. Most of it belonged to

Celia, who had brought books and supplies for the school, plus a large trousseau carefully packed into steamer trunks. They had each paid a landing tax, the sum of two dollars for the support of the Queen's Hospital.

"You are going to have to wait here on the dock for me, Celia," Rebecca instructed crossly. "I want to go and book passage for Kauai." The sparsely populated island of Kauai was where Bertrand Fielding lived.

"But . . . *today*?" Celia was dismayed. Rebecca had been a scold and a burden, but she was familiar, someone from home, and they understood each other.

"I must investigate passage," her cousin declared. "I have talked to Captain Burns, and he says that steamers here can be quite irregular. I don't want to risk being forced to wait here in Honolulu for weeks. Mr. Fielding is expecting me as soon as possible."

"But couldn't you stop and enjoy Honolulu for a bit?" Celia gestured toward the colorful spectacle of the harbor— *lei*-draped natives milling about, dashing brown riders trailing streamers of flowers, and hundreds of tethered horses. "Look at all the fruit for sale! We've never tasted tropical fruit. And there's branch coral—"

"No." Rebecca bit her lip. "I can't, Celia, because . . . if I don't go to Kauai now, I might not want to go at all."

"But I thought you wanted to go. I thought . . ."

Rebecca's sallow face looked woebegone and frightened. "I've never met Bertrand Fielding, Celia. I have only a daguerreotype and some letters. And they don't say much."

Celia felt a spasm of pity. Why, she thought in surprise, Rebecca is being exiled too. Because she is plain and dumpy and barren and was not able to find a husband in Boston, she was forced to come here. And she is afraid.

The cousins clung together, forgetting the stacks of luggage and the swirling crowds around them.

"Becky . . . it will be all right, really it will. Mr. Fielding looks very nice in the picture you showed me. And I'm sure he'll make a fine husband."

Rebecca nodded, and straightened up again, smoothing the flounces of her black dress. She seemed to become her old self again. "Oh, I'm sure. But, Celia, I wanted to tell you

. . . marriage isn't really so bad. It's what a woman is reared to do. It's what life is *for*."

Celia drew back, her mood of affection and pity lessening. She remembered the family conference, the letter from Mama that Rebecca carried in her reticule, the reason for her own trip here. "I want love," she said firmly.

"Love! Oh, Celia . . ."

"I want it, and I mean to have it. And now, you go and talk to someone in the shipping office, Becky. I'll stay here and guard the luggage."

Rebecca sighed, wiping perspiration from her upper lip. A young girl on horseback galloped past them, narrowly missing the corner of a steamer trunk. "Very well. Are you sure you'll be all right while I'm gone?"

"Don't be silly. What can possibly happen to me on the wharf in front of hundreds of people? Besides, am I not going to live here?"

As soon as Rebecca hurried off, her black dress looking funereal among this throng of brightly colored garments, Celia began staring around, looking for Roman. Where was he? She'd spotted him on the deck, finally, as they'd been disembarking, and she had longed to talk to him then. But Rebecca had been gripping her arm firmly, and she had not had the chance.

It couldn't end like this—a few words on a ship's deck, the memory of a kiss, the wild beating of her heart whenever she thought about him. Celia's pride wouldn't let her just quietly slip away without making some sort of reply, confronting him again.

She paced back and forth, growing more and more anxious that she might miss Roman, that he might already have hired a porter and left for the Hawaiian Hotel. It was, they had been told, a brand-new hotel, the only one in town.

Should she desert the luggage and look for him?

An enormously fat brown woman was selling a bunch of yellow fruits, peeling off the skin of one to reveal a white meat. Were these the bananas that Roman had told her about, the forbidden delicacy women had died to taste? Defiantly Celia strode over to the seller and—with sign language and a coin—bought several of the bananas.

She peeled one and bit into the soft fruit. It tasted . . . yes, like delicate sweet pudding and apples, all mixed together. But to give her life for such a treat? She supposed it had just been the idea. . . .

Turning, she glimpsed a man in a light tropical worsted suit hurrying toward a carriage that had pulled up to the docks. A Hawaiian was slinging trunks and bags onto the roof and securing them with ropes.

"Roman!" Celia dropped the bananas and went running, her hem lifted so that she would not trip on the uneven planking of the wharf. Her hair flew out of its pins and some of it tumbled to her shoulders in a thick, heavy mass.

He had been discussing something with the driver, and now he turned, the sunlight glinting in his gray eyes. Eyes that focused on her with a warm, strong glow. He nodded to her politely. "What is it, Miss Griffin?"

She stopped, trying to smooth her hair, to recover her breath. "I . . . That is . . ."

His glance flicked away from her, as if they were two shipboard semistrangers encountering each other on the wharf before they parted, polite but distant. "I suppose you are off to your new life in Honolulu, Miss Griffin," he said.

She reddened. "Yes. The Hawaii Nei school. It is for young American and English boys and is said to be scholastically very fine."

"I've heard of it. Your aunt and uncle are extremely generous with their scholarships."

Silence fell between them, interrupted by cries in Hawaiian as a group of travelers greeted each other. Celia shifted her feet, feeling disheveled and hot. She'd made a fool of herself, racing up to talk to him like this. He had little other than polite interest in her.

"And what will you do?" she said into the awkwardness.

"I'll be in Honolulu for a few weeks, and then go back to Maui and my practice there." Roman shrugged as if this were of little importance. "And now I must finish loading this luggage and go to register at my hotel. I wish you the very best of luck here in the islands. I'm sure that the Hawaii Nei school has found a very capable instructress."

Again Celia flushed. He had said it so *finally*. As if he considered their association finished, as if . . . She was amazed at the sudden lump of pain that formed in her throat, nearly choking her. No other man had dismissed her this easily before.

Proudly she forced her lips into a brilliant smile, a smile that showed him she didn't care. "I'll enjoy my work, I'm sure. Now I'd better get back to my own luggage. There is so much of it. . . ."

She walked back to the stacks of steamer trunks, her stride swift but graceful. Crystal tears prickled her eyelids. She longed to wipe them away—or to smack Roman Burnside right across his wonderfully carved, handsome, standoffish face. Instead, she began looking around for a porter to load the luggage.

3

The sun was hot, the air clear and crystalline, shimmering with light. They rode through town in a carriage heaped high with Celia's trunks. There had been another delay while a perspiring porter separated the cousins' luggage, for Rebecca had booked passage on the *Kilauea*, and it was leaving later in the afternoon, on the tide.

"I had to," Rebecca insisted. "I simply can't linger in Honolulu until the next steamer decides to leave, or I'll lose my courage."

The carriage rattled through the marketplace. Celia glimpsed stalls piled with gourds, objects wrapped around with green leaves, heaps of crimson and opaline fish. There were containers of some purple, pasty-looking stuff. Turtles, sea urchins, seaweed, carcasses of red beef, live pigs and chickens. Everything was strange, and the tropical foliage was so lush and green that it hardly seemed real.

But although Celia was fascinated by the sights they passed—a Chinese shop, a tattooed South Sea islander, houses thatched with grass—a cold nervousness had overtaken her. She sat on the edge of the buggy seat, shivering in spite of the hot glare of the noon sun.

Rebecca planned to drop her off at her aunt's house as if she were a package. And Celia would be left alone on this island where things she couldn't even recognize were sold in the marketplace. She, who had lived in a house crowded with sisters, parents, servants, dogs. Who had never gone anywhere by herself, not even to school.

Rebecca launched into a list of instructions for Celia's behavior in the islands. "You are to work as hard as you can in the school, Celia. There is to be no giggling or lazing about, and *no* flirting with the boys. Follow every one of your aunt's orders implicitly."

"Yes, Becky."

"You're not to cast a look—not even a sidelong one—at a man to whom you've not been properly introduced. And you will wear proper attire at all times. That means a gown with long sleeves, a high neck, and a bonnet. Never leave your hat off, for if you do, you'll expose your skin to sun darkening and freckles, and you'll look quite as dark as any native."

"Of course," Celia murmured, hearing not one word of it. What if Aunt Hatteras scolded, or ridiculed, or insisted on scrupulous neatness? For that was one of Celia's failings. She tended to be untidy, to throw her clothing about her room, a fault that Mama had deplored.

"And there is the matter of your husband," Rebecca continued.

"My . . . ?" Celia jumped.

"You must defer to him in all things. Be mild-voiced and sweet-mannered, *submissive*, if you possibly can. And above all, Celia, curb your tendency to be unconventional. If you don't learn to control yourself, no man will ever want you."

With that warning, Rebecca closed her mouth. Both cousins subsided into silence. Celia felt more and more as if some exotic fish was leaping around inside her, thrashing at her rib cage with its fins. She wondered if she could ever learn to be submissive. She didn't think so.

The buggy rattled uphill over a dusty road composed of crushed coral, sand, and reddish dust. They passed a variety of houses. Some were on posts, some thatched with grass matting, others resembled New England homesteads with clapboard fronts and green-painted shutters. But whatever the style, all the homes were overrun with riots of climbing and blooming flowers. Jasmine, hibiscus, bougainvillea, passion flowers—these were blossoms that Celia had only read about. Now she was seeing them with her own eyes.

Finally they pulled up to a house made of blocks of cream-colored coral. It was festooned with bushes that flamed with red blossoms, while, on a wide veranda, hundreds of plants grew in tubs.

"Could *that* be Hatteras?" Rebecca asked dubiously, narrowing her eyes. "Or is she just a servant?"

Celia looked. In the yard, a tall old woman stood at the base of a palm tree, picking orange fruit into a basket. She wore no bonnet, and her salt-and-pepper hair was pulled into a loose bun at the nape of her neck, stray wisps glowing in the sun. Her scoop-necked white muslin dress exposed leathery brown skin. A necklace of polished dark seeds gleamed at her throat, giving her an exotic look.

"Hello . . . hello, there!" The woman dropped a fruit in the basket and waved vigorously at them.

Rebecca reached in her reticule to consult the letter from Celia's mother. "Well, this *is* the right address. Beretania Street . . ."

A moment later, they had descended from the carriage and Rebecca was explaining who they were.

The tall woman extended both hands to Celia. Her palms felt warm and callused. "I am your Aunt Hatteras. And you're Celia, the youngest of Lydia's girls." Aunt Hatteras held Celia back to inspect her with eyes that were deep blue and unexpectedly beautiful.

"I'm glad to meet you," Celia said nervously.

"And I, you. My, but you're a pretty one, with all those masses of jet-black hair and those flashing dark eyes."

Rebecca frowned, looking at Hatteras' own bonnetless head. "I apologize for our unexpected arrival, but this letter from her mother explains everything. I hope it is not an imposition, but the family thought . . . that is, we hoped . . ."

Hatteras turned. "You're leaving Celia with me, then?"

"Yes, if you will have her. She is intelligent, and she did serve as assistant to the headmistress at her day school. There are reasons—they are all outlined in this letter . . ."

For the first time, Rebecca faltered, while Celia felt a crimson blush creep up from the collar of her dress. Becky was making this sound shameful somehow.

Hatteras nodded, her deeply tanned face assuming an alert expression. She looked at Celia sharply, her eyes lingering at Celia's waistline. "Well, apparently she isn't pregnant."

"Oh, no! I have already investigated, and she is regularly enduring her monthly illness."

Red-faced, Celia stared downward at the ground, where a column of ants labored to carry a white scrap off into the grass. She swallowed hard, feeling sick with shame and apprehension. If her aunt didn't want her here, what would she do? Go to Kauai with Rebecca? She felt sure she would not be welcomed there either.

"Look up, girl. Look me in the eye."

Slowly Celia did as she was ordered. She gazed into the depths of blue eyes that looked as young as her own, although the face that owned them was well over sixty. She tried her best to meet that sharp scrutiny.

Finally Hatteras nodded again, as if well satisfied. She broke the eye contact and turned to Rebecca. "The letter explains everything to me?"

"Indeed. It is most explicit—"

"Knowing my sister, I'm sure it is. But first, you must be thirsty after your ride from the harbor. It's so dusty! The dust here comes from the volcanoes, which serve as bedrock for all of these islands. The trade winds blow it into all of our doors and windows."

Hatteras rang for a servant, then took them to the veranda, where woven grass mats were spread on the floor near rattan chairs covered in green chintz. A fragrant wind swept across the porch, rippling the crimson flowers of the bougainvillea.

Celia sipped her drink of mango juice, barely tasting its strange, rich sweetness. She waited tensely as Hatteras read the first page of the letter, then turned to the second. Mama had shown the letter to Celia before sealing it, and she was all too familiar with its contents.

My daughter is inclined to impulsiveness. She is bright and ought to inspire your pupils, but she needs to be well disciplined herself. I know, my dear Hatteras, that you have had much success dealing with the dusky savages of that far land, and nothing is too formidable for you. . . .

A wry smile curved Hatteras' mouth as she read on, about the hopes for marriage, the requirements for the husband.

"I see you are well provided for," she said finally, taking out the bank draft.

"Yes, ma'am."

"It is her keep and her dowry as well," Rebecca put in. She had tasted the mango drink, then set it down with an air of disgust. "And she's got a trousseau, too. Nightgowns, a beautiful satin wedding dress, petticoats, ball gowns, day dresses, enough to last ten years if she is careful. And yardage of flannel for a layette, when that becomes necessary."

Hatteras smiled. "Does my sister think these islands are the end of the world? We do have dressmakers and dry-goods stores here in Hololulu, a few evidences of civilization." She put down the letter and looked at Celia. "Tell me, Celia, what subjects at school interested you the most?"

"Oh, I liked everything," Celia began. "Mathematics, French, history. I love to read," she went on, growing more confident. "I brought two trunks of books to use in the school, and of course, my notebooks. I like to write. In fact, I had two essays published in—"

"That's enough," Rebecca interrupted hastily. "I'm sure your aunt doesn't wish to be bored."

"On the contrary, I'm fascinated." But for the first time, Celia saw the lines of worry that scored her aunt's sun-browned face. "However, I must admit that your arrival has taken me somewhat by surprise, Celia, and some of your mother's hopes must be thwarted."

Celia's heart sank. They were going to send her back. She sat as straight as she could, preparing herself for the blow.

"You see"—Hatteras' eyes grew sad—"my husband died three months ago of heart failure. It was the end of the Hawaii Nei school; I had to send the boys home for lack of funds. It had been losing money anyway; apparently we had given out too many scholarships. Our creditors called their notes and I was not able to continue operating after I had paid them."

Celia's mouth grew dry. If the school was closed, then she could not teach.

Hatteras leaned forward and clasped both of Celia's hands in her own warm ones. "But you needn't worry, dear, for you are welcome to stay here just as long as you wish. We have the same blood flowing in our veins, although yours is younger and hotter than my own. Besides . . ." Her blue eyes twinkled. "How could I turn away anyone who has been thoughtful enough to bring with her two steamer trunks full of

books? Have you anything on travel? Or gardening? New
reading material is very scarce here.''

Celia and Rebecca kissed each other good-bye, the brims
of their hats knocking together under the hot afternoon sun.

"Do write," Rebecca ordered. "Write to me every week,
without fail. I'm sure a steamer can be found to carry the
letters to Kauai, and of course we can plan visits once I have
settled into my new life.''

Rebecca was flushed bright red, and there was a hectic,
shiny look to her eyes. Celia felt sorry for her.

"I will," she promised.

"Oh, Celia!" Again Rebecca hugged her, this time clinging shamelessly. "I do hope . . . If only Mr. Fielding could
be handsome, or at least pleasant-looking. That picture he
sent me was so faded and stiff . . .''

"Don't worry, Becky, I'm sure he'll be wonderful.''

Finally Rebecca climbed back into the buggy in a flurry of
black faille skirts. The driver cracked his horsewhip and the
carriage rumbled off down Beretania Street, raising clouds of
reddish dust.

Celia watched it go, wondering what would happen to
her cousin now. Kauai was supposed to be incredibly wild
and rugged. Waialeale, the island's volcano, was said to be
the wettest place on earth, getting four hundred inches of
rainfall a year. There were jagged lava cliffs, waterfalls,
pounding surf . . . Try as she might, she could not imagine
Rebecca in such primitive surroundings.

"Come, my dear." Hatteras took Celia's arm. "Let's go
and sit on the veranda again. By the way, we call it a
lanai here in the islands. We'll have a papaya. One must
acquire a taste for them, but they are a very interesting fruit.''

Celia thought that the yellow-orange fruit, eaten like a
melon, tasted like flower blossoms, at once cloying and
sweet. They sat on the veranda while Hatteras talked of the
islands' lush green growth.

"All of the tropical fruits here, including this papaya, have
been imported. Before the Polynesians arrived, Hawaii was
quite bare and windswept. The Polynesians brought breadfruit and bananas and coconut palms. Captain Cook left
seeds, as did Captain Vancouver and countless others. Mis-

sionaries and travelers all brought something. Mango, plum, cactus, sugarcane, eucalyptus . . .''

From where they sat, there was a splendid view of the harbor stretched below. Bristling masts of sailing ships were silhouetted against a backdrop of blue ocean and bluer sky.

"It's so lovely," sighed Celia, finishing her papaya.

"Isn't it? I love to look outward. If one sails far enough over that sea, one reaches Papua, the islands of Japan, the East Indies . . . Ah, well, enough of dreaming. We must talk, Celia."

"Yes?" Again Celia's heart constricted.

"Oh, don't worry, I want you here, I'm delighted that you're to be my guest. But I must confess that the bank draft my sister sent is going to be a godsend. My funds were running precariously low. If you don't mind, I'll deduct an amount for your board, and save the rest for your dowry."

A dowry, as Celia knew, was the large sum of money that a bride brought to her marriage and put at the husband's disposal. It made her a more desirable match. She stared at the harbor, where outrigger canoes formed small, moving dots, and a three-masted bark inched along the horizon.

"Aunt Hatteras, if I am not to teach in your school, then what *am* I to do?"

"Do?" A smile split Hatteras' face. "Why, just keep me company for now. It's dull being alone, with nothing more to do than hoe my garden and harvest my papayas."

Immediately Celia was swept up into exploration of the green valleys of the Koolau and Waianae ranges, through which wound narrow bridle trails, the only road to most settlements. Hatteras provided her with a horse to ride, a sturdy chestnut mare of half-Arabian descent.

"Without horses, we would all perish of boredom here," Hatteras said. "They are a mania here, Celia, among the natives—no matter how underfed or doleful-looking, how knock-kneed or spavined. Horseflesh is a craze here, a passion."

Indeed, the streets were crowded with riders. Men, boys, old women weighing two and three hundred pounds. Beautiful, laughing brown-skinned girls who galloped at full tilt, their horses garlanded with *leis* of flowers. All used the Mexican saddle, with its high horn and immense wooden stirrups, jangling with silver or brass ornaments.

"The Hawaiians love the Mexican influence," Hatteras explained. "About forty years ago, some Mexican longhorn cattle were imported here by King Kamehameha II and released in the hills. A ten-year *tabu* was put on them, in order to allow them to propagate.

"It turned out to be a terrible mistake! They propagated, all right—by the thousands. Aggressive and vicious animals, they marauded in huge herds over the hills, ate crops, broke down stone fences, and terrorized the natives. Finally some Mexican *vaqueros* were imported to kill them. These cowboys captured the imagination of the Hawaiians. They adopted the horses, the colorful trappings, the bandannas. And now many Hawaiians are good cowboys, too. We call them *paniolos*."

Celia had brought several riding habits, each with a full split skirt and fitted jacket that hugged the curves of her bosom. She accompanied her aunt on an expedition to the Nuuanu Valley and the awe-inspiring *pali*, an eight hundred-foot precipice where Kamehameha the Conquerer had once routed the forces of the King of Oahu, driving hundreds of desperate warriors over the cliffs to their death.

"Tell me, Celia," her aunt asked as they were riding back from this trip. "What about those young men you jilted? Your mother was rather guarded about that point, saying only that she considers you rather . . . 'impetuous' was the word she used."

Celia gazed down at her saddle horn. She thought back to handsome Jack Bradleight, a shipping heir every mother in Boston had coveted for her marriageable daughters.

Celia met him at her coming-out party, and noticed him right away. He was tall, blond, good-looking, with the easy, arrogant confidence of the very rich. And he responded to her only too well, sweeping her up into a whirlwind courtship. But one night in the Griffin library, as they were decorously sipping tea, Jack suddenly reached for her and pulled her violently into his arms. His breathing hoarsened as his hands groped all over her, under her skirts, between her legs.

"Jack!" Celia had struggled to push him away.

"You little tease . . . give it to me, give me what you've been waving in front of me. Come on!"

Celia knew, of course, that she had flirted with Jack, perhaps teased him a bit. Didn't all girls behave thus, wasn't that part of a game a debutante played, in a ladylike way, of course? But this . . . Their struggle grew tenser, more violent. Accusing her of "teasing" him, Jack actually ripped the flounces of her petticoats, tearing away strips of lace in his efforts to get at the tenderest part of her body.

Celia was horrified. By threatening to scream, by fighting with all of her strength, she managed to fend off her fiancé. She fled to the safety of her bedroom. Jack had nearly raped her. Well, wasn't that the truth of it? And only a few yards away from her own family. What sort of husband would he make?

For several weeks she agonized over what to do. Finally, two days before the wedding, she sent Jack a careful note. She could not be his wife. She was dreadfully sorry and hoped he would understand.

But Jack Bradleight was furious, and talked angrily about what he called "Celia Griffin's treachery." Celia's mother was beside herself.

"How could you do such a thing, Celia? Have you no sense? You threw away a wonderful chance! Jack is going to be a millionaire when his father dies, and you could have been taken care of for life."

Celia flushed scarlet. What was she to say? "He was too forward," she managed at last.

"*Every* man is forward, Celia, it's part of their base nature. Surely you could have handled it if you'd tried. Now you've earned a reputation as a flirt and a vixen. All I hope is that some other man will still look at you."

For a while, gossip did fly. Celia whirled through the round of Boston parties, aware of the whispers that started as soon as she left the room. *That Griffin girl . . . a beauty, but fast . . . jilted Jack Bradleight. She is a coquette who'll come to no good. . . .*

Six months later, she met Bob Salton, whose patrician family had come over on the *Mayflower*.

"Bob is so rich he can buy and sell all of Beacon Hill," Lydia Griffin instructed her daughter. "I expect you to show some interest in him. After all, you *are* tarnished goods now, in a matter of speaking. You're very lucky he has been eyeing you.''

Reluctantly—for Bob was puffy-faced and inclined to plumpness—Celia did as she was told. She flashed her dimples at the rich, spoiled young man. She gave him long looks from under her lashes, and accepted his compliments.

She also accepted a diamond ring with an oval-cut stone the size of a grape.

"But it became so *dull*," she told Hatteras. "All he could talk about was money and investments and shipping and the horse races. I began to wonder what we would talk about at the breakfast table. And he . . . he perspired too heavily.''

"I see." Hatteras looked amused. "Well, I'm sure that's as good a reason for breaking an engagement as any. You are a wise girl, Celia Griffin.''

"Wise?"

"You're here, aren't you? And we are going to do better for you than that—much better.''

Days passed as Celia sank into the relaxed, gossipy, gregarious social life of Honolulu. There were soirees and "sings," riding parties and veranda parties. Women spent afternoons reading aloud to each other or making fern prints from plants picked in the mountains. Celia endured these afternoons restlessly, her thoughts more on Roman than on the fussy details of pressing the outline of a wild fern onto paper.

His kiss, the way he had held her . . . She couldn't get it out of her mind. She replayed it over and over again in her thoughts, each time growing physically weak at the memory. It was as if something had sprung alive between them, some powerful, irresistible chemistry. She'd never had feelings like this before—she hadn't even known they could exist.

She would awaken in the morning, to pull aside her mosquito netting and wonder if, at the Hawaiian Hotel, Roman was rising too. She fantasized him sending her a note inviting her to ride with him in a carriage or to stroll with him in some gloriously scented tropical garden.

Her nights, too, were filled with restless dreams in which his hands gripped her with hard, virile strength, and his belly arched into her own, pressing so close that she could feel the urgent mound of his manhood.

She wakened from such dreams trembling. Roman had awakened something in her that had, until now, lain dormant. A full, womanly sexuality, desires and longings that she hadn't known she possessed. But she certainly did possess them. They tormented her on these warm Hawaiian nights when she lay alone in her bed, her hands straying restlessly over her own soft skin.

Would Roman ever touch her rich, riped-curved breasts with their pink buds of nipples? Would he ever explore the taut lines of her waist and belly, feel the silken fur that grew between her thighs? Then she twisted away from such explorations with guilt. What was the matter with her? Was it the warm, sensuous, blossom-scented air that teased her desires into life?

"Oh, the tropics do things to people," Hatteras remarked when, on a picnic to the beach, Celia dared to broach this topic in an oblique manner. "It's the warmth of the sun, I think. It melts inhibitions."

Below them, off a magnificent rocky point, huge sprays of surf washed over ridged lava rocks.

Hatteras eyed Celia sharply, then reached into their picnic basket and pulled out a ripe mango and a knife. She began the messy but delectable task of slicing the juicy fruit and eating it. "Have you been troubled lately, Celia, by anything in particular?"

Or *anyone*, Celia amended in her mind, flushing scarlet. "No," she lied, quickly changing the subject to travel, a topic on which her aunt could—and did—discourse for hours.

"I'd like to go around the world," Hatteras confided, Celia's ruse succeeding. "These islands are beautiful, of course, but they are only a small part of the world. The Taj Mahal, the seven ancient wonders of the world . . . I'm only sixty-six, and still healthy as a horse. In fact, a lot healthier than some Hawaiian horses I've observed recently," she observed wryly. "And I intend to go."

"But how?" Celia thought of the strict economies her aunt had to use around the house, in order to survive as a widow.

Mango juice dripped indelicately down Hatteras' fingers, and she had to talk with her mouth full. "Why, I'll earn my passage, my girl! I intend to advertise in the San Francisco and Sacramento newspapers as a companion for a wealthy young lady whose parents wish to send her on a Grand Tour and need a suitable escort for her. I conceived the idea today as we clambered among the rocks.''

"Oh!'' Celia sank back on the picnic blanket, unable to repress a wild, joyous laugh.

"Share the joke with me, Celia.''

"Why, if my mama could see me now, sitting here with you, eating fruit with our fingers, talking about carnal impulses and traveling around the world . . . if they knew what *you* are really like . . .''

Her aunt nodded. "They never did know, Celia, for when I was a young girl I was forced to behave circumspectly, as was the custom. Old age is a wonderful thing. It allows one all sorts of freedom.''

She whisked a stub of pencil and a sheet of paper from her saddlebag and began to write. "And now, the advertisement. What do you think of this? 'Able and educated governess-companion available to accompany young ladies on world tour or travels to far ports.''

It was delicious. It was ironic revenge on Mama and the rest of the family, who'd thought they were sending Celia into stern servitude. Celia loved every minute of it.

4

The trade wind ruffled the flowers on the veranda, bringing with it island sounds: the chatter of birds, the cries of dockworkers as they unloaded a newly arrived vessel. The morning air always carried sound for long distances, Celia had learned.

Celia and Hatteras lingered at breakfast, picking at the remains of muffins spread with guava preserves, and bananas sliced in rich cream. Suddenly Hatteras set down her coffee cup. "I think, Celia, that it's time I followed your mother's wishes."

Celia looked up, startled. The weeks had flown by. She had almost forgotten Mama's letter, with its graceful copperplate script and ironclad request: *You will see to her marriage, won't you, dear Hatteras?*

"Marriage?" she repeated dumbly.

"Why, yes. *I* might be an old woman and able to do as I please, but you are still young. You have an obligation to society. And I have an obligation to my sister. The very fact that I accepted you as a guest is implicit consent to Lydia's request."

Celia felt her heart squeeze with dismay. She began to toy with her muffin crust, playing with the crumbs it made on her plate.

"Celia." Hatteras said it gently. "Did you really think that you could ignore the reason you came here? And your obligations?"

"Do you mean *duty?* My 'lot' in life, as Rebecca chooses to call it?"

"Is duty so terrible? You are young, and it *is* fulfilling to have babies, to care for a family. Millions of women have found it so. And you told me yourself that you like children, isn't that true?"

Celia nodded unwillingly. So, she thought, the joke was on her, after all. Aunt Hatteras ate mangoes with her fingers, rode horseback like a trouper, and had a complexion tanned the shade of old leather. She was fun, and she shaped life into breezy adventure. But inside, she was just like Mama. She was still part of the family, she still subscribed to convention.

"Celia! Surely there's no need to be so downcast. We're obligated to marry you off, true. There's no getting around that. But why can't it be fun? And why can't you get yourself exactly the sort of husband you want?"

Celia looked up. She wanted a man like Roman. His name jumped into her mind, taunting her.

"I've been through all of it before," she said at last. "The parties and introductions, the flirting, the polite games. And I told you how it ended, with two broken engagements. Perhaps I'm not suited for . . . for courtship."

"Don't be silly." Hatteras rose from the table, ringing for Ah Sung with a little India bell. "Fortunately," she went on briskly, "we have enough money to do this properly. We're going to give a *luau*—an enormous Hawaiian-style feast—and we'll invite every eligible man in Honolulu."

"But—"

"What 'buts' could there be about it?" Hatteras' eyes shone with zest. "This is going to be quite stimulating. It will be something for us to do besides reading to each other or making endless trips into the mountains, pleasant as that is."

Ah Sung, a typical Oriental servant, with a black pigtail coiled around his head, clad in spotless white linen, appeared on the *lanai*. He nodded as Hatteras rattled off a market list having to do with the purchase of several pigs and the preparation of something called an *imu*. Apparently several Hawaiians would be enlisted to help him.

"Naturally," Hatteras went on as soon as the servant had departed, "there's also the matter of the guest list. I must do some sharp thinking there."

The suitors, Celia thought. The eligible men from whom she was expected to find a man over forty with firm ideas. She drew a deep, rebellious breath. "I know whom we could invite."

"Who, my dear?" Hatteras frowned into the distance as she scribbled down names.

"His name is Roman Burnside. I met him aboard the *Fair Wind,* and—"

"He is a physician?"

"Why, yes. Do you know him?"

But to Celia's surprise, her aunt's face hardened into a hostile expression. "He is quite out of the question, Celia."

"Why? He is good-looking and certainly very eligible, isn't he?"

"Don't question me, Celia. Now, let's see . . ." Hatteras licked the end of the lead pencil like a child. "There's Roger Whitt, of course. He is the son of Jared Whitt, the shipbuilder. Jared has remarried late in life—you'll meet his new wife. And, yes, William Coffin. They are a whaling family . . ."

Roman had been passed by, exactly as if he were a rather unmentionable social error.

Celia squared her chin, persisting. "*Why* is Roman Burnside out of the question?"

"Because he is. Certain matters in the past . . . Come, now, let's attend to this list. There are a number of planters who should be included. And naval officers from the *California* and *Benicia.* Some, I'm told, are quite handsome."

"Aunt Hatteras, you haven't answered my question."

"I thought I had. He is anathema in Honolulu society, Celia—not accepted in polite company."

"But *why?* What could he have done?" Celia struggled with her shock and dismay. She knew very well what social ostracism meant. The victim was excluded from all parties and invitations. Snubbed. If he was encountered on the street, no one would speak to him. Such societal punishment could follow a person mercilessly for the rest of his life.

"Something happened. It all took place fifteen years ago, but I assure you, Celia, Honolulu has not forgotten it. And for his act, Roman Burnside was banished to the United States."

"Banished!"

"Yes, indeed." Hatteras added two more names to her list, underlining them. "It was assumed—hoped—that he would stay in New York for the rest of his life. But instead he studied for a medical degree and actually had the gall to return here to the islands as soon as he had gotten it. He became a doctor on Maui."

"But . . . I don't understand . . ."

"Roman's practice, Celia, is confined entirely to the brown people. The native Hawaiians, the whalers and sailors who come ashore in need of medical assistance, and plantation workers who fall ill. No one in proper society will go to him."

It was growing more and more incredible. "Why won't they?"

"Because they just *don't*. And now, enough of such talk. Haven't you better things to do than to quiz me?" It was the crossest Celia had ever seen Aunt Hatteras. Her blue eyes glinted.

"But—" Celia began.

"Enough, Celia. We have a party to plan. Are you going to help me with it, or are you going to badger me with matters that have simply no need to be discussed?"

Reluctantly Celia concentrated on plans for the feast, which would include several whole roast pigs, yams, breadfruit, and other delicacies roasted in an underground Hawaiian oven called an *imu*. But there were also going to be Bostonian favorites, too. Teas, ices, coconut pie, sponge cake, trifle, and homemade coconut drops.

The table would be lavishly decorated with flowers and greenery, and the veranda and lawn would be hung with hundreds of colored Chinese lanterns. The effect, Hatteras assured Celia, would be lovely and romantic.

But rebellious thoughts spun in Celia's mind. What had Roman done that was so terrible his family would banish him to the United States, hoping he would stay there for life? Why wouldn't island society accept him as their physician?

She pondered these questions, unable to come to any satisfactory answers. Oddly, there were even certain resemblances to her own situation. She had been exiled to the islands; he had been banished to America.

It seemed to give them a bond.

One night Celia sat in her small bedroom, furnished with a four-post bed, its covering made of calico in a bright pattern. Moonlight spilled through the windows, augmenting the warm glow of the whale-oil lamp. A completed letter to Rebecca lay on the table, ready to be dispatched to the harbor in the morning to go on the *Kilauea*.

Celia picked up another sheet of paper and dipped her pen into the inkwell. Frowning, she began to write: "Dr. Roman Burnside, Hawaiian Hotel."

She paused to inspect her handwriting, for the grace of a woman's handwriting was considered important. Yes, she decided, her script was flowery enough.

Dear Roman.
My aunt and I are giving a *luau* party on the twenty-third and are so much hoping that you can attend. . . .

"Bananas *flambéed* in rum make a spectacular dessert," Aunt Hatteras instructed. "But you must teach your servants carefully, if you don't want them to burn or bruise the fruit."

She demonstrated with a bunch of plump, yellow bananas. "You cut the skins, like this—from end to end, but only peel off one half. Melt the butter and brown sugar in a large skillet. Then, one at a time, lay the bananas in the pan, flesh side down. Carefully peel off the remaining skin . . ."

Celia tried to listen to these pointers on running an island household. She sliced breadfruit, and learned to cut, with a small sharp knife, the fibrous supportive spines of the *ti* leaves with which many Hawaiian dishes were wrapped before being roasted.

She learned to shake a coconut in order to test whether it was edible. If it rattled, it was old, the meat good only for grating. But if it was young, you could drill two holes in its end with a nail or ice pick and pour out the sweet, slightly acid, limpid water with a strong flavor of coconut. The meat was so soft it could be spooned out like jelly.

Now she let her mind wander from her aunt's instructions, and thought instead of Roman. Would he come to the *luau*? Several times she had made an excuse to ride past the

Hawaiian Hotel, but although she had seen several men going in and out, none of them had been the dark-haired doctor.

She fidgeted guiltily, remembering that she hadn't told Aunt Hatteras she had written to Roman. If she knew, Celia felt positive that Hatteras would force her to rescind the invitation. But if Roman just showed up at the party, there was little that Hatteras could do without causing a scene.

It was *her* party too, Celia assured herself. Surely she could invite at least one person she wished.

The day of the *luau* dawned like all other Hawaiian days, in an explosion of sunrise over cobalt sea. By midmorning, whitecaps dotted the Pacific, the color of ocean and sky had deepened, and the clear air seemed to hold the perfume of a thousand blossoms.

Many of those blossoms decorated Hatteras' *lanai* and lawn: flaming hibiscus; ixoria, with its showy scarlet flowers; poinsettias and orchids. Swags of fragrant *maile* vines had been strung everywhere. When night fell, hundreds of Chinese lanterns, each containing a candle, would light the lawn in fiery colors.

At the first rattle of iron buggy wheels, Celia dashed to the mirror in her bedroom to check on her appearance. After much deliberation, they had chosen one of the gowns from her trousseau. It was of white muslin, with tiers of flounces trimmed with shirred bands and delicately tinted pink silk rosettes. There was an enchanting hat trimmed with roses and pink ribbons, and even a pink parasol embellished with a trailing satin bow.

When she had seen the dress, Hatteras had sighed in satisfaction. "That's the one, Celia. Oh, it's going to attract attention! Not that it isn't modest, of course. Still, the bodice is charmingly cut and makes you look as enchanting as a flower."

Now, thinking of that compliment, Celia leaned forward to examine her reflection. Her hair, dramatically dark, was looped into soft, thick curls that showed off glossy highlights. Her eyes were a smoldering black, fringed with thick lashes. Her eyebrows winged in two curves, and her skin was fragile porcelain.

Hatteras had called her a flower. But what sort of flower was she? A Hawaiian blossom, she decided after a moment's

thought. Bold, dramatic, showy. And which of the men to
attend tonight's party would be allowed to pluck that blossom?

Celia jumped, her thoughts scattering as she heard Hatteras
call from the corridor. "Celia, are you coming? The first
carriage has arrived. I think it's the Whitts. Remember what
I told you about them. Young Roger stands to inherit
everything. Now, remember, don't come out yet. Wait until
nearly all the guests have arrived, and then make an entrance."

Celia smiled, and left her room, stepping into the corridor.
Hatteras herself, wearing dark blue *foulard*, stared at her own
reflection in a tin mirror that hung near the arch that led to the
parlor.

"Oh, *dear*." Like a nervous debutante, Hatteras prodded
with a forefinger at the elaborate braids in which she had
done her hair for the occasion. "My hair never stays in place,
no matter how many pins I use."

Celia stifled a grin. "You look lovely, aunt, and your
dress is very becoming."

"Is it?" Hatteras leaned closer to the mirror to adjust a frill
on the gown's high collar. "I think I have grown lax here in
the islands. I'm far more comfortable in old gardening clothes
than in finery."

"But you're making the sacrifice for me."

"Who better to sacrifice for than one's own flesh and
blood? Now, remember my instructions, Celia. When you
enter, keep your spine very straight, and *smile*. Never stop
smiling. You must dazzle everyone who looks at you."

It had begun, the party on which they had worked all
week. Hatteras had hired a small orchestra, which was posi-
tioned on the veranda behind a backdrop of ferns. The air was
already thick with the delicious odor of roasting pork.

Chairs and benches had been placed on the lawn, and
guests would group around these. They would promenade,
flirt, gossip, argue, or listen to the orchestra. There would be
dancing on the *lanai*. Supper would be served at nine by
obsequious white-clad Chinese waiters who had been hired
for the occasion.

Hatteras had planned everything in her efficient manner,
forgetting nothing.

But as a second carriage pulled up, then a third and fourth,
Celia felt a nervous fish of apprehension jump inside her

belly. This wasn't just any ordinary social gathering. This was a parade of suitors who would be brought before her. She would have to choose and be chosen.

A half-hour later, Celia made her prescribed "entrance," her head held high, her lips parted in a smile. She held the smile until her mouth ached, aware of the admiring stares of the guests. The white gown, fashioned from a design in *Godey's*, was the most fashionable of all the ladies' dresses. And, Hatteras whispered proudly to her niece, Celia was certainly the most beautiful.

Her aunt pulled a short man over to meet her. "Celia, this is Roger Whitt. His father runs the Whitt Shipping Company." Celia looked at a stocky, sun-browned man of twenty-five, with nearsighted pale blue eyes that were fixed on her admiringly. The top of his head came exactly even with her own.

"W-welcome to the islands," he stammered, taking her hand. His fingers were damp; she could feel the moisture even through her kid gloves.

"Why, thank you." Celia smiled her brilliant party smile, amused at the reaction it elicited. "I must confess that I had no idea the Sandwich Islands would prove to be so lovely. Do you like living here?"

"Oh, yes." Roger Whitt made awkward social small talk, casting longing glances toward the long tables on which Hatteras had laid out several bowls of fruit punches. One was spiked with *okolehao*, a rumlike liquor distilled from the *ti* plant. She had instructed Celia in its preparation.

After making stilted conversation with the shy Roger, Celia moved on to meet other candidates. Sunburned planters took her hand, their eyes lighting up with interest. A ship's chandler, tall, freckled, and forty, backed Celia into a corner and talked to her at length about breeding wire-haired terriers.

There were whaling captains who walked with swaggering gait, and young officers from the British and American warships, handsome in colorful full-dress uniform. There were slim-hipped young men of twenty-one, and widowers of fifty, with graying hair and faces deeply browned from years of exposure to the tropical sun.

Celia smiled and smiled, and wondered where Roman was, and why he had sent no reply to her invitation.

"Celia." Hatteras drew her into a corner near the orchestra, on the pretext of consulting her about the food. "Your smile looks a little weary, dear. Try to seem happier. All things considered, this is a very good selection of men. Anyway, it's the best we can do here on this remote island."

"I'm sure it is." Celia thought longingly of Roman and his dark, flashing good looks. Disappointment seared her, all the more piercing because she had no right to feel it. Roman Burnside had no obligation to her. They were shipboard acquaintances, no more.

"There is a gentleman who wishes to converse with you, Celia. He is Mr. Fendenstrom, visiting from the island of Kauai. He tells me he has brought something to you from Rebecca."

Celia threaded her way through the laughing, gala crowd of guests. Mr. Fendenstrom turned out to be a mild-mannered man of sixty. He was, he told Celia, a missionary in Waimea, and Rebecca had entrusted a letter to him.

"Oh!" Eagerly Celia took the letter and tore open the wax seal. Two closely written sheets fell out, penned in Rebecca's measured script.

Celia scanned the letter:

I have safely arrived in Waimea, but have been busy getting settled and have not written. I find this island almost frightening in its wild excesses of nature, quite forbidding in some respects. . . . Bertrand and I were married three weeks ago. He is everything I expected, a man of high intellectual achievements and moral character, very busy in the service of the Lord, with much mission still remaining to be accomplished. . . .

There was more. A detailed description of the small frame house with lattices into which the newly wed couple had moved. A description of the village, the school where Bertrand taught. There were complaints about strange food, mosquitoes, an influx of giant-sized tropical cockroaches.

But the letter did not indicate much of Rebecca's personal feelings. Had Bertrand turned out to be good-looking? Was Becky happy? Had she fallen in love with her husband, or hated him on sight?

Celia sighed and tucked the letter into a drawer. What if Rebecca had made a mistake? But Bostonian women did not admit to making errors in marriage, Celia remembered with a shiver. They simply made the best of things and accepted what was.

Emerging onto the veranda again into the throngs of milling guests, Celia felt downcast. She looked around at the knots of suntanned men who stood about talking politics, crops, or island gossip. Some of these men were good-looking, all were eligible, but she found none of them appealing.

At nine, lavish platefuls of pork and vegetables, bananas, sweet potatoes, and other Hawaiian delicacies, roasted for hours underground in a pit lined with hot stones, were served. There were also token portions of *poi*, seaweed, raw shellfish, roast *kukui* nuts, and coarse salt.

Most of the ladies poked at this native fare with their forks, turning instead to the more familiar bread, roast potatoes, and rich desserts.

Celia, too, toyed with her food. Her appetite had fled, both from the reading of Rebecca's letter and from the sight of all these island men. Like her cousin, she was going to have to marry one of them. Like Rebecca, she'd have to spend the rest of her life on a tropical island, far away from familiar Boston.

But finally, as violins and flutes filled the air with gaiety, Celia shook away her dark thoughts. She wasn't Rebecca, full of complaints and fears and moral strictures. She was Celia Griffin. And *she* had the opportunity of selecting her own man.

She intended to take full advantage of it.

5

Hawaii's pitch-black dark had fallen. Without the lanterns glimmering like colored torches, the guests would not have been able to walk on the lawn at all, for the tropical darkness was the most profound that Celia had ever known. Without a lantern, it was possible to trip and fall on your own veranda steps. Ironically, when the moon rose, there would be enough light to read the headlines of a newspaper.

"Why, hello, Miss Griffin. I've been admiring your aunt's Chinese-lantern display. It must have taken hours to light them all."

Celia turned to see one of the planters, a man who had caught her attention by his resemblance to Roman. Tall and wide-shouldered, this man had coarser features than Roman but had the same bold look. A crest of gray-black hair flowed back from his forehead, lending force to his expression, and his skin was tanned a deep mahogany, scored with deeply engraved sun lines. Celia estimated him to be about fifty.

"I'm John Burnside," he told her, extending a large hand that was callused from work. "We were introduced earlier, on the veranda, but I don't think you heard my name."

No, she hadn't. Now she stared at this tall, attractive older man, her heart pumping wildly. *Burnside.* And his resemblance to Roman . . . Of course. Why hadn't she guessed it right away?

"Is something wrong, Miss Griffin? You look upset."

"No, I . . . Of course not." She fought to recover her

equilibrium. This man was in his fifties, and Roman was somewhere in his early thirties. Could John Burnside be Roman's father? A part of the family that had banished him to the United States?

"You're staring," John Burnside said sharply. "Do you find me strange-looking?"

Celia tried to smooth over her breach of manners. "Of course not. Whatever would make you think like that?" She smiled up at him. "In fact, I think you're very attractive."

"Ah, I see." He seemed mollified. Eyes like Roman's regarded her. "And I must confess that I find you the same. In fact, you're quite the loveliest woman here tonight, Miss Griffin."

"Why, thank you." She strolled with him among the colored lanterns. In the distance they could hear the thunder of the surf, coming from several miles away, a counterpoint to the party noises and laughter.

John Burnside told her that he was a sugarcane planter and owned a large plantation on the island of Maui, called Mountain View. He was a widower who had lost two wives in childbirth, and had a grown son and an eight-year-old daughter.

"Do you know a Roman Burnside?" she finally blurted.

"Why do you ask?"

"Your resemblance to him. He was aboard the ship when I sailed to the islands."

"He is my half-brother." John Burnside's voice grew suddenly cold. "But if you don't mind, Miss Griffin, I don't wish to talk about him. Would you like more punch?"

She was startled at the rebuff. "Why . . . yes."

John Burnside escorted her back to the veranda, and while he went to get the punch, Celia was drawn by a circle of men into a heated political debate about the conviction in New York of "Boss Tweed," a corrupt politician.

Celia voiced her own opinions, which she had gained from reading several daily newspapers. As she spoke, she was surrounded by admiring men. Suddenly the conversation died away as a latecomer arrived at the party. Celia turned to see Roman stride across the veranda.

His walk was sinewy and aggressive, his wide shoulders giving him a powerful look. He wore an impeccably tailored evening coat, the contrast of elegance and power only making him look more formidable.

Compared to the other male guests, Roman seemed like a lion in the midst of domesticated cattle, Celia decided. And she was not the only one to sense this. As Roman approached, crowds of guests moved aside to let him pass, the women eyeing the man's lean, animal grace, the men bristling. Celia glimpsed Hatteras' dismayed expression.

Calmly Roman walked straight to her. He bent over Celia's hand, lifting it to touch his lips. As his lips touched her skin, Celia felt an electric shock run through her.

"Hello, Miss Griffin," he murmured, glancing at the men, their discussion interrupted by his arrival. "I see that you're surrounded by a crowd of admirers. Apparently that's nothing unusual for you."

She dropped his hand and glared at him. "We were discussing politics. I had no idea that you would finally decide to join us."

"I was delivering a baby until the last moment and didn't know if Mother Nature would cooperate. Happily, she did, and here I am."

The other guests moved away, forming their own conversation groups, pointedly excluding them. Roger Whitt's new young wife gave Celia a venomous look, and Hatteras, conversing with a pair of middle-aged matrons, looked angry.

"Cordial, aren't they?" Roman's color deepened, and his full-carved lips twisted with irony.

"Why do they act like that?" she began. "Why—?"

But before she could finish, she was interrupted by a voice behind them. "Celia, here is your punch."

John Burnside stood balancing two cups of punch with the caution of a man accustomed to dealing with heavier, more solid objects.

"Good evening, John." Roman said it calmly.

"*You.*" With an angry movement John Burnside set both cups of punch on a tabletop. "Fancy meeting you here, in polite company."

"I go anywhere I'm invited."

"I see!"

The two men glared at each other like fighting cocks about to break into full battle. Celia's heart sank as she realized that

Hatteras was watching with an angry and exasperated expression, that all the other guests were staring too. Obviously Roman and John were enemies. And unwittingly she'd brought them together.

Knowing that she had to separate the two somehow, Celia glided forward, giving Roman her most enchanting smile. "My aunt has planted some pretty mango trees in the yard, and they are charmingly hung with lanterns. Would you like to see them?"

Roman scowled at her. "Not particularly."

"Oh, but please!" Desperately Celia flashed her dimples, and grasped Roman's arm firmly. Through the fabric of his coat she could feel the hard-ridged muscles of his forearm. "I'd so enjoy showing you the wonders of our garden—I suppose beautiful flowers seem old to *you*, but to me they are very new. And shouldn't a newcomer to the islands be humored?"

It wasn't very clever, but it was the best she could do, and it left Roman with very little choice. He could either snub her or accompany her. He chose the latter, giving her a reluctant smile as he escorted her toward the steps.

"You're a sly little devil. Do you always manage your guests with such aplomb? Or is such treatment reserved only for the renegades, like me?"

Celia gave him a sidelong look. "Oh, only for those like you."

They started across the lawn toward where the two young trees had been planted near a little hillock. Colored lanterns created jewel glows of color, and the moon had begun to rise. It flamed above the horizon, its flamboyant beauty totally unlike any pallid moon Celia had ever seen in Boston.

She drew a deep breath. "Why did everyone stare at you like that? And why did you and your brother bristle so? I was afraid you were going to hit each other."

"Ah." He shrugged. The moonlight carved out his high cheekbones, shaping the chiseled lines of his face. "I suppose we could have—it would not have been the first time."

"You nearly ruined my party with your sparring at each other, like two wild bulls penned in a field!" She was trembling; she hadn't realized that she was so angry. And she knew that her fury wasn't only for tonight, but for the casual way Roman had treated her on the wharf, his remoteness, the way he had ignored her invitation until the very last minute, the hurtful things he had said to her.

"Celia, why did you invite me here, when you knew my brother would be present?"

"But I didn't know he was your brother, how could I? I didn't even know he was on the invitation list."

Roman's black eyebrows lifted ironically. "You didn't know?"

"No." A flush reddened her cheeks, and she was sure he could detect her heightened color, even in the moonlight. "I didn't look at the list. And I didn't consult with my aunt before I invited you," she added miserably.

"So I gathered. I certainly would never have come here if I had known that I wasn't welcome."

Celia wanted to sink into the feathery lawn, to close the reddish volcanic earth over her head.

"You *were* welcome. *I* wanted you. I . . . I wanted to see you."

He gave her a long look. "You certainly accomplished that. But you should have had your aunt's permission. Since you didn't . . ." He stepped away from her. "I must take my leave. And you shouldn't have meddled in matters you don't understand."

Tears of rejection stung her eyelids, and she furiously blinked them back, afraid that he would see. "That's just it—I *don't* understand! Maybe if I had, I wouldn't have caused a social flap by inviting you. Why does everyone dislike you so? What did you do that was so terrible? What's all the mystery?"

" 'Mystery'?" Roman's lips curved in the suggestion of a smile. "Suffice it to say, Miss Griffin, that the problem dates back a long time, cannot be changed, and is none of your business anyway, my headstrong beauty."

"I'm not headstrong! Why do you call me such things? Why do you dislike me? You make fun of me. You—"

"I must go. Charming as all of this has been."

"Roman!" The evening had fallen apart and she didn't know how to retrieve it, what to say to him.

"Good night, Miss Griffin."

She started forward in dismay, but he had already turned

on his heel and was striding across the lawn, melting into the shadows of the palms that formed a thicket. She heard the crunch of his shoes on gravel as he walked toward the road with its line of waiting carriages.

Hatteras was furious at Celia's deception. After the guests had gone home, leaving the lawn and veranda a litter of punch cups, Sèvres plates, crumpled napkins, and wilted flower petals, among which the Chinese servants moved with quiet efficiency, she took her niece to task.

"I really don't understand how you could have done such a foolish thing, when we expressly discussed the matter of Roman Burnside and I told you where matters stood."

"But you didn't tell me where matters stood! You didn't tell me a thing. You merely hinted, and made it sound as if Roman had done something awful, when I don't know how he could have."

"Well, he could have, and he did." They were in Hatteras' bedroom. Celia's aunt was unpinning her braids, releasing iron-gray hair to straggle about her shoulders. She reached for her brush and began to wield it with angry strokes.

"What did he do?" Celia demanded. "I *don't* understand why it was so terrible to invite him."

"Enough." Hatteras' voice held all the firmness of a Victorian matriarch. "It's late, and my digestion is upset from all that rich food. I simply don't wish to discuss it further."

"But—"

"We'll talk some other time about the sins of Roman Burnside. Meanwhile, you'd better go to bed if you don't want your eyes to be puffy from lack of sleep. No doubt the house will be crowded with callers tomorrow."

"Callers?"

Hatteras' face softened slightly. "Suitors, my dear! Why else did we roast two pigs and entertain all those people? I believe the men found you most attractive, and I'm sure they'll prove it by lining up at our veranda. You'll be able to pick and choose."

Celia stared at her aunt, whose anger apparently had dissolved into a brisk self-satisfaction with the results of the evening. It was as if the matter of Roman Burnside had been tabled, not to be referred to again.

"However," Hatteras went on, brushing vigorously, "you *are* going to have to watch yourself, Celia. You're opinionated. You do things in a headstrong rush. If you want a husband, you're going to have to follow advice, not race off like a filly at the gate."

Celia shook her head. If *she* wanted a husband? She looked gloomily down at the tortoiseshell box where Hatteras kept a variety of pearl, jet, and garnet jewelry, most of which she never wore. There would be a long line of suitors, all right—but none of them would be Roman. Roman Burnside would not be allowed. As far as Hatteras was concerned, he didn't exist.

"He is handsome, though, you must admit." The defiant words popped out of her mouth unbidden.

"Who is?"

"Roman Burnside." Celia flushed. "He was the best-looking man there, far handsomer even than his half-brother, John."

For an instant Hatteras' hand paused in her brushing, and her eyes seemed to focus on some faraway point, as if she were recalling some warm past memory.

"Yes, he is handsome," she sighed at last. "And that's the trouble. He's entirely too attractive. If he were as plain as a hedge fence, you would never have disobeyed me and caused a hubbub by inviting him here. He's trouble, Celia! I insist that you stay away from him. Will you obey me?"

Celia lifted her eyes to meet her aunt's sharp blue ones. Finally she nodded. But she knew that her heart wasn't in it, that she would spend most of tonight lying awake thinking of Roman's dark good looks and of the force as powerful as the surging surf that drew her to him.

By eleven o'clock the following morning, eight baskets of flowers had been delivered, ranging from delicate orchids to lilies and magnolias. Notes, invitations, and small gifts had arrived, too, including a *lei* made of what Hatteras said was called candlenut, or *kukui*.

Celia fingered the polished dark surfaces of the nuts and

read the note that had come with them: *"You are the most beautiful woman in the islands. Your servant, John Burnside."*

Celia crumpled the note in sudden pique. Why couldn't it have been from Roman? There had been no letter from him, no flowers or gift, nothing. It was as if he had just vanished into the darkness.

He had treated her like a silly schoolgirl, she thought angrily. Was it her fault that no one had told her what terrible thing he had once done?

"Roman Burnside's arrival at our little party created a great deal of gossip," Hatteras reminded her, "but it will all subside in a few days, when people get their teeth into something else. Meanwhile, my girl, you are to create no new scandal. Do you hear me?"

Celia heard, and she tried to cooperate. More days slid by, but now there was little time for reading aloud, or for jaunts to mountain valleys. Suitors for Celia's hand crowded the *lanai* every evening after supper. They arrived unannounced with their lanterns, and they stayed for hours, to flirt with Celia, to debate with Hatteras and with each other, and generally to treat Hatteras' home as a meeting place.

Celia was invited to a party aboard the warship *California*, where a military band played gay tunes and couples twirled and danced on the deck. She attended a royal garden party at the Winter Palace, and met King Kamehameha V. She shook the hand of the brown-skinned Hawaiian ruler, called "Lot," clad in his gaudy military uniform decorated with epaulets, cordons, and lace. His dark, flashing eyes admired her openly.

But, pleasant as it was to be the center of male attention, to be complimented endlessly on her beauty, to receive gifts, flowers, and even a few clumsy poems, Celia grew restless. It was Roman she wanted, not any of these others. Although she had sent another note to the Hawaiian Hotel, there had been no response. What if he had already left for Maui? If he had, she had no way of knowing, and dared not risk open inquiries.

Hadn't she promised her aunt she would create no new scandal?

One morning Celia slid out of bed and pushed aside the filmy draperies of her mosquito netting. Hot tropical sun flooded into her room, sending waves of heat across her body. Last night she had danced aboard the *Benicia*, whirled in the arms of one young officer after another. But now it all seemed a blur, and she could not even remember the name of the man who had escorted her.

She padded barefoot to the window. A tan gecko clung with its suckered feet to the other side of the glass, its pale underbelly heaving slightly as it breathed. Celia tapped the glass lightly under it; the tiny creature did not move.

"Hello, lizard," she greeted it. "Are you out looking for insects to eat?"

The gecko stared at her knowingly, its eyes tiny black dots.

"Well? And what shall I do today, little lizard? Shall I ride with John Burnside in a carriage, dressed in my finest satin-de-Lyon gown for all to admire? Shall I entertain yet another group of adoring suitors, who endlessly repeat the same island gossip?"

The gecko still did not move, and Celia heaved a sigh. The truth was, she was growing bored with her life and its apparent aimlessness. She thought of the school Aunt Hatteras and Uncle Jud had run before, and wondered if she would have enjoyed teaching there. She still had her books, slates, pens, pen-wipes, maps, and other things she had purchased in Boston, thinking that she was to be a teacher.

She hadn't read a book in weeks!

Decisively Celia moved away from the window. She by-passed the ecru silk ballgown she had worn last night, which lay crumpled on a chair, and hurried to her closet. She threw on a blue broadcloth riding dress with frog trimmings, altered so that it had a split skirt, enabling her to ride astride, rather than the more perilous sidesaddle, which was ill-suited to the steep hills of Hawaii. She brushed back her heavy hair with swift strokes, tying it at the nape of her neck with a ribbon. Today she was going to do what *she* wanted to do.

She gulped down a hasty breakfast and packed a saddlebag with several books she had been longing to read, a sketchbook, and enough food and drink to last her and her horse the day.

"Wherever are you going, Celia?" Hatteras came into the kitchen, pulling off a pair of heavy gardening gloves. She usually gardened in the early morning before the heat grew too intense.

"I thought I'd go riding."

"But I wanted to take you shopping today. I wanted to find

some good French organdy for another ball dress. Most of
yours are too heavy for the tropics. Did you hang up your
gown from last night?''

Celia flushed guiltily, remembering the untidy clutter of
her room. ''I'll hang it up before I leave. And tomorrow I'll
shop. But today I just have to get away.''

''Celia—''

''No,'' her niece said firmly. ''I don't intend to waste
another day on the veranda sipping orange punch. I want to
be out in the sun!''

Before Hatteras could object further, Celia hurried through
the house and out to the small stable where her aunt kept two
horses. The glossy chestnut mare nuzzled her, and she saddled it eagerly, looking forward to the day ahead.

Fifteen minutes later she was cantering down Beretania to
Ke'eaumoku. A fresh, hot wind ruffled her hair, picking out
ebony strands from the ribbon that bound it. Celia paused by
a hibiscus hedge to pluck a blossom for her hair, and wound
branches of pink bougainvillea into a garland for the mare.
Today she'd be as flower-bedecked and free as the Hawaiian
girls she'd seen in the streets.

She rode through the market, which she found endlessly
fascinating. One could see an occasional Samoan, embellished
with blue tatooing. Today she saw one man who had actually
tattooed his tongue.

Poi merchants squatted in the shade, selling a purplish
paste made from the root of the *taro* plant. Groups of Hawaiians crouched around open communal bowls of the stuff,
dipping it up with their fingers.

There were also sellers of *awa*, a potent drink that, Hatteras said, caused addiction and a bad skin disease. Chinese
streets beckoned, with rows of exotic shops and Oriental
signs. From one came laughter and the clicking sound of
mah-jongg pieces.

More shops caught Celia's eye. A milliner had moved a
plaster bust onto the sidewalk, and here displayed her fanciest
creation of Swiss straw, with loops of velvet, grosgrain
ribbon, black lace, and fluffy black ostrich tips.

Celia slowed the mare to gaze at the bonnet and picture it
on her own head. Then, with a laugh, she spurred her horse

to a gallop. What did she care about hats today? Didn't she
already own enough to last her for ten years?

She rode on, her riding skirt billowing out behind her, the
wreath of bougainvillea casting back a sweet perfume.

She finally found a beach located near the crater of Diamond Head, a jewellike span of sand protected on either side
by outcroppings of lava rock that gave it privacy. Homes of
well-do-do foreigners, or *haoles*, were being built now along
the shoreline, but thus far civilization had not intruded here.

Celia shaded her eyes, gazing up at the famous profile of
Diamond Head. The dormant crater dominated the entire
shoreline from Maunalua Bay to Ewa Beach. British sailors,
exploring its slopes in 1825, had discovered sparkling stones
there which they thought were diamonds. Jubilant, they had
named the site of their discovery "Diamond Hill," but later,
the diamonds were found to be only calcite crystals.

Thinking of the disappointed sailors, Celia dismounted.
She looped the mare's bridle over the branch of a thorny
kiawe that grew in a protected area, and fed the mare some
oats from her saddlebag, along with a canteen of water.

She patted the mare's nose and looked around her with
pleasure. The sky was a deep, strong blue. The sea was tinted
turquoise, its color so intense that it almost looked dyed. A
three-foot surf rolled in, foam creating lazy patterns in the
golden sand.

Celia took out her books. She found an extra saddle
blanket and spread it on the sand about fifty yards from where
her horse waited patiently. She sighed in contentment. She
had the whole day ahead of her! No suitors to whom she must
pay attention, or polite conversation to make. It was going to
be heavenly. . . .

An hour later, she had read exactly four pages. Her eyes
constantly lifted from the page of the novel to focus on the
ocean with its ebb and flow of waves and choppy currents.
Some of the waves had formed semicircular crescents in the
sand, washing back with magnificently slow grace.

A lone bird wheeled overhead, but generally there were not
very many birds on Hawaiian beaches. Imported birds had
brought disease with them, Hatteras claimed, killing off many
of the native species. But tiny sand crabs scuttled about,

digging themselves in and out of little holes near Celia's blanket. She watched them, fascinated.

The beach was utterly deserted; she had never been this far away from people before, never this alone.

Noon came, bringing a blazing sun that made Celia pull the brim of her hat well down over her forehead. She dug in her saddlebag for her lunch, and sat munching chicken, cold biscuits, and bananas. She had packed a jug of orange juice and she gulped it thirstily.

By one o'clock she was bored with sitting, and wandered down to the edge of the waves. She sat down to dangle her bare feet off a flat-topped rock, cooling her skin in the water. Delicious! Water splashed farther and farther up her legs, dampening the hem of her riding dress. Impulsively Celia pulled up the dress, and finally—feeling very daring—she stripped down to her camisole and petticoats.

She felt the sun touch her bare shoulders with a shiver of forbidden joy. Was this pleasure what the Hawaiian women felt as they played and sported on the beaches?

She waded into the surf, gasping as the waves sucked at the hem of her petticoats. The pull of the water was surprisingly strong.

Joyously she ran along the surf line, braving the wild pull of the waves, feeling totally free. She shouted with pleasure as a bigger wave buffeted her; her heart seemed to expand with happiness. She was totally at one with the sea and the waves; she could do this forever. . . .

She played for hours, giving herself up totally to the walls of tumbling water, the crescent patterns carved out by the surf against the waiting sand. And then, suddenly, her feet sank into a hollow in the sand beneath her. She staggered, caught off balance in water up to her waist.

Another wave crashed in, pushing at her with full force.

Celia lost her balance, tumbling over sideways. Panic flooded her as she flailed her hands, struggling to stay upright. But instead, she was tumbled by the surf, lifted up and tossed as if she were of no more importance than a tiny chip of wood.

6

Salt water burned her eyes. The surf tossed her like a doll, lifting her up, then hurling her against the sandy bottom, so that grit abraded her skin mercilessly. She choked and struggled, too frightened to think coherently. She was going to drown. . . .

My God, she was going to drown here on this deserted beach where no one would ever know what had happened to her.

Then Celia felt strong hands grip her arms and drag her unceremoniously out of the water. She was being hauled onto the sand as if she were a bale of straw.

"What the hell . . ."

She lay where she had been thrown, gagging and coughing up water. Her sinuses burned, her eyes stung with salt, and her skin was painfully scoured from abrasion against the gritty sand.

She heard rich male laughter.

"Well, Celia? It *is* Celia Griffin, isn't it, whom I've pulled up gasping like a beached fish?"

Her eyes flew open. A pair of bare feet was rooted in the sand near her face, attached to bare, brown, sinewy legs. Her eyes moved upward. He wore nothing but a brief loinstrap that covered his bulging masculinity. He had taut, hard thighs, a flat belly ridged with muscle, and curls of black hair that marched in a narrow line upward from the loinstrap to form a thatch on his massive chest.

"Roman!" Her voice came out a shocked whisper. "Roman Burnside!"

She struggled to sit up, pushing against the resistance of the heavy, wet sand.

"Here," he said in a rich, amused voice. "On your feet."

He reached down and pulled her easily upward, setting her upright as if she were a doll brought to life. Celia stood dripping, for the first time aware of how she must look. She was soaking wet, her petticoats dragging in the sand. There was more sand stuck to her skin in wide swaths, and gritty particles of sand and coral matted in her hair. Which was also dripping wet and hung in tangles about her face.

Worse, the damp fabric clung to her like a second skin, revealing every outline and contour of her body.

"Oh . . . oh!" Humiliated, she tried to cover herself, sand falling off her as she did so.

Roman laughed, his teeth very white against his burnished skin. "I like the way sand looks on you, especially a great deal of it. It lends a certain charm to your appearance."

"Charm!" Celia glowered at him as she brushed at the gritty bunches of sand, at the same time trying to shield herself from the intense interest of his look. She was beginning to shiver. She had nearly drowned. She could have died here on this deserted beach and her Aunt Hatteras might never have known what happened to her. Her teeth chattering, she wanted to collapse in a mound and simply give herself up to relief that she was still alive.

But in front of Roman, half-naked, his skin glistening like oiled satin, amusement glinting in his gray eyes? No, she wouldn't give him the satisfaction!

"I was just coming out of the water when you happened to find me," she said defiantly, fighting the chill.

"You were turning end to end like a cork in a floodtide. If I hadn't pulled you out, you would have swallowed half of Mamala Bay."

"I wouldn't. I was fine!"

"Oh, certainly! Yes, indeed." His eyes admired her, lingering on the wet fabric that strained against her full breasts.

"Stop it!" she snapped. "Stop looking at me that way!"

His mouth quirked in a smile. "I'm sorry, I'm not being a gentleman, am I? But you must admit that you are well worth looking at, Celia. I may call you Celia, mayn't I, since we seem to be in such informal circumstances?''

But before Celia could react, Roman frowned. "You're shivering! I didn't realize—come, I think we'd better warm you up.''

Roman pulled her up the slope to where her blanket still lay, along with her novel. He picked up the sun-warmed blanket and shook it free of dry sand, then draped the warm wool over Celia's shoulders.

It was a curiously intimate act—the sudden warmth touching her, the feel of his hands through the wool as he adjusted the blanket. On the outside of the wool, he began to rub and massage her back, forcing the circulation back into her shocked system.

"Here, Celia . . . you're shaking so . . ." His voice soothed, caressed. "This will warm you. You were a fool to go into the surf like that, when you can't swim. You could have drowned, and now you're in mild shock.''

Roman soothed her, rubbing her down through the thick wool as if she were the little chestnut mare, exhausted after a day's run. Mindlessly Celia leaned against him, giving herself up to his stroking. How warm and comforting it felt to be held by him, how gentle his touch was. His hands seemed to know exactly how to touch her. . . .

After a few minutes, the warmth of the blanket and Roman's patient rubbing began to warm her. Celia's healthy body began to revive.

"Well, that's a little better," he said in satisfaction. "Your color is back. I've got some brandy in my saddlebag, and I want you to drink some.''

"But I don't need anyth—''

"I'm the doctor here. And for once you're going to do what I tell you to.''

Roman strode over the sand to where he had tethered his horse, a large gray gelding, beside her own. The saddlebags contained, presumably, a medical bag and other supplies. He returned with the brandy, which he had poured into a tin camp cup. "Here, drink this. All of it.''

Obediently Celia tilted the cup to her lips. The fiery liquor burned her throat, causing tingles of warmth to radiate down her arms and legs.

"This is better," she admitted. "I know I shouldn't have gone in the water . . . I can't swim. But the surf was so beautiful and powerful, and it was such fun to play in it. I wanted to see what it would do."

"And you found out, all right." Roman's eyes suddenly caught hers, pinning her helpless under his gaze. "Celia, Celia . . ."

He leaned forward and kissed her, taking her mouth as casually as if he owned it. At first his kiss was soft; then his mouth grew hard and demanding. His arms crushed her to him, bent her so that her body had no choice but to curve into his. The salty, male smell of him, the demands of his mouth and tongue—she thought she would die of sheer pleasure. If he did not stop crushing her close like this, if his lips didn't stop searching out the very center of her, her slamming heart would surely burst through her chest.

Then Roman pulled away, holding her at arm's length. His smile teased her. "Take off your petticoats, Celia."

"What?" She stared at him, feeling shaken, drugged by the kiss.

"I meant what I said. I'm sure you're wrapped in about six heavy layers of cotton, whalebone, and lace. Strip some of it off and we'll spread it on the sand to dry. Don't worry, no one will see you here, this beach is deserted. Besides, you'll still have a few odds and ends left on, won't you? That should be enough to save your modesty."

But *he* would see her. Her shift and corselet, soaked by the water, would be almost the same as total nudity. No decent young woman of Celia's class would ever dare to appear nearly naked in front of a man—any man. Yet something painful and sweet seemed to turn in Celia's belly.

She wanted to . . .

"Go on," he urged. "Do it. I'm going to teach you how to swim. It's shameful that a woman could live here in the islands and be totally at the mercy of a little four-foot surf."

Roman told her that he had seen her riding through town as he had left his hotel, and had impulsively followed her, losing track of her when her mare had left the beach trail. He had tried several of the beaches, and had stumbled on her here only by accident.

"If I had arrived here ten minutes later . . ." Roman didn't complete the sentence, but his meaning was clear. The look he gave her swept her with fire from head to toe.

Shyly Celia dropped the blanket and stripped off her outer layers of clothing, as he had ordered her to do. Her hands shook as she managed buttons and ribbon ties. But finally she wore little more than he did—a corset cover trimmed with lace and embroidery, and cotton drawers that ended just above the knee, also lavish with embroidery.

For a moment Roman was silent, his eyes appreciating the full curves of the figure that Rebecca had called "scandalous." She thought she saw his breathing quicken.

"Ah, God, but you're beautiful," he murmured huskily. "A nymph, a lovely naiad."

Waves crested with lacy caps of foam. Magnificent rushes of water that peaked, crashed, and withdrew in whispering patterns along the shore. And a blue sky so intense that it hurt the eyes to look at it. The afternoon passed for Celia like a stolen dream, one that she would always treasure.

Roman showed her how to walk into the waves, turning her body sideways so that she would offer less resistance to the force of the water. Later, when she was more experienced, he would show her how to dive *under* each approaching wave, so that it would not buffet her about.

"Under?" Celia remembered all too well the gagging salt water and pounding force of the waves.

"Yes, my girl, under. Now I'm going to swim you past the breakers, and we'll practice getting your face wet. Relax and hold on to me. I promise that I won't let you go."

Roman was endlessly patient, a strong swimmer who could tread water effortlessly, holding up Celia's weight as if she were a feather. He supported her with his strong arms, teased her when she choked, praised her when she managed to duck her face underwater.

His black curly hair clung to his skull like a cap. "You're very brave to try this, Celia, especially after your unfortunate experience. What couldn't you accomplish if you were allowed to swim every day? I daresay I'd have you surfing after a few weeks."

"Surfing?"

"It's a marvelous Hawaiian game with the waves, the most

exhilarating thing one can do in the water. Someday I'll show you.''

Whether casually or not, he had spoken of a *someday*. Sun-dazed and thoroughly tired, Celia allowed Roman to tow her back to the beach through the pounding surf that now did not seem quite so frightening. She took the blanket he handed her and dried herself, forgetting to be self-conscious of her body.

"There's more brandy, Celia, and I have food, too. Are you hungry?''

"Ravenous!''

They pooled their supplies and devoured ham, bread, and fruit. Celia's skin tingled, and she knew already that she would have a fiery sunburn by nightfall. If Hatteras ever saw how extensive that sunburn was . . .

She giggled.

"Why are you laughing, witch?''

"Never you mind.'' Teasing, Celia threw a crumpled papaya skin at him, and Roman hurled it back. Laughing, they battled with the remains of their lunch like two unruly schoolchildren.

At last Roman spread his hands over his face in mock surrender. "Enough! I have papaya dripping from my cheeks, and you have it in your hair. Let's spread out the blanket and bake in the sun like sensible people.''

So they splashed off their hands and faces in the sea, and then lay belly-down on the blanket, side by side, their bodies nearly, but not not quite, touching.

After a while, Roman began to talk. He told her stories of his childhood on Maui, the last-born son of a sugar planter and his young second wife, who had died in giving birth to Roman. He had been instructed in water sports by Hawaiians from a nearby village.

"There's nothing that Hawaiians don't know about the water, Celia. They learn to swim almost from infancy. They can free-dive to amazing depths, and remain underwater for incredible lengths of time.''

He had learned to surf on a board measuring seventeen feet in length and weighing two hundred pounds, carved from a tree with a stone adz.

"Diving, body-surfing, fishing canoeing—it was the most

golden part of my childhood, an experience I never forgot, even when I was in New York, wading around in huge drifts of snow for the first time in my life. Snow!'' Roman grimaced. ''You can't believe how cold and alien that white stuff seemed to me, Celia.''

She gathered her courage to ask, ''Why did you go to America?''

The long, lean body stretched beside her suddenly tensed. ''There are certain matters that are painful to me. I don't want to talk about them.''

''I'm sorry.'' Celia flushed, sitting up. For a while there'd been easy communication between them. But now the lazy, carefree mood between them was gone, totally destroyed by just a few words. But some demon of curiosity made her persist. ''Did you marry your wife . . . Hope . . . in New York?''

Roman's jaw knotted, and with a swift unfolding of limbs he sat up too. For a long time he sat still, gazing outward at the cobalt water, where the sun created swaths of diamond glitter.

''I told you about Hope before, Celia. I loved her very much. After she died, I was distraught. I went to Boston to study under Dr. Devalle, who was famed for his research in obstetrics, his innovative use of forceps, and his use of carbolic as a disinfectant. That is a procedure that many doctors consider quackery, but some are saving lives with it. I wanted to learn what might have saved my wife. I studied five months under Devalle, doing deliveries, and I did save the lives of several dozen infants and mothers who might otherwise have died.''

Roman's eyes might have been polished gray stones filled with a tormented inner light.

''Now I'm back in Honolulu, trying to impart what I learned to the doctors of this fair town. They might ostracize me socially, but they aren't too proud to learn from me,'' he added bitterly. ''They consider that I've 'practiced' on my Hawaiian patients and on the charity patients I treated in Boston. They are resistant to the idea of carbolic, but I'm trying to pound it into their heads.''

Roman subsided into silence, and Celia sat beside him, unable to think of anything more to say. His private feelings seemed to close her out, and she felt a wave of painful envy for the unknown Hope, whom Roman had loved. Whose death had left him heartbroken.

She cleared her throat, breaking the silence. "Could we go swimming again?" She hoped that in the water they might recapture their earlier joyous mood.

"No."

"But I'm rested, and your lessons were so good, perhaps I can swim farther this time—"

"Look at the sun." Roman pointed to the horizon, where the sun had begun to sink, casting long, golden shadows on the golden hillocks of the beach sand. "It's too late."

Uneasily Celia nodded. She knew that the ride back would be long, and if darkness fell before she reached home, it could be dangerous. Before moonrise, the tropical night was impenetrably black.

"You'd better get ready to leave," he told her. "Your aunt will be wondering where you are, and I see that you didn't provide yourself with a lantern."

Again he was treating her like a schoolchild. She bristled, feeling rejected at his cool tone. "I'm so *sorry* that I forgot! Perhaps you would escort me back to town, then, since you seem so concerned over my welfare! I'm sure *you* thought of bringing a light."

"As a matter of fact, I did, and I'll give it to you. I always carry gear in case I'm out late at night, and I also carry a pistol as protection. But I won't accompany you."

"Why not?"

"Gossip, Celia. This town thrives on it. I am already anathema here. Do you wish to share in my notoriety?"

She stared at him, her face reddening. She knew very well what he meant, of course. For the two of them to ride back from the deserted beach trails, her riding dress crumpled, her hair tangled and salty . . . Scandal would erupt again, worse than what she'd created in Boston.

Still, she felt a certain anger. Roman had no right to treat her like this, to fob her off like a schoolgirl or a servant who had been too stupid to bring a lantern. All she knew was that he had kissed her. Spent the day with her, held her in his arms in the water, saved her life. Now he talked coldly of gossip, making what they had shared seem dirty somehow, and soiled.

She jumped to her feet, grabbing furiously for her clothes. "Turn your back!" she snapped. She began yanking on her petticoats, fastening their ribbons with shaking hands. "Oh, all right! I'll go, then—by myself! And believe me, I'm glad to do so. You are the rudest man I have ever met! The most maddening, the most incorrigible . . ."

"I?" To her surprise, Roman suddenly grinned. "I would say that *you* are the incorrigible one, Miss Griffin. You are the one who went swimming in her undergarments in the company of a renegade. Do you make a habit of such daring behavior? I'm sure your Aunt Hatteras would find it extremely shocking, not to mention the rest of Honolulu society."

She wanted to punch him. "Oh! *Oh!* I did it because you . . . because you told me to!"

His laughter followed her across the beach as she stalked to her mare, tightened the saddle girth, and mounted. Slapping the bridle against the horse's neck, she galloped off, her face burning as red as the setting sun.

That night Celia avoided Hatteras' scrutiny by claiming a sun headache. She retired early to her bedroom, where she rubbed salve into her burning skin and sat fuming, thinking of Roman.

How dare he insist on teaching her to swim, then torment her because she'd done the very thing he wanted? Men! There was no understanding them, and in her present angry mood, Celia wasn't even sure that she wanted to.

She began cutting the pages of a novel, ripping the knife tip through fine vellum paper with swift, furious strokes. She thought of Roman's kiss. His smile. The smoky, intent look in his eyes. In the water, he had held her so closely, there had been nothing between them but a scanty layer of cloth . . .

Finally she put away the book knife, not even caring when the novel slid off the bed to the floor. Was it always to be like this between them? Celia pulled to Roman as irresistibly as a moth is drawn to a lamp? Then to be singed and hurt, flung away in pain? What did he want of her?

The next morning, when she came down to the veranda for

breakfast, she found a huge bouquet of pink tea roses waiting. She snatched at the note, unfolding it with hands that shook.

Then she put down the note in disappointment. It was from John Burnside, not Roman. "Will you see me today? I would like to take you riding. I will pick you up at eleven."

She crumpled the note and tossed it to the floor, stunned at the intensity of her feeling of loss. Roman had never sent her flowers. He had never invited her anywhere, whereas his half-brother plainly liked her, wanted to be with her.

She stooped and retrieved the balled-up note, carefully smoothing it out.

"Why, Celia, what are you doing, scrabbling about on the floor like that?" Hatteras wanted to know, coming onto the veranda. "You look so flushed."

It was her sunburn, of course, that Hatteras had noticed. Celia spoke hastily. "I'm going to go riding today," she told her aunt. "With John Burnside."

"Indeed?" Hatteras nodded with approval.

Celia penned a note of reply and dispatched it to John's lodgings, telling him that she would love to go riding with him and was looking forward to seeing him.

She lifted her chin defiantly. She hoped that they'd ride by the Hawaiian Hotel, and that Roman would be on the veranda where he could see her in the company of the brother he hated.

Yes, she'd flaunt herself in front of Roman. She'd smile up into his brother's eyes, giving him her most dazzling smile. Why not? She would make Roman sorry for the rude way he had treated her.

Two mornings later, Celia sat glumly out on the lawn in the rattan swing that Hatteras had recently strung up between two palm tress. In the thicket, two mynah birds were squabbling like spoiled children, and near the horizon Celia could see the sails of a ship inbound from some far port.

Her plans to taunt Roman had failed miserably. He hadn't been anywhere near the Hawaiian Hotel, and her efforts to appear joyously happy and in command of herself had only resulted in John Burnside's growing more attentive to her.

In fact, John was becoming infatuated—

"Celia." Hatteras interrupted her thoughts, her long skirts

rustling across the grass as she approached the swing. "An invitation came this morning from the Whitts. We're to attend a gala tonight."

Celia nodded without much interest. They had been present at many such impromptu gatherings, and she supposed that the same collection of people would be there.

"Celia! Your eyes look so faraway, I swear you are on another star. All you do these days is daydream. You've been to dinner and riding with John Burnside twice this week. Could it be that you're falling in love with him?"

Celia jerked her head up. "In love?"

"Why, yes, my dear. I must say that John would be a very good catch. His sugar plantation, Mountain View, is very prosperous, and he owns a number of shipping investments as well. Even if he is a widower with two children, many women consider him very handsome."

"Oh, he is," Celia mumbled.

"Why are you flushing, Celia? I must say that your face has been very ruddy lately. Have you been neglecting to wear your sun hat?"

Celia shifted about uncomfortably. Her sunburn had been hard to conceal, even with dabbings of rice powder, and if Hatteras knew that it extended to most of her body . . . She drew breath, thinking to change the subject to something less dangerous.

But Hatteras was back to the topic of men. "Naturally, John Burnside is a major suitor. But Roger Whitt is interested in you too. Twice he has sent flowers, and his attentions to you have been most pronounced—for a man of his type, that is."

Celia couldn't help giggling. Roger was painfully shy and had spoken to her only in monosyllables.

"What *is* his type, Aunt Hatteras? You know he can barely say four words if he isn't coached by his father or by his young, pretty stepmother."

Hatteras gave a hoot of laughter. "You may be right. But you are going to have to curb that tongue of yours if you expect to make a good impression tonight. And beware of Kathryn Whitt. She might be young, but she is someone to be reckoned with."

*   *   *

Celia descended from the carriage in a swirl of India linen printed with a delicate pattern of rosebuds and tiny leaves. Dusk was falling, the rose-and-salmon afterglow of a magnificent sunset still visible. The Whitts had sent servants to light their way with lanterns, and Celia and Hatteras followed a Chinese serving man along a scented garden pathway.

In the carriage, Hatteras had talked about the ads she had placed in the California papers, speculating on what sort of replies she might receive. In only a few months she might receive a response. She wished, she said, to have Celia safely married off before she left on her world tour.

Celia had only half-listened, responding automatically. She felt restless tonight, out of sorts. At Hatteras' insistence she had taken a nap this afternoon. But she had not slept well, and a tepid bath had not soothed her. Now her full-skirted dress seemed too bland, its pattern displeasing. Her *curacoa* kid slippers felt too small, and one of them chafed the instep of her foot. She had found an ugly run in one of her silk stockings, and had thrown it away in a fit of sudden displeasure.

Now, as they passed beneath a charming latticed trellis overgrown with wisteria, Celia slapped a mosquito that had landed on her arm. She hit harder than was necessary, and was rewarded by the sting of her palm against her own flesh.

The pain didn't make her feel any better. Nothing did. She dreaded the thought of this party, exactly like all the others. She was suddenly tired of this game of suitors. Why had she consented to it?

They entered the house and were caught up in a flood of greetings. Their hostess swept forward to meet them, a brittle woman of thirty with dark blond hair who enjoyed a local reputation as a beauty.

"Hatteras . . . Celia . . . so lovely to see you."

Kathryn Whitt gave both of them pecking kisses, then focused on Celia a challenging smile. "I have seen you escorted about town by a most handsome gentleman—is it anything serious? Ah, are you blushing, my dear, or is that a bit of sunburn I see on your cheeks? We women have to be deadly careful of the sun. It is certain to age us."

Celia smiled back evenly.

"Was your dress sewn here, Celia?" Kathryn drawled. "If

only there was a really *good* dressmaker here in the islands. I myself try to buy as many things in Paris as I can."

Why was Kathryn being so catty? But before Celia could respond, there was another hubbub at the door as more guests arrived. All three women turned to see John Burnside enter, along with a group of officers from the *California*. In evening wear, his graying hair combed back from his blunt-carved face, John was striking.

Kathryn hurried forward to greet her guests, her cheeks suddenly flushed a hectic red. She gave perfunctory smiles to the officers, then extended both hands to John Burnside. Her voice trilled, "John, it's *so* good to see you! Everyone has seen you riding about town, and yet you never stop here to pay *us* a call. Are you angry at us?"

At the arch tone in Kathryn's voice, Celia suddenly realized why their hostess had been so venomous. She was jealous! Kathryn was married to a dry old man of sixty, and John Burnside was handsome and vigorous.

"*I'm* going to monopolize him tonight, Celia, dear," Kathryn said, drawing John past her. "You had him all this week, and now it's my turn, since I see him so seldom. He is an old friend, you know."

The Whitt drawing room was lavishly furnished in the style of a Southern mansion, with white-painted carved moldings and Oriental rugs. A tall, gilded harp stood near the fireplace, and Celia tried to imagine Kathryn Whitt playing it. A large table had been spread with the inevitable punch bowls, one for the ladies, another, stronger version for the gentlemen.

Celia wandered about, greeting those she knew, smiling or nodding at those she did not. Aunt Hatteras was deep in conversation with a whaling captain recently returned from the Bering Straits, where thirty-three ships had had to be abandoned in the Arctic ice floes, a tragedy for the whaling industry.

"Would . . . would you like a cup of punch, Celia?" Roger Whitt approached her nervously, his face as flushed as his deep suntan would allow. His voice was already slurred from drink. "I would be glad to get you one."

She smiled warmly, waiting while the shy Roger fetched her punch. Near the tall windows, Kathryn Whitt had cornered John and was laughing up into his eyes. Celia felt a spurt of annoyance. Roger handed the cup to her with exaggerated care and waited while she took a sip.

"I hope you like it, Celia." He paused to moisten his lips nervously. "I thought . . . that is, I was wondering if you would . . . There is a picnic that some of the women are organizing, to the Nuuanu Valley . . ."

Celia drank more punch, noting its rather strong flavor. It seemed to flow directly into her veins, making her feel reckless and tingly. Could it be possible that Roger had mistakenly given her the wrong, spiked punch? Accidentally or perhaps even deliberately? She gazed at him from under her lashes as she drained the cup.

"Roger, are you asking me to accompany you on the picnic? I think I would like that very much. But do you think you could bring me another cup of that wonderful punch? It tastes delicious, and I'm really so thirsty."

Three cups of punch later, Celia's edgy mood had completely disappeared. Now everything seemed to surround her in a halo of warm, happy light. Jokes seemed funnier, gossip incredibly interesting.

Why had she dreaded coming to this party? She circulated among the guests, airily ignoring Hatteras' sharp look. She had a soft smile for Roger, a flirtatious look for Adam Benson, one of the Navy officers who had squired her aboard the *California*. She even startled dry, dusty old Jared Whitt with a brilliantly sexy smile. She felt good. Yes, she felt wonderful. . . .

Finally John Burnside approached her and asked if she would like to stroll with him in the Whitts' garden.

Celia gazed up at him, widening her eyes in a way that many men had found devastating. "I thought you'd want to be with Kathryn Whitt."

"When I can talk to you instead? Kathryn is an old friend, nothing more. No matter what she might think."

Celia wondered what their brittle blond hostess would say if she could hear that. "Then, why, yes, I'd love to walk with you. But we shouldn't be too long, should we? It wouldn't be proper."

Her teasing caused John's face to redden, and she felt a

flash of triumph. Let Kathryn smile into his eyes. She, too, possessed power over him.

They walked under a sky lavishly dusted with stars. The garden smelled of sweet pink *plumeria*, a tree often planted in Hawaiian graveyards but adopted by the foreigners for its scented beauty. The moon had risen, casting its enchantment everywhere.

John touched her hand lightly. "My God, but you are stunningly beautiful in the moonlight, Celia. It touches you with magic."

At the compliment, some of the night's spell seeped away. Celia looked down at the ground. She was here with the wrong man. It should be Roman saying such lovely things to her.

"Tell me about Maui," she said.

He smiled down at her, a handsome older man smitten by her looks. "I've already talked about the island, and Mountain View, until you're sure to be tired of hearing of it."

"No. Tell me more. I really want to hear."

"Very well, then. Since you insist!"

As John talked on about the plantation his family had owned for two generations, Celia listened, rapt. To her, Maui sounded like paradise. A dormant volcano, Haleakala, dominated the large end of the island. There were green-clad tropical valleys and craggy mountain slopes of incredible beauty. Mountain View, John had told her, was situated on the smaller end of the island, on the slopes of the West Maui Mountains.

"It enjoys a rare, double view. To the front, an incredible sweeping vista of blue sea. To the rear, the jagged green mountain slopes and valleys.

"It's incredibly lovely, a wonderful place. And the house is straight from Connecticut, every lath, nail, and stick of wood shipped over from Westport by my father. I'd love to show it to you, Celia. Will you come sometime?"

She looked at him, at the serious expression in his eyes. And suddenly she was being pulled into John Burnside's arms and enfolded in a warm, hard embrace.

"John . . . please . . ."

She tried to pull away, but he would not let her. His mouth

plunged down on hers, his urgent tongue forcing her lips open to probe her mouth.

"You're so damn lovely. So provocative . . . My God, but I want you."

The night seemed to swirl around them, enclosing them in perfumed flower scent. Celia gave up struggling and permitted John's kiss, feeling a pleasurable physical sensation. He might not be Roman, but he was definitely virile. . . .

Suddenly John pulled away from her. "I will take you to Maui with me."

"What?"

"I want you for my wife, Celia. I need you, I love you, I have to have you."

Celia caught her breath, looking at John's handsome features. The silver light exaggerated his strong features, making him look more than ever like an older, coarser Roman. Her heart had begun to race. Well? Didn't Aunt Hatteras insist that she marry someone? Wasn't that the entire purpose of this party and of all the others she had attended, to find the man who would make her a good husband?

And John Burnside was even over forty, she thought with a little inward giggle. Would he be strict, curbing her the way Mama wanted?

"Why do you hesitate?" he demanded.

"I . . . I don't know."

"Is there someone else? Another suitor?"

"No."

She had drunk too much punch; it was making her thinking fuzzy. *Roman*, she thought, in a last desperate grab at reality. She realized that John had grasped her upper arms, was pulling her forward, forcing her to look up into his eyes.

His eyes were blue, not gray.

"You like me, Celia, I know you do. I know I could make you happy. I'd spend my life trying."

She felt herself sway, and the stars seemed to swoop downward, then move away again, like faraway lanterns. Why not? she thought recklessly. Why, indeed, not? Let Roman see how he liked having her married to his brother.

"All right." She heard her own consent with a sense of dizzy surprise. "I'll marry you."

"You will! By God!" An expression of amazement and

joy burst across John Burnside's face. He scooped Celia off her feet and whirled her around in triumph, until the stars swirled and the moon became a silver blur.

By the time he had set her down, she felt dizzy and slightly nauseated. She clung to John's arm, wishing that she could be alone for a few moments. As he pulled her back toward the house, she had to stop to wipe her suddenly perspiring face.

Had she really said that she would marry him?

Apparently she had.

Five minutes later, John Burnside made the impromptu announcement to the houseful of more than eighty guests. As soon as the ceremony could be arranged, he and Celia Griffin would be married.

7

The bedroom of Kathryn and Jared Whitt was dominated by two huge maple four-poster beds, one, apparently, for each of them. There were hooked rugs and decorative pieces of blue Sandwich glass, while more Sandwich lamps in jewel tones of red and blue cast a flickering glow.

Celia sank down in a rocking chair, fighting the waves of dizziness that had plagued her ever since John had whirled her about in the garden. Thank God she was alone here in her hostess's bedroom, which had been set aside for the ladies to freshen up. A table was laden with an assortment of sewing materials, perfumes, smelling salts, and pins.

What had possessed her to drink so much punch?

She could barely remember what she had said to John now, only that awful moment when he'd propelled her in front of eighty people to announce she would soon be his wife. Instantly she'd been surrounded by tumult. Shrieks, cries, congratulations. Hatteras had swept her up in a joyous embrace. A white-faced Kathryn Whitt had offered congratulations. Only Roger Whitt had withdrawn to a corner to sulk.

Now Celia rubbed her aching temples and wondered how it could have happened so quickly. One moment she was arriving at the party in a grumpy mood. Then suddenly she had drunk too much punch and was engaged.

"So . . . you're to be married!"

Celia looked up. Kathryn herself had entered the bedroom,

her long pink silk skirts making angry swishing sounds as she walked. Her lips formed an unpleasant straight line.

Celia rose. "Yes, I was just freshening up, and I should get back to—"

"In a minute. There's no harm in the two of us talking, is there? Woman to woman?" Without waiting for a reply, Kathryn closed the bedroom door behind her and moved to stand by one of the four-posters. She was breathing deeply.

Celia eyed her. She knew why Kathryn was so angry. "What do you wish to talk about? If it's John Burnside, I don't think you have any reason to be upset. After all, you are already married, aren't you?"

Kathryn stiffened. "Yes, I'm married. But did you know that John was in love with me before I met Jared? *I* was the one who refused *him*."

Celia wondered if this were the truth. "I didn't know that."

"Well, it's true. And I ought to warn you. If you marry John, you'll be in for trouble. He's told you about those children of his, hasn't he?"

Celia nodded. John, a widower twice over, had a twenty-three-year-old son, Beau, by his first marriage, and an eight-year-old daughter, Tina, by his second.

"Well, they're a handful. He lets Tina run half-wild, and I don't think her hair gets combed from one week to the next. As for Beau, he made a fool of himself in the California gold fields. Daddy," Kathryn mocked, "had to go to the Coast to fetch him home. Now Beau is back under his father's thumb. He roams about Mountain View making ugly paintings—he considers himself an artist. He's moody and difficult and is bound to give you a hard time."

"I . . . I see."

"I hope you do see." Kathryn fixed Celia with hard blue, jealous eyes. "And then, of course, there's the Burnside curse."

"A curse?" This had gone too far. Celia stared at Kathryn, wondering if she were joking. But apparently her hostess was not.

Kathryn reached out to the little table of toilet articles and unstoppered a bottle of heliotrope essence. With quick, furious movements she dabbed the scent on her throat and wrists.

"Don't pretend to be so innocent. The Burnside graveyard is full of the graves of women. Old Amos lost two wives in childbirth, and both of John's wives died the same way. Although in the case of the second wife, it happened when Tina was two years old, of complications from a miscarriage. And Roman's wife, Hope—she, too, died in childbirth. Of course, she was buried on the mainland."

Celia was shaking. "But childbirth—it has always been dangerous for women. It's a fact of life, everyone knows that."

"Not that dangerous—not for *every* women who marries into a family."

"Coincidence," Celia said.

"You think so? Two generations? And I'll wager it goes even further back into the family tree, if you were willing to check. I'd think twice if I were you, before I—"

"Stop!" Celia clapped her hands over her ears. "I . . . I don't want to hear this!"

"If you're marrying John, you'd better hear it," Kathryn went on with vicious satisfaction. "And there's more. That house—the plantation—it's torn apart."

"What do you mean?"

Kathryn put the stopper back in the perfume bottle with a decisive click. "Hate. Dissension. And . . ." She paused. "Near-murder."

Celia's heart gave a horrid, twisting thump.

"Those two brothers," Kathryn went on, smiling tightly. "They fought bitterly over Mountain View."

Celia moistened dry lips. She knew she was about to hear why Roman had been banished, the reason he was ostracized from Honolulu society, the basis for the scandal that Hatteras had hinted at.

"Please, Kathryn, you must tell me everything about it. I . . . I have to know."

The Sandwich lamps flickered, sending out a glow into the well-furnished bedroom as the two women talked, Kathryn forgetting some of her anger as she recalled the enmity between the two half-brothers.

"John is sixteen years older than Roman, he is stable,

while Roman is the wild one, a spoiled baby born when his father was old and inclined to dote on him.

"Roman grew up quickly, a hotheaded youth who ran wild with the Hawaiians, as at home in the water as they were. Charming, bright, handsome, he was his father's favorite, while John was always the dependable one, the plodder. John began to work on the sugar plantation, and it was always understood that he, as the elder, would inherit Mountain View, the shipping, and the other prudent investments Amos Burnside had made. But one day Amos Burnside—who worked fifteen hours a day in the mill office—died at his desk of a heart attack.''

Kathryn paused dramatically.

"Please, go on," Celia begged.

"The will was read. It divided Mountain View and the other property equally between the brothers, stipulating that the firstborn male heir of each would inherit his father's share if either Roman or John were to die. Since John had already been working in the mill, he would function as its manager and would have the right to live in the plantation house— which, by the way, is very beautiful."

"I see."

Kathryn shrugged. "It was a fair enough settlement, most people thought. After all, John was the elder and had already been working in the mill office, while Roman had been running wild doing exactly as he pleased. Anyway, after the will was read, Roman stalked off. *He* was angry because he'd been his father's favorite, and he'd expected more.''

Celia shifted uneasily. Spoiled, petulant—this didn't sound like the Roman she knew, and she was about to say so when Kathryn continued.

"Later that day, Roman surprised his older brother on the beach near Pu'unoa Point. Roman was a very strong young man of sixteen, his muscles well developed from years of surfing and swimming. He attacked John.''

"*No!*" Celia's cry was involuntary.

"Oh, yes, indeed. Roman was quite wild, beside himself with rage. He dragged John out into the surf, pulling him toward an outcropping of lava rocks. He attempted to brain him to death on those rocks.''

He attempted to brain him to death on those rocks. Celia

stared at Kathryn while the ugly words spun through her mind, drilling her with their shock.

"No, I . . . I can't believe . . ."

"It's true. Everything is documented by the testimony of the servants at the time, the Hawaiians who found them and pulled Roman off his brother before he could kill him. There is even a scar on John's face, near the hairline, put there by his brother on that day. That's why Roman Burnside was sent to the United States, because he tried to murder his brother and almost succeeded."

Celia sat silent, trying to make sense of it. The accusation against Roman, the "Burnside curse," the rivalry between the brothers. Her thoughts whirled with confusion. No, it wasn't possible that Roman had attempted murder; she simply could not believe it. She had talked to Roman, had seen the despairing look in his eyes when he talked about his dead wife, the way he talked about his patients.

She heard Kathryn continue. "John Burnside had hoped that his younger brother would stay permanently in exile, never returning to the islands, and allowing him full sway over the plantation. Instead, Roman studied medicine in the United States and returned to start a medical practice in Lahaina. Since then, the brothers have been forced to run Mountain View together, a project," Kathryn said, "that causes endless quarrels. They both have fierce tempers."

Celia moistened her lips. "Then Roman will be often at Mountain View in the months to come?"

"Oh, yes. It's necessary in order to run the place. But he would be there anyway, I'm afraid," Kathryn went on. "He has a woman there."

"A . . . woman?"

Celia sat rigidly, her hands clenched tightly together. A spasm of jealousy possessed her, so strong that it left her gasping for breath. A woman. Roman had a woman. . . . But what did she expect? He was a good-looking man in the prime of his life.

The venomous tone was back in Kathryn's voice as she noted Celia's reaction. "I thought it was John that you liked, Celia. My, but you *do* seem attracted to the Burnsides, don't you?"

Celia had had enough. "I really must be getting back downstairs," she said, jumping to her feet so hastily that the rocker began to move back and forth.

"Burnsides are trouble for any woman," Kathryn said, smiling tightly. "That's why I refused to marry John. *I* have no desire to cope with all of it, not to mention dying in childbirth." And she picked up a comb, pulling it delicately through her white-blond ringlets. "No, I think more of myself than that. Of course, some women will be fools, won't they?"

Celia paused in the hallway to collect herself before returning downstairs. A mirror hung on the wall, its carved frame heavily encrusted with gilt, reflecting her movements as she brought shaking hands to her temples.

Her mind spun with anger and horror. Roman wasn't a murderer, he just wasn't! As for the "Burnside curse," that was only the talk of a woman who had been spurned. Realistically speaking, women did die giving birth, and many men outlived one, two, or even more wives. But the reverse could also be true. Many women were brought to childbed six, seven, or even a dozen times and lived to a ripe old age.

Celia's own three sisters had seven healthy babies among them.

Just as she was turning to go downstairs again, she heard feminine giggles. Three young wives came chattering up the stairs, evidently headed toward the hostess's bedroom to refresh themselves.

"Celia! Oh, isn't it exciting!"

Audra McNally and Patience Bird were both young Honolulu matrons, each the mother of several young children.

"Your engagement happened so *suddenly*—not that we didn't expect something to happen, of course. John has been so attentive to you . . ."

John. His name was like a dash of cold water, sweeping over Celia and bringing her back to reality. Her engagement—she'd almost forgotten it! She forced a smile, accepting their congratulations. The effects of the spiked punch were long gone now; Kathryn Whitt's little "talk" had certainly accomplished that. What a fool she'd been! Whatever had possessed her to accept John Burnside's proposal?

"You'll be going to Mountain View soon, I suppose?"
Audra McNally said enviously. "They say it's gorgeous there."

"Yes, I . . . I imagine."

"Of course, John isn't the only Burnside at Mountain
View. His brother comes there often, too." Audra eyed
Celia, as if to see what reaction this statement could elicit,
and she was unpleasantly reminded of the power of island
gossip. "Will you mind that, Celia?"

Celia flushed scarlet. "I hadn't even thought about it," she
lied.

That night Celia slept restlessly, dreaming of green mountains crowned by masses of dark, shifting clouds. In her
dream, Roman strode along those craggy hillsides, his black
hair windblown.

I didn't kill anyone, he whispered. *Don't you believe me,
Celia?*

She overslept the next morning, wakening to the hot sun
that blazed into the room. She pushed aside the mosquito
netting and slid out of bed, going to the window. The tan
gecko was still there, gazing at her with tiny eyes.

Celia watched the lizard, feeling pinned under the sun's
heat, her eyes crusty with sleep. What was she going to do?
What *could* she do?

"Celia! Oh, Celia!" A rapping at her bedroom door interrupted her confused thoughts. It was Hatteras, her voice
sounding so cheerful that Celia winced.

"Yes, aunt?"

"Are you up? You're such a lazybones this morning. . . .
Flowers have come for you. Whole masses of them—they are
going to overflow every vase I own. I don't know *where* I
can put them."

Celia reached for a blue silk dressing gown and pulled it
on, fastening the belt at the waist. She felt old . . . about a
hundred years old, she thought dully. Every muscle in her
body ached. She must have been clenching her body in her
sleep, she decided.

"Did John send them?"

"I should hope so!" Hatteras bustled into Celia's room,
clad in an old loose-fitting muslin dress. "Who else would
send them, dear girl, now that you're engaged? And I imag-

ine that you'll receive a ring soon. I'd think that John might go to the jeweler's today and order a setting for you. Or perhaps he'll give you an old family stone."

Celia felt a chill. "A ring?"

"Of course." Hatteras stared at her. "I must say you do look pale this morning. Perhaps you should have a nap this afternoon—unless John wants to come by and take you for a drive, of course."

John . . . John . . . With just a few words, how quickly her life had changed! Celia tried to smile at her aunt, postponing talk about wedding plans. Her mind kept running in frantic circles. What was she going to do?

She sat tensely over breakfast, toying with her scrambled eggs.

"Whatever is the matter with you?" Hatteras demanded sharply. "You certainly don't act as an engaged girl should."

"Perhaps it's because I've been engaged twice before."

"Ah?" This explanation did not seem to satisfy her aunt. "If you ask me, you've been acting strange for days now. Getting engaged so quickly . . . and that day you went riding, you returned with a sunburn you tried to conceal from me."

Celia was barely listening. She sat up straight, as the idea suddenly came to her, full-fledged and daring. She shouldn't—it wasn't right—but it was *possible*, and it was her chance, and if she didn't take it, she'd regret it for the rest of her life.

"Celia, child, whatever is the matter with you? You look as if you'd suddenly seen a vision."

Celia mumbled an excuse, pushing back from the table.

"Celia." At the sight of her, John Burnside's face lit up with genuine pleasure. "What are you doing here—couldn't you stay away?" He laughed, but Celia knew that he was only half-joking. "I suppose you stopped to see me on your morning ride. Well, you've already completed my day. You're beautiful."

His eyes admired her in the tight-fitting green riding habit that accented Celia's full breasts, and made her complexion look as fine as pure alabaster. She had looped her heavy, thick hair back in several elegant coils, threading a string of pearls among them. It was an elaborate coiffure for riding, she knew, but she had felt that it would give her confidence for the difficult thing she wished to say.

John was staying at a small, respectable boardinghouse while he completed banking business in Honolulu, and he had received her in a sitting room that opened onto a veranda crowded with potted plants.

They sat down in wicker chairs. Celia adjusted the folds of her riding habit, wondering how she should begin. On the ride here, she had rehearsed her speech: John, I've been thinking over my decision of last night, and I've come to some conclusions. . . .

"Would you like some fruit juice or tea?" John was effusively cordial. "I'm sure I can persuade my landlady to provide them—she is all agog over our engagement. In fact, the news is all over Honolulu by now, and probably traveling to the other islands too," he added in satisfaction.

Celia knew he was right. She felt a stab of guilt.

"John . . . I've been thinking over my action of last night. I believe that I might have been . . ." She twisted her hands together, unable to look at him. "A bit hasty."

The smile vanished from John's face. Under his deep Hawaiian suntan, his skin went ashen. "Celia, have you changed your mind?"

Celia felt another pang, but then she hardened herself against it. She wasn't going to hurt John—not really. She had to refuse him anyway, so what harm if she waited a few more months to do so?

She moistened her lips and began to speak carefully. "John, we haven't gotten to know each other very well. I need a lot more time to feel really comfortable with you."

His eyes watched her, full of distress, and Celia felt her heart sink. But she *wasn't* doing anything wrong, she told herself.

She hurried on. "As you know, I really came here to the islands to teach in the Hawaii Nei school. But it closed before I arrived, and I was out of a job."

"I'm aware of that," he said stiffly.

"I still want to teach. I'm a good teacher, I know I am. I brought two trunks of books and supplies here to the islands, and I long to be able to use them."

John frowned. "I don't understand. What does that have to do with your marrying me?"

Celia lost her composure for a moment. She had not known this would be so hard, that she would feel such uncomfortable prickings of conscience. "I . . . I can't accept a ring from you yet. I need time . . . I scarcely know you yet, I . . ."

"Celia! You're frightened, that's all. But I do love you, and I know you love me. I saw it in your eyes last night, I felt it when you kissed me in the garden. I want to prove I can be a good husband to you."

John rose from his chair and came to kneel beside Celia's, putting his arms around her. He was strong and manly, and he smelled of shaving soap, hair pomade, and good, clean perspiration. But she didn't love this man, she loved his brother, Celia reminded herself desperately. Roman was the only man she wanted, and she'd do anything to have him—even lie.

"Please." She pushed John away, shaking herself free of his embrace. "Let me finish what I was saying."

Reluctantly he released her. "Very well."

"I need time to . . . to accustom myself to being your wife. Therefore I would like to come to Mountain View for a long visit. I will teach in the plantation school there, and you can pay me a small salary."

It was as if she'd asked for a piece of property on the moon. John stared at her, dumbfounded, and finally he threw back his head and gave the hearty laugh of a man who has heard something preposterous. "What? You want to come to Mountain View as my *employee?* Don't be ridiculous!"

"On the contrary, I'm utterly serious. You told me yourself that you have several hundred workers, and some of them must have children. And your own young daughter is desperately in need of learning, if what I hear about her is true."

He scowled. "Tina is all right."

"Running half-wild, allowed to do exactly as she pleases? Do you want her to grow up illiterate, unable to read or write?"

As John looked thunderous, Celia pressed her advantage. "Besides, I want to teach. I've been bored here, with little to do but explore the island on horseback or attend veranda parties.

I want to be useful. And if you don't allow me to come to Mountain View, then I'll go somewhere else."

"No. I don't want you anywhere else." John reached for her hand, gripping it in his two large, warm, callused ones. "Celia, I just don't understand. You're having second thoughts about marrying me, but you want to teach at my school. . . . I don't even *have* a school."

"But you could build one."

She gave him her prettiest smile, filling it with all the charm she could muster. She held eye contact with him, using all the power of her femininity.

"Yes," John sighed at last, his blue eyes regarding her yearningly. "I suppose I could."

Then suddenly his arms lifted her up and squeezed her so tightly that Celia feared her ribs would cave in. His lips sought hers, his tongue insistent, demanding. Trembling, Celia allowed the kiss.

"All right," he whispered. "You can come to Mountain View, I'll build you a school. I'll humor you in that. But you'll teach only for a while, my darling. Only for a month or two. Then we'll marry. And I'll hear no more refusals."

He grabbed her and kissed her again. She wasn't doing anything wrong, Celia told herself feverishly as their lips melted together. She was merely giving John two months of happiness that he wouldn't otherwise have had. And she'd be a good teacher, she vowed. She'd work long and hard. She would not cheat John in that.

But if she came to Mountain View, she'd see Roman. She'd get another chance to make him fall in love with her.

And that was all that counted.

Hatteras was horrified when Celia gleefully returned from riding to announce her plans.

"Do you mean to tell me that you're going to Maui to live on the plantation of a man to whom you aren't even married?"

Hatteras had been repotting some anthuriums, with their dramatically waxy red blooms and long pistils. A smear of dirt marred her right cheek.

"Why, yes, I am." Celia faced her aunt, determined not to back down.

"And you're doing it because you need time to *think*?"

"Yes. Of course, John is reluctant," Celia admitted. "But he is humoring me on the hope that we'll be married in a few months."

Hatteras looked troubled. "I see."

"I really *do* want to teach!" Celia burst out. "I want to be useful, and I do have to think. Marriage is such a serious step . . ."

Hatteras sighed. "In view of your past history of jilting two fiancés, if you say you need time to think, then you probably do. I know you've been bored here in Honolulu. Still, we're faced with the problem of gossip. If you go to Maui and live at Mountain View without marriage vows, people will think the worst."

Celia's heart sank. She knew that what her aunt said was true.

"But it isn't fair that a woman can be damaged by merely being in the presence of a man to whom she's not wed, while a man can go about as he chooses, doing whatever suits him!"

Hatteras pulled off her gardening gloves with an air of decision. "Who said life was fair? But I've solved everything —if you don't mind a companion for a month or two, that is."

"What do you mean?"

"Why, simply this. I'll come with you. I'll be your chaperon. *That* should silence any wagging tongues!"

"Oh, aunt!" Hatteras intended to stand behind her, to back up Celia's behavior with her own utterly respectable presence. Celia felt her eyes moisten with sudden emotion—and another spasm of guilt. If Hatteras knew why she really wanted to go to Maui . . .

She hugged her aunt, smelling Hatteras' oddly mingled scents of rosewater, perspiration, and garden earth. "What would I ever do without you, Aunt Hatteras?"

Hatteras laughed. "Goodness, who knows? Anyway, you aren't going to be tested. I'm coming, and frankly, I intend to see to it that you *do* end up marrying John Burnside just as planned. Remember, I did make a promise to your mother. I think this is the only way I'm ever going to be able to keep it."

8

Just that quickly, Celia's life took a whirling change. Two days later, John left for Maui in order to prepare for their arrival and to start building the school according to the instructions Celia had given him.

Celia and Hatteras began a feverish round of packing. All the items in Celia's large trousseau had to be rewrapped carefully in tissue paper and put into trunks. There was even a wedding dress, a lace-and-satin creation sewn in Boston by Celia's mother's society dressmaker, boasting layers of flounces and a long, flowing train sewn with thousands of tiny seed pearls.

Celia eyed the dress as it was being tucked away, squaring her chin with resolve. She wasn't going to wear it to marry John. If Roman wasn't to be her husband, then she wouldn't wear it at all.

She spent several days scouring the Honolulu market, searching out more books, pencils, slates, and copybooks. This was a task that drew her enthusiasm. Already she could picture her pupils. There would be Tina, young and eager for learning. The native Hawaiians, too, were bright, quick learners, Hatteras had said, and they adored the written word. Surely it would be a joy to teach such children.

"You're really enjoying this, aren't you, Celia?" Hatteras said one afternoon as they struggled, with the aid of two shop assistants, to load more boxes of books into a carriage. "I've seen how hard you worked, preparing your lesson plans. I believe you really *do* want to teach."

"Of course I do." Celia stared at her aunt, surprised. "Didn't you believe me?"

"I thought . . ." Then Hatteras' hand went out to clasp Celia's. "You're a good girl, Celia. However could I have doubted you?"

The steamer that would ferry them to Maui was the same one that Rebecca had taken, the *Kilauea*. It was a rather shabby ship of four hundred tons that looked as if it had received plenty of battering in *kona* storms. Its keel, Hatteras said, had scraped off the branch coral on reefs around all of the islands.

The morning of their departure dawned hot and sunny. Masses of fluffy clouds were banked behind the Koolau range in their usual high-piled display. However, the rest of the sky was clear, its color an intense, paint-box blue. The waves inside the harbor reef were choppy and capped with white.

Celia felt suffused with a wild excitement that she could scarcely hold in check. The deck of the *Kilauea* was crammed with Hawaiians draped in flower *leis*. These passengers had brought their own supplies for the journey—calabashes of *poi*, water jugs, coconuts, bananas, dried fish. The afterdeck of the dining saloon was heaped high with the travelers' Mexican saddles and saddlebags, for although horses were easy to come by in the islands, saddlery was not.

They left the harbor, towed by a small tugboat. By dusk the deck was covered with mats and mattresses, and nearly two hundred natives sat, slept, chatted, or snoozed in happy abandon. Down below, Celia and her aunt had been given quarters in a large stern cabin that held twelve or more passengers.

As Celia started to turn down the thin cotton blanket that covered her bunk, a cockroach scuttled across her pillow. It was fat and shiny, about two inches long.

"Oh!" Celia shuddered and leaped backward.

Hatteras laughed. "Oh, it won't hurt you, Celia." She went after the insect with the heel of her shoe. "Before the whites came to Hawaii, there were no cockroaches, rats, mice, scorpions, or mosquitos here. We brought them all on our ships. Now we must suffer from them. It's poetic justice, don't you think?"

On the second day of the voyage, the *Kilauea*'s machinery

broke down. The steamer lay tossing and rolling on the swells for five hours in what the captain said was a heavy gale.

Celia believed him. She spent a miserable night in her sweat-soaked clothing, listening to the sounds of those around her being sick. In the middle of the night, water began to flood through the skylight of the cabin, and soon the floor was sloshing in seawater four inches deep.

Celia lay stiffly in her bunk, her excitement gone. Had she made a mistake in deciding to go to Mountain View? Surely John would try to pressure her into wedding him, and Hatteras had already made it clear she intended to see Celia married.

But her stay would be for only two months or so, Celia assured herself, twisting about on the narrow bunk. Surely she could put John off for that length of time. And Roman would surely come often to Mountain View. She'd see him, attract his interest, show him how desirable she was . . .

The following day, Maui loomed out of the water. Celia hung over the rail, her excitement rekindling. How beautiful it was! The island rode the horizon, its large end dominated by the huge bluish-green, brooding bulk of Haleakala, capped by dark clouds at its summit.

More mountains loomed at the smaller end of the island, cloud-crowned, eerily majestic.

"It looks like something out of a fairy tale," Celia exulted, while Hatteras smiled indulgently at her enthusiasm. "As if a king and queen could live there." She shaded her eyes against the glare of the sun on the water.

"Well, in a manner of speaking, you may be right," Hatteras said. "Mountain View is supposed to be stunningly lovely, and to be mistress there will be a real feather in your cap. I've already written your mother a long letter explaining everything. I'm certain she'll be very pleased with your choice."

So the news would travel to Boston, too. What else had she expected? Celia's hands clutched the rail of the *Kilauea*, and she felt perspiration spring out on her forehead at the thought of what she planned to do. But she'd come too far now, she reminded herself. She wanted Roman, she intended to have him, and there was no looking back.

* * *

That afternoon they docked in Lahaina, a little whaling town whose harbor was crammed with sailing ships, its streets lined with grog shops, sleazy hotels, brothels, grass houses, and the homes of missionaries. They bought food in the marketplace and hired a bullock cart to take them to Mountain View.

Two hours later they were jouncing uphill along a trail carved out of the shoulders of the West Maui Mountains. Mattresses placed on the floor of the cart barely cushioned them against the roughness of the ride.

But the scenery was worth the battering about. They passed gorges carved into the hills, cliffs that plunged hundreds of feet toward boiling surf. The landscape seemed to Celia larger than life, fitting in with her own tumultuous feelings. Nothing here on Maui could ever be ordinary or prosaic.

"Well, my girl, what do you think?"

Celia struggled to find words. "It's so . . . dramatic, so *big*. I already love it. I think I belong here."

"I sincerely hope so. Since you've promised to marry a man who makes his home here."

Celia flushed and said nothing.

The road continued to wind upward, presenting views that grew ever more breathtaking. The sea glittered below, a faded, glorious blue. On the horizon lay the islands of Lanai and Molokai, distance giving them a blue-green, mysterious cast. Magic islands, Celia thought, her heart giving a little leap. Everything today seemed magic.

Finally they saw their first cane field. It lay before them, an undulating, wavy mass of bright green, rather like a field of giant grass. As the cart drew closer, Celia saw that this "grass" was formed of giant stalks that grew man-high, sun glistening on their blades. The wind created ripples of sound as the blades rubbed together.

She stared into the cane, transfixed. It made her think of fairy tales, of Jack and the beanstalk. . . . She jerked herself away from the fancy. Grow up, Celia Griffin! she scolded herself. You're a grown woman, not a child. Still, the green fields drew her eye, hinting at dreams only half-realized.

Suddenly, as they rounded a bend in the road, Mountain View appeared before them. Celia caught her breath. There was an avenue of tall, massive trees with heavy, divided trunks. At the end of the avenue was a house, set in a lawn stunning in its green beauty, where red blossoms had been set in large stone urns.

But it was the house itself that drew Celia's gaze. It was white and rambling, its style Georgian, its lines gracefully balanced, a pleasure to the eye. There were gracious green-painted shutters, a Federal-style porch, a Palladian window, scroll-topped dormers, and further wings set with long verandas.

This house didn't belong in Hawaii at all, but in New England. And yet, Celia realized, her heart pounding, it did belong here, too. Masses of flowering trees and shrubs had been planted around the house, melding it with the tropical landscape. A riot of vines and flowers hung from the verandas, and grew close to the main entrance.

"*Oh* . . ." Celia breathed. She couldn't stop looking at the wonderful, improbable house. So this was Mountain View. Then she pressed her hands together, feeling a sudden aching surge of loss. She'd never be mistress here, for she didn't intend to marry John.

"It is indeed a pretty place," Hatteras remarked briskly, holding on to the edge of the rattling cart. "But I imagine a good deal of work to run. Have you noticed the outbuildings? There seem to be a goodly number of those, too."

Obediently Celia gazed around. Visible through the trees were other plantation buildings. Houses, grass-thatched sheds, a huge building with a corrugated-iron roof. There was a scattering of frame homes, a stone church, and even—just visible over a field of cane—a small Hawaiian village. It seemed to be a whole community.

A Hawaiian galloped past on a horse, intent on some errand. He kicked at the animal's sides, shouting at it. More horses, Celia now saw, were tethered to a nearby rail, and other riders trotted here and there, giving the place an air of activity. Somewhere in the distance she heard a mechanical hum and roar, and the bellow of oxen.

The wind had been blowing away from them, but now it shifted, and for the first time Celia became aware of a thick, heavy, fermenting odor.

"What's that smell?" she asked her aunt.

Hatteras grimaced. "I believe it is sugar, my sweet. For all of this loveliness, one must pay a penalty. Fermenting molasses has quite a noxious stench sometimes. But you'll get used to it.''

The plantation wasn't to be hers . . . and it smelled. While Hatteras climbed out of the cart to examine a flaming red bush, Celia struggled to assume a more realistic attitude. What had she expected, paradise? she asked herself crossly.

Suddenly there were childish giggles.

Celia turned, to see a clutch of small, barefoot brown boys who had raced forward at the sight of the cart, and now watched from a distance, giggling and pushing each other. In their midst was a small white girl with flaming red hair.

"Why, hello." Celia smiled at them.

The children stared at her. Then a boy called something in Hawaiian to another one, and they all laughed hilariously.

Hatteras came back from her inspection of the bush. "Your pupils are skittish creatures, aren't they? You'll be hard put to tame them, I would think.''

But before Celia could comment, the children giggled and ran away, and Hatteras nudged her. "There is our host now, coming down the avenue to greet us. Do smile at him, Celia. I know how glad you are to see your fiancé.''

John Burnside strode toward them, a handsome, vital man of middle years, his gait so like Roman's that Celia's heart gave an absurd skipping jump. Hatless, he wore black broadcloth pants and a white shirt with sleeves rolled up to reveal brown, muscular forearms.

In deference to the presence of the older woman, John did not sweep Celia into his arms, although it was plain that he wanted to do so. His face had lighted up with joy on seeing her. "Celia . . . so you're here, really here. Welcome, both of you.''

Celia could not contain herself any longer. "Your plantation . . . it's gorgeous! The house, the setting—it's far lovelier even than you told me!''

John looked pleased at the compliment. "I hope you'll like it here, Celia. This is going to be your home too, my darling, as soon as I can persuade you to stop this teaching silliness.''

"It isn't silly. You need a school desperately. I've already seen some of my future pupils, and they look as skittish as wild deer.''

John sighed. ''Yes, yes, I suppose you're right. And my daughter, no doubt, was among them. Well, come into the house, both of you, and I'll show you the quarters I've arranged for you. I've given you adjoining suites, and there is a private veranda that has been walled off for your use. It has a wonderful view of the sunset. I assure you, Celia, Maui sunsets are very special. Flaming reds and purples and magentas. It's as if God himself went berserk, drunk on color and beauty.''

Celia thought her bedroom charming, with its woven grass matting, its walls hung with *tapa* fabrics woven by Hawaiian women in Mountain View's own village. On one wall there was a huge painting of the sea, powerfully depicted in bold brush strokes. Celia looked at it, caught by the scrawled signature in one corner. It said, simply, ''Beau.'' Was this the work of John's son?

Everywhere, in honor of her arrival, vases of flowers had been arranged. Hibiscus, gaudy bougainvillea, gardenias, roses, *ohia*, jasmine, others that Celia couldn't recognize. Their combined scents flooded the room, drowning out the background smell of sugar that permeated the plantation.

Arranged on Celia's pillow like an offering was a tiny collection of seashells, pink and polished, with delicate whorling. They had been laid out in a slightly lopsided manner, as if placed by a child. Immediately Celia thought of the small red-haired girl who had been standing with the Hawaiian boys, and smiled to herself. She guessed that the shells were from Tina.

She freshened up, taking a bath in a tin tub that a pretty Hawaiian servant girl brought her. Then she opened one of her trunks and changed to a fresh day dress. It was made of airy dotted swiss, lavishly decorated with embroidery and silk ribbons. Into her mass of dark hair she tucked a red hibiscus.

She descended the magnificent curved staircase.

''There you are.'' John Burnside was suddenly beside her. ''There's so much to show you, Celia, I can't wait to begin. Just having you here is going to be wonderful.''

Celia gazed around her with astonishment. A large drawing

room opened off the large center foyer, done in warm shades of red, rust, and cream, with accents of mossy green. An Aubusson rug was woven in shell-like patterns, its center a beautiful faded brick.

All the doorways had curved arches, the moldings painted a rosy beige that contrasted with the paler cream of the walls. There was moss-green furniture, some of it Sheraton and Chippendale, and through an archway she saw another room, painted a deep orange-rust. Here curio shelves had been filled with collections of minerals, volcanic specimens, and native artifacts.

A gun collection hung on one wall, a number of antique pistols and a few modern ones. And there were more of Beau's paintings, each having the harsh power of the one that hung in Celia's room.

"My father shipped this house over from Connecticut, every beam and arch," John told her proudly. "It was an enormous undertaking, one of the few foolish things he ever did. But the house has gradually adapted to the islands. Those paintings are my son's," he added.

Celia walked about, feeling more and more enthralled with what she saw. It was a home of brilliant color and spirit, she thought, a place meant for magnificence, for women in long-trained gowns, their throats glittering with diamonds and rubies.

Already she loved the plantation house—and felt a sharp pang that she would not be able to live here for long. For it was John's wife who would be mistress here.

She realized that he was looking at her, and wondered how much of her regret showed on her face.

"Now that you've seen the house, I'd like you to meet the rest of my family," John said. "Tina is outdoors somewhere— she's as hard to catch as the trade winds. But I have summoned my son, Beau, to meet you."

Celia turned to see a young man framed in one of the beautiful arched doors. He was in his early twenties, slim and handsome in an arrogant way, with a mop of brown curls that fell over his forehead. His eyes were amber, almost golden, but there was something sulky about the narrow face.

"So this is our new teacher." Beau gave her a lazy smile, as if enjoying some secret known only to himself. "I hope you can cope with the kind of pupils we grow here at Mountain View. We did have a school once before—years ago—and I'm afraid their last teacher was quite intimidated.''

Celia lifted her chin. ''I thought there had never been a school here.''

''One of your predecessors, Ariadne, who was Tina's mother, ran it. Until she was frightened away, that is. She was squeamish, quite ill-suited for the tropics, scared of the lizards that lived in the schoolhouse.''

''The geckos? I rather like them.'' Celia wanted to laugh. If Beau was trying to scare her, he would have to do better than that.

Hatteras had come down the stairs, and John went to greet her. The two moved to the other room, where John was showing Hatteras the small carved figure of a war god. Celia was left to continue the awkward conversation with John's son.

He made her uneasy. She didn't know why; perhaps it was those amber eyes that glinted so mockingly. She searched for a topic of conversation. ''Your paintings are very remarkable, Beau.''

He shrugged.

''I have never seen any like them before,'' she floundered on. ''All those landscapes and seascapes filled with mysterious clouds and jagged brush strokes. It's as if you both loved the island and hated it.''

For the first time, Beau showed a reaction. Color spread over his fair, fine-grained skin. ''Ah, but I must have something to do to keep me from madness. Maui might look beautiful to you, but to me it is the ends of the earth. A rocky island, trapping all its residents in a prison from which they cannot escape.''

She stared at him. ''What an odd way to talk.''

''Didn't my father tell you? I was dragged back here in disgrace after I lost all my money trying to find gold in California, and ended up in a jail in Sacramento. I am the black sheep,'' he added resentfully. ''Brought back to Maui to molder.''

Celia did not know what to say. ''I don't see how anyone could dislike it here.''

Beau's eyes glittered. ''Well, I do. I hate it. And you will, too, soon enough. Everyone who's been here long enough gets island fever.''

Celia glanced toward the other room, wishing Hatteras and John would rescue her from this uncomfortable conversation. Beau's eyes seemed to consume her, traveling restlessly from her face to her bodice, then back again to her face.

"I don't think I could ever get island fever," she said. "I could stay here forever, gazing at that wonderful view.''

"You'll change. At least in California there was always the hope of finding a big gold nugget and making your fortune. Here . . . ." Beau's face twisted. "There is nothing but sugar. You'll grow to hate it soon enough. All the other wives did.''

"You seem intent on making it clear to me that I'm only one in a succession," she snapped, voicing her annoyance at last.

"Well, you *are* going to be number three, aren't you? But there have been even more women than that. My father is a lusty man, and the village is, of course, close at hand. Hawaiian women make pretty, passionate mistresses.''

Beau leaned closer, obviously enjoying tormenting her. "But that shouldn't concern *you.* You're only to be a teacher. And the chaperon you've brought with you will protect you from all unwanted advances—from my father or from anyone else.''

Did he mean from himself?

What a confusing, disconcerting man Beau was! As Hatteras and John finished their conversation and again entered the drawing room, Celia greeted their approach with relief. Kathryn Whitt had been right, she thought with a shiver of misgiving. Beau was indeed going to be difficult.

John sent a servant to fetch Tina. While they waited, he arranged for tea to be brought to the veranda. They sat at a table, enjoying the gorgeous view.

While Hatteras and John discussed island politics and the sugar market, Celia daydreamed, her eyes focused on the shimmering cobalt sea.

"Is this my teacher?" a childish voice interrupted her reverie. She turned to see the red-haired girl clambering like a boy up the railing of the veranda. Down on the lawn, a gray dog capered, its tail forming a nearly perfect semicircle. It did not bark, but made strange, half-whining sounds.

"Tina!" John Burnside interrupted his conversation to speak sharply to his daughter. "Get down from that railing at once and climb the steps like a proper girl. And go and change your dress. You look a disgrace! Don't you *ever* brush your hair?"

The child grinned impishly, but finally jumped down and did as she was told. Celia regarded her. Tina had flaming dark red hair, its natural curls matted into a wild mass. Her heart-shaped face was darkly suntanned, emphasizing the golden hazel of her eyes, which were nearly the same color as Beau's.

However, Celia noted with amusement, Tina certainly did resemble a little wild creature. Her knee-length white dress had evidently been dragged endlessly through red Maui dust, rocks, brambles, and mud. Scratches marred her brown arms and legs, and her bare feet were callused and dirty.

"Are you the one who left the lovely shells on my pillow?" Celia asked, smiling.

The child's face lit up. "Yes, did you like them? I've collected lots and lots of them. You have to dig out the animal inside, you know. They make a frightful stink. Papa won't let me keep my shells to dry on the veranda anymore, he says I'll drive us out of house and home. So I leave them outside for the ants to pick clean."

Celia was captivated by the girl's natural charm. She engaged Tina in conversation about her shells, asking her where she had collected them.

"Enough, enough," John protested at last. "This girl is barely civilized. She owns hundreds of shells, but do you know that she cannot write any of their names?"

At the rebuke, the excitement faded from Tina's face. She hung her head.

"Then we'll have to teach her," Celia said quickly. "I can see right now that she'll be a very fast learner."

John snorted. "Fast? I've been after her for eight years to wear shoes, and she hasn't learned that quickly. In fact, she hasn't learned it at all."

"But what do shoes have to do with writing?" Celia

wanted to know. "Unless you happen to write with your toes, that is."

Tina giggled. Her laugh was silvery and infectious, and with relief, Celia smiled back. She hoped that she had made at least one friend here at Mountain View.

Later that day, John called the servants to the main hallway and introduced each one to Celia and Hatteras. There were seven or eight young Hawaiians from the village. The men were smooth-skinned and big-boned, with wide faces. The girls were pretty and giggly, their eyes dark, lustrous. Celia could not help wondering which of them had been John's mistress, and then, almost violently, she pushed away the speculation. What did it matter which of these girls John Burnside had slept with? Or if he had taken any other women at all?

Leinani was the girl who had brought Celia her bath, a plump girl in a bright-flowered *holoku*. She greeted Celia in a "pidgen" dialect that was a hodgepodge of English and Hawaiian words, spoken fast and difficult to understand.

But Kinau, another maidservant, spoke perfect English.

Celia looked at her curiously. Kinau was taller than the other girls, and slimmer, her body lithe. She had black hair that fell like silk to her waist, glistening with a rich sheen. Her dark eyes were sultry. She wore a white flower tucked behind her ear.

"I hope you like it here at Mountain View," Kinau shyly welcomed Celia. "If you wish, I'll take you to a pool I know, and teach you how to swim."

Celia was delighted at the invitation. "Oh, I'd love that. How did you learn to speak such good English, Kinau?"

"I learned at the missionary school in Lahaina. I worked there, too, once, in the hospital."

"I see." Celia was relieved that there would be someone here of approximately her own age, and looked forward to taking Kinau up on her invitation.

Chang Liu was the cook, a slim, immaculate man who—like the Chinese servants in Honolulu—wore his head partially shaved. A glossy black pigtail, woven with silk cord, was wound several times around his head. Chang smiled at

Celia and told her, in broken English, that she and her aunt could be served breakfast on their veranda if they wished.

"Anything missy want, she can have," he added obsequiously.

"Chang lives in the village with his Hawaiian wife," John explained after the cook had gone back to the kitchen. "They have five children."

The gray dog that Celia had seen earlier came padding into the house, flopping onto the Aubusson rug with a sigh of contentment.

"The Orientals were brought here to the islands to work in the fields, but most of them prefer other work," John went on. "Chang speaks English, Hawaiian, and Cantonese, and runs a little store for the workers here at Mountain View. It's also rumored that he has other, more disreputable business in Lahaina."

"Oh?"

"Of course, if I knew that for certain, I'd fire him, and he knows it. But Chang enjoys his place here. The work is easy and his Hawaiian wife apparently contents him well enough. As long as he does the work and minds his own business, it's all that I ask."

Celia nodded, reaching down to pat the short gray fur of Tina's pet. The dog licked her hand happily.

"Have you any more questions?" John wanted to know.

Celia laughed. "This is really a silly question, but I have to ask it. I was wondering about Tina's dog."

"Hili? Ah, yes . . ."

"Why doesn't she bark?"

"Hili is descended from the original Polynesian dogs. They had no bark, and probably whined or made singing sounds like the barkless dogs of New Guinea. Anyway, they were brought to these islands centuries ago as food."

Celia started. "As *food?*"

"Indeed." At Celia's gasp, John laughed. "Dog flesh was considered by the old Hawaiians to be superior to pork, and as many as two hundred dogs were sometimes baked for a single feast. They were considered a very useful beast. Their bones served as fishhooks, and their teeth were used in dancers' anklets—"

"Stop, stop!" Celia cried, looking at the innocently snoozing canine. "I hope for Tina's sake that nobody intends to eat Hili."

"Of course not." John extended an arm to Celia. "And now, come, there's much more I want to show you. My pride, my work, and the whole reason for the existence of Mountain View . . . sugar."

Celia remembered what Beau had said, that after a while, like the other wives, she would come to hate sugar. But, she reminded herself, she wasn't going to be a wife. Not John's wife.

When was Roman coming to Mountain View? She fervently hoped it would be soon.

9

Later, Celia's first tour of the sugar mill would blur in her mind, becoming an endless succession of buildings. The plantation office, which still contained the old leather chair that Amos Burnside had died in. The cooper's shed, the carpenter's shop, a machinist's shed, a drying house where the discarded cane stalks were turned into fuel for the mill fires.

There were barracks for the workers, who numbered more than two hundred and whose nationality ranged from Hawaiian to Japanese to Samoan. And everywhere, churning up the red Maui dust, were the oxen, rumbling back and forth with huge wagonloads of cane. Drivers shouted and cursed, cracking bullwhips just inches away from the flanks of the straining animals.

"So many oxen!" Celia exclaimed to John, inhaling the thick, fermenting odor of sugar mixed with cattle droppings, dust, and flower blossoms—an odd combination, she thought.

John laughed. "We have more than a thousand," he boasted. "And we need every one of them. This place runs on water and animal power. To haul the cane, to cut wood in the mountains and haul that, to transport our sugar to the port—without oxen, and the men to handle them, Mountain View would be nothing."

Celia felt a spurt of excitement as John escorted her toward a big building made of corrugated iron, crowned by several smokestacks that belched steam.

"My mill," he explained proudly.

As they approached the building, Celia heard the rush of water over the mill dam, and loud, pounding noises of machinery coming from inside. As soon as they stepped inside the door, the stench hit them. Gross, powerful, it permeated the senses.

"The smell," Celia said, reeling backward.

John frowned impatiently. "Oh, you'll get used to it—I have. I never even notice it much anymore. Mind your step, now, this place can be dangerous for those who grow careless. I want you to see the crushing."

After the bright glare of sunlight, the interior of the mill seemed dim and steamy. It clanged with noise: the grinding of machinery, the shouts of workers in strange languages, all echoing against metal walls.

John led her to where four Japanese workmen were gathered around a pair of big stone rollers. The cylinders turned slowly, while a man fed an armload of cane stalks, one at a time, into their maw.

Pale green juice, flecked with bits of dirt and cane, flowed into a trough below.

"See? That's going to be sugar! And those rollers are made of granite, imported all the way from China. They weigh three and a half tons each."

Celia gazed at the green, scummy liquid, wrinkling her nose. She had always thought of sugar as a pure-white crystal that she dropped into her coffee, pretty and neat.

"But how . . . ? I mean, that juice is certainly not very clean," she finally said.

John frowned, as if she had said something heretical. "Of course it isn't—not yet. This is only the start of the process."

They went deeper into the mill. A room glowed with heat, rich with the stench of boiling sugar. Five shallow iron pots, bolted together in a long row, were set in a brick oven tended by a big Japanese, naked except for a loincloth. His skin glistened with perspiration as he threw chunks of wood and cane trash onto the fire.

"This is where we clarify the cane juice," John explained. "Believe me, it's a tricky process." As he went on to talk of milk of lime and chemical processes, Celia stared at the lurid scene before her. The fire created huge dancing shadows against the walls. The pots bubbled and gurgled like devil's brew—and smelled like it, too, she thought.

"More wood! More wood!" A fat man paced back and forth on a platform above, shouting at the workers. "Are you lazy dogs who want to lie around in the sun all day? Get moving, get ready for the strike!"

Everything became urgent.

Frantically the workmen began ladling the turbid, scummy juice from pot to pot, while the man on the platform paced back and forth, shook his fist, and screamed at the workers.

But finally it was done, and they left the shed. John wiped perspiration from his forehead, and unobtrusively, Celia did the same.

"Why all the hurry and shouting?" she asked.

"Because it was time for the strike. No two batches of sugar are exactly alike. The sugar boiler has to know exactly when the maximum number of grains have been formed. That's when we take it off the fire and put it in the cooling vats. It's an art, believe me. My father was very good at it, and he taught me. Now I have McRory. He's a cantankerous Scot who drinks too much, but nobody knows better how to make sugar."

There was more. A centrifugal machine that separated the sugar grains from the molasses. Other machines, storage vats, testing apparatus. John explained all of it to Celia in detail. But the thick, fermenting stench of sugar had begun to affect Celia's stomach, and she was relieved when they finally left the mill and started back toward the house.

"Do you think you'll grow to like sugar?" John asked her. By the way he said it, Celia realized this was no idle question.

"Why, I . . . I did find it fascinating."

"But can you stand it? Both of my wives hated the stuff. Susan kept all the windows of the house shut, no matter how blazing hot it got inside. She said sugar nauseated her. As for Ariadne, she refused even to put sugar in her tea. Said she might have to live here, but she didn't have to eat it herself."

"I see." Celia had wondered what those two previous marriages had been like, and thought that what John said gave her a clue.

"Did Susan and Ariadne like living on Maui?" she ventured. "Aside from the smell of sugar, I mean."

John's jaw knotted. "Not really, I am sorry to say. Susan longed to return to Georgia, which was where I met her. She always missed Atlanta, and she is the one who planted most of the flowering trees here—they reminded her of home, she said. As for Ariadne, she, too, felt trapped here on the island, and was always longing to be somewhere else."

Island fever, Celia thought. But she knew that *she* would never feel that way. It was too beautiful here—and even sugar held an excitement. She supposed that in time a person could even get used to the thick smell of it.

John took her hand and pressed it tightly between his own two large ones. "But let's not talk of them—they're gone now, and those days are past. Now we have only the future, and each other. I love you, Celia, and you're going to be my real wife, the wife of my heart. The only one who counts."

It was a beautiful thing to say, and it stabbed Celia, flooding her with guilt. She tried to smile at her husband-to-be, and found that she could not.

The following morning, Celia walked to the schoolhouse that had been built for her use. She walked around its perimeter, gazing at it in dismay. The structure had been built in the island fashion, its lower half constructed of lava rock, its upper of wooden beams bound together with grass thatch. The roof was thatched with old cane stalks.

Celia stared at the building, her heart sinking. John had given her explicit directions for finding the building, so this had to be the place he had meant.

She stepped inside. The interior smelled aromatically of grasses. The floor, made of dirt, was spread over with clean, woven *lau hala* mats. But the furnishings were pitifully sparse—rows of hand-hewn wooden benches, one table, and one wooden chair, presumably for her. She dropped her supply bag on the table and sank into the chair. How crude the building was, how primitive! Why, they might as well hold their classes outdoors!

She had given John such careful instructions on the dimensions of the school, the need for a privy, for desks and blackboards, a bell with which to call the pupils. And it was as if he had mocked her every instruction. The school was roofed with cane. The benches looked so uncomfortable that she was sure they would be torture for the children. And, the final ignominy, there was no bell. How was she to call her pupils to class?

It was as if John had given only lip service to the idea of a school. Why bother to make it permanent when she was only going to be playing at teaching for a month or so?

Fuming, she unloaded her supplies and decided to have the servants bring the rest of the boxes to the school later in the day. Finally she slumped back into the chair and stared out one of the windows, where a view of green mountains was magnificently framed.

Tears of frustration stung her eyes, and she knew they were not only for the inadequacies of the school, but also for her own situation.

Nothing had turned out as she had anticipated. She had thought it would be easy to be at Mountain View, to keep John Burnside happy with a few smiles and polite evasions, to earn her way by teaching. Instead, John was genuinely in love with her. He had called her the wife of his heart. Guilt tore at Celia, and she felt like banging her fist on the rough tabletop.

She hadn't known it would be so hard to deceive! For she really was deceiving, wasn't she? She had come here under false pretenses, with no intention of marrying John. All along, she'd had another man in her mind. Roman.

She picked up a slate and began turning it restlessly, gazing at its fresh surface, as yet unmarred by childish scratches or initials. Where *was* Roman? Kathryn had implied that he would be often at the plantation in order to see to its business. Yet he had not come.

Last night before dinner, Celia had tried subtly to learn from Beau when Roman might be expected.

"Let sleeping dogs lie," he had told her, scowling. "Or, rather, sleeping murderers. We tolerate Roman here at Mountain View because he is half-owner, because my grandfather's will stipulates he has a right to be here. He has financed some of our irrigation projects and advanced us several large loans. But never think he is welcome here. Because he isn't. And he never will be."

"Isn't it a little crass, to accept the money he lends, without accepting him?" some imp made Celia say.

"It is the way things are done," Beau had responded stiffly.

Now a noise outside the school building interrupted her thoughts. Celia looked up to see Tina pad barefoot into the school. The child lugged a basket filled with some fragrant, vivid green vine.

"I brought these. They are *maile*, they grow in the mountains. Don't they have a good smell? We can hang them on the walls."

Celia looked at the little girl, whose red mop of hair today looked as wild as ever, ringlets flowing down her back in a tangle. A schoolhouse hung with vines? But this was Hawaii, she reminded herself. The Sandwich Islands.

"Why, yes, we could do that. They certainly do smell wonderful. And we ought to bring in some flowers, too. We'll study botany."

"Botany?" At the word, Tina wrinkled a pretty, tip-tilted nose. She roamed curiously to the table, picking up one of Celia's books to examine it.

"That means studying the structure of the plants. It means . . ." Then, at Tina's puzzled look, Celia smiled. "Never mind, it's going to be fun. Oh, that's a book called *Little Women*. It's about four sisters—Meg, Jo, Beth, and Amy— and their lives. When you've learned to read, we can read it aloud to each other."

Tina wriggled her shoulders, as if the idea didn't appeal to her. She pawed again in the stack of books, volumes on Greek mythology, Latin, and history. "Are there any books about Maui?"

"The island? No, I don't have any, but perhaps—"

"No, not the island. *Maui*," Tina insisted. "Hina was his mother, and she had trouble drying her bark cloth because the day was too short. So Maui went to the sun and lassoed it with his rope to make it go more slowly."

Tina chattered on, telling more stories of Maui, who apparently was a figure of Hawaiian legend, a prankster with many exploits. Thoughtfully Celia put away the Louisa May Alcott book and went about her task of arranging the school. There was so much about the islands that she didn't know. And how strange that an eight-year-old should begin to teach her.

*   *   *

"I need a bell," Celia said firmly that night as she and John walked along the edge of the lawn, gazing outward at the afterglow left by the sinking sun, lavish sweeps of fading purples and magentas. "John, you didn't provide me with one, and I can't summon my pupils without some way to call them."

"Must you?"

"Must I what?" She stopped strolling, to stare at him.

"Must you call them at all? Celia, won't you reconsider this strange idea of yours? If there must be a school at all, let your Aunt Hatteras teach it. Didn't she and her husband run a school in Honolulu for more than twenty years?"

Celia bit her lip. "My aunt has already told me that her teaching days are finished. She says that she is too old, and there are too many other things she wishes to do instead. But I *do* want to teach, and I intend to do so. And if you can't rig up some sort of a bell for me, I . . . I'll find one for myself. There must be some sort of factory bell down there at the mill. I'll go and ask Mr. McRory to help me, I'm sure he'd be more than happy to oblige."

John frowned. "I happen to have a bell. It weighs forty pounds, though, and might be too heavy for you to manage."

"Then we'll build a frame to hold it. I *am* going to teach those children, John, whether you make it easy for me or not." Then she softened her words, smiling at him gently. "But of course I know you'll help me, you are a kind man, and after all, Tina, too, will benefit. Surely you couldn't deny your own daughter, could you?"

It was one argument—at least—that she had won.

Two days later, Celia walked quickly down the path that led to the school, her color high. It was a wonderful island morning, the sky washed clean blue except for the usual gray blanket that hung over Haleakala, and the puffier white clouds fluffed over the West Maui Mountains. In the distance, the Pacific lay calm, traces of wind patterns etched on its vast surface.

She opened the schoolhouse door and gazed around with satisfaction. She and four servants had worked all day yesterday. Shelves and tables had been carried out from the house, and a makeshift blackboard constructed. Celia had nailed maps and

pictures to the wood framing, and the room was lavish with
maile and freshly picked *ohia*.

She sat down and began to look through her lesson plans,
excitement filling her. She had tutored younger pupils at Miss
Tanny's Day School, enjoying every minute of it. She was
proud of the fact that her giggly young-girl students had
adored her, that the headmistress had praised her for her work
with them.

She could hardly wait to get started. Where were the
children?

Then, belatedly, she remembered the bell. She stepped
outside the door, where the heavy iron bell had been sus-
pended from a wooden frame. She lifted the handle, and the
clapper clanged against the bell. Sound pealed into the clear
air, carrying for miles.

A few minutes later, as if by magic, the school building
swarmed with children. Some were Hawaiian, clad in rumpled cotton pants or just loincloth *malos*. Others, Chang's
children, were half-Chinese, and there were also Japanese
and Samoans. Two freckled brothers were apparently the sons
of McRory, the sugar boiler.

All of the children were barefoot, all had faces darkened
from the sun, and all were full of riotous good spirits. One
freckled boy threw a fragment of cane scrap at another one. A
brown boy leaped on a bench, then jumped from it to a
neighboring bench, shouting in pidgen Hawaiian. Hili, Tina's
dog, raced about in hysterical joy.

More children joined the jumping. Tina was in the thick of
it, leaping from bench to bench, farther than most of the
boys. Her red hair flamed, and her cheeks were flushed with
exertion.

"Boys and girls! Boys and girls!" In vain Celia tried to get
their attention. A bench crashed to its side, carrying with it
three howling, gasping boys. "Please . . . will you come to
order?"

The laughing and horseplay went on, more frenzied than
ever. Celia realized that her pupils, overexcited by the nov-
elty of school, had no intention of coming to order. The
benches were a fabulous new game, and they intended to
enjoy it to the fullest.

A tiny girl, her hair a cloud of black, fell and skinned a

knee. The others ignored her wails, continuing to leap and dance.

Celia ran to the crying child. She picked her up and inspected the bleeding knee. The shouts of the children had reached a frantic crescendo in which the weeping of the little Japanese girl could scarcely be heard.

Dismay plummeted through Celia. This was chaos. She had lost control of the children before school had even begun; she'd never be able to teach. At the thought, she wanted to cry out with frustration. Without schooling, these children would grow up as ignorant as wild beasts. Tina, too, would never be able to read a sign or handle money. Like any illiterate, she'd have to count on her fingers or depend on others to help her.

And this adorable, sobbing Japanese child whom she held in her arms . . . *No*, Celia thought violently. She couldn't let it happen, and she wouldn't.

She set the Japanese girl down and marched grimly out of the building toward the school bell. She yanked on its handle, causing the bell to peal. Clang after clang reverberated, drowning out the children's shouts. Again and again Celia rang the bell, filling the air with its din.

Then Tina hopped down from the bench, giving Celia a shamed look. In a moment, the two freckled boys followed. Within three minutes the children were standing in rows in front of the benches and silence and order reigned in the schoolhouse. Thirty-five pairs of round, awed eyes stared at her.

Celia gazed sternly back, not allowing one trace of a smile to lighten her expression. Her hands shook from the effort of slamming the big bell, but she made her voice as deep and impressive as she could.

"Good morning, boys and girls. I'm Miss Griffin, your new teacher."

The day sped by. Celia worked on the alphabet, and several of the children, Tina included, mastered most of it. A freckled boy, Kevin McRory, rivaled Tina for brightest pupil.

As the heat of the afternoon grew more intense, Celia was stunned to glance at her *chatelaine* watch and realize it was already three o'clock. Hastily she rang the bell again, and

Julia Grice

waited while her pupils scampered out of the building as magically as they had entered it. Within seconds the school was empty.

Celia sank into her chair, exhaustion filling her like a tide. It had been an effort to be stern-faced all day, to hide the smiles that came so naturally to her, to remember thirty-five foreign names, to show thirty-five sets of grubby little hands how to hold slate and chalk. How could she ever have thought that teaching would be easy?

"Well, I see that your pupils have not yet torn you limb from limb," a voice mocked from the doorway. She looked up to see Beau slouch in, his crooked grin challenging her. His mop of brown curls was untidy, giving him a rakish look.

Annoyed, Celia began gathering up her papers. She spoke evenly. "I think the day went very well."

"Oh, indeed. Miss Prim, are we? I saw the debacle this morning. I couldn't resist walking by the school to see just what sort of mess you might make of it." He grinned maddeningly. "It was loud enough to be heard for miles."

Celia reddened. "I had trouble at first, yes, but I did get my pupils under control. How dare you stand around outside the school hoping I'd make a fool of myself?" Fury spurred her words. "Have you nothing better to do than that?"

Beau shrugged. "I was on my way to the mill office—I help with the books sometimes. When he is in a good mood, my father deigns to permit it."

"Well, the office is a good half-mile that way," Celia flared, pointing. "So I think you walked a mile out of your way."

They glared at each other, and Celia felt inordinately pleased when Beau was the first to glance away. "Oh, well." Again he shrugged. "I merely wanted to see if you intended to follow in your predecessor's rather shaky footsteps."

"Do you mean Tina's mother?"

"Who else? As I told you, Ariadne screamed at the sight of the geckos. She cried in class when the pupils refused to do their numbers, and when two boys got into a fight, she put her hands over her face and fled the schoolhouse. She never came back, either."

"And how do you know so much about it?"

Beau's eyes glinted with sudden bitter amusement. "As a matter of fact, I was one of the boys who fought."

"I see!" Celia was angry enough to kick him. "Well, I don't permit fighting in my classroom." She grabbed up her books. "And now, if you'll excuse me, I believe I'll walk back to the house."

"I'll accompany you."

"Don't bother." She flounced on ahead of him, uncomfortably aware of his eyes boring into her back, inspecting every detail of the blue day dress she wore, with its modest ribbon trim. And probably the flesh underneath it, too, she thought with annoyance.

For a few paces they formed an odd single file as John's son followed her.

"Stop following me!" she turned to snap. "You're disconcerting and terribly rude!"

"Am I?" He laughed. "Ah, Celia, you have a temper, don't you? I'd love to paint you when you're mad." He went on mockingly, "Do let me know if you need help with the school. As an old pupil, a former bad boy, I'm sure I can give you many pointers."

Then Beau gave another harsh laugh and strode on ahead of her, leaving Celia to stare after him.

The dining room at Mountain View was elegant, its walls painted a glowing rust, its fireplace mantel decorated with rare Chinese porcelain. A Waterford chandelier dripped leaded glass pendants that caught the lamplight in rainbow facets. The dining-room chairs, with their airy, fluted lines, were Philadelphia Chippendale, the sideboard a burnished Hepplewhite.

But although the room was gracious, the meal certainly was not. John and his son had made everyone uncomfortable by arguing, mostly about Beau's work at the mill that day. Apparently he had made several major accounting errors, compounding them by losing a book containing six months' accounts.

"And you claim that you can run a mill by yourself?" Celia had never seen John so coldly furious. "You can't even find your way to the mill office without a guide, much less locate a chair to sit in."

"Your father's chair?" Beau sneered. "I'm amazed you keep it there. What a relic! The chair old Amos Burnside died in! Do you think I plan to keep around the chair *you* die in, old man?"

John stiffened with outrage, and Hatteras, ever the well-bred hostess, quickly stepped in to change the subject. "I'd like to do some touring of the island," she began. "I understand the Iao Valley is very curious, with a pointed mountainous formation called the Iao Needle."

John and Beau glowered at each other, ignoring her.

"You never let me do anything around the mill," Beau muttered.

"Why should I, when you only ruin everything you touch? Last week, two sugar batches! Three other planters depend on us to process their cane, and you let them down badly. Do you think you know more than McRory?"

As the two wrangled, Tina ducked her head and made an excuse, leaving the table to flee to her room. Celia wished fervently that she could join her. Why did John have to pick at his son like this? It happened, if not every night, then entirely too often, and made her feel sorry for Beau. No wonder he thought Maui a prison. He was treated as if he were less than useless.

Later, after the difficult meal finally wound to a close with the serving of plum tarts, Celia wandered out to the veranda. She stared restlessly at the night's sunset, a spectacular sweep of molten gold and violet. There never had been sunsets like these in Boston, so beautiful that they seemed to cut straight to the heart, taunting the viewer with their glory.

"What are you doing out here alone?" It was John, striding out to join her. His dinner jacket revealed the wide thrust of his shoulders, and the evening shadows molded his features, making him look younger than his fifty years.

"I'm just thinking." She frowned at the sunset, then burst out with what had been bothering her. "Why do you treat Beau so harshly?"

"I'm not harsh to him at all. I'm simply trying to teach him how to run Mountain View. After all, he'll inherit my share when I'm gone."

"But you're so hard on him, shaming him in front of all of

us." No wonder he is resentful. I would be too, if I were treated in that manner."

"But you are not treated so. Beau is moody and difficult—I'm sure you've observed that by now. His personality is unpredictable. Do you know, I found him in jail in California when I went there to fetch him? He had been accused of theft. *Theft*, Celia! My son!"

"Was he guilty?"

"I hope to God not. I bought his way out and took him home with me."

"And you've been punishing him ever since," Celia said quietly, remembering that Beau's mother, Susan, had died in giving birth to him. Did John blame his son for that, too?

For some moments they were both silent, gazing out at the colorful display of sunset.

"Are you happy here?" John asked suddenly.

"Happy?" Celia was startled at the abrupt change in topic.

"Yes. Are you glad you came to Maui?" Suddenly John's arms went around her, pulling her close, his grip so powerful that she could not struggle away. "Celia! Oh, God, this is impossible, totally impossible! Do you think I'm made of iron? To have you so close to me, to see you every day, and yet be unable to take you as my wife . . ."

He crushed kisses on the hollow of her neck, the bristles of his cheeks scraping her skin. She managed to wriggle partially free.

"John, please! Someone might come out to the veranda and see us."

"Who? The servants? I pay them, they can see what they please. Or is it your aunt you're worried about, your damned chaperon?" John's voice had roughened, taking on a commanding note. "Celia, it's time we married. We'll do it in the village church next Sunday."

"No," she whispered.

"Why not?"

"Because . . ." But this had gone far enough; she couldn't bear her spasms of conscience any longer. "Because I came here under false pretenses. I don't really intend—"

Roughly he cut her off before she could finish. "I don't care what you intend. If you're worried about the school, I'll get a teacher from the mainland. Teachers aren't hard to find.

Wives are. Look at that sunset!'' Angrily he gestured. ''Do you think I want to enjoy it alone? I've had enough of being alone. It's been six years now. Six years since Ariadne died. Celia, I need you!''

Again his kisses smothered her. John didn't want to listen to her message, Celia realized. Didn't want to hear it. But she had to persist.

''John, I don't love you. I shouldn't have come to Maui, it was a mistake. I . . . I think I should book passage back to Honolulu as soon as I can.''

Finally her words penetrated. The burly planter jerked back from her as if she had slapped him. His ruddy face darkened as he turned on his heel and stalked to the *lanai* railing.

''Stop saying such things! You did come here, you did promise to marry me. You couldn't have done it if you didn't hold some love for me. You're just nervous, that's all. You need more time to accustom yourself to me. Well, I'm going to give it to you. I won't let you leave Maui. Do you hear me? If you try to go, I'll stop you.''

This was incredible.

''You can't mean that,'' she said finally. ''You wouldn't actually stop me physically from going.''

''I'd do anything. Believe me.'' John's eyes fastened on hers, filled with pain and mute pleading. ''Stay here,'' he begged. ''Learn to love me. It's all I ask of you.''

Later, Celia lay in bed, perspiring in her long nightgown under the draperies of mosquito netting. The scene with John whirled in her head. How ironic it was! She'd tried to tell him the truth, but he'd refused to accept it. He *wanted* her here, despite the fact that he knew she didn't love him.

So, the traitorous thought came to her, what was the harm in staying just a little while longer? There was still the chance of seeing Roman. Her desire for him had become an obsession, to be satisfied only by face-to-face contact, by touch and embrace.

10

In the mornings, from the private veranda she shared with her aunt, Celia could sometimes see the crown of Haleakala. It reared hazy blue in the distance, looming over its circlet of gray clouds. A mysterious giant, the volcano brooded over the island it had itself created aeons before.

In fact, John had told her that a new, hardened lava flow lay near La Perouse Bay, dating only from the 1790s. There were many cinder cones on the island, and lava tubes that had formed caves. Lava rock was everywhere, a reminder of cataclysm.

But here at Mountain View, nature's excesses seemed very distant. In the morning, peaceful sounds carried in the clear air: bird calls, hammer blows, the rattle of carts, the bellow of oxen. There was laughter from the servants, the wail of a baby in the village. Several times Celia had heard gunshots as native hunters fired at wild pigs in the hills.

But even those were normal sounds, familiar ones, comforting in their ordinariness.

The days had slipped by. First, of course, came the school, the thirty-five children Celia had grown to love. Tina was her best student, her mind avid and quick, thirsty for everything Celia could give. Competition with her made the rest, especially Kevin McRory, work even harder.

Then there were the others. Tiny Aiko, with her sweet oval face and soft questions. Melani, at eleven already a beauty. Kaweo and Keoni were Hawaiian youths full of irrepressible high spirits. Hamada, a Japanese boy, persisted every day in bringing Celia a small blossom to lay on her table.

What a medley of languages the school held! Ripples of pure Hawaiian clashed with the pidgen dialect used by many of the children. Chang Liu's three youngsters spoke Cantonese and Hawaiian with equal ease. Some of the pupils spoke Japanese, others Samoan, and all knew enough English to get by.

But it was Hawaiian—soft, liquid, musical—that the children enjoyed the most. Soon Celia, too, began to pick up certain basic phrases. *Kaukau* was "food," and if a child said, "I'm *pau*," and rubbed his belly, it meant that he was full and had had enough.

Pilikia meant "trouble," and, to Celia's amusement, the word could be stretched to mean everything from a slight difficulty, such as a child skinning a knee, to downright disaster.

Makai meant "on the seaside," and *mauka* was "on the mountainside," essential words in the islands for giving directions. Celia learned that she herself was a *haole*, which meant "white foreigner," and two of her pupils with half white blood were *hapa-haoles*, or "half-foreign." *Kanaka* was "man," *wahine* was "woman," and "child" was *keiki*.

"Sugarcane" was *ko*.

Once Celia heard some children giggling and pointing to the small, hard buttocks of a brown boy. She picked up a ribald addition to her vocabulary: *akoli*.

On days when she wasn't in school, Celia rode Misty, the horse that John had given her, a spirited gray gelding accustomed to the steep island trails. She explored the boundaries of the plantation, following the cane fields almost to the sea. She visited the little Hawaiian village and wandered along deep-carved gulches where foliage grew in riotous confusion and lava caves beckoned. She discovered a stone *heiau*, or temple, where the old Hawaiians had worshiped and made sacrifices to their gods.

She collected leaves to press, and sent to Honolulu for more books on Hawaiian history. And all the while, Roman never left her mind. When would he come to Mountain View? She was tired of waiting!

One morning Kinau and Leinani came to her room to ask her if she would like to go swimming with them.

Celia looked at the two Hawaiian girls dressed in their long bright garments that hinted at curves beneath, the velvet beauty of brown skin.

"Swimming? I'd love it! But what should I wear?"

Leinani nudged Kinau, and both giggled.

"Whatever you choose," Kinau finally told her. "But today we're not going to the beach, but to Pele's Pool."

"Pele's Pool?"

"It's lovely and cool there, you'll see."

Half an hour later they set off, the Hawaiian girls on a pair of old, scrawny mares that looked to Celia to be more than ready for pasture. But along the way, Kinau stopped to weave a crown of white blossoms for herself, and both girls draped their mounts lavishly with vivid *leis*.

After a while the steep trail wound along plunging cliffs, the drop more than two hundred feet. Celia's horse was next in line behind Kinau.

"Do you like working at Mountain View?" she asked the girl.

Kinau glanced back over her shoulder. "I don't work there all the time. Sometimes I am in Lahaina. But I think John Burnside is a good employer. He lends me books to read when I wish."

They cantered along companionably. "Do you like to read?"

"Sometimes." Kinau shrugged. "When there is not something else to do. I do not much like being quiet."

The trail zigzagged along the rim of a gulch, until at last, rounding a bend, they saw a pool of water set like a cup in a lava fissure. Ferns and wild *taro* reflected green images in the crystal water. A stream fed the pool, splashing into it with a pretty, lacy waterfall, and below the pool, the stream continued, deepened between walls of rock. Somewhere Celia heard the rush of a bigger waterfall as water tumbled over an invisible drop.

"Oh!" she breathed, enthralled by the pristine beauty of it. "This is wonderful!"

"This place is Pele's," Kinau said.

"Who is Pele?"

"She is the goddess of volcanoes, a most frightening person who can hurl her red-hot vengeance on all she chooses. She makes her home in the crater of Kilauea, on the island of Hawaii, but often wanders about the islands at will. Sometimes she is fearsome and ugly, a horrid old crone. But at other times she is a beautiful young woman. It is in that form that Pele visits this pool. It is her favorite.''

The idea of a beautiful goddess swimming in the clear pool enchanted Celia. Following the example of the two Hawaiian girls, she dismounted, tethering her horse to a nearby tree. Kinau and Leinani were already stripping, to reveal bare brown bodies and full breasts tipped with dark nipples. The crown of white blossoms in Kinau's hair gave her the look of some exotic naked princess.

Celia stared, shocked. "You don't mean that you intend to swim that way?''

Both girls nodded and giggled.

"But—''

"What other way is there to swim? It is the way of all women,'' Kinau said, shrugging. "Come, Celia, what are you waiting for?''

Leinani had already clambered to the rocks that edged the pool. She stood poised to dive, a plump brown nymph with dimpled buttocks. She dived in with a neat splash. In a second Kinau was in the water, too, her black hair floating behind her in feathery fronds.

Celia caught her breath, envying the freedom of these young Hawaiian women, the carefree attitude toward their bodies. Modesty was a part of every Victorian girl's upbringing, a code drilled into every little girl from babyhood. Yet her skin did feel moist and sticky from the long ride. And this *was* Hawaii, she reminded herself. She was thousands of miles away from Boston now.

From the water, Leinani tittered, plainly amused at Celia's indecision. Without giving herself time to think, Celia tugged at the jet buttons of her green riding habit. She struggled with its tight bodice, the ribbon fastenings of her split petticoats.

But at last she, too, was naked. It felt daringly, deliciously free. The sun warmed her breasts as she walked barefoot to the rim of the pool.

"Come.'' Kinau splashed a silvery spray of water up at

her. "We'll teach you to swim, Celia, we'll turn you into a swimmer like the *ono*."

"What's an *ono?*" Celia lowered herself into the cool water. It invaded the secret parts of her body, thrilling the nerve ends of her skin. Her full breasts bobbed upward, feeling delightfully weightless. Her entire body felt lithe, sinuous, alive. It was wonderful to swim naked, she realized with a spurt of delight.

"An *ono* is a fish! *Ono* means 'sweet,' Celia." Kinau burst out with merriment. "And you will make a very sweet fish for someone to catch, won't you?"

That night, as Celia was dressing for dinner, Hatteras came into her bedroom. Celia felt her aunt's sharp eyes on her as she shrugged into a petticoat.

"Your skin seems awfully ruddy, Celia. Have you been watching your exposure to the sun?"

"Of course," Celia lied.

Hatteras did not look convinced. "Did you declare a school holiday this afternoon? I saw you ride off with those two Hawaiian girls."

"Yes, we rode up the mountain to a pretty little natural pool."

"To see it? Ah, you must be careful, my dear, in consorting too much with servants. The Hawaiians are charming, of course, but you do belong to two different worlds. Soon you'll be mistress here at Mountain View, with a position to consider. And proper behavior."

Her aunt was wrong; she wasn't going to be mistress at Mountain View. Celia's red cheeks grew even more scarlet. "I don't consider it wrong to go riding with Kinau and Leinani. I like them, and there are no other girls here my own age."

"Then you will have to find some. I'm sure there are other planters' wives with whom you can socialize, once you are married to John. After all, you will have obligations then, and a duty to entertain."

Celia stared at her aunt. "How exactly like Mama you sound sometimes."

Hatteras smiled a trifle sadly. "I *am* Lydia's sister, after all; we were brought up in the same household."

Later, in her room, Celia sat by an oil lamp, composing a letter to Cousin Rebecca, for she had tried to keep her promise in corresponding with her cousin. But more and more, Rebecca seemed a stranger, a representative of Mama and all the tight strictures of Boston. Besides, it had been months since she had seen her cousin. Rebecca's terse monthly reports covered life in the village where she and her husband lived, and were filled with complaints about the climate and the difficulties of leading what Becky referred to as a "civilized existence."

Now Celia struggled to compose a sentence. *Have you been learning to swim, Becky? I have, and find the water very invigorating. Today we went to a place called Pele's Pool, supposed to be haunted by a volcano goddess. However, we didn't see her. . . .*

She stopped writing and stared at the words she had written. What would Rebecca think of such fancies? She couldn't imagine her cousin swimming naked. Rebecca was never naked. Even when she bathed, she removed only parts of her clothing at a time, so as to expose as little skin as possible. And never when there was anyone about to view her.

Celia thrust the letter into a drawer, deciding to finish it later. As she did so, she wondered what was making her violate her strict Bostonian upbringing. Was it the seductive heat of the sun on her skin? Or the sweet Maui breezes, the silvery splashes of moonlight that transformed every night into an enchantment?

Had all of these things weakened her somehow, creating in her a kind of madness?

That night Celia tossed and turned, thinking again of Roman. Her body seemed filled with strange sensation, a taut urgency that could not be dispelled. A warm, molten ache centered in her groin, torturing her with a need that could not be fulfilled. . . .

More days passed, blending into weeks, marked off by the growth of the cane. The stalks grew thicker, their blades meeting overhead to form green jungles. Right now, the crop was thriving, John said, but soon the dry season would be here. Water would be scarce.

As John spent more and more nights in the plantation

office, Celia and Aunt Hatteras were thrown on their own resources. They read aloud and played chess, teaching Tina the game. To Celia's delight, Tina proved to be a wily chess player. "Check! And mate!" she would squeal joyfully.

After one such victory, Celia hugged the child, smoothing her fiery hair, now kept reasonably well brushed. "You're going to beat us all, Tina-girl! You're so smart that soon there will be no stopping you. Someday you'll have to leave the island for better schooling than we can provide you here."

Tina thrust out her lower lip, abruptly mutinous. She threw her thin arms around Celia. "I want to learn from you, Celia. *You're* my teacher! I won't go away from Maui, I won't, I won't!"

One hot afternoon, Celia was out on the sloping green lawn playing a game of quoits with Tina and Kinau. The three of them chatted lazily as they tossed iron rings toward a stake sunk in the ground. Celia did not even bother to glance up at the sound of a horse's hooves. It was a commonplace sound here, for nearly everyone owned a horse, and workers were always galloping back and forth from the mill on errands.

It was Kinau who suddenly dropped the iron ring that she held. The girl's eyes widened as she stared through the grove of *koas*.

Curious, Celia turned too.

Roman rode toward the plantation house on his gray gelding. Roman! Celia felt the blood wash away from her face, her knees grow suddenly shaky.

How handsome he looked as he approached, sitting erectly in the saddle, his black hair, under the brim of his riding hat, ruffled in the wind. The intense sun cast shadows on his face, highlighting his carved cheekbones, the full, arrogant mouth.

"Roman!"

Did she shout out, or was it only a cry of the heart, not even spoken? Beside her, Tina and Kinau seemed to fade into the sunny afternoon, and she was aware of only Roman. She had despaired of seeing him, and now he really was here.

She hurried toward him, nearly stumbling over a half-buried tree root in her single-minded need to be near him.

But Kinau was faster. With a glad cry, the beautiful Hawaiian girl darted past Celia and ran toward horse and rider, flinging herself into Roman's arms.

Somehow Celia managed to make her way back into the plantation house, to find the privacy of her own bedroom, without revealing her profound hurt and shock. It was Kinau who had rushed up to Roman, who had hurled herself into his embrace like a lover. Who *was* surely his lover.

Why, why hadn't she realized it before?

Certainly there had been enough clues. Kathryn Whitt had even told her that Roman had a woman at Mountain View. There had been Beau's remark about what passionate mistresses Hawaiian girls made. And even Kinau's casual statement that she spent time in Lahaina. . . .

She fought for calm, to reason with herself against the pain she felt. Roman was a man, in the full prime of his life. Men *did* have mistresses, women able to satisfy certain basic urges; this was something Celia had been taught to accept. She had even, at times, suspected her own father of having a woman on the side.

And yet . . .

She flung herself facedown on her bed and burst into tears. Kinau! No, she didn't want Roman's mistress to be Kinau, the girl of such velvet brown beauty, who had looked like a princess in her crown of white flowers, whose flawless body Celia had seen for herself, totally naked.

Roman had caressed that body. Had kissed those perfect dark-tipped breasts. In an agony of jealousy, Celia pounded the feather pillow, hitting it over and over again.

She heard a hesitant knock on the door.

"Who is it?" She reared up from the pillow.

"Leinani. Have missy's bath."

It was impossible. Leinani had been with them that day at Pele's Pool, was Kinau's friend.

Pain made Celia's tone sharp. "No! I don't want a bath— not now! Leave the tub here, and I'll ring later for water."

"But, missy—"

"I said I'd bathe later!"

Leinani scurried away, hurt, and Celia flung herself on the

bed again, feeling worse than ever for having shouted at a
servant. This wasn't Leinani's fault. She lay for a long hour,
her hands clapped over her ears so that all she could hear was
the frantic beat of her own pulse.

Roman. Oh, God, all these weeks she'd been thinking of
him, dreaming of him, creating fantasies about him. Imagining the way it would feel to be held in his arms, to melt under
his kiss. . . .

But he had not been thinking of her. No. Celia tortured
herself thinking of the days when Kinau had not worked in
the plantation house. Had she been in Lahaina then, with
Roman?

The pictures that flooded her mind were vivid, and would
not go away.

But after a while, her pride roused her from her bed. She
was Celia Griffin, not a sulking child, and besides, she knew
she would be humiliated beyond belief if Roman ever found
out what her reaction had been to Kinau's headlong embrace.

She sent for bathwater. It arrived, as always, with a few
fragrant petals of gardenias floating on its surface. She forced
herself to bathe, afterward perfuming herself with light fragrance of heliotrope. With a wet cloth she made a compress
to hold over her eyes. Roman would be at dinner tonight; he
must not know she had been crying.

Defiantly she went to the closet where her gowns hung,
padded with tissue paper to keep them from crumpling. She
riffled through them, dissatisfied with all of them. This one
Roman had already seen, on board the *Fair Wind*. The blue
silk was too plain, and the white piqué seemed too girlish, its
flounces too frilly.

At last she settled on an apple-green shot silk that gleamed
with subtle highlights. The gown hugged her waist, emphasizing the full, womanly swell of her breasts. Its matching
underskirt was trimmed with pleated flounces and dark green
velvet ribbons. In Boston, such a gown would be worn to
intimate little suppers or musical galas. She examined her
reflection carefully, hoping that the dress brought out her
dramatic brunette beauty.

What was she going to do with her hair? Although she had
managed, with no fuss, a coiffure every night of her stay here

at Mountain View, suddenly tonight nothing seemed suitable. She combed and recombed, sweeping her hair up into thick, glossy curls, as she'd seen in *Godey's*. Then she tried for a smoother, more elegant effect.

Finally she twisted her hair into a coronet, threading a rope of pearls among the braids. Their nacreous luster contrasted with the deep blue-black shine of her own hair, creating a dramatic effect. As a last effect, she slapped color into her cheeks until they glowed deep pink.

She was ready. She descended the Burnside staircase, her skirts sweeping behind her, a dazzling smile on her lips. But to her disappointment, she had made her entrance too early. In the library, visible through the open doorway, Tina sat curled on a couch with a book, but no one else had yet appeared. Celia hesitated, feeling uncertain. Should she go upstairs and try again? But that was ridiculous, to make two entrances.

Then Beau appeared from the smaller of the two drawing rooms, giving her a sardonic bow. "My, but you look smashing tonight. What's the occasion?"

Her already pinkened cheeks burned a deep red. "No occasion. I just thought I would begin to wear some of the dresses I brought with me from Boston. Otherwise they will mildew in my closet."

"Ah? Of course, the fact that we have a guest tonight wouldn't have anything to do with your elegance, would it?"

"Of course not, I . . ."

But her reply had to be stifled as Hatteras appeared, clad in her usual black evening silk, followed by John and Roman. The brothers seemed to have been arguing, for John wore a glowering look and Roman's face was an expressionless mask.

"Good evening, Celia, darling," John greeted her. "As you can see, we have a guest tonight."

She stared at Roman, unable to find words.

"Hello, Celia."

There seemed an aura of coiled-up power to Roman tonight. It hung about him like a cloud of energy, giving Celia a curious thrill in the pit of her stomach. Time seemed to spin between them, stopping everything. Celia managed to hold her smile, gliding forward to extend a hand to him. She felt him touch her, the wild, electric contact of his skin on hers, and thought she would scream out.

Fiercely she pushed back the feeling he gave her—what was the matter with her?—and spoke politely. "It's good to see you again. I hope your medical practice has not been keeping you too busy. Did you have a good ride from Lahaina?"

"As good as can be expected on our rough Maui roads, where the potholes are big enough to swallow a king's palace." Roman's gray eyes seemed inscrutable tonight, hiding his thoughts. He had changed from his riding clothes and now wore evening wear, beautifully tailored. His skin, in the lamplight, looked deeply burnished.

As the four of them made small talk about the poor condition of the Lahaina road, Celia eyed the two brothers. Now that they were side by side, she wondered that she could ever have found more than a superficial resemblance between them.

Both men were handsome, of course, tall with wide shoulders and an aggressive, muscular build. Yet Roman was leaner than John, his body a rangy tiger to John's heavier-set, bull-like quality. Roman's face was finer-chiseled, his mouth fuller and more sensitive than John's coarser features. And of course, she reminded herself, Roman was younger. Sixteen years younger.

The meal that night consisted of pork ribs marinated in Oriental sauce, a dish that Celia ordinarily found delicious. But tonight she could only pick at her food, all too aware of the tension that simmered around the table. Even Tina seemed to feel it, as she ate silently, her eyes large.

The brothers began to argue about an irrigation ditch that Roman wanted to build in order to divert water from the mountains into the cane fields.

"Sure—a ditch to drain away money," John scoffed. "What if the water doesn't flow, what then? Or if it flows too much? If the cane gets too much water, it'll rot."

"There are always risks in growing sugar or any other food crop," Roman responded.

"Do you think I don't know that? If the crop is good, and the price of sugar is up, the owners can make plenty of money. But if it doesn't rain, or the cane doesn't have enough sugar content, or the cane borer gets you, or the price drops . . .'' John shrugged. ''Failure. I have seen enough sugar planters go broke. I don't intend to be one of them.''

''We won't be. Irrigation is the coming thing; in a generation, everyone is going to be using it.''

''Not at Mountain View,'' John said violently.

''Shall we talk of something else?'' Celia interjected, fearing an explosion. Soon Hatteras was chattering about trips she wanted to make around the island, especially to the crater of Haleakala, which she said was one of the wonders of the world.

But tension still clouded the air, and after a while Celia began to realize that some of it centered around herself. It was a sexual tension, she realized with a spurt of unease. All three men kept looking at her, were subtly *aware* of her, like male animals scenting a female. John's look was openly possessive. Beau eyed her mockingly. And when Roman glanced in her direction, his look was lingering and smoky, making her shiver.

Three Burnside men, she thought. And each so different. John, the aging plantation owner, openly in love with her. Beau, the wastrel son, moody, sardonic, restless. And Roman, the hated half-brother, brooding and withdrawn, with an aura of power about him. . . .

Drawn out by Hatteras' questions, Roman began to talk about his medical practice. He had treated everything from lockjaw to Asiatic cholera and the skin disease caused by overindulgence in *awa*.

''Recently I even diagnosed a case of leprosy,'' Roman went on, frowning. ''She is a young Hawaiian mother only twenty years old. She'll have to go to Molokai, of course. What's worse, her infant has it too, and will have to go with her.''

''*Oh!*'' Both Celia and Hatteras gave gasps of horror, and Tina's eyes opened wide. Leprosy was said to be a hideous disease. Advanced sufferers had swollen, decaying limbs and glassy eyes set in bloated faces. Lepers were condemned to an isolated settlement on Molokai, where they stayed until they died.

''Will the girl die?'' Tina wanted to know.

''Yes, I am afraid so.''

"But . . . the baby!" Celia cried involuntarily.

"It, too, of course." Roman looked angry. "Life is often cruel, and it wrung my heart to have to make such a diagnosis and to send them away. But the disease is communicable, and the Hawaiians are so gregarious, they share everything, from sleeping mats to dishes of *poi*. We can't allow the rest of the people in her village to become lepers too."

As Roman told of the facilities for lepers at the Molokai settlement called Kalawao, Celia tried to imagine him with Kinau. Kinau spoke perfect English and had worked in a hospital before. Did Roman talk to her about his cases? Did she soothe his frustration when he encountered a case as pathetic as the baby dying of leprosy?

She felt a hard ache in her throat that would not go away.

To her relief, the meal was at last over, and John and Roman departed for the plantation office to go over the books. Beau insisted on accompanying them. Tina scampered back to the library, while Hatteras went to the kitchen to consult with Chang Liu on the following day's menu.

Celia fled to the veranda. She sank into a wicker chair and stared blindly out at yet another magnificent Maui sunset. More sweeps of rosy clouds, purples and oranges and magentas. The beauty, so out of step with her own mood, seemed to mock her.

"Celia?" Tina had come to stand by her chair. Tonight the little girl wore a white muslin frock and her fiery hair had been disciplined and tied with pink silk ribbon. There was an unaccustomed serious look on the child's face. "Celia, do you think that *I* could ever get leprosy?"

"You?" Celia was horrified at the thought. "Oh, no, darling, *no*. I'm sure not."

"But that Hawaiian baby got it."

"Yes, Tina, I know, but leprosy is spread by human contact, remember what Roman said? I'm sure that if you wash every day and keep yourself clean, such a thing can't happen to you."

Celia didn't know if this was true, but Tina seemed satisfied. Immediately her eyes brightened. "How long do you suppose Uncle Roman will be here this time?" she wondered.

"How long does he usually stay?"

"Oh, sometimes days. Sometimes only hours—it depends on how angry he gets at my father, and how much my father yells back at him," the child explained. "Sometimes they yell quite a lot. And Beau shouts, too."

At this simple picture of plantation life, Celia stifled a smile. Then she realized that Tina presented her the opportunity to learn more about Roman.

"What does your Uncle Roman do to amuse himself while he is here?" she ventured.

"Oh, he rides. And swims. Sometimes he goes into the village." The village, Celia knew, was the collection of grass houses near the plantation occupied by the Hawaiian workers and their families, plus a large number of horses, dogs, and cats.

"What does he do there?"

"He takes care of the sick mothers and babies. And the men, too, if they get hurt at the mill. Once he cut off a hand."

"What!"

Tina's eyes shone as she related this exciting event. "He used ether to make the man sleep. Then he got out a big saw . . . I know, because I watched it outside through the window. It was ever so interesting."

"I see." Celia listened to the tale of the operation, meanwhile formulating her own questions. "There is so much about Mountain View that I don't know yet. For instance, what about the people here, like Kinau? Does she have children in the village, or a husband?"

Tina looked puzzled. "I don't think so."

"And does Roman ever go . . . riding . . . with Kinau?"

"I think he goes into a bed with her." Tina said it casually. "And I have seen them before, kissing. Roman loves to kiss Kinau, and I think she likes to kiss him back, too. Would you like to come outdoors with me, Celia? My cat is about to have kittens and I want to see if any of them have come yet."

Celia fought her shock, following Tina outdoors. It took all of her fortitude to admire the orange tabby, to listen to Tina's chatter about her pets. *I think he goes into a bed with her.* It was confirmation of her worst fears.

The next morning, she sat on the private veranda she shared with Hatteras, feeling dulled from lack of sleep. She had tossed and turned all night, tormented by visions of Roman and Kinau in bed.

"Good morning, Celia." Hatteras came onto the *lanai*, wearing a dressing gown of white Indian mull. She poured herself coffee and uncovered the salvers of egg and sausage that had been left there for them. There was fresh juice from Kauai oranges, and Hatteras briskly poured two glasses, handing one to Celia.

"Here. You haven't had your juice yet. Ah, such a lovely day! I think I'll go for a tramp in the hills. I'm looking for some good plants to dig up. I want to put a garden along the avenue where the road approaches the house. No one has planted a thing here since Susan Burnside died, and John has given me permission."

Celia nodded politely, sipping the sweet juice. At this moment, she didn't care whether Hatteras made a garden, or if, indeed, the entire plantation house fell down around their ears.

"Whatever is the matter with you this morning, girl? You have dark circles under your eyes, and the corners of your mouth turn down like a crescent moon."

"I . . . didn't sleep very well last night."

"Why not? You've slept splendidly every other night, haven't you?"

Celia said nothing.

"It's him, isn't it? That rogue, Roman Burnside. He's the one who has you upset."

"I . . ." But Celia couldn't lie to her aunt. She floundered and finally gave up, focusing her eyes stubbornly on the sea view visible from their *lanai*.

"You know what happened in the past, Celia, you know the attack that Roman Burnside made on his brother."

"But . . . maybe it didn't happen that way! Maybe there is an explanation, something to exonerate Roman."

"No. Servants saw the whole thing, and in fact saved John's life. Now Roman is accepted here in this house only because he is half-owner and because it is his money that finances many projects. And, of course, because of his skill as a physician. He treats the workers here when they need medical help."

Celia squared her chin, gazing rebelliously ahead.

Hatteras spoke sharply. "Celia, you have come here as John Burnside's fiancée. *John's*. Don't forget it."

Celia looked at her aunt, seeing the plain warning in her eyes. "I won't," she said.

But she knew that she lied.

11

Somehow the days of Roman's stay passed. The brothers walked the hills over the plantation, marking out the site for the irrigation ditch, which would be more than five miles long and would require blasting through hillsides. At night, both men appeared at dinner with tense expressions. It was plain that their enforced association was wearing thin.

Roman's room at Mountain View was located only a few doors from Celia's own, and several times she encountered him in the corridor on his way downstairs.

Each time he nodded at her politely. Celia wanted to cry out with frustration. Didn't he remember the day they'd shared on the beach near Diamond Head? The way he had held her, had taught her to swim, had pulled the blanket around her shoulders, massaging warmth back into her cold body?

Yet now his expression was inscrutable, and he behaved as if they were two strangers meeting in a hotel corridor.

"Here are your flowers today, Celia."

Dressing for school one morning, Celia jumped and turned as Kinau entered her bedroom, carrying a basket of freshly picked Mexican creeper. The flowers looked like chains of small pink hearts, and in fact the Mexican name for them was *cadena de amor*—chain of love.

Celia had always loved these flowers, but today she felt a spurt of revulsion as she looked at them. She didn't want it to be Kinau who brought them to her. In fact, it was getting so that she hated the sight of the sultry Hawaiian girl as she moved about her household duties.

As the girl began, unbidden, to arrange the flowers in vases, Celia looked at her. This morning Kinau wore a flaming hibiscus behind her ear, its red petals glowing against her silky black hair. Her movements were sinuous, graceful, feminine. In fact, Celia decided in resentment, Roman's mistress was entirely *too* feminine.

"Stop," she snapped suddenly. "I'll arrange those flowers myself."

"But your aunt told me to bring them. You always have flowers. Don't you want some to put in your hair?"

"No! I don't! And I don't want you here in my room anymore, either. Tell my aunt to find one of the other girls to serve me."

Kinau's lustrous dark eyes showed no emotion. "Have I displeased you, then?"

Celia stared at her, wondering what to say. *I love the man you love. I dream of him each night, he fills up my thoughts all during the day.* A bitter laugh welled up in her. How could she possibly say such a thing to Kinau? And was it the girl's fault that Roman had chosen her?

"No," she said at last. "You haven't displeased me, Kinau. And I'm sorry I spoke sharply to you. It . . . it is the wrong time of the month for me."

The other girl nodded. "Then if you do not wish further help, I'll go."

In a rustle of cotton skirts, Kinau was gone, leaving behind her the scent of some musky perfume. *French* perfume, Celia realized with a little indrawn gasp.

That morning she rang the school bell with more vehemence than usual. It was as if she pounded out her frustrations on the iron, taking satisfaction in the loud ringing that reverberated over the plantation and could be heard for miles.

The children rushed in. They were in their usual flurry of giggles, laughter, and high spirits. Today Hili romped in with them, her tail thumping, and flopped down on the floor near Tina's bench.

"Missy, we go study plants today?" Aiko, the little Japanese girl, wanted to know.

"Today we're going to study one plant, *ko*. Sugarcane!

Everything about it, from first planting to harvest. . . . Who can tell me what a *rattoon* is?''

Kaweo, a sturdy Hawaiian boy of twelve, raised a hand. ''Ratoon—everyone know—he more than one crop from allasame planting,'' he said in pidgen, grinning. ''I plant once—I drive ox!''

The day had begun. Celia was forced to put aside her troubling thoughts to concentrate on her pupils, who demanded every shred of her attention. By late afternoon the children were laboriously copying words like ''ox,'' ''cane,'' ''plow,'' and ''sugar.'' Tina, however, finished her assignment early and sat fidgeting on her bench.

''Would you like to write a special story, Tina?'' Celia approached the red-haired girl.

''Oh, yes. A book! I'll write a long, long book!''

Celia smiled at the child's artless enthusiasm. ''Well, then, why don't you write about Mountain View? Since you've lived here all your life, you know everything about it—and I'd love to read its story.''

She supplied Tina with paper, pen, and inkwell and left to work with the others. When she rang the afternoon bell, Tina was still at work, her tangled curls trailing across her paper until Celia did not see how the child could write at all.

As the children rushed out of the school, Tina belatedly among them, Celia began to put away her books. Suddenly she felt tired, weariness settling about her shoulders like a cape. And she knew it was a tiredness caused not by the children, but by her own tumultuous thoughts.

Had she made a mistake in falling in love with a man who paid no attention to her, who kept another mistress of indisputable beauty? Of course she had! Why had she done it? Why couldn't she get Roman Burnside out of her mind and heart? Damn him. . . .

A knock on the framing of the open door startled her. One of the Japanese workers stepped inside the school. ''*Konnichi wa*,'' he said, bowing and giving the traditional Japanese greeting.

''*Konnichi wa*.''

The man, dressed in the wrinkled cotton shirt and pants provided by the plantation for its workers, was slight, homely,

almost scrawny in appearance. His facial bones were prominent in his face, his eyes dark pools of intelligence.

"Missy, you teach me read and talk English? Talk good,
so *haole* man talk to me? And I can speak to him?"

"Why . . . yes, I could," she said slowly. "If you really
want to learn. . . . What is your name?"

"Genzo. Hard Nippon worker, very, very hard. I learn
quick-quick."

"I'm sure you do." Celia was already calculating what
time she would have available. And would the other workers
come to her, once she began to teach Genzo? The thought
filled her with excitement. She could do some good here. To
teach an adult to read and speak, to be more at home on the
island where he now lived—surely that was terribly important.

"Would you like your first lesson now?"

The wide grin on Genzo's face was more than answer
enough. Pushing away her weariness, Celia got out her books
again. For three hours she sat with Genzo, teaching him the
alphabet, which he learned as quickly as Tina had.

When dusky shadows crept into the school and they could
no longer see to work, Celia sent Genzo back to the workers'
compound. She started up the path, lined with bougainvillea
and Barbados lilies. She still felt tired, but now it was an
entirely different feeling—bone-deep, satisfied.

With slow surprise she realized that she loved this crude
schoolhouse thatched with dried cane, its unwieldy bell and
rough benches. She loved her pupils, too. Tina, Aiko, Kaweo,
Kevin, all of them. They needed her, for she was their
lifeline to a whole world that lay beyond Maui.

Celia walked back to the house, where the lamps had
already been lighted for the night.

"I don't believe this! I can't believe that you could have
enticed this child into writing such a thing!" John waved
Tina's paper in front of him as if it were something
unspeakable. His face held a thunderous expression that reminded Celia all too vividly of her father when he had read
her essays in *Scribner's*.

"Why, I think Tina's 'book,' as she calls it, is an excellent
example of scholarship," she told John evenly. They were in
the plantation office, with its pigeonhole desk, clutter of

wooden files, and large ceiling fan that whirred lazily. Pushed up against one wall, unused now, was the old horsehair chair in which Amos Burnside had had his heart attack. "True, many of the words are misspelled—it will take time for her to master spelling—but the fact that she could write this at all is a tremendous achievement. She has marvelous potential. She is truly gifted, I think."

"Gifted! I don't care about that! Will you just listen to what she has written?" John held up the untidily scrawled paper, and read aloud from it.

" 'Workers get yelled at by Papa and Mr. McRory and their pay is docked when they . . .' What is this damn word?"

" 'Ruin,' " Celia supplied.

" '. . . when they ruin a sugar batch. Papa does not trust the workers and says they cheat. He does not give them enough good food. Uncle Roman says two men died because of . . .' I can't read these hen scratches. What's this word?"

" 'Weakness.' "

"Yes, 'weakness.' Her printing is atrocious, you really should teach her better penmanship." John hurled the pages into the air, where they fluttered in the breeze generated by the fan before falling to the floor. "My own daughter, accusing me of starving my workmen so that some of them die of malnutrition! That's what she really meant, isn't it? It's all a lie!"

Celia met his glare. "Is it?"

"Indeed it is! It's Roman's opinion she gives in this accursed paper, and you know how Roman is—nothing I do is right. True, two Japanese did die of pneumonia, but they were sickly when they arrived here, and I gave them triple rations of food. Triple, do you hear me? I refuse to be accused of being some cruel slave driver who kills his workers!"

"I'm sure Tina didn't mean any such thing. You know how dramatic children are."

"Yes, I know how children are! I'm not going to have my daughter turned into an obnoxious little muckraker who accuses me of infamy—and I'll close the school if you can't teach her any better than this!"

Celia's heart sank.

"Have you ever taken your daughter through the mill and explained what goes on to her yourself?"

"Why . . . no."

"Perhaps Tina made some mistakes in her essay because she doesn't know what really goes on. You can't deny, John, that you've been too busy to include her, just as you've also left Beau out of your life. The fact that she couldn't read until I arrived here is plain evidence that you did neglect Tina. I suggest you remedy that."

John seemed about to explode again, but finally he slumped in a veranda chair, expelling his breath in a long sigh.

"I suppose you're right. I'm sorry, Celia. You're not the one I'm angry at, not really. I took my temper out on you. And as you can see, I *do* have a temper."

She smiled. "I accept your apology."

"It's just that, with Roman here—you know what the enmity is between us, it's been no secret. And further, I must confess that your presence is proving most unsettling to me."

"My—?"

But before she could finish, John had pulled her to him. As before, he crushed his lips down on hers, pushing his body against her with demanding pressure, so that she could feel the hard ridges of his muscles, the push of his masculinity. Never before had he transmitted to her such a message of fierce desire.

But it was a desire she didn't reciprocate.

"Celia," he murmured hoarsely into her neck.

She wriggled free. "John, you forget yourself!"

"I know, but I have to ask you again, I'm beyond pride. Will you marry me soon? I know I've been busy, but that doesn't mean I haven't been thinking about you constantly. I need you. You don't know how much. I've never felt this way about any other woman before, you've got to believe me."

Looking at the tension, the desire and longing written plainly on John's face, Celia did believe him. *Roman*, she thought. Why couldn't it be John's brother who was entreating her, whose need for her was so desperately urgent? She realized that the same agony of the heart that she felt about Roman, John felt about her. Love! How strange it was, how cruel.

"I've told you already how I feel," she whispered. "I shouldn't be here, I came under false pretenses, I—"

But as before, John stopped her, putting a hand over her lips. "Hush, I won't listen to your refusals."

She rose and smoothed her skirts, feeling the color rise high to her cheeks. "But I must refuse—at least for now, John. I'm simply not ready to make up my mind yet, and you're going to have to understand that."

That night after dinner, Celia was alone on the veranda, staring out at the sinking sun, when she heard a noise beside her and turned to see Roman. The fading salmon glow of sun lit his face, softening its lines.

"I have to apologize to you," he began quietly.

Celia's heart gave a little twisting leap.

"It has to do with Tina," he went on. "The other night at the dinner table, I should never have talked about leprosy as I did, for today she came to me and demanded to know all about the disease. Apparently she is worried that it may infect her and the other children in the school here at Mountain View."

So it was Tina he wished to talk about, rather than their own relationship, the way he had treated her. Celia held herself very still, replying to him coolly, "It was good of you to talk to Tina. She is a very bright child, and she is warmhearted, concerned about others."

For a few moments they discussed Tina, while an evening wind ruffled the hair near Roman's temples, making Celia long to reach out and touch it, to feel the texture of him with her fingertips. This physical attraction she had for him—she'd never felt anything like it before, so intense that when she was with him she sometimes felt weak, her knees trembly.

She had to get him out of her mind. Expunge him, get rid of him. And yet how could she? It would be like denying a part of herself, a new, frightening, beguiling part of herself that until now she had not known she possessed.

She realized that Roman had turned, was preparing to leave the veranda. He nodded to her courteously. "I'll take my leave now, Celia. I have some reading I wish to do. Good night."

"Good night," she said, staring after him.

The next morning, to escape her thoughts, she rose early, hurrying out to the stables to saddle Misty, the gray gelding she usually liked to ride. Roman's horse was already gone— was he out riding, too? she asked herself furiously. But who cared? Let him ride anywhere he wished, let him go back to Lahaina if that pleased him.

Riding alone, she spurred her mount up the winding bridle trail that led toward Pele's Pool. In places the path was marred by depressions made by storm water, and lava rocks jutted up, making passage difficult. But Celia didn't care. She had to get away, had to think.

Had she made a mistake in coming to Maui? She'd accomplished nothing, she told herself bitterly. Nothing at all as far as Roman was concerned. She was no closer to him than she'd been in Honolulu. Why couldn't she get him out of her mind? It was insane, these feelings she had for Roman Burnside.

She heard the rushing of a waterfall and passed the steep cliff where it fell. Rounding a bend in the trail, she came upon Pele's Pool, shimmering like a silver mirror in the sun. The pool was utterly deserted. Not even the song of a bird broke the pristine silence.

Celia tethered her mount to the same tree that the Hawaiian girls had used before, and walked toward the water, shining in its cup of rock. She remembered how Kinau had looked, bathing nude in its clear waters, a crown of white flowers woven in her hair.

Tiny fish darted in the shallows, skittering away as she dipped a finger into the crystal water. She lifted her hand and watched water fall like diamonds. Roman didn't want her. She had to accept that fact, to cleanse him from her heart. She'd been a fool to love him, and she knew it.

The sun on her face and neck felt hot, and after a time Celia loosened the neck of her gown. Finally she stripped it off, folding her dress carefully on a rock. She pulled off her petticoats, too, stopping only when she had reached her camisole and drawers.

She stepped into the cool water, shivering with delight as the liquid found her skin. A fish nibbled at her toe and then darted away as if daring her to play.

Celia looked through the clear layers of water at the tiny

swimming creature and laughed aloud. She began paddling and floating, splashing up jewel sprays of water. The flimsy cambric, she noticed, clung to her body, the flesh tones of her skin showing through provocatively.

But no one was here to see. And, after all, wasn't her dress folded on a rock only a few feet away, easy to reach if she needed it?

After about twenty minutes of swimming, she grew cold, for the pool was spring-fed from a source far up the mountain. She had started to paddle toward the edge when suddenly she saw a movement among the candlenut trees that grew near the stream.

"Who . . . who's there?" she called nervously. She ducked down in the water until only her face and shoulders were visible, thankful she hadn't ventured into the pool naked.

"Only me."

"You?"

To her shock, Roman appeared from the trees, striding over the scattered lava rocks toward Pele's Pool.

"What are you doing, splashing around as naked as a *wahine?*" He stood gazing down at her, his eyes glinting with amusement. He wore riding clothes and was hatless, his black hair ruffled from the wind.

"I'm not naked!"

"Why don't you stand up, then?" he teased.

For a fleeting moment Celia was angry. But almost as soon as she felt it, her anger vanished, to be replaced by an odd, daring gaiety. She laughed, a pretty, silvery laugh. "I won't stand up until you turn your back!" she responded pertly.

"And what if I don't wish to turn it?"

"But you must." Daringly she splashed him.

Roman knelt by the water's edge and scooped up water in his hands and splashed her back.

It was a game they played, an exciting game fueled by the smoky look in Roman's eyes and by Celia's own burningly physical awareness of him. Still in the water, she could not tear her eyes away from his maleness. His riding shirt was open at the throat, his skin sheened by perspiration, revealing silky curls of black hair. With a shudder of desire, she wondered what it would be like to bury a kiss at the hollow of

Roman's throat, to taste with her tongue the musky, salt-sweet odor of his skin.

For a few moments longer they bantered and teased. Celia swam about, well aware of the intriguing picture she made. Cream shoulders, ivory skin, silken hair. Sooner or later, both of them knew, she would have to come out. The soaking-wet cloth of her undergarments would cling to her flesh, revealing every inch of her to his gaze.

Finally, smiling, Roman picked up her riding dress and tossed it to her.

"Here, catch! All teasing aside, you'd better get out of that water, Celia, before you freeze. I've been in that pool before, and I know it can get cold."

With whom had he swum in Pele's Pool before? Some of Celia's daring mood seeped away as she contemplated this. She began to shiver, as if in response to Roman's suggestion.

"Hurry," he urged. "Or you'll be covered with goose bumps."

Still in the water, she took the dress and held it modestly in front of her as she climbed out. As soon as the air hit her exposed skin, she began to shake more violently. She *had* stayed in the water too long. She fumbled with the dress, miserably aware that her nipples had hardened with the cold, that her entire body was virtually revealed to him.

What was he thinking as he stared at her with those smoky eyes? Did he think her beautiful, desirable?

"Don't tell me that you're going to pull that dress on over your wet clothes," Roman exclaimed.

It was exactly her plan; what else was she to do?

"Well, if you do, you'll catch your death of pneumonia."

Before she could move, Roman took the dress from her and began to undress her, peeling the wet camisole away from her skin. His skin was warm; his touch seemed to burn her. She felt her desire for him, stirring in her like the blooming of a rose. Abruptly this had become more than a game. It was deadly serious. There was nothing else in the world but this.

She tried belatedly to cover herself. "No," she whispered. "No, please, I . . ."

But her breasts were already bared to him, full-curved and perfect, the nipples hard pink buds. As his hands brushed her flesh, a shiver of sensation rippled through her body, centering in her groin.

"Don't be a fool. I'm a doctor." She thought Roman's voice sounded hoarser than usual. "Even the Hawaiians have more sense than to let themselves be chilled."

He was pulling off the clothing below her waist now, his touch gentle. Standing frozen, her heart slamming in her throat, Celia allowed it. She had never felt anything like this before, the sexuality that burned between them. Roman's hands lingered, tasting the roundness of her buttocks. She could hear his breathing quicken; everything seemed to hang between them, every possibility. What was going to happen? Celia knew, and yet somehow her mind seemed utterly frozen in this moment.

She was Roman's. She belonged to him. She would do anything, anything he asked. . . .

He stripped off his own shirt, to uncover the bronzed glory of his chest, smooth skin over rippled muscles, the tufts of hair that so intrigued her. He smelled wonderfully of perspiration; the musky odor of him made Celia gasp. She stood trembling as he draped his shirt over her shoulders, enclosing her in its voluminous folds that smelled of his own scent.

"I don't . . . You shouldn't . . ." She didn't even know what she had begun to say. Words failed her, and helplessly she allowed herself to be folded in warmth, to experience the sensuous feeling as Roman rubbed her dry through the shirt fabric.

"You shouldn't what? Shouldn't be dried off and gotten warm?" Every word was a caress, a wooing. "What kind of man would I be if I didn't help you, Celia?"

Roman's hands moved more deliberately now. Slow. Wonderful. She wanted it to go on and on, never to stop, his hands exploring every curve of her, every softness. He touched her only through the cloth, his hands tracing the mounds of her breasts, the soft curves of her upper arms, the delicate tracery of her rib cage.

She responded under his touch like a kitten being stroked, totally giving herself up to him.

"I love your breasts," he murmured. "They're beautiful. . . . I love them, tipped with pink. . . ." Gently he

opened the shirt and cupped her left breast in his hand as if it
were infinitely precious. His fingers kneaded her flesh, stroking the tender nipples until she thought she would cry out
with pleasure.

Now Roman kissed her right breast, first in tiny, soft
butterfly licks. Then he encircled her nipple with his tongue,
flicking it with soft moistness, teasing, enticing, inflaming.

Soft fire bloomed in the pit of Celia's belly, filling her.
She clung to him, gasping, as he lifted her up and carried her
toward a little clearing.

He laid her down on a bed of ferns and grasses. The shirt
fell away and she lay trembling, allowing him to look, his
hungry eyes to seek out every secret part of her, to desire her
totally.

"Celia . . . ah, God . . ."

She was no longer cold. Her skin seemed to burn, and her
breath came in deep, ragged gasps. He was going to make
love to her. At last, at last. And she wanted it, longed for it
as she had never longed for anything else in her life.

He lowered himself beside her and pulled her to him for a
long, rapturous kiss, his tongue exploring her mouth, weaken-
ing her beyond imagining. Kisses melted into further kisses,
each one deeper than the last.

"I've never . . . Roman, I have never made love before
. . ." She blurted out the truth.

"It doesn't matter. I'll help you. I promise . . ." They
whispered and murmured, said what all lovers say, caught in
the throes of their passion. Roman pulled off his own clothes
and came back to her, pressing the full, virile length of his
body against her own.

Feverishly they wound their bodies around each other,
straining to be closer than was humanly, physically possible.
They caressed; they kissed; they stroked and loved. They
pressed together, skin to skin. Celia shivered, caught up in a
force that was far beyond mere pleasure, but total involvement.
His heavy breathing affected her like a powerful aphrodisiac.
She was beyond thought, beyond reason, knowing only that
this joy was the sharpest she had ever known. Everything in
her cried out for it to go on to the culmination. . . .

And then they heard the abrupt loud creak of wagon wheels.

Roman sat up, grabbing for his shirt to fling around Celia's nakedness.

"Roman? What. . . . ?" She felt confused, drugged by lovemaking. She could not seem to come down from the heights to which he had lifted her, to deal with this reality.

"*Shhh!* Someone's on the path!"

He pulled her farther into the glade, into the shelter of a patch of wild *taro,* pushing her down among the large heart-shaped leaves. Celia crouched, shaking, feeling as if her very soul had been violated. One moment she had been in Roman's arms, transported to the beginning of ecstasy. Now she was crouched in a thicket like a criminal. The sharp edges of the leaves cut her skin.

They waited. Endlessly. The creak of wagon wheels grew nearer, and they heard voices joking in Hawaiian, bursts of male laughter. Squatting in the little glade, pinned by Roman's arms, Celia felt an insect crawl on her ankle. Beside her Roman breathed lightly.

"It's mill workers, probably a lumber crew. They're always having to cut new wood for molasses barrels. If we're lucky, maybe they'll go right on by."

Or maybe the workers would decide to stop at the pool for a swim or a drink of the cool mountain water. Or maybe they would see the two tethered horses, the scattered clothing, and draw their own conclusions. Celia was in an agony of suspense. She felt as if her nerves were exposed raw and vulnerable. If they were to be discovered here . . .

More voices. The bellow of an ox, the crack of a whip.

Were they going to be exposed?

And then, like a reprieve, the creak of wagon wheels grew less. Celia sagged with relief; the workers were going away. They were safe.

Roman relaxed too. "Thank God, they took the higher fork. They're gone now."

He rose to his feet, totally naked, to Celia a beautiful sight with sunlight dappled across his skin. She rose too, clutching the shirt to her, feeling suddenly awkward. The day had been exploded apart, their feelings scattered beyond recapture.

"Come on, Celia. By some miracle we've been spared, but you'd better get dressed in case that work party comes back."

They got dressed. It was all cool and efficient, pulling on

her dress, fastening buttons and ribbons. Where was their lovemaking, the sweet cocoon of desire that, only minutes before, had surrounded them like a beautiful dream? Celia felt robbed, bereft.

"We shouldn't have made love today," Roman said harshly.

She stared at him.

"I mean it. It was as if some madness came upon me . . ." Roman was fully dressed now, the way she had seen him when he first arrived at the pool. His eyes seemed dark and unreadable, cold granite, and Celia knew he had withdrawn from her, retreating into a deep privacy of self where she could not reach him.

"If it was madness, then I was mad too," she told him softly.

"I imagine!"

"What . . . what do you mean?"

To her amazement, he glowered at her. "Simply this, my beautiful young witch. A woman as lovely as you . . . Surely I'm not the first lover you've had?"

"But I've never . . . I told you . . ." she stammered, the blood suffusing her cheeks. "I am a virgin."

"I wonder. You seem so passionately skilled at lovemaking . . . and the way you flirt at the dinner table, carefully manipulating the interest of *three* men."

She was shocked, stunned that he would talk to her like this. All she had done was to give herself to him, to love him. . . . With angry gestures she finished buttoning the bodice of her riding dress, jerking the jet buttons through their holes. "Explain yourself, Roman!"

Anger spun between them.

"That's easy enough. John devours you with his eyes. And his son . . . Beau, too, desires you. Haven't you noticed that, Celia? Wasn't it you who engineered it? Does it please you, to have all of us at your beck and call? John, Beau, and myself?"

"I don't even know which of your unfair accusations to answer first," she responded hotly. "Despite what *you* say, I'm a virgin. I can't help it that John is in love with me. As for Beau, it is not my fault that he—"

"Stop." Roman's eyes burned into hers. "Do you really expect me to believe such nonsense? An extravagantly pretty girl like you, sent away from her home to these far-flung islands! I'm not a fool, Celia. No upper-crust Bostonian family sends a daughter that far away unless there are reasons. And those reasons are invariably sexual.''

Celia thought she would die from the crystal pain of held-back tears. ''No! It . . . it isn't true.''

''It *is* true, and you know it. Since you weren't pregnant when you arrived here, then the explanation has to be that you are a coquette. A flirt. You bask in the attention of men and need to test their admiration. Well? Isn't that true, Celia?''

''*No.*''

''Don't lie to yourself, my beauty, or to me. The evidence is to the contrary. Two broken engagements, three men at the Burnside dinner table, each desiring your body, which, by the way, is very lovely, well worth the wanting.'' Roman's jaw knotted. ''Didn't you come to Mountain View as my brother's fiancée?'' He spat out the word. ''And where do you find yourself? Here at Pele's Pool, dallying with *me*.''

''But . . . I can explain . . .''

''Don't bother, Celia. I don't think I want to listen. And by the way, I would suggest that you wait here for a while after I have left, before you return to Mountain View. That way no one will suspect we've been together. You don't wish your 'fiancé' to become suspicious, do you?''

Roman stood gazing at her for a moment, his face dark with anger. Then he turned on his heel and went to his horse. Grimly he tightened the saddle girth, mounted, and rode away without looking at her again.

12

Celia had returned from Pele's Pool in a dark mood, as close to despair as she had ever felt. Roman's accusations swirled in her, heavy with the weight of his judgment. *Flirt, coquette . . .*

Somehow she managed to get through the rest of that endlessly long day without revealing how deeply he had hurt her. But that night, in bed, at last she gave way to tears. And finally, her eyes reddened from crying, she flung out of bed and walked in her nightgown out to the veranda, to stand staring at the moonlit sea.

The spectacle of moonlight glimmering in silver splashes on the far-off surf was lovely, but it offered little comfort. Finally she went back to her room, and that was when she heard the noise in the corridor.

Was it Tina, crying out in the throes of a nightmare?

Concerned, forgetting her own distress, Celia hastily pulled on a dressing gown and went to investigate.

But as soon as she had reached the corridor, she realized that it wasn't Tina she had heard at all, but a woman's giggle. High, soft, abandoned, and all too familiar. The sound seemed to come from the room that Roman had been given.

And didn't she smell, lingering in the air like a caress, the soft odor of French perfume?

Celia stood frozen, one hand held to her chest as if to keep her heart from pounding its way out of her body. Kinau was in Roman's bedroom. The realization slammed sickeningly through her. What other explanation could there possibly be?

She had smelled the girl's perfume, recognized her laugh. It was the middle of the night. There were no servant's duties that could possibly take Kinau into a man's quarters at this hour. No duties except . . .

But *that* was not a duty.

Celia's mouth went suddenly, horribly dry. She clapped her hands over her ears and fled back into her own room.

The flowering trees of Hawaii were beautiful, and Mountain View possessed a number of them, planted by Susan Burnside, Beau's mother. There was a tree called the "bestill," an oleander with trumpet-shaped yellow flowers and narrow green leaves that never seemed to hold still, always shimmering in the wind. There were dwarf poincianas, with clusters of flaming red blooms. Several "shower trees" dripped with breathtaking, fluffy masses of peach and apricot.

And there were plumerias. Fragrant, waxy flowers in white, yellow, pink, cerise. In India and in the temple gardens of Ceylon, from which it had been imported, the flower was known as frangipani.

Here in Hawaii it was *melia*. And it was often planted in graveyards.

The day after her disastrous lovemaking with Roman at Pele's Pool, Celia wandered to the small Mountain View burial plot. She wasn't sure what drove her: was it that she wished to be surrounded by an atmosphere as bleak as the way she felt?

Now, as she entered the small plantation graveyard, Celia breathed in the deep, sweet fragrance of *melia*. Frilly redcoral hibiscus grew wild, and overgrown bushes of bougainvillea created explosions of magenta and purple. The little graveyard was untended, insects buzzing among its wild grasses and weeds.

Driven by some impulse she could not explain, Celia wandered among the two rows of gravestones. Some were made of stone, others were only of wood, their carvings blurred by weather, seasons of *kona* storms and tropical rains.

One of the wooden markers was for a servant: "Annie Langue, Trusted Nurse, dyed of Diphtheria, Febr. 1849. Aged 23 Yrs." Next to it, was a tiny, pathetic stone: "Henry Burnside, Aged 1 Yr. Dyed of Diphtheria, Febr. 1849."

A baby who must have perished, along with his nurse. Celia caught her breath, wondering if Henry could have been an infant brother of Beau's. Yes, the year would seem to indicate so. Poor Susan Burnside. Celia had seen a portrait of John's first wife, a tall, slender woman with an oval face and reserved expression. Susan had been uprooted from her life in Atlanta, brought here as a bride. She had lost a child, then died in childbirth herself, leaving behind her only Beau and some flowering trees. . . .

Tears filled Celia's eyes, and a rush of sadness swept over her, so intense that it left her shaking. And she wasn't entirely sure whom it was for—Susan, the dead infant, or herself.

She walked on, seeing the gravestone of Amos Burnside himself, the founder of Mountain View, the patriarch who had shipped over the plantation house from Connecticut piece by piece. His epitaph read: "A Tomb Now Suffices Him for Whom the Whole World Was Not Sufficient."

Celia paused, remembering how Amos had died at his work. Slowly she continued, seeing the markers for Amos' two wives, for Ariadne, who had been John's second wife. The Burnside women, dead of the "Burnside curse," as Kathryn Whitt had said. Celia shivered. Somehow, in this graveyard, the idea did not seem as farfetched as it had before.

"Well, what have we here? A mourner? How touching!" Beau's voice interrupted her reverie. He leaned against the cemetery gate, a hat pulled rakishly over his mop of brown curls. He looked young, handsome, and arrogant.

Celia was annoyed at the intrusion on her privacy. "I was just out walking and decided to look at the gravestones."

"Oh? You find such ghoulishness enjoyable?"

"No! I . . . Anyway," she recovered herself, "what are you doing here? Did you follow me?"

"As a matter of fact, yes. I happened to see you on the path and I was curious to know where you were going."

They faced each other. Her cheeks stinging, Celia remembered Roman's accusation that Beau looked at her with desire. Yes, she realized with a spurt of anger. His amber eyes *were* focused on her intently, moving from her face to her breasts and waist, lingering on her soft curves.

"I've told you before, I don't like you following me," she snapped. "And stop staring at me like that."

"I wasn't staring, Celia, it's only your imagination. Anyway, I was on the path for a purpose. I intended to paint."

Beau motioned behind him, where for the first time Celia saw a folded easel and a paint-spattered box.

"I . . . I see."

"I like to do graveyards," Beau told her. "They have a mystery to them, don't you think? A bleakness. Time stands still here and never moves on. It's all static, nothing changes. Except for the gravestones. They tilt."

Beau kicked out at the marker for the nurse, and Celia gasped as it sagged to one side.

"Oh!" She hurried to straighten it. "You shouldn't have done that—desecrating a grave . . ."

"I'll own Mountain View someday. I'll own this graveyard too, and every headstone in it." Beau paced about restlessly. His eyes looked dark today, Celia thought, the pupils narrowed to tiny pinpoints by the light. "When are you going to pose for me?" Beau asked suddenly.

"Pose?" Celia stared at him. Beau always made her uneasy, with his mockery, those golden eyes that seemed both to covet and to hate her, to know all about her.

"Why, yes. I imagine that my father will want a portrait of you, won't he? Assuming that you *are* going to marry him, of course."

"What do you mean by that?"

He shrugged. "Nothing. What should I mean?"

"Beau, you talk in riddles and in nasty hints that lead nowhere. If you have something to say to me, then please say it. If not, then I think I'll go back to the house. I have some schoolwork to go over."

Without waiting for a reply, she turned and began to stalk off through the cemetery gate and up the dusty path. Beau came after her.

"You really think you're something, don't you, Celia Griffin?"

She hurried on, ignoring him.

"Prancing about here . . . teaching school . . . making eyes at my father and at Roman . . ."

She reddened, snapping about to face him. "I haven't been making eyes at anyone!"

Beau grinned. "You have. You're like a pot of honey, my beauty—and there are a lot of bees buzzing about you. However," Beau added, "there is one bee who won't buzz any longer."

Celia had had enough of Beau's insults and innuendos. "What *do* you mean?"

"Simply that Roman has gone back to Lahaina. He left this morning, lock, stock, and medical bag—and good riddance to him, I say. We don't need would-be murderers here at Mountain View, even if they do have money to lend us for ditches."

Beau's eyes gleamed at her maliciously. "I would imagine that he took his mistress with him. She is lovely, isn't she? Hawaiian women sometimes run to fat, but not this one—she is all woman."

Celia felt as if candle tallow had congealed in her veins, as if she could barely move. "I . . . I am going back to the house now," she told Beau woodenly. "Don't try to follow me again, or I'll tell your father."

"Whatever is the matter with you, Celia? You look as if you had lost your best friend." Hatteras looked up from a flower bed as Celia hurried past, walking blindly. Hatteras had been gardening, and her old day dress was earth-stained at the hem.

Celia could only look at her aunt, wondering if all of her feelings were written on her face for the world to see.

"Goodness, I think I'd better make you a tonic, something to perk you up a bit, put some enthusiasm back into you."

Hatteras' blue eyes inspected her niece with all the sharpness they had employed on the day she had first arrived in Honolulu. Celia fought not to quail under their scrutiny.

"I feel fine, dear aunt."

"You feel rotten, and don't lie to me, Celia, I know you too well for that. Do you have island fever?"

"Island . . . Oh, no. I love it here. I merely feel restless today, that's all."

Hatteras nodded. "I've been thinking, Celia. It's about time we visited the crater of Haleakala, don't you think?"

She gestured toward the faraway volcano, swathed in its layers of clouds.

"I suppose we could go," Celia said mechanically.

"We'll make a holiday of it. I'll speak to John about it tonight at dinner. I'm sure he'll give his consent."

That night's meal seemed endless to Celia. Roman's absence seemed to cast a huge void into the room, and questions taunted her. She hadn't seen Kinau today; as Beau had suggested, was the girl in Lahaina with Roman?

Tina chattered on and on about a toy house she and Aiko wanted to build, begging Hatteras to help them with construction. Half-listening, Celia sat quietly, immersed in her own gloomy thoughts. Beau, too, was silent, his expression sullen, his eyes avoiding Celia.

Finally Hatteras broached the topic of a trip to the crater.

John cleared his throat. "Why shouldn't you go, if you wish, and take Tina? I certainly have no objections. Beau will escort you."

Beau looked up, startled, and Celia, too, let out a gasp of dismay. She could not imagine anyone she would *less* wish to escort her on a trip than John's arrogant and difficult son.

"Aren't you coming?" she asked John.

"I don't have time, Celia. I have the irrigation ditch to see to, and there is other pressing plantation business. Harvest is almost upon us, and as you know, three other planters also utilize the mill operations here at Mountain View."

"But—"

"Enough." John gestured impatiently. "If you want to go at all, you'll take Beau. Anyway, you'll have menservants along, so you can't get into any real trouble, no matter how incompetent my son proves to be."

Although Beau was their ostensible leader, it was really Hatteras who planned the Haleakala expedition. The party would consist of Hatteras, Celia, Beau, Tina, and four male servants, including Maka, a large, heavyset Hawaiian with a gentle smile. All would be on horseback, with extra mounts. They would carry their own tents and food, and Hatteras was already filling a saddlebag with small items that might prove useful on the journey: a knife, horseshoe nails, glycerine, thread, twine, leather thongs, spoons, drinking flasks.

"I hope you don't have a tendency to low blood pressure or wooziness, Celia," Hatteras remarked as she went through Celia's closet to decide which of her riding clothes should be packed for the trip. The altitude on the volcano's summit was ten thousand feet, and temperatures could drop drastically.

"Why, no. I've never fainted in my life."

"Good. Nor have I. And I don't intend to."

Celia smiled to herself, thinking what an efficient paragon her aunt was. This week, Hatteras had finally received a response to her advertisement in the San Francisco paper. It had come from a wealthy gold magnate, a widower with neat handwriting who described twin blond seventeen-year-old grand-daughters who needed, as he put it, "much more supervision than their overworked grandfather can provide." The rich gold miner sounded as if he might possess a sense of humor.

Celia could imagine Hatteras shuttling two spirited girls through Europe or India, leading them on adventures. And perhaps even the trip to Haleakala would be fun. Certainly it would be a change of scene. And perhaps, if Celia were to get away from Mountain View for a few days, she could regain her equilibrium somehow.

Two days later their party of eight set off down the trail that would take them around the small end of the island, across the dry, sandy, desertlike Wailuku Valley, and finally, in switchback trails, up the vast shoulders of Haleakala.

Beau insisted on being at the head of the line. "I've been to Haleakala a dozen times," he boasted. "I've picked silverswords and bounced them down the slopes like cannon-balls. They are a monstrous sort of plant with an odd beauty," he added. "They grow only on Haleakala."

"I hope you left some for the rest of us," Hatteras murmured.

"Oh, yes, there are plenty. They are shipped out to the Orient as ornaments, did you know that? The Chinese prize them."

As they rode, Celia's mood of gloom at Roman's treatment of her gradually lifted. She had to admit that it did feel good to be riding along with the wind blowing in her hair. Overhead the sky arched a deep blue, and even the fluffy clouds that drifted over the West Maui Mountains had a fresh-washed look. Ahead of them, nearly always visible, was the cobalt Pacific.

How beautiful this island is! she thought. With a twist of her heart, she remembered a sunset she had watched with Roman, quiet moments they had shared. If only he were riding beside her now. How happy she'd be, how gloriously content.

Stop it, she ordered herself fiercely. Roman was back in his surgery now, treating his patients, and that was where she prayed he would stay. She must not think of him. What good could it possibly do? He had Kinau, and his own life. Let him keep them. Her feeling that something wonderful and precious hung between them was only illusion—a dream.

They cantered along a track where the wind swirled reddish sand among shifting sandhills. Patches of grass, thistle, indigo, and *pohuehue*, the beach morning glory, formed tangles. Here Maka had to act as guide, for the wind obliterated wheel- and footprints almost as soon as they were made.

His hat pulled over his eyes against blowing sand, Beau spurred his horse to ride beside Celia. "The Hawaiians love Haleakala, Celia, they perform all sorts of religious ceremonies there. You'll see why, when we get there."

"It's impressive, then?"

"Oh, very." This was a new Beau, more open and enthusiastic than she had seen him. "The crater is truly stunning if you are lucky enough to catch it on a clear day, when the clouds don't obscure everything. People usually go up in the afternoon and camp near the summit. They freeze all night long, and then the next morning they get up to see the grand spectacle of the sunrise."

The trail to Haleakala led upward again, into farming country where groves of eucalyptus had been planted, and someday would shade the road, sending out their pungent odor to tantalize the nostrils. As they rode, Beau talked to Celia about his life at Mountain View.

"I'm not wanted here, not really. If I make a suggestion, my father barely listens to it. He thinks I'm less competent than a Hawaiian servant—than Maka, for pity's sake. He just wants me here under his thumb, that's all."

"That must be very difficult to endure," Celia remarked cautiously.

"It is. Believe me, Celia, it is." Then, giving a kick to the side of his horse, Beau suddenly galloped ahead, leaving Celia to ride by herself.

By evening they had ridden through the cloud layer, a chill gray mist, and were above the treeline. While they bundled up in sweaters and made camp, Tina rushed around excitedly, chattering about a wild pig she claimed to have seen in the scrubby hummocks that grew here.

Thoughtfully Celia helped with the camp preparations, thinking of what Beau had told her. He was displaced here at Mountain View, as useless as he had been in California. It was not just petulant complaining, for she had observed this for herself: John treated his son with barely concealed contempt.

No wonder Beau was bitter and difficult. Somehow, knowing these facts about John's son made him easier to like.

That night Celia lay alone in her tent, struggling to keep warm against the high-altitude wind that whipped through crevices in the canvas, slapping a loose rope with monotonous regularity.

She stared upward into darkness, her thoughts assailing her again. Roman . . . Restlessly she turned, pulling her sweaters and wool comforter tighter about her. Why was it that Roman still tormented her, even though she had made up her mind to put him out of her thoughts forever?

The sound of the tent flap startled her. Celia felt a gust of chilly air, and then someone crawled in beside her. She smelled the pungent odor of *okolehao*.

"Who . . . ?" She struggled to sit up, fighting the layers of sweaters and wool that impeded her.

"It's just me. I wanted to talk to you." Beau's voice sounded faintly slurred.

"Beau, it's the middle of the night!" More annoyed than alarmed, Celia edged as far away from him as she could get. He had blocked the tent's entrance with his body, and ground stakes had driven the canvas sides securely into the hard earth, trapping her here.

"I couldn't sleep."

"I'm sorry that you can't sleep, but surely you're aware that it's totally improper for you to be in my tent. I must ask you to leave."

"And what if I don't wish to?" Suddenly Beau clutched at Celia's arms, caressing her with feverish intensity.

A spurt of fear wriggled in her chest. "Beau! Must I scream? Or call Maka to help me?"

It was not a very effective threat, for the wind screeched loudly around the summit of the volcano, so noisy that even if she were to scream, she doubted if she could be heard. Still, the prospect seemed to hold Beau back, for he released her.

"You're the only one who listens to me here, Celia. The only one who understands."

"Beau . . ." she tried again. "You really must go."

"Not yet. I love you, Celia. Oh, yes," he added as shock reeled through her. "Does that startle you? Did you think that I was only my father's offspring, John Burnside's lazy young whelp who wanders about Mountain View with his paints, doing nothing useful?"

Beau was full of endless uncomfortable surprises. For him to trap her in a dark tent, to say such impossible things to her—how was she to respond?

"Beau. Please, you must leave this tent at once, before you say things you will regret in the morning."

"You don't love my father. You love me. I know you do, I feel it."

She felt as if she were trying to swim in quicksand, the morass created by Beau's confused emotions. "Beau! When did I ever give you that impression? I . . . I like you very much, of course . . ."

But soft excuses designed for the drawing rooms of Boston did not work very well in a cramped tent on the rim of a dormant volcano. Beau suddenly muttered something and pulled Celia toward him, smearing a whiskey-flavored kiss across her lips. "Don't lie to me. *I hate lies.* I'll have you if I want, I'll take you away from my father."

"Beau, no . . ."

Horrified by his words, by the situation, Celia used all of her strength to push Beau away, shoving him toward the tent entrance. "You must leave here at once! Do you hear me? And don't talk to me of love again. Or I'll be forced to tell your father of your behavior."

It was not the only time she had had to use that threat. This

time Beau jerked away from her as if she had stabbed him.
"You wouldn't."

"I would. I will. I mean it, Beau."

"Very well. Oh, very well, then." Beau crawled out of the
tent, pulling the canvas flap aside to admit another cold gust
of wind. "But you haven't heard the last of me, Celia
Griffin. I'm going to have you. One way or the other. I'm
going to take you away from my father, mark my words."

Celia secured the tent flap with strips torn from the hem of
one of her petticoats, cursing herself for not having done this
previously. In the morning, if anyone asked, she could say
she'd done it against the wind.

Trapped in the wind-buffeted canvas, she lay awake the
rest of the night. Beau, in love with her! She could hardly
believe it possible. Surely it was only the *okolehao* talking,
and in the morning Beau would be shamefaced, barely able to
recall the incident in the tent.

She certainly hoped that was the end of the matter. She
didn't look forward to trying to explain to John that his son
had crawled uninvited into her tent and announced he planned
to take her away from him.

But the next morning, to Celia's relief, Beau paced about the
campsite exactly as usual. His attitude toward her was the
same as before—sometimes ebullient, sometimes taunting,
always unpredictable. Celia decided that he had been drunk
after all. She would say nothing further about it.

The sun rose in a blaze of reds and golds. They climbed
over the rim and sat on a rocky cliff scattered with cinders
and hardened lava "bombs." The usual gray canopy of clouds
that hung over Haleakala had lifted, and they stared out at the
most magnificent sight Celia had ever seen.

The crater stretched before them, a painted wasteland of
cinder cones. Rusts, purples, browns—there were a dozen
subtle colors to the old lava flows that had been worked on by
erosion to create a primeval and utterly beautiful scene.

"Look, look!" Tina wriggled on slippery cinders as close
to the edge of the precipice as she could get. "It's so big, and
it goes so far. Miles, Celia!"

"One might imagine this the surface of the moon," Hatteras mused. "Sere, yet with a terrible grandeur."

"Sere," Tina repeated, obviously enthralled by the unfamiliar word. She squirmed about, picking up a chunk of hardened lava and pitching it downslope. With fascination they all watched the rock slide endlessly, creating a sandfall as it went.

"Be careful, Tina," Celia cautioned. "It's very steep here."

"Oh, let her roll downhill," Beau said carelessly. "We can see how high she'll bounce at the bottom." He paced about, kicking at cinders, as if already bored.

"Beau!"

"Well, you must admit she's been nothing but a chattering nuisance for the entire trip. Claiming she sees wild pigs . . . I for one am growing quite sick of her."

Celia was again angered at Beau. Surely he was himself nothing but a spoiled, petulant child! But she managed to make peace, taking Tina with her to where a number of the silversword plants grew, with their daggerlike silvery leaves and exotic clusters of flower heads.

That night they camped again at the rim, and this time Celia prudently invited Tina to share her tent. She was not troubled with any more of Beau's invasions.

The next morning they resaddled their horses and started downslope again. But the visibility that they had enjoyed before was gone. Now a bank of dirty gray clouds hung below them, a mist that thickened as they entered it.

Celia swayed in her saddle, staring into the damp mist. Suddenly she heard a cry and looked up to see Hatteras go flying off her mount, tumbling into the scrub growth that grew along the trail. The mare, too, rolled among cinders, whinnying.

"Aunt Hatteras!" Celia pulled up her own horse and jumped off. She went running to her aunt, who lay small and diminished in the rust-colored volcanic dirt. Her aunt's face was furrowed with pain.

"I'm perfectly all right, Celia. My horse tripped on a hole. . . . I just think I might have broken a bone. I believe it could be my hip."

"Well, Celia," Beau said flatly, "I hope you know something about medicine." He gestured toward the deserted trail, fogged over with heavy gray clouds that exuded a damp chill. "Because it's a very long way to civilization."

The servants had ridden up and stood about in clusters, talking in Hawaiian, their faces fearful. Celia heard the word *moo*, pronounced "moh-oh," which meant "lizard."

"They think that a *moo* brought Hatteras bad luck," Beau added sourly. "Pele doesn't want us here, or something to that effect. These people will believe anything."

Tina was crying, and Celia, too, felt anxious as she looked down at Hatteras' pain-twisted features. A broken hip! What was she to do? She knew nothing about broken bones, other than having watched a doctor set her oldest sister's broken arm years ago. The arm had healed. But Celia knew that a broken hip was indeed serious. Already Hatteras' face was dotted with clammy perspiration and she had begun to shiver violently. And how were they to get her down the mountainside?

"Blankets," Celia said quickly to Maka. At least this was one thing she knew about. "We must warm her at once. And . . . we'll have to make something to carry her in."

The big Hawaiian stared at her, uncomprehending.

"A litter. Something for . . . carry-carry," Celia tried in pidgen.

She forced herself to think of necessities. She sent one of the Hawaiians on ahead to fetch Roman, telling him that the party would continue along the trail, meeting him. The clouds made it chilly and damp here, and she felt sure that the rarefied atmosphere could not be good for Hatteras in her injured condition.

By the time Hatteras had been wrapped in blankets and servants had been dispatched to find several long, strong branches with which to make carrying poles, a half-hour had passed. Celia held her aunt's hand, wishing there was more she could do for her.

"Celia . . . I don't intend to die, you know."

A pang knifed across Celia's heart. "Of course you're not going to die!"

"There is always that chance, my dear. I'm an old woman now."

"You're not. Not in your heart."

"I'm old," Hatteras insisted. But she managed a crooked smile and patted Celia's hand. "You're doing the right thing, dear girl. Get me down out of these clouds and back to Mountain View—that's exactly what you should do.''

But they soon learned it was not going to be easy. The three Hawaiians and Beau carried the makeshift litter, slipping along the rough bridle trail, while Celia and Tina led the riderless horses.

It was a slow, agonizing progress, for the walkers had to proceed slowly, and several times Celia heard her aunt's involuntary cry of pain.

"You're being very brave, aunt," she told Hatteras at the next rest stop, smoothing back gray hair now matted with perspiration.

"Nonsense. I'm a coward about pain, always have been." Hatteras' voice sank to a whisper. "It looks as if I won't be making that Grand Tour, my dear—not for a while."

"You'll go. Roman is going to meet us on the trail, and he'll fix you up."

But Hatteras' eyes had closed, and she turned her face tiredly to the side.

13

They had descended through the layer of cloud and were in farming country again, near the groves of young eucalyptus. When Celia spotted a cloud of dust along the trail, she sagged with relief, knowing that it must be Roman.

He rode up, his horse covered with great swaths of red dust, lathered and nearly foundering. His clothes were dusty, and a bristle of dark beard on his cheeks gave him a wild, fierce look that made Celia's heart turn over.

She flew to meet him. "Roman! Please, hurry, she's in so much pain."

"Show me."

Roman swung down from his mount and half-ran to where Hatteras lay on her stretcher, a pathetic mound under gray saddle blankets. He bent over the old woman.

"I'm going to have to examine her hip, Celia. Tell the servants and Beau to go some distance away. I want you to stay and assist me." Always, a woman's modesty had to be considered. In fact, Celia knew, male physicians often were expected to prescribe treatment for a fully dressed female patient without ever having examined her.

Thankful that Hatteras would get treatment, Celia busied herself with carrying out Roman's orders. She stood by to shield her aunt while Roman lifted her aunt's riding dress to reveal a pale, naked flank. Carefully Roman probed. Hatteras stiffened and bit down on her lip, trying not to moan.

"Yes." Roman frowned. "It's broken. . . . We'll take

you back to Mountain View, Hatteras, and then I'll make a support frame for you. It will be devilishly uncomfortable and you'll need help to do everything, since you'll be bedridden for a while. But I believe that you're going to walk again."

"And ride?" Hatteras whispered.

"And ride." Roman said it firmly, although Celia saw a muscle knot in his jawline. "Right now, I'm going to give you some laudanum. That will help with the pain and make it a lot easier for us to get you home."

After Hatteras had swallowed the liquid tincture of opium, her eyes nodded shut. Roman made adjustments to the litter and they were on their slow way again, Roman taking his turn at helping to carry the stretcher.

An hour later, Celia caught up to him as he relinquished his place on the stretcher. "Roman, is my aunt going to be all right?"

Roman hesitated. "I don't know." At Celia's stricken expression, he reached out to touch her hand briefly. For an instant she felt the warmth of his skin on her own. "But she is strong, and that counts for a good deal. By the way, I must compliment you on the carrying litter you devised. It's very serviceable."

Celia glowed at the compliment.

"Women like your aunt have remarkable recuperative powers," Roman went on thoughtfully. "Nothing will stop her if she is determined to get well. Besides that, she is a true lady, warm and loving to others, and courteous to me, even though I know she disapproves of me."

Roman said this with such admiration that Celia felt a swift stab of jealousy. He had never talked about her like that, and she would have given anything if he had.

John met them at Mountain View. He had sent servants out to assist with the litter, and now he walked alongside the stretcher as they carried Hatteras into the house, a handsome man in the prime of life, master of Mountain View and all the hills and cane fields around it.

He took the old woman's hand. "Hatteras, I'm sorry this happened to you. Was it the result of some kind of neglect?" As he said this, he glanced pointedly at Beau, who flushed.

"Oh, no," Hatteras murmured. "My horse stumbled . . . it was an accident."

"Let's get her inside," Roman interrupted impatiently.

John ignored his brother. "Hatteras, if there is anything you need, I will provide it. My guests here at Mountain View are treated properly—I see to that."

"I'm going to need wood, tools, and cloth material for padding," Roman said. "And a competent assistant."

"Very well. I'll give you Chang Liu. The Chinese is very good with his hands, and he understands English."

"No, Celia will do. She's capable enough for what I need."

Inside the house, Hatteras was taken upstairs, and Roman began work on a wooden device that would hold her hip and leg in place while the fracture healed.

"If we're very lucky, the break may heal naturally. I'm sorry to say, Celia, that hip fractures are generally considered untreatable. But I saw a compound fracture of the thigh treated successfully in Boston, and your aunt has told me that she does not object to my trying."

Untreatable. Celia's heart twisted with pity. "Will she be . . . ?" But she could not say the word.

"I don't know, dammit." Roman's eyes darkened with frustration. "There are times when I think that doctors are only charlatans, doing more harm than good to their patients. If only we could see into the body, know more about why some patients survive and others die. We know so little about the human body, Celia! But I am going to try."

When the device was completed and padded with soft strips of flannel, Celia assisted with its fitting. Once, when Hatteras moaned as they tried to turn her, Celia felt herself go white. She clutched at the back of a chair, fighting waves of blackness.

"Hand me those scissors, please," Roman ordered, looking at her sharply. "Quickly. We don't want to tire her any more than necessary."

Celia fought swirling darkness to do as she was told.

When they had Hatteras encased in her large, awkward brace, Celia fed her aunt some soup and fruit juice and sponged her face. She tried to seem cheerful. "I know you'll feel better by tomorrow, aunt. We're going to have plenty of time for reading aloud and just talking. We'll enjoy it.''

Hatteras sniffed. "I don't wish to be trapped in my bedroom like a mollusk in a shell."

"Then we'll move you during the day to the veranda."

"Only the veranda? I want to go everywhere, and I intend to. What did you do with that litter thing you got me down the mountain with? I hope you didn't throw it away, because I intend to use it again."

"Of course, it will be a good way for you to get about," Celia agreed, not voicing her fear that Hatteras would have to use the litter permanently. Roman nodded to her, signaling that it was time to leave the room. By the time they had closed the door behind them, Hatteras was sound asleep.

"Laudanum," Roman said. "It works wonders. Celia, what are you going to do about nursing her? You already have the responsibility of the school and your pupils."

She thought. "I'll get one of the servant girls to help."

"Kinau is a very intelligent girl and has had experience nursing her mother when she was dying of a tumor."

Roman said it casually, but Celia felt her body stiffen, jealousy spurting through her. "I don't want Kinau."

"Oh?"

Something seemed to leap between them, and they gazed at each other, their eyes locking.

"I prefer to use Leinani."

"Why?"

"Because she is . . . cheerful, and I'm sure my aunt will appreciate that."

"But she speaks only pidgen," Roman objected, "and can be slothful. However, if you insist . . ."

They glared at each other. "I do insist."

Roman shrugged. "Very well. I'll stay here tonight, and then in the morning I'll return to Lahaina. I'll leave more laudanam for her pain, and you must summon me at once if your aunt has any problems."

They walked down the hallway together and stood at the top of the stairs. Celia found that her heart was beating ridiculously fast, and to counteract her physical reaction to him, she walked past him, holding tight to the carved wooden baluster. "I doubt if we will have any problems," she told him with a defiant lift of her chin.

She was positive she saw Roman's face darken.

"Good," he murmured in cool response. "Then I won't need to have Mountain View on my mind, will I?" *Or you, Celia,* his tone seemed to imply.

"I never thought I'd be trussed up like this, like a piece of meat at the butcher's," Hatteras complained the next morning when Roman came in to examine her one last time before departing.

"Who would want to buy you? You'd be much too tough and stringy," Roman joked, smiling. This morning he seemed in a jocular mood. Celia watched as he bantered with her aunt, amazed that this was the same Roman Burnside who had spoken to her so coolly the previous day.

What a puzzling, complicated man he was! Sometimes cold and withdrawn, at other times wonderfully tender. She had seen the devoted care he gave to his patients, the despair he felt when the medicine of the day proved inadequate. Would she ever understand him? What drew her to him, what weakness of her mind and senses pulled her into his spell?

Later, John Burnside accompanied his half-brother out to the avenue of *koas*, where Roman's horse was already saddled and waiting. Celia walked with them, glancing up at wispy clouds that seemed to pulsate against a domed sky of brilliant blue.

"We are grateful for your help in this emergency," John told his brother stiffly, the tone of his voice indicating the opposite. "But I am sure your patients need you in Lahaina, and we must not keep you."

The brothers gazed at each other. Roman's jaw knotted. "Let me know if she has problems," he said, swinging onto his horse. He looked down, his eyes granite. "Meanwhile . . . good day to you, Celia."

He was gone, wheeling his horse about and galloping through the heavy old trees, headed back in the direction of the whaling town.

As he disappeared from sight, John heaved a heavy sigh. "Well, that's that. Good riddance to him."

"Why do you hate him so much?" Celia dared to say.

"Surely what happened fifteen years ago doesn't matter now. Roman was only a boy then."

"As the boy grows, so does the man." Abruptly John lifted his luxuriant graying forelock and pointed to a thickened whitish scar hidden by his hair. "My half-brother tried to murder me once—here is evidence. I suffer him at Mountain View when I must—it was a stipulation of our father's will. But I don't have to love him. And I'm going to get another doctor for your aunt. Roman can stay where he is, treating Hawaiians and prostitutes."

"But—"

"Don't try to dissuade me. *I* am master here at Mountain View, Celia. And that should be sufficient."

As the days passed, Hatteras recovered her strength and began to chafe at her enforced restriction in the castlike wooden frame. "I'm a prisoner," she griped. "Walled up in a wooden box! Tomorrow, Celia, I want you to have that flighty Leinani prepare a picnic for me. I itch to get out-of-doors, and I think I'd like to go down to my gardens, just to see how they are coming."

"Very well, but—"

"No objections!" Hatteras snapped. "This wooden device is not going to be anything more than an inconvenience. Call Leinani, Celia, at once. And please see if you can find my gardening gloves. I may even spade up some of the plants."

Two weeks later, Celia rose from bed on a Saturday morning, smelling the tropical breezes that blew through her windows, scented with bougainvillea, a dozen blossoming trees, and the inevitable sugar. After breakfasting with Hatteras and seeing to it that her aunt was carried to her favorite gardening spot, she felt at loose ends.

Below Mountain View, morning sun glinted off the Pacific, and the wave surface was calm today, with only a hint of baby whitecaps. Overhead, the sky burned blue.

Celia paced the lawn restlessly, unsure what to do with herself. It was a school holiday, and she didn't feel like browsing in Mountain View's small library or curling up in a chair with a book. Hatteras was happily occupied with her flowers, with servants to care for her needs.

John was at the plantation office, and harum-scarum Tina was off playing with Aiko.

Celia found that she had begun walking toward the stables, and allowed her feet to take her there. Inside the stable, she stood breathing in the pungent odor of manure and straw. Her gelding, Misty, whickered at her from his stall.

"Do you want out, Misty? Do you want to go somewhere?"

She stroked the horse's long muzzle, looking into his intelligent eyes, and finally, impulsively, she saddled him. Then she tethered him to a rail while she went in through the back door of the kitchen to beg a picnic lunch from Chang Liu.

"You go ride, missy?" The Chinese cook seemed agitated at this change in routine. He puttered about the big kitchen with its coal range, wooden icebox, and tables covered with oilcloth.

"Yes, I thought I might. In fact," she added recklessly, "why don't you give me food enough for two meals, in case I return late."

"Two meals? You not home for dinner?"

"I don't know when I'll be home. Just give me a big box of chicken and fruit, and maybe some cold biscuits, anything to tide me over."

She was impatient to be going; she could hardly wait for Chang to cut the chicken, wrap it in oiled paper, load a small wicker basket for her. She left a note for her aunt and then set off.

She had ridden for some time before she realized she had chosen the trail that led to Lahaina. Lahaina—where Roman was. She squared her chin defiantly, deciding not to change her route. She had a right to go where she pleased, didn't she? And she'd never traveled this road before, not the full distance on horseback.

She took her time, savoring the day, enjoying the warmth of the sun on her shoulders, the spectacular scenery. The afternoon sun was lowering itself over the West Maui Mountains as she finally rode into Lahaina.

Celia looked about her with eager interest. A generation ago, when whaling had been in its heyday, the little town had burst apart at the seams with roistering sailors bent on pleasuring themselves in its grog shops and brothels. There were still plenty of sailors, lounging in the streets, eyeing Celia or whistling at her as she cantered past on Alanui Moi, the King's Road.

"Eh, there, my beauty! Whyn't you stop and say hello?" a bearded sailor called to her. "What is it, you're too haughty?"

From the doorway of a clapboard building, two dark-skinned girls peered at Celia, giggling behind their hands. An old Chinese man peered from an upper window, his queue wrapped around his head, his face scored with wrinkles and creases.

It was at the end of a little cul-de-sac, sandwiched between a saloon and a ships' chandlery, that she found Roman's surgery. It was a small building made of coral blocks, a sign over the door proclaiming "Dr. Roman Burnside, Surgeon."

Celia's mouth suddenly went dry, and she realized that this had been her destination from the start, even if she had not wished to admit it to herself. She drew up her horse and stared at the clumps of palms that grew near the surgery, the trade wind making a papery, rustling sound through their fronds.

What if Roman didn't want her here? What if Kinau were with him and she had interrupted them at an inopportune time? Doubt assailed her, and she almost slapped the bridle to ride away. What sort of blind fool had she been, to come here uninvited and unannounced?

But something stopped her. Her heart hammering in her throat, she dismounted and walked up to the surgery door. Her hand was trembling as she knocked.

Roman had been shaving, and a lather of soap covered the right side of his jaw but had been scraped from the left. He was shirtless, and his muscular bare chest gleamed a rich brown. "My God. Celia." He stared at her, his large body bulking in the doorway, filling it with his presence.

"H-hello," she managed to stammer. "I've come for a refill of Hatteras' laudanum."

"Indeed? And you didn't see fit to send a servant on such an errand?"

She flushed hotly and looked away, miserably aware of the flimsiness of the lie and Roman's own knowledge that it was only an excuse.

"May I come in?" she forced herself to say.

"If you don't mind being present while I finish shaving, why not? Be my guest."

As she followed him inside, Celia hardly knew where to look, what to do with her eyes. She had seen Roman naked before—she remembered vividly every outline of his body, every beloved contour. Still, it was a fresh surprise to see again the wide, massive shoulders, the smooth muscles that rippled underneath his skin. She had been held against that satiny skin. She had gloried in the feel of those hard, hard muscles.

As if sensing her confusion, Roman went to a chair where a starched shirt had been flung, and began to put it on. "There. That's a little more proper, don't you agree?"

Proper. When they had been together as naked and abandoned as it was possible for a man and a woman to be. . . .

In confusion she looked around the surgery. It was immaculately clean, its glassed-in cabinets filled with surgical knives, forceps, saws, and other tools, the use of which she could only guess. There was a high table on which she supposed surgery was performed. The office smelled of carbolic and some ammoniac disinfectant.

Roman went to a small oak mirror that hung on one wall and completed shaving, with the aid of a brush dipped in a mug of shaving soap. In fascination Celia watched the straight razor move across his skin. "Your office is very interesting." She said the first thing that came into her head. "Do you perform much surgery here?"

"A fair bit." Roman tilted his chin back and shaved the cleft.

"But do you live here too?" she asked him. "This surgery looks much too small for that."

He gave a dry laugh. "It is, and I don't relish sleeping on a hard surgical table. I have an apartment behind the surgery. Perhaps you would like to inspect it before you leave? With the laudanum you came for, of course. My pharmacy happens to be in my apartment."

"If you insist," she managed to retort, glad he had his back to her so that he could not see the fiery blush of her cheeks.

Minutes later Roman led her into a four-room apartment

with cool walls of whitewashed coral block. Grass matting was spread on the floor, and there were a few pieces of rattan furniture covered in chintz, and bamboo shades to shield the room from the worst of the tropical sun.

On the walls hung a collection of Hawaiian weapons. Roman began to explain some of them to her, talking of the tribal warfare and human sacrifice with which the history of these islands was rife. "Someday I'll lend you some of these to show to your students," he said, smiling. "I'm sure they'll love the grand stories of bravery and death."

She drew a deep breath. "I didn't come to bother you," she said quickly. "I know you must have dozens of patients who require your attention."

"As a matter of fact, I just came from one." Roman's expression tightened. "A sailor who died of infection after injury with a whaling harpoon. I couldn't save him."

He looked abruptly weary, and Celia realized that he must have been going since early morning, and that when she had seen him shaving, it had been his first opportunity to do so.

"As I told you, I came for some laudanum for my aunt," she hurried to say. "If you could make some up, I'll take it back to her and she will be most grateful. I have brought money to pay for it."

"No, I won't accept money. If you'll wait just a moment, I'll get some for her."

Roman went to a cabinet and pulled it open, revealing an extensive collection of pills and powders, pastes, liquids, jellies, and ointments, all carefully labeled. He rummaged among them, finally pulling out a large bottle. He poured from this into a smaller bottle, and carefully put in the stopper.

"There. That should be sufficient. But don't give her too much of this, Celia, unless she needs it to sleep. Laudanum is a derivative of opium, and is addictive. Too many people seek the temporary relief of some patent medicine, only to discover too late that it is liberally laced with opium. Unwitting addiction is the result. And it isn't pleasant."

"I'll tell her," Celia promised. "And now that you've made this up, I should be getting back to Mountain View before it grows dark."

Roman frowned. "You won't make it all the way back before darkness, Celia. You set off too late."

"I . . ."

Her color deepened. It was, of course, the truth. She'd set off casually, without really thinking of the dangerous black tropical darkness. Now she was uncomfortably aware of Roman's quizzical look. Did he think that she had deliberately put herself in this position in order to find her way into his bed? Yes, she could tell by his expression that he did.

She drew herself up and said sharply, "I brought my own lantern, of course, so I should be fine. If you think that I came here to seduce you, Roman Burnside, you are sadly mistaken! I wouldn't . . . I'd never . . ."

"You are a beautiful little witch, Celia, and I'm sure you have your own tactics to get what you want."

"Well, I don't want *you*." She clutched the bottle of laudanum so tightly that the edge of its stopper cut into her skin. "Anyway," she added sarcastically, "thank you for the medicine for my aunt. I'll convey to her your regards."

"Please do," he told her, his voice maddeningly calm.

Celia slammed the door as she left Roman's apartment, but the act gave her little satisfaction. And she was forced to stop in town at a general store in order to buy the lantern she had told Roman that she carried.

Hatteras was angry with Celia for riding all the way to Lahaina by herself, returning late at night.

"Whatever got into you, Celia Griffin? To go so far by yourself, a lone woman . . . Your horse could have fallen, you could have been attacked by brigands, or lost your way . . . There are times when I think you should be turned over someone's knee and spanked soundly."

"I . . . I'm sorry, Aunt Hatteras."

"As well you should be. Celia . . . I'm a garrulous old woman, and sometimes I say too much. I know well enough that broken hips are considered a lost cause. Usually nothing is done for them except to make the patient comfortable. I am grateful to Roman Burnside for trying. However, I admit that he worries me."

"What . . . what do you mean?"

"Are you in love with him?" The question caught Celia by surprise. She started, her face flushing dark.

"Oh, girl, don't blush so! I saw you when you were putting this wooden thing on me. You trembled every time he looked at you or accidentally touched you. You have never reacted to John Burnside like that. And John is your fiancé, the man you have promised to marry, the man whom, presumably, you love."

Celia looked downward at the bedside table, where a half-finished letter lay, addressed to the widower in California.

"I . . . I was merely assisting Roman in his duties as your doctor."

"I might have been injured, but I still have eyes to see. And I have seen other things, as well. Beau, too, is enamored of you."

Celia caught her breath. "Beau has been far too forward," she said at last.

"Beau is a hot-blooded young man," Hatteras said tartly.

"Three men," she mused. "Beau. John. Roman. This is dangerous, Celia, what you're doing, and sooner or later you're going to have to choose one of them. I hope you're prepared for that."

Harvesttime. All summer the cane had grown, from chest-high to head-high, a green, leafy jungle. Now it stood so tall that a man on horseback could not look over it.

"I've been fortunate this year," John said in satisfaction, surveying the green expanse. "No blight, no hurricane, and the sugar content looks to be high. We may make as much as ten tons to the acre."

"I imagine that you and your workers will be very busy," Celia said.

"It's the ox carts that will be busy, my girl, hauling cane. An ox moves at exactly one mile per hour, so we have to use a good many of them."

One morning Celia awakened to smell the harsh, acrid odor of smoke. In a panic she jumped out of bed and grabbed for her dressing gown, racing for the door. Tina! she thought, her heart in her throat. And Hatteras, helpless in her heavy wooden hip frame.

She found her aunt propped up in bed munching a piece of

toas. while Leinani brushed her long gray hair. Tina was curled at the foot of the bed, leafing through a book on Tibet, her red curls falling across her cheeks. None of the three seemed much concerned about the thick smoky odor drifting in through the jalousied windows.

Celia skidded to a stop. "Aunt Hatteras! There's a fire!"

Tina giggled.

"Of course there is, my dear," Hatteras said calmly. "Sugarcane—acres of it. It's harvesttime, and John is burning away the dried leaves to get to the stalks."

Celia reddened, feeling like a fool. "I . . . I see."

"He does the burning in the early morning or late evening, when the trade winds are light and there's less danger of the fire spreading."

The cane fires, with their huge gray plumes of smoke, filled the air with cinders for days. Soon Celia grew accustomed to the thick odor, which permeated the house and all of their clothing, bedding, and food. Every day they heard the rattle of iron wheels, the curses of wagon drivers, and the crack of whips. Hundreds of wagons rolled back and forth, each with a load of cane stalks for the mill.

During this time, Celia saw little of John, for he rose at dawn each day to supervise the fires and sometimes did not return until dusk. His complexion, already sun-darkened, grew more leathery.

Rejected from the plantation office, Beau wandered about Mountain View with his paint box. Celia had seen his current painting—a depiction of the cane fires as a lurid scene from hell, heavy with smoke and tendrils of red flame.

There was something about Beau's work that she found unsettling. He was talented; of that she held no doubt. Yet his landscapes seethed with vivid color and angular brush strokes. His portraits made his subjects look like dark mirror images of themselves. Celia was glad she had never submitted to sitting for Beau; she felt sure she would not like his rendition of her.

By the third day of harvest, however, Beau had retreated to his quarters, a suite in the west wing of the house, separated from the others by storage rooms and a long corridor. Celia glimpsed Chang Liu, the cook, bringing Beau his meals on a covered tray.

She sent a manservant to investigate. Was Beau ill? But the Hawaiian returned to bob his head and grin at her. "Beau, he *lolo*." He made a gesture to indicate the brain.

"*Lolo?*"

"He *lolo*," the man repeated, grinning as he turned to leave.

"What is wrong with Beau?" Celia asked John that night when his son did not appear for the dinner hour.

"He's sulking—what else? It's a habit of his, to wall himself up in his room whenever something does not please him."

"Perhaps he does it because he wants to be more a part of the harvest and a help to you," Celia ventured.

"A help! I've tried that, dear girl, and it didn't work. Beau is so temperamental that the workers refuse to work under him. He can't command their respect. Workers are at a premium here, and I can't afford to lose any. Mountain View is mine, and I know what needs to be done to preserve it."

Thoughtfully Celia nodded. John and Roman, she knew, owned the sugar plantation jointly. Yet John persisted in calling Mountain View his. She supposed that in his mind it *was* his. No wonder he and Roman clashed so often, she thought. And he and Beau as well. What complicated threads of rivalry were woven through Mountain View!

"Are you ready for the big party?" she heard John ask her now.

"Are we giving a party?"

"We certainly are. As soon as the harvest is over, I plan to celebrate. I've already sent out the invitations." John named a number of local planters, and others from the islands of Kauai and Hawaii. "Many of us attended Punahoe School in Honolulu together. Is there anyone you wish to invite, Celia?"

Celia thought. She had made many casual acquaintances in Honolulu, but no real friends. "We could ask my cousin Rebecca," she finally said. "Becky traveled all the way to Kauai to marry a man she had never met. I must confess I have been thinking about her, wondering whether she is happy."

"Then we'll send her a message. It will do you good to see her."

"Oh, thank you!" Impulsively Celia hugged John, and was dismayed when he wrapped his arms around her, refusing to allow her to leave his embrace.

"Celia, Celia," he muttered into her neck. "What are you trying to do, drive me half-wild with desire? You know why I'm throwing this party, don't you?"

"Why, you said to celebrate the harvest . . ."

"Yes, but also to announce our wedding date. It's time we were married."

Celia swallowed, feeling a sudden lump clog her throat. She should have known this would happen again. Had she been living in a fool's paradise, dreaming along in a fantasy that things could go on as they were, that John would not try to claim what he thought was his? She *was* his fiancée.

She managed to pull a fraction of an inch away from his strong, insistent grip. "John, I . . . I . . ."

"No," he insisted. "No more excuses. I want an answer, Celia, you owe me that much. And I want to make the formal announcement at the party. So I suggest that you do some thinking, darling. About what you want as a wedding gift from me."

Preparations began for the harvest celebration. Some of the guests would stay in the house, being put up in guest rooms and in Beau's large suite. Others would stay in the clapboard home of McRory, the sugar boiler, or Kenneday, the plantation foreman, both of whom would be moved out of their dwellings for the occasion.

From her bed, Hatteras planned menus and ordered the preparation of roast pigs and all the other feast trimmings. Already Celia's pupils were buzzing excitedly about a *hula*. On the isolated plantation, where there was seldom any excitement, the harvest feast was going to be a real occasion.

But each day pushed Celia closer toward an unwelcome decision. She buried herself in her teaching, working long hours after class with the adult workers, anything to keep her mind busy. If only she'd spoken up to John earlier! If only she had insisted more vehemently that she didn't love him, forced him to believe her.

Instead, she'd worked herself into an untenable position.

John was in love with her, and expected her to marry him. If she jilted him now, he would be desperately hurt and she would have no alternative but to leave Mountain View.

And did she really want to leave yet?

She knew that she did not.

14

On the day the first guests were to arrive, Celia awoke with a trembling, uneasy knot in the pit of her stomach. She rose and dressed, donning a pink shot-silk gown that, with its layered flounces, emphasized the slimness of her waistline, the glossy sheen of her dark hair.

She leaned forward to frown at her reflection in the mirror. Her cheeks were flushed and her eyes held a hectic glow. She had had days to mull over her answer to John. Yet she knew to her shame that she was no closer to a solution than she had been.

The house echoed with the chatter of servants as they made last-minute preparations. At noon a servant came racing to the veranda, where Celia, Tina, and Hatteras were eating a light lunch. "A wagon, a wagon, missy! Someone here, *wiki wiki!*"

Celia rose and went to the railing, from where a wagon could be seen pulling up in a cloud of red Maui dust. She felt a light shiver travel over her body. These people—whoever they were—would be the audience, if John had his way, for their wedding announcement.

"What a bumpy and dusty ride. I declare, I don't think I've ever been so battered about in my life. That cart had no padding whatsoever, and I don't think that Maui wagoners have ever heard of wagon springs!"

Cousin Rebecca stood up in the ox cart with an air of aggrieved dignity, slapping dust out of her black dress. More dust and perspiration coated her upper lip.

"There, now, will you wait until I can help you down?"
The man accompanying Rebecca said it pettishly. He looked
to be about forty-five, stocky and plain.

"Very well, then, Mr. Fielding," Rebecca said. "I only
thought—"

"I do not wish you to harm yourself," Bertrand Fielding
said sharply to his new wife. With an air of authority he
helped Rebecca down and then turned to greet Celia. "Miss
Griffin, I presume? We have read your letters on the sugarcane industry and find them most interesting."

John Burnside came striding out of the house to greet his
first guests, and soon a hubbub of voices and activity filled
Mountain View, permeating every corridor and room.

Celia took her cousin on a tour of the house. As they
walked through verandas, two drawing rooms, library, kitchen,
buttery, and storage rooms, Rebecca lost some of her cowed
look. "My," she said, looking around her with interest.
"This is certainly an elegant house, isn't it, Celia? So big! Is
it true it was transported in its entirety from Connecticut?
And those lurid paintings—who on earth did them?"

Celia began to explain Beau's role as artist.

"I don't like his work at all." Rebecca frowned at the
painting of the cane fires. "It's much too sharp and harsh for
my taste."

"I think Beau possesses artisic genius." To her surprise,
Celia found herself defending John's son.

"Oh, I suppose. But I'm glad I don't have to have those
things hanging on *my* walls. They make me feel uneasy."

At last, when they had reached Celia's bedroom and Celia
had shown Rebecca the large collection of shells that Tina
and the other children had given her, Rebecca plopped down
on Celia's bed and gave a gusty sigh. "I must confess I'm
tired. Not that I don't have a right to be. . . . I'm pregnant.
At thirty-one, can you imagine such a thing? In my ten years
of marriage to my previous husband, I had come to believe
that I was barren. But apparently he was sterile, rather than
myself."

"Congratulations, Becky!" Celia hugged her cousin, who
still seemed a stranger in the tight black dress that emphasized new lines of anxiety about her eyes and mouth.

"Yes, I've always wanted a baby . . . although to rear it

here in the islands, among heathen . . ." Again Rebecca sighed. "But I suppose that is the burden that the Lord places on us women." Then Rebecca frowned and changed the subject. "I must say I was rather surprised to receive an invitation here."

"Why so?"

"Well, you are not in exactly an official position to extend invitations, are you?"

Celia flushed and said nothing.

Rebecca smoothed her brown hair and rose to pace around Celia's bedroom, gazing critically at details of the furniture and lamps. "I must tell you that I came here in my delicate condition for only one reason, and that was to talk to you. To inform you what scandal you are creating."

Celia shivered. "Scandal?"

"Why, of course! It's all over the islands, your living in the house of a man to whom you're not married, queening it over his dinner table, carrying on a flirtation with his son, and even with Roman Burnside."

How had such news traveled? Had it been through servants? Celia stared at Rebecca, feeling chilled. "If you know all that, Becky, then you also know that I have a chaperon. Aunt Hatteras is here, too."

But Rebecca sniffed. "She is bedridden now, from what we hear. And therefore, I'm sure, helpless to act in that capacity."

Celia wanted to cry out at the unfairness of it all. "Hatteras is far from helpless," she defended her aunt. "She planned this entire party, she runs the house, and has even supervised the gardening. She is carried everywhere she wishes to go—"

"But can she go under the trees at night, and into the bedroom of the master of the household?"

Celia looked at Rebecca's plump, self-righteous expression. "What are you trying to imply, Rebecca?"

"Why, that people will think you are John Burnside's mistress. What else? Celia, you are scandalizing the islands! The situation is shocking, and as a representative of your family, I must insist that you remedy it at once. I urge that you marry John Burnside as soon as he'll have you."

People will think you are John Burnside's mistress. Was that the island gossip? Celia's thoughts raced. She had defied

Rebecca, speaking to her cousin coldly, but inwardly she seethed with shame. She had brought all of this upon herself. She knew she had, and the knowledge did not make her feel better.

All day long, more guests streamed in. Ruark Cousineau and his wife came from the far end of the island, near Hana. George Wilcox had traveled from Kauai. Local planters included Henry Baldwin and Sam Alexander, their families, and others. Children raced and giggled, and wives caught up on gossip. Men gathered in knots to discuss island politics or sugar prices.

The dining room had been banked, in honor of the occasion, with huge bouquets and baskets of flowers, their scent overwhelmingly sweet. *Pointe de Venise* lace mats and runners decorated the table, adorned with fresh green vines. Two huge candelabra flamed with light.

Celia sat uncomfortably at table, picking at her rare roast beef. On her left, at the head of the table, sat John, resplendent in evening dress, his sun-browned face a handsome contrast to his starched white shirt and silk cravat. Often, as the meal progressed, John's eyes rested on her.

She forced herself not to squirm under his scrutiny. She hadn't given him her answer yet. What was she going to say to him? She didn't want to leave Mountain View. And she didn't wish to be John's wife.

Jewel-bedecked women laughed and chattered, flirting decorously with planters whom they had not seen in months. Celia tried to pay attention to the conversation, joining it when she could. Was Rebecca right—did all these people assume she was John's mistress? She felt miserable. Would this long meal never end?

But at last the bananas flambé was served, and the men retired to the library, where John had brandy and choice Cuban cigars to offer them. Celia and the other women withdrew to Hatteras' bedroom to freshen up.

Women surged about the room's two mirrors, peering into wavy glass to pat stiff curls and elaborate braided coiffures. Was it Celia's imagination, or did their eyes touch her and then move pointedly away?

"I suppose you're very busy at the school here," Melanie Cousineau said to Celia as they stood combing their hair in front of the mirror. Melanie was younger than the others, only twenty-two, plumply pretty, with a scattering of freckles.

"Yes, I am, and I am teaching seven adults to read, too," Celia said, relieved to have someone to talk to. She told Melanie about the school, and several trips that she had planned for her pupils.

"Is it true that you're going to marry John Burnside?" the other burst out at last. "That you'll be mistress here soon?"

"I—" Celia began.

"Oh, I do hope you are! Because I'd like to have you over to visit us. It does get lonely where we are. Hana is almost nothing but ocean and *taro* patches and banana trees and natives, so boring."

"Is it?"

Melanie chattered on. "They say John is going to make the announcement soon, Celia, but you don't have to worry, I'll pretend I don't know anything about it. I'm sure once you marry him, all the gossip will die away."

Then there *was* gossip. Her cousin had been right, and she had not misread the attitude of these planters' wives. Somehow Celia managed a reply, wondering how she was going to get through the remaining eight days of this long house party.

The following afternoon, Celia fled the incessant chatter of the planters' wives for the relative peace of the schoolhouse. She sat correcting papers, feeling the push of the hot trade wind that brought with it the scent of dust, flowers, and fermenting sugar.

"Celia?" She heard the door slam and then Tina trotted into the school, her red hair flowing down her back. "Celia, I wondered where you were. Don't you like the party?"

"Yes, of course I do."

"They talk a lot, don't they? Oh, but it's going to be fun when we start playing quoits and croquet. And the *hula*! Leinani is going to dance, and lots of others. They have already been practicing for days. I know, 'cause I watched."

Tina lingered to prowl about the schoolroom, chattering artlessly in her high, sweet voice.

"Are you really going to marry my father?" she asked Celia suddenly. "I heard the ladies talking. They said if you didn't marry him, you'd have to leave. Go back to the mainland, back to Boston.''

Celia caught her breath, stricken. How was she to explain to a child of eight that she had falsely accepted her father's proposal of marriage?

"If you marry him, you'll be my mother, won't you?"

"You already had a real mother, who must have loved you very much," Celia pointed out gently.

"Yes, but I want *you*. I want you to stay here on the island—I want you to be my teacher forever and ever. I never want you to leave, never, never!"

"Tina . . . oh, love." Touched, Celia pulled the little girl to her. The child squirmed into her embrace, all knobby elbows, smelling of little girl, soap, and sunlight.

"Promise me, Celia! Promise me you won't go!"

"Tina, I can't make any promises just yet. I told your father I would marry him, but . . . but I need more time to think. Marriage is an enormous decision to make."

"I just want you here. I don't want you to go . . . promise me you won't."

Later, as Celia changed for dinner, putting on a fresh white lace gown and threading a glowing red hibiscus in her dark hair, she could not get Tina out of her mind. The child loved her. And she loved Tina. It hurt to think that, once she left Maui, she'd probably never see John's daughter again.

What would happen to Tina after she left? Would she revert to the half-wild hoyden she had been before, with tangled hair and bare feet? Ignorant of reading, mostly ignored by her father and brother?

The decision she made about John was going to have repercussions, Celia realized, about which she had not thought before.

"This, Celia, is a song in which the lover pours into the ear of his beloved the story of his passion."

John leaned toward Celia, smiling, as Hawaiian voices filled the air with liquid music. There were the rhythmic sounds of nose flutes, *hula* drums, gourds, and rattles, the smell of flowers, the coconut oil worn by the dancers, the pungent whiff of burning *kukui* torches.

" 'Two flowers there are that bloom in your garden . . .

entwine them into a garland, emblem and crown of our love . . .' '' John's eyes fastened on Celia's as he translated. ''This *hula* was danced for me long ago. I have forgotten some of the words, but it's one of my favorites.''

The harvest celebration had lasted more than a week. For the guests, who included most of the island's leaders, there had been a succession of elaborate dinners, a *luau*, and several forays to the beach. Now, seated in a garden chair next to John with the other guests, Celia listened to the pound of native instruments.

Eighteen young men and women danced for them tonight, their oiled bodies glistening. Celia watched the swaying dancers with pleasure. What a joyous, carefree people the Hawaiians were, in spite of the diseases that had decimated their numbers, the religion and other burdens of civilization that had been put upon them.

Nearby, Beau sat with a sketchbook, capturing the fluid lines of the dancers, intent on his work. The young women were especially beautiful, Celia thought, in their grass skirts, their long hair gleaming in the torchlight.

Then there was a drum burst, a change in the rhythm of voices as another dancer appeared from behind a bank of flowers.

Celia drew a breath of surprise. Kinau. She wore a short *pau,* white blossoms hung around her neck. Her long black hair, like a length of perfect silk, swayed when she did. The girl was superb, her eyes flashing, her body supple, as, with undulating hips and arms, she commanded the dance.

Celia heard the appreciative murmur of the other guests. Nearby, Rebecca's mouth hung open, her expression mesmerized. Celia swallowed hard, feeling as if she could barely breathe. Had Kinau ever danced like this, so sensuously, for Roman? Had he ever pulled her into the shadows, as she had seen several other men doing with the girl dancers, tumbling them into the grass to make love to them?

That, too, she sensed, the lovemaking, the physical contact of two bodies, was a part of the *hula*. . . .

''Well, what do you think? Isn't she a splendid dancer?'' John wanted to know.

''Yes, she is . . . very skilled.''

"I thought you would enjoy this. Kinau is our best dancer. I invited her especially to be a part of it." His voice changed, growing more husky, as if the rhythmic, sensual beat of the music had had an effect on him. "Celia . . ."

She froze, knowing what was coming. He was going to touch her, put his arm around her, beg her to set a date to marry him. Celia felt a sudden smothering feeling of being trapped. Impulsively, aware of the stares of the other guests, she rose from her seat. Ignoring John's cry, she lifted the hem of her skirts against the evening dew and hurried across the grass into the night.

It felt good to get away. Like a soft, mocking song, the music of the *hula* followed her. She breathed deeply. The air was full of flower scents. Overhead glowed a huge silver moon set against blackness strewn with millions of diamond-chip stars. Light glimmered on the grass, turning the lace of Celia's evening gown into silver filigree.

Roman, Celia thought in despair. Oh, Roman. Why can't I stop loving you, why do you interfere with what I know I ought to do?

Be sensible, she ordered herself, walking through a splash of moonlight and then into soft shadow. Marrying John would certainly be the prudent thing to do. As Rebecca suggested, she would preserve her reputation. This certainly was no small consideration. But there were many more good reasons for her to marry John. She'd acquire a stepdaughter, Tina, whom she already loved. She would be mistress of Mountain View, with all the luxury and privilege that meant. Certainly marriage to John would be a far better bargain than most women got.

Finally Celia sank to the ground, folding her skirts around her. A knot seemed to fill her throat, choking her. Was a "bargain" in marriage what she really wanted? Making do, accepting a man she didn't really love merely for the sake of expedience?

But, she reminded herself, it was what many women did. Rebecca had done so. And who was to say that their marriages didn't turn out as happily as those made for love?

"Well, look who's here. Don't you like the *hula*?"

Celia jumped. She turned to see Beau approaching, his sketchbook still in hand.

"I . . . I wanted to be alone."

"Ah, the prenuptial jitters? I suppose you are going to announce your wedding to my father soon."

She said nothing, jumping to her feet to hurry across the lawn toward the plantation house.

"Don't do it, don't marry him." Beau caught up to her and grasped her arm. She felt the wiry strength of him. "My father is thirty years older than you are. He's old and tired, he's used up two wives already. You need someone who could please you—"

"Stop!" She whirled on him. "Beau, don't you remember what I told you at Haleakala?"

"I remember." He said it sullenly. "You ordered me never to speak to you of love. Well, I'll do it if I wish. You're a fool if you choose my father over me. I'll inherit Mountain View. I'll be master here one day, I'll run everything."

He was like a petulant child thwarted in an urge for candy. Celia shook free of him, furious at herself for getting into such an awkward situation with Beau. Why couldn't he leave her alone?

"Celia . . . listen to me!" Like an actor in some ridiculous comedy, Beau strode after her. Celia hastened her steps, her face burning. She should never have left the *hula*.

To her relief, she heard a horse's hooves on the road, and turned, heading toward the welcome sound. Beau wouldn't dare to bother her in the presence of anyone else, even a mill worker or servant.

"Celia! I want you to talk to me! I want you to listen to me!"

Celia darted for protection toward the horseman, who was no more than a dark silhouette, moonlight glinting on metal harness decorations. Beau fell back, just as she had hoped.

"All right, I'll talk to you later, Celia. I won't forget this. No, I won't forget!" the son of the household shouted after her. Then, apparently vanquished, he disappeared up the avenue and was gone.

She heard the jingle of metal as someone dismounted.

"I see you have yet another admirer," the rider drawled. "Does it never stop, Celia, the men who are interested in you?"

Roman: somehow he was here, come to attend the *hula*, Celia supposed, to see Kinau dance. She fought to govern her pulse. "I suppose you've come to see the dancing," she blurted.

He was walking toward her, a wide-shouldered man whose dark hair and black riding clothes made him seem like some easy, confident devil. "Is that why you think I've come?"

"Why else would you? Kinau is . . . That is, she's your . . . I was told that you and she . . ." Her cheeks flaming, she subsided into miserable silence.

In the silver light, Roman's face was an expressionless mask. "Yes," he said heavily, "she's my mistress, if that's what you mean. I won't hide that from you. But it isn't Kinau I've come here to see tonight, but to deliver a package for my brother from our bankers in Honolulu."

"Oh!" But she didn't care, Celia thought defiantly, why he'd come. They walked on in a thick silence punctuated only by the distant noises of the dance, the lilting Hawaiian voices and instruments. Why couldn't he get on his horse again and leave; why did he have to torment her like this with his very presence? Even now her heart was pounding with sick weakness, and she knew that she responded to him. With her breath, her heart, every reflex of her body.

Cinders crunched under their feet, accentuating the space between them, the silence. Finally she heard Roman's soft, indrawn breath. "Celia, you play with men. You enjoy having them at your disposal, don't you?"

"No." A thick lump clogged her throat.

"Ah? Remember, I witnessed that touching little scene with Beau back there in the moonlight. I heard his plaintive words. 'Celia,' " Roman mimicked, " 'I want you to talk to me.' "

"Stop it!" she snapped. "It wasn't as it appeared! Beau is foolish and impetuous, he's very young."

"He is older than you are, my sweet."

"That's . . . that's not what I mean. I don't love Beau, I

never invited his attentions. As for John, I . . . I don't love him either.''

"No? Coquettes seldom do feel love, you know. To them love is a sport, a fascinating game, no more. Face it for once, Celia, face the truth.''

Tears of hurt brimmed in her eyes. "Is that what you think of me, Roman? That I play a game? Well, I don't. I . . . I love you,'' she whispered painfully.

"Me?'' Roman laughed. "I doubt that, Celia. I doubt it very much. Flirts don't love any man—they can't.'' With that he swung astride his horse again, his face carved and cold. "Now I believe I'll ride on up to the house to wait for my brother. The bankers entrusted a package to me, and I wish to deliver it to him. Good night, Celia.''

Roman cantered into the shadows cast by the *koas* and was gone. Celia stared after him, trembling. *Flirts don't love any man—they can't.* His words had cut her to the heart. She'd made a fool of herself, declaring her love for him, and he'd sliced away at her emotions with words as sharp as knives.

She stumbled into the house, using the kitchen entrance, and fled to her room to wash her hot face. A flirt, a coquette! Was Roman right in calling her such things? *Did* she toy with men, make love into a sportive game?

Celia sank trembling into a chair. Certainly, she thought, her mouth going dry, the evidence supported what Roman said. She had enjoyed the attention and compliments of men, the heady pleasure of feeling beautiful. She *had* jilted two fiancés on their wedding eves. She had also accepted John Burnside's proposal when she had no intention of marrying him. That meant another, inevitable jilting, her third. . . .

Face it for once, Celia. Face the truth. . . .

But . . . Her confused thoughts swirled in turmoil. But Roman was wrong about one thing. She did love him. It was why she'd come here to Mountain View, because of him. She had only hoped to have a chance to win his love.

So Roman was wrong in saying that flirts couldn't love, because she did. She loved him. . . .

Celia rose from the chair, moving to her closet, where rows of trousseau gowns hung, as if to mock her. The satin wedding dress with its expensive embroidered pearls glimmered on a hanger. She stared at it, her eyes fixed on its ornate flounces. She had no right to be here at Mountain View. She'd done John a terrible wrong in coming here, and she should leave. Now, tonight, before she could change her mind.

She'd pack her trunks, load them in an ox wagon, and pay a servant to drive her to Lahaina, where she'd wait for the next steamer to Honolulu.

Yet as soon as she began to take out dresses, laying them on her bed in a welter of silk and cambric, she went cold. Ignoring the heaps of fashionable gowns, she sank down into the chair again and put her hands to her temples, rubbing away a sudden sharp headache. What was she doing? Had the moonlight and Roman's accusations addled her brain?

She might be a coquette, but she couldn't leave like a thief in the night. She couldn't hurt Tina that way, or Aunt Hatteras, or John. John was a good, kind, decent man and she owed him more than that.

Quickly Celia rehung the dresses and brushed her glossy dark hair. She patted rice powder onto her face to hide its flush, and smoothed the folds of her dress. The guests would be returning soon from the *hula*, and she must go downstairs and mingle with them. She would let no one see how upset she was; she would hide behind a mask of gaiety.

She would tell John that she needed a few more weeks, and during that time she would prepare both him and Tina for her departure. Gently, kindly, she would try to leave without causing any more pain than necessary.

And after she left . . .?

But beyond that, she could not think.

"I see that no wedding date has been set yet," Rebecca remarked two days later as the Fieldings were preparing to depart. The plantation house was again a flurry of activity as servants lugged trunks and portmanteaus out to waiting buggies and ox wagons. Rebecca and Bertrand Fielding were among the last to go.

"I'm still thinking, Becky," Celia told her cousin.

"Thinking! Don't be a fool, Celia. John Burnside is very eligible and there are plenty of other women eager to snap him up if you won't." Rebecca fixed Celia with a long look. "I expect to receive a letter from you soon, telling me that you're safely wed. If I don't get one, I intend to write your mother at once."

Celia thought of Mama, thousands of miles away in Boston. "And just what do you expect her to do, Rebecca? Turn me over her knee and spank me? It's difficult to do that through the mails."

"Don't be sassy. I was enlisted by your family to escort you here to the islands, and I'm still responsible for you, whether you wish it or not."

Celia didn't think so, not when Rebecca had dumped Celia off at Hatteras' house in Honolulu like an onerous package, not when the letters from her cousin had diminished to a few monthly notes of complaint. But there was no time to argue. Tina was jumping and bouncing between them, begging to say good-bye, and then John appeared to give the Fieldings last-minute instructions for their trip.

Still, as the Fieldings' cart pulled out of sight down the road, Celia drew a long breath. What *would* Lydia Griffin say if she knew her daughter's situation now?

Celia could imagine Mama's soft, yet cutting voice: *"So, daughter, you're planning to jilt yet another man? You're in love with a renegade doctor who's considered an outcast in polite society? You would give anything, even your honor, to have him? I was right—right to banish you—wasn't I?"*

As if in sullen retribution for Celia's rejection of him, as soon as the guests left, Beau again retreated to his rooms—to sulk, Celia supposed. Yet she could not help being relieved to have John's difficult son safely out of the way.

But John, the master of Mountain View, was very much present, attentive, insistent. As the days slipped past, Celia tried to find the words to let him down gently, to tell him what she must.

One afternoon she suggested a ride, and she and John saddled horses and rode upward along the bridle trails that wound along the edge of a deep gorge that had been cut in the hills by water action over the centuries, after heavy storms.

But today all was calm, hot and sunny, and they passed several tiny waterfalls that glittered over rocks, bits of silver magic among lush greenery.

"I'm a fool, Celia." John wiped perspiration from his

suntanned face. Had he lost weight in recent days? Surely he looked thinner, Celia thought uneasily. "Allowing you to keep me dangling like this, waiting for a decision from you. No woman has ever done this to me before. It shows the power you have over me."

Power. That word came uncomfortably close to the things Roman had said about her.

"I don't want to have such power."

"Nevertheless, you do possess it; your beauty gives it to you. I know you're unsure, but I also know that I can teach you to love me. And I will."

"No, John," she began heavily. "I'm afraid that can never happen. I must return to—"

"Never!" He nearly shouted it at her. "I told you, Celia, that I would stop you from leaving Maui, and I meant it. I won't let you go until you consent to be my wife."

More days passed, each one more difficult than the last as John continued to press her, refusing to listen to her protests. Celia tried to bury herself in the routine of the school, glad that the children kept her busy, that Genzo and her adult students also demanded her attention.

One day she took her pupils on an expedition to Olowalu, a beach near Lahaina where, in 1790, there had been a bloody massacre of Hawaiians by an American sea captain in a quarrel over the theft of a longboat and the killing of a guard. In revenge, the Olowalu chief had captured Metcalf's ship and killed the entire crew except for one man.

"Boom! Boom! You're dead!" Kaweo, Kevin McRory, and the other boys were delighted with the idea of cannon, which none of them had ever seen. They raced about the beach, reenacting the grisly tale. But little Aiko had had tears in her eyes when Celia finished telling the story.

Tina, too, looked shocked. "Eighty people?" she said. "Why, Celia, that's as many people as there are in our village at Mountain View."

"Yes, it is, my darling. People do many cruel and ugly things in the name of pride."

It was grim truth for a group of schoolchildren, but she had wanted them to know. Even children, Celia believed, should be able to learn and profit from the mistakes of the past.

Later, sitting on the sand while the children played in the

surf, Celia gazed at the craggy profile of the mountains, split
by the huge sawtooth pass called Olowalu Gorge. Ghosts, she
thought. This island was full of them. Those who had died
here at Olowalu. The Burnside wives who had died in childbirth and now lay in rows in the graveyard at Mountain View.
Old Amos himself, the founder of the plantation, the one who
had built it.

As the children raced in and out of the waves, shrieking
with pleasure, Celia wondered if it was on a beach like this,
almost a generation ago, that Roman had supposedly attacked
his brother.

Hatred between brothers, desires and passions that smol-
dered for years, flaring, dying, then igniting again. And now,
unwittingly, she had become a part of it all.

Celia knew she could not keep John waiting indefinitely,
and finally she set a date on which she would give him her
decision. Surely, she felt, this would ease the tension at
Mountain View and forestall the looks that John kept giving
her, alternately passionate, entreating, angry.

She decided upon the end of the month, a day that happened to be her own birthday, on which she would turn
twenty-three.

But the act of setting a specific date, instead of easing
John's anxiety, only increased it. He wrote her notes, even
copying a poem from one of the leather-bound volumes in his
library. He flooded her bedroom with huge bouquets of fragrant flowers, each one a mute plea. One evening, when
Celia pulled aside her mosquito netting to climb into bed, she
found a diamond bracelet lying on her pillow.

Awed, she picked up the bracelet. Its gold circlet was set
with dozens of large brilliant-cut stones, each one worth a
fortune. Even Celia, who had moved in Boston society,
where women bedecked themselves in diamonds and emeralds,
had never seen such magnificence. When she held the bracelet up to the light, the diamonds refracted it in arrogant
rainbows.

Quickly Celia put down the bracelet. It was impossible for
her to keep it. No respectable woman accepted such a gift
from a man who was not her husband, and especially not
under these circumstances.

Half an hour later, she entered the veranda with the bracelet carefully wrapped in tissue paper, hidden so that the servants would not see it. "I can't possibly keep this, John," she said in a low voice, handing the package to him.

He thrust it back at her. "It's yours."

"But—"

"Keep it, Celia, no matter what happens between us. I had it delivered from Honolulu, I can well afford it, and I don't wish to be denied the pleasure of giving it to you."

Was this the package that Roman had delivered to his half-brother on the night of the *luau*? Thoughtfully Celia went back to her room, where she tucked the bracelet, still in its package, in a drawer of her dressing table. She didn't want it. And somehow she'd think of a way to give it back to John later.

On the morning that she was to give John her answer, Celia slept late. She awoke to find sunlight streaming over her bed. It bathed her in a hot, yellow light. She stirred and yawned, rubbing her eyes, wondering why they burned, why her head had begun to throb so.

It was her birthday. She remembered that first, and then the other, more important fact: today she must tell John that she could not marry him. She never should have put it off so long.

She twisted under the sheets, trying to frame her answer. *I don't love you. . . .*

No, that was too stark, too cruel. It was the truth, however.

She tried again. *John, I wronged you. I came here under false pretenses. I did it because I wanted to be near Roman, your brother, because I love him, not you. . . .*

No! Oh, dear God, what was she to say? There was no way to get out of the situation now without inflicting pain; she had come too far. Roman was all too correct, she told herself miserably; she'd given very little thought to John's feelings until it was too late. Now she'd worked herself into a real mess.

Despairing, she let her thoughts drift, thinking of what she would do once she left Mountain View. She would have to return to Honolulu, she supposed, with her aunt. And once back at Hatteras' house on Beretania overlooking the harbor, what then? Was her aunt to hold yet another *luau*, invite another selection of eligible bachelors from which Celia could choose?

Would the whole search for a husband begin anew? In sudden agony she clenched her fists, pounding them into her pillow. She wanted Roman. Not another carefully selected husband, someone "eligible" and "proper," but the man she loved, the man she still adored, in spite of his mistress, in spite of their quarrels and the conflict that seemed always to surge between them. Roman was the only one she'd ever love.

Gradually she became aware of a clatter outside the bedroom, the pound of a horse's hooves. Celia lifted her head, alerted by an urgency not usually present in the rattling comings and goings of Mountain View servants.

"*Pilikia!* Much *pilikia*!" a servant shouted from underneath Celia's window. She stiffened. *Pilikia*, the Hawaiian word for "trouble."

As the cries grew louder, she got out of bed and padded in her nightgown to the window to investigate.

The servant was one of the Hawaiian mill workers, clad in the gray cotton trousers and shirt supplied by Mountain View to its employees. He rode a spavined old mare, his eyes wide with alarm.

"Trouble! Oh, trouble at the mill!"

Celia cranked open the window and leaned out. "What's wrong?" she called.

The rider looked up at her, veering his mount uncertainly. "Master Burnside . . . Master Burnside! He hurt . . . the crushers . . . he hurt at the mill."

15

Celia flew to get dressed, flinging on the first gown her hands touched. She jammed her feet into a pair of shoes, not bothering with stockings or petticoats, and ran out of the bedroom. Then she stopped, ran back, and grabbed a stack of clean linen towels that had been left on the dressing table by one of the servants.

She raced outdoors.

"Missy, you hurry . . . *wiki wiki* . . ." His face twisted in distress, the Hawaiian leaned down to scoop her up on the mare behind him. "Blood," he gabbled. "Master Burnside all blood. Much blood, much!"

"We'd better go—hurry!" she urged.

He spurred the old horse, and as they jounced along, Celia clung to the saddle in order to keep from being thrown off. *Blood,* she thought in horror. What had happened? Injuries in the mill, she knew, were common. A month ago, one of the Japanese workers had lost four fingers after a cut with a cane knife. Roman usually treated several such accidents each time he came to the plantation.

But John . . .

The ride under the *koas* and along the dusty mill road seemed endless. When the main mill building finally loomed ahead, Celia slid down from the horse, clutching at the towels she'd managed to bring with her. They'd be useful in stanching blood, she thought wildly. Oh, God . . .

"*Moo,*" the Hawaiian moaned. "Lizard did this. A curse."

Julia Grice

"What are you talking about?" she snapped. "Go for Dr. Burnside in Lahaina, at his surgery. Go—quickly!"

The man gazed down at her, his mouth working open and shut, but finally he did as he was told, wheeling the mare down the road, her hooves churning up red dust.

Celia hurried toward the big building made of corrugated iron. Her heart sank as she saw the knots of frightened men standing about. The usual mill noises had ceased, and all was eerily silent except for the workers' whispers in Japanese, Hawaiian, and Samoan.

"Missy? You help him? You stop blood?" Ashido, one of the Japanese to whom she was teaching English, grabbed at her as she ran inside. Celia shook him away. Did he think that she had magical powers, that she could stop death at will? Fear clutched at her stomach, and she thought she would be sick.

In the mill, heat reached out to surround her. The air was full of the thick, sickening stench of processing sugar and molasses. Celia ran through several rooms, past the iron vats full of sugar juice that John had once shown her so proudly.

"Where is he?" she shouted as McRory, the fat sugar boiler, emerged from a doorway. There was blood spattered all over his shirt.

"In there." He pointed. "Damn fool caught his arm in the rollers."

"The . . . No . . ." The rollers were made of granite and weighed three tons each; John had shown her those, too, on her first trip through the mill. Celia reeled, feeling her stomach clutch with nausea.

McRory leaned against the wall, beads of perspiration dripping down his face. "Crushed the arm, peeled the flesh right off. He's going to die, me girl. You'd better get the preacher for him, that's what I say. He needs the last rites."

Celia fought terror. *No,* her mind screamed. It wasn't so, it hadn't happened, surely the seriousness of this was exaggerated.

She walked on, into the next room. Yes, there were the huge rollers she'd seen before, silent now, with a crowd of men standing about. A litter of cane stalks was scattered on the floor, dyed with red. Red, everywhere. On the men, on the rollers, on the floor. And something else lay on the floor, too. Something that looked like a bloodied heap of clothing.

Celia forced herself to walk closer. As she did so, the crowd of workers backed away, revealing the prone body of John Burnside. He was covered with blood, his right arm fastened in a crude, bloody tourniquet. The arm, Celia saw with a spurt of horror, didn't seem to be the proper length. . . .

She fought nausea. John's face was ashen, Celia saw, but he was still alive.

"Missy, I tried to stop the bleeding."

It was Genzo, the Japanese who had once come to Celia begging to learn English. Now he knelt near John, holding the tourniquet, his face tense with anxiety.

Celia felt as if she were in a slow, foggy, unreal dream as she knelt by John.

"Celia . . ." he whispered through bloodless lips.

"I came as fast as I could. One of the workers brought me."

"The damn rollers. They were stuck and I reached in my hand to free them."

How gray John's face was, Celia thought, still trapped in the slow, terrible dream. And the blood everywhere made her think of a slaughterhouse.

"Missy." Urgently Genzo pointed to the folded towels, and Celia came to her senses. She grabbed the first towel and pressed it over the terrible wound. All too quickly, it was soaked with red.

"Glad . . . glad you came," John whispered. "I was thinking about you. . . ."

She barely heard him, so hard was she concentrating on the task of stopping the bleeding. She pressed more towels on top of the first one, while Genzo helped her to hold them steady. "Blankets," she told the Japanese. "Any kind, and quickly. He must be kept warm."

Genzo spoke to another man, and she sensed movement about her as the workers scurried to carry out her orders. She was in charge, she realized. She fought to think. The cane litter on the floor was making movements difficult, and was full of dirt and insects. And the milling, anxious workers were impeding their efforts to help the injured man.

"We must move him," she decided. "Come, we need four men to lift him. We'll carry him to Mr. McRory's office."

*   *   *

How long? Celia wondered in desperation. How long did it take for a frantic Hawaiian to ride to Lahaina and back with help? And how long did it take for a man to die from loss of blood? She prayed that they had stopped the bleeding in time.

McRory told Celia that John had been trying to free a snag in the rollers when his fingers became caught. The rollers pulled the skin from his arm, like stripping off a sleeve.

"He didn't cry out, he just told me to make the rollers go backward, to eject the arm. Saved it from being taken off at the shoulder, poor sod. Of course, he's goin' to die anyway. But he was brave."

McRory added that the master of Mountain View had seemed troubled today, as if something were on his mind. "Got careless, he did. Poor man. It don't pay to have bad thoughts when you're around machinery."

Celia managed a reply, fighting a wave of guilt. *I was thinking about you.* John had told her that himself. And it did not take much imagination to realize that it was her decision about marrying him that had upset John so much that he had grown careless with the cane crushers.

A few minutes later, Hatteras arrived, carried on her litter by two male servants. With sharp eyes she assessed the situation. "Looks as if you've done everything you can, Celia. But he's going to need surgery, if he survives this. I'll go back to the house and prepare. I'm sure Roman will have the necessary ether and surgical instruments with him."

Celia nodded. "How is Tina taking this?"

"She is crying, of course. She loves her father very much."

After Hatteras left, Celia busied herself with her patient, saying a silent prayer. *God, please, let him live. I didn't mean to hurt him. I didn't mean to hurt anyone.*

Time inched past.

"Cold," John muttered. He groaned, jerking and twisting spasmodically under the blankets with which they had covered him. The look of youthful sun-browned vigor that John Burnside once had possessed was gone now. He seemed suddenly an old man, his cheeks sunken. He gasped for air as if he could not breathe deeply enough.

Celia flung open the windows in the tiny office, hoping for

a gust of fresh air. What else could she do for him? What could she give him?

Then she remembered the laudanum she had fetched from Roman's surgery for Hatteras, and sent Genzo riding to the house to get it. That would help with the pain. Or would the tincture of opium only depress John's bodily functions, making it even more difficult to save him?

But when the laudanum came, John was groaning with pain. Celia made the split-second decision to give him the opium. To her relief, the narcotic took effect at once. John relaxed and seemed to rally, his eyelids fluttering as he looked at her. "Celia . . . I did love you . . ."

"Hush." She pushed back a sob. "You mustn't talk, you must save your strength until Roman gets here."

"Roman. So it is my brother who will save me." The bluish lips parted in a grim smile.

"Please, don't try to talk. Just rest."

"I'll have enough rest. God, yes, enough . . ."

But for a time John did subside into a restless doze. Celia sat beside him, periodically covering the blood-soaked bandages with fresh ones. Dimly she was aware of others coming and going. Genzo, McRory, and finally Beau, who appeared at the door of the little office, looking shaken.

"My father . . ." Beau whispered.

"We have stopped the bleeding," Celia told him. "And I've summoned Roman—we're expecting him at any time."

"Roman!" Beau's expression darkened. "We don't want him here now, he doesn't belong here."

Celia couldn't believe Beau could carry petty angers into a desperate time like this. "He is a doctor," she said, shocked.

She left the bedside so that Beau could spend a few moments with his father. Beau leaned over the bed, and then they all heard John's hoarse cry: *"Get him out of here!"*

"But, Father . . ." Beau began in a strangled voice.

"Go, Beau. *Go from me.* You'll ruin Mountain View, do you hear me? You'll ruin everything I built!"

Celia couldn't help feeling sorry for Beau as he stalked out of McRory's office, his back stiff, his face twisted with grief. Celia brought John a gourd of water, holding it up so he could take brief sips.

"You shouldn't have spoken so to your son," she murmured,

unable to stop herself. "He does love you, even though he may not show it."

"Beau loves no one. He is weak. In ugly ways you know nothing about. And I've seen the way he looks at you." John coughed, and his uninjured hand clutched at hers. "Celia . . . I'm going to die."

"No. Please. Don't say such things."

"I'll be down there in the Burnside graveyard . . . beside my wives."

Celia wanted to weep. "No, Roman is coming to help you, you're going to be all right. He'll fix your arm."

"With what? Even if I survive this loss of blood, there will be infection, that cane was filthy . . ." John stirred and groaned, seeming to lose track of what he was saying.

As the hours passed, Celia gave him more laudanum. He tossed and turned restlessly, crying out unintelligible words. Once his entire body stiffened and he sat up straight, knocking aside the blankets. ". . . water . . . cold . . . *the surf! The surf!"*

Celia realized that John had slipped over some narrow edge of consciousness and was reliving some previous moment. She did her best to soothe him, sponging his face and giving him small sips of water.

"Roman!" John shouted. "You little bastard, come and get me. Father's favorite, father's favorite! Oh, you're puny, you're a weakling, you're *afraid."*

Frightened by the words, by the taunting quality of them, Celia tried to push the dying man back onto the couch. "Hush. Roman is coming soon, he'll clean your wound and perform surgery . . ."

John was unaware of her, totally back in the past, his voice an angry grate. "Roman, you're just the second son. *I'm* the firstborn. Mountain View should be mine, all of it. Come on, come on, swim out here and see if you can get me."

As John sank down again, apparently exhausted by his effort, Celia froze. Those words . . . a taunt . . . Of course! John was reliving that day at the beach long ago, the day after the reading of Amos Burnside's will, when the brothers had fought.

She retucked the blankets around John, and adjusted the thick bandages. His skin felt cold, and she couldn't imagine where he had found the strength to sit up like that. And the implication of his cries swirled in her mind.

See if you can get me.

That sounded as if John had egged his younger brother on to attack him! Yes, as if he had provoked the fight himself.

But why? Why would John have done such a thing? Had he been that jealous of his younger brother?

"Celia?" Abruptly John's eyes, which had been glazed over, focused on hers. Dark, hooded, sunken, they were the staring eyes of a dying man.

Celia bit her lip, fighting not to cry. "Yes, John, I'm here."

"I know I'm going to die. . . . I wanted to kill him. I wanted it to look like self-defense." A brief ghost of a smile twisted John's lips. "But he was the better man. . . . The servants broke it up. I told them . . . told them it was Roman who attacked me, and they believed me. Everyone believed it. . . ."

Celia sat very still, her heart thumping. Roman wasn't a would-be murderer, after all. John was.

He had just confessed it.

Night had fallen, and the moon had risen over the mill roof, its mottled surface half-obscured by thin clouds. Celia walked out of the mill feeling numb and drained. Not five minutes ago, John Burnside had died in her arms, calling out her name and that of his brother, Roman.

"I'm sorry," he had wept at the end. "Tell him . . . tell Roman . . . forgive me . . ."

Then John had sighed and his body had jerked convulsively. A huge breath of air had left his lungs, and he had not breathed in again.

Now Celia drew in great gulps of night air, feeling her body shiver all over. Overhead, the Milky Way was an enormous glittering swath, the stars numerous beyond counting. Was John one of those stars now that he had begged absolution for his guilt?

She walked slowly back to the plantation house. She had told the servants to wash the body and prepare it for burial, and this would be done. In a tropical climate, the dead had to be buried quickly. There were messages to send to local planters, to all who had known John, a funeral to arrange. . . .

Celia swayed with exhaustion. She was so tired, and she hadn't eaten since the previous night. My God, had she been in the mill all day, was it night now?

She stumbled into the house, soothed by its familiar lines, the gracious architecture and antiques that she'd grown to love. She walked across the great foyer and into the largest drawing room, where she sank onto a turkey-red couch, feeling the soft cushions draw her body into them.

"Missy? *Oh* . . ." Leinani's dark eyes were wide with fear as they swept up and down Celia's gown. Awakened from the restless sleep into which she had fallen, Celia glanced down at the day dress she'd flung on this morning, and recoiled in horror. The blue muslin was stained with spotches of dried blood, hideous evidence of death.

She shuddered violently. "I . . . I'll need a clean dress, Leinani. And a bath, please."

"Yes, missy, yes." Leinani pressed a fist to her mouth, looking as if she might bolt. But finally she trotted from the room. Celia leaned back against the couch and closed her eyes tiredly.

John . . . his confession . . . the grayness of his face . . . Her mind rejected these images, sinking her into a dark pit that went down forever and forever, spiraling her with it into oblivion, her screams echoing.

"Celia! Celia!" a voice called to her insistently, penetrating the darkness. Celia didn't want to hear it. She covered her eyes with her arm and burrowed deeper into the pit, the blank exhaustion that took away all thought.

"Celia, wake up!"

"No," she moaned. "No, please . . ."

But she woke up anyway, opening her eyes to see an exhausted-looking Roman, his face dusty, deep circles under his eyes.

"I came as fast as I could, but it was too late, he was already dead. Leinani tells me you've been screaming in your sleep."

"Screaming?" Celia struggled to sit up, feeling dazed.

How long had she been asleep? Roman's arm supported her to a sitting position and she sagged against its strength, feeling drained by the nightmare in the mill.

"Yes, you woke the whole house with your cries. The servants are already terrified of lizards, and now some of them have fled to the village." She had never heard Roman's voice so tender before. "Celia, oh, God . . . Darling, you're covered in blood."

"He died." The day flooded back to her, all its horror. She clung to him frantically. "Oh, Roman, he . . . I couldn't stop it, I didn't know what to do to help him!"

Strong hands stroked her, comforted, as if she were a child. "It's all right. It's all right."

"It isn't! I didn't know what to *do*! He's dead, Roman. *Dead*!"

"I know, Celia. I examined him. The servants are laying him out now."

She was quivering violently. "He . . . he talked about you, he said he was sorry, and begged for your forgiveness."

"I see."

"It wasn't your fault that day, it was his. He accused you unfairly, he provoked you, he wanted you to attack him so he could kill you and say it was self-defense. He admitted it, Roman!"

"Enough, Celia."

"But—"

Roman's voice roughened. "I suppose that I forgave John long ago for what he did. He was a proud and difficult man—as I am also, I know. And now the past is finished. Nothing can be done to go back and alter words that were said, deeds that were done or not done. Let it rest, Celia."

She couldn't understand. "But aren't you going to exonerate yourself? Tell people that John lied?"

"Those who know me, know my character, already realize that I could never have tried to kill anyone. As for the others, I don't care about them, Celia. *I* know who I am. I don't need to beg anyone to accept me."

Roman's voice softened, and he held her to him, stroking her back, her hair, her shoulders, his touch unutterably gentle. "McRory told me that you were with my brother all day, that you never left his side, even to eat. You were very valiant, Celia. Now you must try to get some rest. It's over. You did everything you could.''

But she could not relax, could not stop shivering. ''No, it isn't over. . . . I . . . I think I helped to kill him.''

''What!''

Exhaustion and grief had chipped away at her defenses, leaving her vulnerable. Tears burned Celia's eyes as she struggled to speak. ''Because . . . because today I was going to tell him that I couldn't marry him. I was going to refuse him, and John knew it. He . . . he was upset. Thinking about me. That's why he had the accident!''

Roman folded her to him, petting her as if she were some small, fragile kitten. ''No, darling, you didn't do anything, you weren't responsible. Those rollers were always dangerous. Other men had been hurt in them before, and John knew it. He was careless, that's all.''

Tears streamed down Celia's face and she shook in a misery of guilt. ''But it was my f-fault . . .''

''Stop it.'' He shook her. ''Stop blaming yourself! You're exhausted, Celia. Damn those servants for not taking care of you.''

Before she could protest, he had suddenly lifted her and was carrying her up the staircase. She clung to him, to his warmth and strength. ''You *don't* have to feel guilty,'' he emphasized. ''You fought like a tiger to save him. McRory told me all about it.''

When they reached her room, Roman laid her gently on her bed. Tears exploded out of her, hot, painful, choking.

''There . . . it's all right.'' He held her and rocked her, and she felt his strength flow into her, a strength she had never known he could give. ''Go ahead, darling. Let it out, cry. Cry all you want. I'm here. I'm here.''

It seemed only minutes later that Celia awakened, alone in her room, to hear the sound of voices coming from downstairs. She sat up in bed, blinking her eyes in the darkness. Roman's voice. Yes, and wasn't that Beau's shout, too? And their anger could be heard even on the upper floor.

She struggled out of bed and found her dressing gown,

pulling shut its frog fasteners and belting it. She hurried into the hallway and started down the staircase, where two wall sconces still burned, casting fitful shadows against the walls.

"You!" Beau practically screamed the word, his voice vibrating with fury. "You caused his death, you!"

Celia froze on the stairs.

"I?" Roman drawled. "And how did I do that? I wasn't the one who forced my brother's arm into that cane crusher. I am afraid he accomplished that act all by himself, may the Lord have mercy on him."

"That isn't what I meant!" Beau shouted. "If you had hurried, if you'd tried to get here sooner, my father might still be alive!"

Celia edged a step downward. By leaning forward, she could see the two men. Beau, white-faced and rumpled, dark circles under his eyes. And Roman, tired-looking, still wearing the same dusty clothes in which he had ridden here. His medical bag sat at his feet, coated with dust from the road.

"I was doing surgery when your servant arrived. I sewed up my patient and came as quickly as I could. I rode at breakneck speed to get here, nearly foundering my horse. Your stable servants will attest to that. There was no way I could have gotten here any faster."

Beau's glance darted toward his uncle, then away. Something flickered across his face, pinpointed in his eyes. "Well, he's dead now, isn't he? Let me tell you something. *I've* got my father's share of Mountain View now, and the right to live in this house. I inherit that. And I intend to buy you out."

Roman raised a dark eyebrow. "Oh?"

"I have a bit of money set aside from my mother." Beau paced back and forth, his movements jerky. "Before, my father kept it from me, but now I can do what I want with it, and I aim to have your share of the plantation. Mountain View has seen the last of you."

At this challenge, Celia saw Roman shift slightly on the balls of his feet. She realized that he was holding back his anger, trying to be civil to a distraught young man who had just lost his father.

"You're overwrought, Beau, you don't know what you're

saying. I suggest that you have a glass of brandy and go to bed, son. Tomorrow we'll sort things out.''

"Don't call me son! No. They kept me away from my father, and I won't be shuffled off like a child. I'm tired of that. *I'm* master of Mountain View now.''

"Beau, you're angry and under stress. Go to bed, try to get some sleep.''

Beau's face reddened, and his shouts echoed through the house. "Sleep! How can I? You killed my father by not getting here in time, just as you tried to kill him long ago. Now you think you can just step in and take over. Well, you can't, not as long as I'm here. I'll buy you out! I never want to see you around here again!''

Celia heard a creaking sound, and saw the door that led to the kitchen corridor inch open. She peered in that direction, surprised, for she had thought the servants had all left the house. She expected to see Leinani or one of the other servant girls. Instead, it was Kinau who peered from the kitchen, her lovely face solemn, black hair streaming around her shoulders like witch's silk.

Kinau. Like Celia, she also watched, her eyes flicking from Beau to Roman, then back to Roman.

Beau's tirade continued for several more minutes, growing progressively more intense, until at last he stood panting, shaken with the vehemence of his emotions. Celia felt an unexpected spasm of pity for him. Beau *had* been shunted aside—both during John's lifetime and again at his death. No wonder he was so confused and angry.

Evidently Roman had had a similar thought, for it was with compassion that he said, "Things will look better in the morning, Beau, for all of us. Do you want a sedative?'' He started toward his bag. "I think I have something I can give you to calm you and let you sleep.''

He opened the bag and took out a small glass vial.

"I said I don't want to sleep!'' Savagely Beau knocked the vial out of Roman's hand. It crashed against the wall and shattered. From the doorway Celia heard Kinau's gasp.

"I don't *want* a sedative,'' Beau raged. "I want what's coming to me. My father's estate. Everything he would have had. Everything!''

As he said this, Beau happened to look toward the staircase, seeing Celia for the first time. "Celia! What are you doing here?"

This, she realized, was her opportunity to make peace. She started downstairs, her dressing gown rustling. "Beau, I think you should take a sedative, as Roman suggests. It has been a terrible, shocking day, and—"

"No! I want him out of this house tonight!" In a frenzy, Beau rushed toward Roman, his steps crunching broken glass. "You'll sign papers—you'll sign them tonight!"

Roman responded calmly, his voice even. "No one can force me to sell if I don't wish to. You know that, Beau. Mountain View is as much mine as it is yours, and we're going to have to work together now." He picked up his bag, starting toward the door. "Go to bed, Beau. There are funeral details to take care of in the morning. Since you are *master* of Mountain View, surely the responsibility is all yours."

Roman pulled open the carved front door and left, while Beau stared after him, his mouth opening and closing in surprise. Then suddenly Celia saw a blur of color dart across the foyer.

It was Kinau. The Hawaiian girl's movements were fluid, graceful, as she ran to the door, pushed it open again, and hurried after Roman.

Celia stood stock-still, feeling hurt and jealousy pour over her like flaming lava. Only a few hours ago, Roman had tenderly carried her upstairs and held her, soothed her, giving to her of his own strength. Now Kinau had run after him, and Celia could picture all too vividly what would happen next.

She had thought . . . Oh, she had thought . . .

She swallowed over the thick lump that filled her throat. It was *pity* Roman had felt for her tonight, nothing more! He had felt sorry for her because of her grief and exhaustion, and that was why he had comforted her. How could she have been such a fool as to think it anything else?

"Whatever is the matter with you—you look as if you'd seen a ghost," Beau said in a sudden eerie switch of moods. Celia jumped, touching her tousled hair, the fasteners of her dressing gown. She'd been so engrossed in her own pain, she'd completely forgotten about Beau.

"It's . . . all right," she managed to say. "It has been a long and awful day, Beau. For all of us."

"Yes." Beau scowled. "But I know why you look so weak and sick right now, and it isn't because of my father dying, is it? Oh, no, it isn't because of him at all!"

Celia could only stare at him.

"My Uncle Roman is the one who has turned your face so appealingly pale. Oh, I saw your expression when Kinau ran after him. And do you know what they are doing right now?" Beau's hazel eyes were fixed on hers with a bright, almost feverish look. "I'll wager they've headed down to the village, where Kinau keeps a little house. That's where they'll go—to make love."

"No!"

"Didn't you know? He has had her as his mistress for years, off and on. She goes to Lahaina, he comes here—a nice arrangement, don't you agree?"

Was this terrible day never going to end? Celia struggled not to reveal how much Beau's words hurt her. A fool—oh, what a fool she'd been to fall in love with Roman!

But Roman had never told her he loved her, she reminded herself, feeling sick. It had been only her own mind, imagining such things, creating a dream where nothing real existed. She'd been as romantic as a silly schoolgirl treasuring a crush on a teacher who barely knows she exists.

Beau was smiling, as if pleased by the reaction he had caused. "Come, Celia. Perhaps my uncle was right when he said I needed a sedative. Only I think I'll have the pleasant kind, something to relax us both."

He had taken her arm and was leading her into the library, where John had kept a large collection of leather-bound volumes. Soft chairs lined the walls, and there were several velvet-covered couches. More pistols from John's extensive gun collection had been hung high over the shelves, out of Tina's reach.

Beau reached into a small mahogany cabinet and pulled out a Waterford decanter whose crystal facets gleamed in the lamplight. "Brandy," he announced. "That's the sedative *I* intend to have. And I suggest that you join me."

Celia looked at the golden liquid that filled the decanter

three-quarters full, and thought of the long, lonely night hours that still stretched ahead of her, crowded with guilt and regrets and pain. If she went to bed now, she'd only think about Roman and Kinau, tormenting herself with a dream that never could come true.

"All right," she agreed. "I'll have one drink, then."

Beau was already pouring.

16

What a confusing man Beau was! His moods were intense, his passions strong, his anger great. Yet Celia could not help feeling pity for the young man who sloshed brandy into two glasses and then drained his own, almost in one gulp.

"There," he said, immediately reaching for the decanter to pour another. "That's better. My father's best brandy—and now it's mine."

Celia sipped her own drink, feeling it heat its way down her throat. "And what of Tina?" something made her say. "Doesn't half of that brandy belong to your sister now—in a manner of speaking?"

Beau shook his head. "No. My father left a trust fund for her that she'll receive when she's twenty-one, or when she marries, whichever comes first. But Mountain View is mine."

"Half yours," Celia reminded him, remembering how John, too, had always referred to the plantation as if Roman did not exist.

Beau sank into morose silence, and Celia sipped more brandy, uneasily aware that she wore only a nightgown and dressing gown, her hair tumbled in a thick mass down her shoulders. But Beau did not seem to notice her dishevelment, engrossed in his own bleak thoughts.

For a time they sat silently, sharing an odd sort of communion, while Celia finished her second glass of brandy. It was making her faintly light-headed. Finally she started to rise from her chair. "I really should get to bed," she began. "There will be much to do in the morning."

Beau suddenly jumped up, pressing his hands down on her shoulders to stop her from leaving. "No, Celia . . . Ah, God, not tonight. Don't leave me alone tonight."

"But—"

"I can't be alone tonight."

Celia heard the naked plea in Beau's words, one that she could not, with any humanity, deny. Reluctantly she sat down again and accepted the third glass of brandy that Beau poured for her. She took a sip, feeling its warm glow spread through her. She was perspiring slightly, she noticed, and unobtrusively she loosened the neck of her dressing gown. "Do you want to talk, Beau?"

"Talk?"

"Why . . . about your father. Perhaps you would like to remember him."

"Remember what? The way he brought me home from California like a criminal? All because of a trumped-up and unjust charge that never should have been made? He shunted me aside here at Mountain View, Celia, like a wayward child. He never paid any attention to my suggestions—treated me as if I were worthless. You can't deny he did, you saw him, you know." Beau tilted his glass and drained it, reaching for another. "Well, I'm going to finish what he started. I'll build the irrigation ditch. I'll pipe more water to the fields than he ever dreamed possible."

Celia settled in her chair to wait this out. Love and hate, she thought, inextricably mixed. That was what Beau felt for his father. As he talked, she continued to sip the brandy, finding that it did indeed relax her own tension. In fact, the aromatic spirits seemed to create a pleasant, filmy blur across her emotions.

How easy it seemed just to sit here, to listen to Beau's droning voice, and not to think. . . .

Now Beau was talking about Kinau again—she wasn't sure how he had gotten back on this subject. "She is barren, you know," he was saying. "Many Hawaiian girls are—it is one reason their race is dying out, don't you know? In a generation or two, there may be damn few of them left."

Celia murmured something. At this moment, nothing seemed

very real to her; the brandy was softening all the hard edges of her pain. What did it matter whether or not Kinau could have babies? Celia was glad that she couldn't, glad that she could not give Roman a child. . . .

Beau talked and talked, and Celia continued to sit with her glass, no longer hearing anything he said, immersed in her own private cloud of grief. For John, for Roman, for destroyed dreams. Beau finished the decanter and then rummaged at the back of the mahogany cabinet for another bottle, which he finally found. He splashed golden liquid into the decanter, spilling a good deal of it on the tabletop.

Laughing, Celia tried to wipe away the spilled brandy, her hands encountering Beau's as he, too, tried to mop up the spill. His hands closed over hers with a grip surprisingly firm. "Celia . . . I don't want to be alone with myself . . . I can't."

She felt as if she were dreaming all of this, and would wake up at any moment to find herself tangled in the sheets, perspiring heavily. "What a coincidence," she said, hearing herself giggle. "I don't want to be alone with myself, either."

"Then let's not be. Let's not be alone at all. You and I, Celia . . . Oh, God, you and I."

I don't want to be alone with myself . . . I can't. Was it pity for Beau that made her reach out for him and put her arms around him? He had been hurt too, just as she had. He suffered, just as she did. . . .

She felt Beau's arms tighten around her. She could smell the brandy he had drunk, hear his heavy breathing. She seemed immersed in a golden brandy dream, an unreal illusion that Beau caressed her urgently, his hands sliding over her back, finding the fasteners of her dressing gown. She wanted to laugh. Felt a giggle welling up in her like bubbles.

"Celia," Beau whispered urgently. "Oh, *God* . . . strip off your clothes for me. I want to see you naked. Please."

The words penetrated through the cloud of liquor. She pulled away from him, his thickened gasps finally bringing her to her senses. "Beau!" She pushed away his groping hands. "Beau, no, you're insane."

But it had gone too far. Beau no longer seemed to hear her, to be aware of her protests at all. Drunkenly he yanked at her dressing gown, pulling it away from her. He tugged the nightgown up. His hands kneaded her bare breasts, squeezing the nipples with a sensation both painful and pleasurable.

"*Beau* . . . please don't . . ."

"I have to have you, Celia. You don't know, you don't know how it's been, to be laughed at, not to be able to . . ." Beau's hands groped, pushing her, and then he almost seemed to fall toward her, shoving her back onto the velvet couch. His heavy weight pushed her down, so that she could not move.

"Celia . . . Celia . . ." His voice was hoarse, incoherent.

Celia lay pressed under Beau's weight, reality flooding back to her. This wasn't a dream, this was real. Horribly, Beau was fumbling at his clothes, revealing his bare flesh. She struggled to get free, pushing at him. He rolled atop her erratically as she struggled, pounding at him with frantic fists.

Then suddenly he passed out on top of her.

Celia had never realized just how heavy the deadweight of an unconscious man could be. It nearly forced the breath out of her, and she felt the stirring of panic as she shoved at him with all of her strength, managing to roll him to one side so that she could wriggle free.

Choking back a sob, she scrambled to her feet. She snatched the folds of the nightgown down over her nudity. Beau snored loudly on the couch, his limbs sprawled, his body exposed where his clothing had fallen away. If he should be found like this . . . But Celia felt a wave of revulsion at the thought of touching him.

She picked up the dressing gown and flung it around her, fleeing from the library as if a devil were after her.

In her room, with shaking hands, Celia stripped off the nightgown and scrubbed herself with the pitcher of water always kept in the room. She rubbed and rubbed at her flesh, punishing herself until her skin burned. Finally she stumbled into bed. She lay staring into the first pearl light of dawn, feeling soiled and filthy.

Beau. She had let Beau touch her. No, she amended in her mind with disgust, she hadn't let him, she had fought, but he had been stronger. Thank God he had passed out before he'd had his way with her. Yet she knew that she'd provoked his attentions by putting her arms around him, by pitying him. Why had she drunk so much brandy? What had possessed her?

Celia tossed and turned, alternately huddling under the sheets, then flinging them off. Images tormented her. Beau's arms pulling her to him, his hoarse breathing, the feel of his skin. The heavy weight of his body.

I was thinking about you, John had whispered as he lay dying. *I . . . did love you.*

And Roman had held her tenderly, giving her comfort. *Go ahead, darling. Let it out, cry. Cry all you want. I'm here. I'm here.*

She had betrayed both of them. She had betrayed her family, her upbringing, every part of the code she had lived by. Well, hadn't she?

She could not seem to find rest, for her mind or her body, but as daylight filled the room, she finally lay listening to the sounds of the new day. The morning chatter of a pair of mynah birds, the sound of horses' hooves. Probably servants were already being dispatched to spread the news of John's death to the other planters on the island.

Today funeral arrangements would have to be made.

Tiredly Celia rubbed her burning eyes, forcing herself to get out of bed. Weariness made her movements slow as she went to her closet and looked among her wardrobe for a black dress. She had always disliked black, and it was not practical for a warm climate. But finally she found a black faille that her mother had insisted she pack.

She took out the dress, unfolding the tissue paper in which it had been wrapped. Suddenly she heard rapid, childish steps in the corridor, and then Tina burst into her room.

This morning the girl was a pale wraith with reddened eyes and hair streaming in an ungovernable tangle down her back. Seeing John's daughter, Celia felt a violent spasm of guilt. *Last night . . .* She forced away the memory of what had so nearly happened with Beau.

"Celia, oh, Celia!"

Celia knelt to take Tina into her arms, where the child clung, gripping her with surprising strength.

"He died . . . my Daddy died. . . ."

"I know, baby, I know."

"Why did he? Why did God take him?"

At this moment the question seemed too large for Celia, but she put aside her own grief and struggled to answer it. She hugged Tina, stroking her hair, and at last buried her face in the fragrant hair. For long moments they clung together, and Celia found herself drawing an odd sort of comfort from the child's presence.

Hatteras lay on a chaise longue in her bedroom, pen in hand as she consulted the list of those who had been invited to John's funeral. It was basically the same people who had attended the harvest celebration, except that those from other islands would not be able to arrive in time. Hatteras had taken charge of the burial arrangements, for no one else in the house seemed capable of it. Beau had withdrawn to his quarters, no one had seen him today, and Celia, numbed with exhaustion from the ordeal of John's death and the nightmare with Beau, felt as if she could bear no more. She just longed for this day to be over.

"Celia," Hatteras said, "I know you're grieving, but you really must pull yourself together. We are going to have dozens of guests here for John's funeral, and you will need to deal with them."

Celia drew a deep, shaky breath. She didn't care about the funeral guests; she barely knew most of them. Her mind felt numb. John was dead. He'd be buried tomorrow. She had betrayed him. Hurt him.

She must leave here, of course.

But how could she, when Tina depended on her, loved her? The thought tormented her. And there were her pupils, who could not be callously deserted.

And Mountain View itself. She loved this plantation, she realized with a twist of her heart. The gracious plantation house with its sweeping view of cobalt sea and far islands. The serrated green hills that loomed behind it, the rippling fields of cane, the *koas*, the gorgeous flowering trees that bloomed everywhere. Even the mill, with its smell, its noisy machines and hurry. She felt as if she belonged here.

But you don't belong here, she reminded herself fiercely. You have no right to love this place.

She spent the rest of the day helping with the funeral plans and trying to comfort Tina. The little girl seemed dazed and fretful, and clung constantly to Celia, scarcely leaving her presence. When the child asked about her brother, Celia had to explain that Beau had gone to his rooms to grieve in privacy.

That night Celia slept heavily, her mind fighting confused dreams. The following morning dawned as usual, hot, clear, and blue except for a blanket of gray-white clouds that hung over the mountains, indicating rainstorms in progress over the Iao Valley.

Celia rose and put on the black faille, her hands cold as she fastened its long row of jet buttons. She adjusted the overskirt and rummaged in her dresser for a black veil. Critically she examined herself in the mirror. Her face looked smooth and calm, belying the turmoil of her mind.

Leinani brought her breakfast on a tray—rolls, a papaya half, coffee. But Celia could not eat. Finally she put aside the tray and went to Tina's room to see that the child was properly dressed for the services.

Clad only in petticoats and shift, her collarbones looking frail and angular, Tina flung herself into Celia's arms, weeping. "I don't want to go to the church."

"But, darling, you must."

"I don't want to! I don't want to see my daddy dead."

"But, honey, you won't be seeing your daddy. He is gone up to heaven to become a star in the sky. Inside the church will be only his mortal body, his remains. They don't have anything to do with him now, they are only the shell he left behind him."

As she said this, Celia struggled with her own confused thoughts. Why could not life be easy and straightforward? Why *had* John had to die?

The little plantation church was built of mortared lava, its interior painted, a generation ago, by an itinerant Portuguese artist in subtle colors depicting biblical scenes. Painted-on columns supported a barrel-vaulted ceiling, and banks of flowers had been arranged at the altar, their heavy scents permeating the air.

As they entered the church, Tina gripped Celia's hand tightly. Hatteras followed behind, carried by two strong male servants. Beau followed, darkly handsome in his black frock coat, his expression somber. Was it Celia's imagination, or did he seem thinner, his eyes curiously dark and fixed? But of course, she told herself, Beau had probably eaten little since his father's death. She hadn't felt like eating either.

Miserably Celia seated herself between Tina and her aunt. The little church was densely packed with people. There were sun-browned Maui planters and their wives. McRory, the fat sugar boiler, sweating profusely in the heat, filled up nearly a third of a pew himself. Kinau, in a loose black dress that emphasized the velvet texture of her perfect skin, sat next to a solemn Leinani.

The back rows of the church were filled with the other house servants and with those mill workers who had been able to crowd in. The remainder clustered at the door or crowded outdoors at each open window.

Celia saw some of the men cast anxious glances at Beau, and she knew they were wondering what kind of employer he would make and whether they would be able to get along with him. One of Chang Liu's daughters began to play the organ, the notes pealing out sonorously as Kilohana Gregory, the pastor, walked into the church.

Then Celia heard a stir in the congregation and turned to see Roman stride down the aisle. He sat down next to Beau and stared stonily ahead. As the pastor began to intone the burial service, Celia sat with her hands pressed tightly together. Even through the fabric of her gloves, she could feel the sharp pain of her fingernails biting into skin.

After what seemed an interminable time, the funeral party filed out of the church and walked down the path toward the Burnside graveyard, where John would be buried between his two wives.

Overhead, the sun baked down, and Celia felt perspiration spring out under the black faille, moistening her skin. She hated black, she decided. She'd never wear this dress again; she'd have the servants burn it as soon as was decently possible.

Along the path, bougainvillea grew, insects humming among the blossoms. Today the air seemed heavy, thick with the smell of sugar that John, after a lifetime of living here, no longer had smelled. But Celia breathed deeply of its odor, thinking that sugarcane had shaped John Burnside's entire life, virtually from cradle to grave. It had even killed him.

They stood by the open grave, a yawning reddish hole that had had to be hacked out of the rock-studded earth. Slowly the coffin was lowered, and a red-faced Tina stepped forward to drop the first blossom onto the casket.

Beau tossed a hibiscus, and then, one by one, the mourners filed past, each adding a fragrant flower, until the casket was covered with a blanket of exotic Hawaiian blooms. Celia blinked back tears.

But finally it was done, and the mourners filed away. Tina dropped Celia's hand and hurried ahead to walk beside Hatteras. Celia's steps slowed as she started through the headstones toward the gate. The black mourning gown seemed to drag at her, its skirts heavy and cumbersome, and the veil seemed almost to strangle away her breath.

Gasping, she lifted it from her face.

"Someday," Beau whispered beside her, "we will be buried here, you and I."

"*What*?" She turned, startled.

Beau stood beside her, his eyes burning into hers. He pointed to an empty spot. "There's a place for you. And one beside it—that's the site I choose."

She stared at John's son, horrified. Husbands and wives were customarily buried side by side. Was this some sort of macabre marriage proposal?

"That remark was in very poor taste," she hissed in an undertone so that the guests would not hear. "I won't lie beside you, Beau."

He leaned toward her sardonically. "You already have, my dear. Or, rather, under me."

A cold repast had been laid out in the dining room on the long burnished mahogany table once shipped out from Connecticut. Hatteras, propped in a chaise, presided over the meal, drawing out from the planters and ranchers who had attended the funeral, reminiscences of the man who had run Mountain View for fifteen years.

Beau seemed in a sullen mood, interrupting stories as he attempted to change the subject to cattle ranching and sugar. Roman, too, held aloof from the others, talking little.

"I suppose you'll be returning to Honolulu, Celia?" Melanie Cousineau remarked as the guests dispersed, some going onto the veranda, others milling about in the largest of the two drawing rooms. The women wore black dresses marked with storage creases, and unaccustomed black bonnets, while the men were uncomfortable in starched collars, cravats, and black frock coats.

"I imagine so," Celia responded after a hesitation.

"Beau will have to raise Tina, then?"

Celia stared at the inquisitive young rancher's wife, her heart sinking. Beau, rearing Tina? Beau, who at the volcano crater had joked about tossing his sister down the escarpment to see if she would bounce? Who had given the girl little attention, treating her always as an annoyance?

The remark hung in Celia's mind as she extricated herself from the crowd of mourners and started toward the stairs. It was as she reached the balustrade that Beau found her.

"Celia. You look beautiful today. Your eyes seem almost to glow. You are without a doubt the loveliest woman present."

To Celia the remark seemed wildly inappropriate at a funeral, and, coldly, she said so.

Beau raised an eyebrow. "If I want to compliment you, I will. I like you in black, Celia. I wish you to wear it often. It makes your skin look almost translucent, like the finest alabaster."

Her funeral pallor, caused by grief, guilt, and lack of sleep. She stared at him. "Beau, what are you going to do about Tina after Aunt Hatteras and I leave?"

His eyes met hers, then looked away. "I'll manage."

"But how? She's still only a little girl, she's going to need supervision, love, caring. How can you give her that? Maybe you should think about sending her to boarding school. A good school in Honolulu or on the mainland—"

"She'll be all right." Suddenly Beau grasped Celia's arm and escorted her toward the large drawing room, the strength of his grip giving her no option but to follow him. He pulled her into the center of the room, where most of the mourners had now gathered. Roman stood with McRory, and Tina sat on the piano bench, leafing through some sheet music.

"Beau, what are you doing?"

"Hush, Celia. I want to say something to them. Attention, everyone, attention!" Beau's raised voice silenced conversation, and faces turned expectantly toward them. Did Beau intend to make some sort of announcement about Tina? Celia assumed so, and stood waiting to hear what he would say.

The new young master of Mountain View cleared his throat self-importantly. "Friends, I have something to say. I know this comes at a poor time, only two days after my father's unfortunate death. But under the circumstances, I know you will all understand when I announce that Celia Griffin and I plan to be married within the week."

The words dropped like a bomb into the crowded drawing room. There were gasps, exclamations of surprise, and Celia saw the color drain from Roman's face.

"Beau!" Stunned, she clutched at Beau's arm. "Beau, you can't mean such a thing!"

But Beau was not even looking at her. His eyes were focused on those in the drawing room, the surprised faces of the planters who had come to mourn his father.

"It is for Tina's sake, of course, that we're doing this," he told the assembled guests. "My sister desperately needs a mother. And Mountain View needs a mistress. I hope all of you will attend our wedding."

17

Minutes later, Celia confronted Beau in the library, her body trembling with anger. "How could you have done this to me? Beau, you told all those people we were going to be married!"

He looked at her, a slim young man with the sort of sardonic good looks that attracted women. Celia knew that many of her friends in Boston would have been smitten by him, would have been thrilled at the prospect of marriage to Beau.

"But of course I knew you would consent, once you thought about it. After all, codes, manners . . . the usual thing."

"What *are* you talking about?"

Beau looked at her, and then Celia flushed dark red. His meaning was clear. There was the very velvet couch, its cushions still disordered from his assault on her.

As Beau continued to stare at her triumphantly, Celia took a step backward, her heart slamming. Drops of perspiration sheened her skin. Honor was vitally important; when a man seduced a decent woman, he was then responsible for her. This was the code under which both of them had been reared.

Now she moistened her lips, all too aware of Beau's eyes gleaming with satisfaction. To him this had been a clever chess game, in which she had been pawn.

"I . . . I won't be your wife!"

Beau glanced significantly down at the couch, his meaning plain. "You must have wished to marry me, or you wouldn't have allowed me to make love to you. Anyhow," he pointed out, "you are getting a very good bargain. I plan to double Mountain View's profits, we'll be rich beyond the sights of most men here in the islands. You'll give me an heir to Mountain View, and I'll pamper you. I'll give you anything you want. I'll make you happy, Celia, I swear it!"

"I . . . can't decide so quickly," she said in a panic. "I must have time to think."

"What is there to think about? I've already made the announcement and accepted congratulations. All we need do now is make the arrangements at the church. We'll have a small, quiet ceremony, befitting the circumstances. Your aunt can manage it—she's good at things like that."

Beau took Celia's arm and steered her firmly toward the library door. "Besides," he added, "there is Tina. She needs a mother, and what is to happen to her if you don't marry me? You know how my father let her go half-wild. I'll probably do the same thing. As you yourself pointed out, she does need supervision. Love. Care."

He was parroting her own words back to her. *Blackmail*, Celia thought angrily. What was she to reply?

In the foyer, they were stopped by Chang Liu, the cook, who had something to say privately to Beau, and Celia seized the opportunity to flee. She hurried to the end of the hallway and out onto the veranda, with its rows of wicker chairs, hanging vines and plants, its sweeping view of the Pacific that had so enthralled her when she first arrived at Mountain View.

She sank into one of the chairs and stared blindly ahead. Beau . . . to marry Beau. It had been announced to the world, effectively trapping her. As, of course, Beau had known it would.

"Shall I congratulate the bride-to-be?" The voice came from the chair next to her, which had also been turned toward the view.

Her heart sinking, Celia turned to see a pair of long black-clad legs, their muscles flexing against black broadcloth. Roman. He leaned forward to fix her with a hot gray stare.

"My God, Celia, how could you? To allow that young idler to claim you like that, only two days after his father's death! Are you that hungry for a man—any man—that you'd accept such a shabby proposal?''

She had never seen Roman so enraged. His eyes sparked fury at her, and his mouth formed a grim, tight line. She stiffened. ''Beau is half-owner of Mountain View, and that hardly makes him 'shabby.' ''

''Is that so!'' Roman threw back his head and laughed savagely. ''You're a damned little fool! After the way you stood by John, struggling to save him, refusing to leave his side, I thought you had matured. Become a real woman instead of a silly, flirtatious girl. I see that I was mistaken! You hunger for men, you crave them. You can't even let *two days* go by after you lose one before you sink your claws into another!''

It was an insult that struck to the heart of her like a sword blow. Celia felt hot shivers ripple over her skin. ''How dare you!'' she shouted. ''Is that what you really think of me, Roman? That I'm some sort of . . . of predatory animal, a man-hungry tigress, for heaven's sake?''

''Aren't you?''

''No! I'm not!'' She wanted to weep with her rage and frustration. ''I want you to know, in case you've *forgotten*, that there's a child involved here. A little girl who was left without a mother and now has no father either. Tina loves me, she depends on me. I don't intend to desert her.''

''Oh?'' Roman scowled, his dark brows beetling together. ''Isn't that a fine sentiment? Yes, indeed! You're using that child, Celia, as an excuse for your own lust.'' As she gasped, he went on. ''Are you really so greedy and impatient that you'd settle for a wastrel like Beau, a drifter from the gold fields, successful at nothing? Within six months Beau will let Mountain View go to the dogs. Or,'' he sneered, ''do you harbor the mistaken notion that he's going to make you rich?''

Insults, one after the other, stabbing her to the quick. Celia drew in a deep, shuddering breath. In this moment, she hated Roman. She wanted to scream out her pain, she wanted to hurt him if she could, to lash back.

She jumped out of the wicker chair, pushing it back violently. ''Oh, you're wrong, wrong! I don't think Beau will make me rich—I don't *want* to be rich. Anyway, I love Beau, do you hear me? I love him!''

The lie flew out of her mouth. It seemed to spin recklessly in the air. Roman paled, his nostrils flaring. Even Celia was horrified at what she had just said. But it was too late, for now Roman, too, rose from his chair. She had never seen his eyes such a chilly granite.

''Very well, then, Celia. I can't save you from being a fool, can I?''

She lifted her chin. ''No, you can't. Maybe it is too soon after John's death, but I don't care. Beau is handsome, and he loves me, which is more than I can say for *you*. You don't care for me, you never have. It's Kinau who fascinates you! Your mistress, your 'passionate lover.' ''

She had gone too far. At the mention of Kinau, Roman's face darkened. For a terrible moment Celia feared he would hit her. But then he did not, although the violence still remained in his eyes and in the harsh line of his mouth.

''All right,'' he said heavily. ''I won't stop you, Celia. Obviously you must go your own way—it's what you've wanted all along, isn't it? Beau Burnside. My God, that young puppy, *Beau*.''

Celia stood stricken.

''I'm leaving, Celia. I'm going back to Lahaina early tomorrow morning. Be kind enough to give my regards to your Aunt Hatteras. And to the *master* of Mountain View.''

And he was gone, moving lightly into the drawing room. Celia stood swaying, horrified at what had happened, the irrevocable words she had said, splitting them apart forever.

Later the mourners began to depart, news of the sudden marriage buzzing among them. Celia watched them go, feeling sick. Word would fly around the islands, spread on the interisland steamers by word of mouth. Within days, those on Oahu, on Molokai and Lanai, would know everything there was to know. Even Cousin Rebecca, on far Kauai, would hear.

Beau Burnside, Roman had said in scorn. *My God, that young puppy, Beau*.

Melanie Cousineau hung about, chattering excitedly, want-

ing to know every detail of their plans. She seemed amazed
when Celia told her that she did not know.

"But of course you know! What are you going to wear to
be married in?"

"It's a dress I brought from Boston," she responded dully.
She remembered the heavy pearl-encrusted white satin gown
that her mother had insisted on including as part of her
trousseau. It would still be worn, after all—to wed a man
much younger than the over-forty-year-old stern widower
whom Lydia Griffin had envisioned.

Somehow Celia's consent to all of this had occurred. She
was really going to be Beau's wife. Why not? she asked
herself defiantly. Since Roman didn't want her, since she and
Roman hated each other . . .

"Celia, darling niece." Hatteras reached for Celia's hand
to pull her down on a footstool next to the chaise where she
had held court all day. "We haven't had a minute to talk, not
one minute. I confess I was startled when Beau made his
announcement."

Celia tried not to flinch from Hatteras' keen blue eyes.
"I'm happy," she lied. She forced a smile. "Of course I am!
It's just that . . . John's terrible death, and then Beau's
announcement coming so quickly. I'm concerned about what
people think."

"Celia, you don't have to do this, you know. Even if Beau
has given the word to a roomful of people, the decision is not
irrevocable." Hatteras frowned. "There is something unsta-
ble about Beau, I think. Something very brooding and erratic."

Celia found herself defending Beau. "That's because he
felt out of place before, always shunted away from any real
work at Mountain View, made to feel like a fifth wheel. But
now things will be different."

"I hope so." Hatteras relaxed. "Anyway, this does relieve
a worry for me—a worry that you wouldn't be settled, that I
would fail in carrying out my obligation to your family. As
soon as the ceremony takes place, I'll write your mother all
about it. I'm sure she'll be very happy."

Happy? Celia thought of her mother, far away in Boston,
receiving first a letter that she was to marry John Burnside,
then a second letter announcing her marriage to Beau's *son*.
Surely Lydia would be surprised, even stunned. Yet hadn't

they sent her here, the family, wasn't this what they had envisioned for her?

Finally the guests had gone, leaving the house feeling oddly empty. Servants moved about, cleaning up the remains of the funeral supper. The interminably long day continued. Tina dogged Celia's footsteps, chattering to her, stopping to plant moist kisses on Celia's cheeks and neck, an eager, pathetic puppy of a child whose yearning eyes tore at Celia's heart.

"Oh, I'm *so* glad you'll be here with me, Celia!" Tina cried. "We'll do so many things. We'll go to Hana to visit the Cousineaus. We'll see some waterfalls, and pick bananas, and there's a place called the Seven Pools of Kipahulu. We'll swim there . . . oh, it'll be such fun. And we won't take Beau, will we, because he'll only be cross . . . Oh!" Tina clapped her hand over her mouth. "We will have to take him with us, won't we, since he'll be your husband now."

Celia stared at the child, the reality of her marriage beginning to sink home to her. "Yes, he will be," she managed to say.

Tina frowned, as if certain thoughts had just occurred to her. "But will you have to kiss Beau, then, Celia? And sleep in his bed with him?"

"Why, I suppose . . ."

"But Beau never lets anyone go into his quarters. He shouted at me when I went there once, when I asked him about the smell."

"The smell?"

"Oh, sometimes it smells like flowers in Beau's rooms. Rich, sweet flowers. The odor almost makes you sick."

Celia suggested that it was probably a bouquet left to rot, or a pomander gone bad. The child nodded, and Celia was glad when the topic passed to something else. She was in no mood to hear about Beau's habits. She would learn them soon enough, she knew. He *was* moody and erratic; her aunt was correct about that.

But he could do whatever he pleased, she decided, as long as he treated her well and cared properly for Tina. As for the clouded moments in the library when Beau had lain on top of her, his breathing hoarse . . . She shivered, pushing the memory away. She wouldn't think about that anymore. She would pretend that it had never happened.

"Celia?" Tina's face twisted anxiously. "Why are you frowning?"

"Am I?"

"You are . . . you *were*. Do you love my brother?"

"Love?" Celia hesitated, unable to think of anything to say. Finally, knowing that the little girl needed reassurance, she went on. "I know I will learn to love him. I'll live here at Mountain View for the rest of my life—this will be my home now. And you will be my sister, Tina, in every way that you can be, except by birth."

Tina sighed with pleasure. "Oh, good. I love you, Celia."

"And I love you." Gently Celia hugged the child, stroking the fiery red hair. It was too late, she knew, too late to change her mind, for such a cruel act would cause pain to this dear little girl. She blinked away the tears that she knew she could never let Tina see.

Night came at last, fragrant with flowers, a soft trade wind rustling at Celia's mosquito draperies, stimulating her restless thoughts. She sat at her dressing table, brushing her hair with long strokes. Lamplight flickered, creating a long shadow as her arm moved. Such an endless day it had been. It seemed a thousand years since she had awakened this morning and put on the black funeral gown.

Doggedly she pulled the brush, the motion automatic. If she married Beau, she would never know what it would have been like with Roman. The thought came like a secret stab to the heart. Would it have been wonderful, full of passion, an ecstasy of which she could only dream?

Stop it! Celia ordered herself fiercely. *Stop thinking of him, of his arms, his lips, his body . . .*

But instead of stopping, her thoughts only intensified as she pictured in her mind their previous lovemaking—a passion never consummated fully. She completed one hundred strokes and then put her brush down and leaned forward to stare at her reflection in the glass.

Dark eyes gazed back at her, and the lamp cast gentle shadows on her face, giving it a soft beauty. She wore a cambric nightgown with a tucked yoke of Valenciennes lace and tiny satin bows. It had been part of her trousseau, and soon Beau would be the one to see her in it, to take it from her body and make love to her.

Beau, not Roman.

Slowly, dreamily, Celia's hand went to the little row of pearl buttons that fastened the yoke of the gown. She loosened them, revealing the creamy skin of her breasts and shoulders, rounded and lovely. For long moments she stared at herself.

Roman would never see her naked again.

From now on, it would only be Beau's hands that touched her, Beau's mouth to kiss hers. . . . Celia felt harsh tears burn again at the back of her eyes. If only she could touch Roman again, just once. Feel the beloved texture of his skin, look deeply at his face, drink in the look of the man she still loved above all. For now that night had fallen, her hate for Roman had evaporated. She knew she'd never really hated him at all.

Celia found that she had risen, that she stood tensely, her hands clenched at her sides, her fingernails biting into her skin. Roman slept only a few doors from her. If she were to pad into the hall barefoot, to move very, very quietly . . .

She reached over to turn off the lamp. Then, drawn by an impulse impossible to resist, Celia glided to her bedroom door and pushed it silently open.

The upstairs hallway of Mountain View was dark and deserted as Celia crept toward the door of Roman's bedroom, her heart slamming in her throat like a wild thing. What she was doing was foolish—crazy, insane. To steal into Roman's room, drawn by an irresistible desire to look upon her love as he slept . . .

Cautiously she pushed open the door of his room, wincing as it creaked. She froze, waiting for a sound, a stir of alarm. But there was nothing except Roman's heavy, regular breathing. After a while, her own breathing slowed, and she gathered her courage to step inside.

At first she was aware only of the darkness. Heavy draperies had been drawn at the windows, blocking out all but a small shaft of moonlight. Regular breathing continued to fill the room with even sound; Roman was asleep, a mounded shadow in the four-poster bed.

Celia felt a tight band of excitement cut across her throat as she realized the danger of what she did. If Roman were to stir and wake, to rouse the household . . . She should turn at once, tiptoe out of here while there was still time.

Yet something rooted her where she was. Would she ever stand again like this, hearing the deep, even regularity of his breathing? If only she could touch him. Just one last time feel his flesh against her own!

A demon of daring seemed to prick at her as she glided forward a step, her heart trip-hammering. As she neared the bed, Roman gave a soft groan in his sleep and turned over, throwing off the sheet that had covered him.

Celia stared down, her mouth going dry, every thought flying out of her head. He lay naked, half-tangled in the sheets, arms and legs flung out in abandon.

How beautiful he was, she thought with an indrawn breath, how totally male. The strong, muscled arms, the wide chest that tapered to a flat waist. The long thighs partly hidden by the sheets, but revealing the nest of dark, curly hair and the tumid maleness that drew her eyes irresistibly.

Roman. Her lips formed the word, but nothing came out. She stood frozen, unable to move forward or back away, able to do nothing except look at him hungrily, imprinting every detail of him on her mind.

Suddenly Roman awoke. "Ah, God . . ."

The sudden drowsy exclamation startled her, and then like a god coming to life, Roman sat up, his hands reaching for her. With easy strength he pulled her onto the bed.

Did he think she was Kinau, his mistress, crawling into bed with him? Or was he awake enough to know that it was Celia he held in his arms?

Celia didn't know, and, her heart hammering fiercely, at this moment she did not care. They were together, touching, caressing. Deep, deep kisses explored her, drew her, trembling, into the spell of this dream. For it *was* a dream, sharp, vivid, totally wonderful.

"Oh, God. God . . ." Which of them cried out the words? And what did it matter? They were deep in the communion of their bodies, the endless rapt kisses. Roman's hands caressed her and she moaned with pleasure, totally past all control, lost, encompassed in him. She could have given anything, done anything for him. She wanted it to go on forever, the glorious kisses, the stroking caresses, the tight locking of hip against hip.

They were molded together, skin against skin, and a frenzy overtook them both, sweeping them along like chips in a flood. Roman guided Celia's legs open, entering her with a swift, sure thrust. She cried out and clung to him as they rocked together. Lost . . . lost forever in each other. . . . They ebbed and flowed, thrust and received, their pleasure growing ever more intense.

It was love, it was more than love, painful in its intensity, savage in its passion, sweet in its joy. It was everything, everything she had ever wanted.

Roman's movements in her grew more intense, her rocking response more frenzied, until he spasmed with sudden shuddering thrusts. As he did so, Celia felt an explosion of pleasure, of pure, exquisite sensation so powerful that it swept away her self, overflowing in rapture.

18

Dawn. Celia stirred and sighed luxuriously, deep in a dream of warmth and happiness in which she was being cradled in Roman's arms, breathing the sweet scent of his breath. Half-awakening, she reached out her arms to embrace him, only to feel instead the coolness of linen sheets.

He wasn't there. Her heart gave a strange little twist as her body completed the task of waking up. She opened her eyes. She was in a strange bedroom, full of dim, unfamiliar shadows. Draperies, pulled over windows, shut out the morning sunlight. She was in Roman's room, not her own.

She sat up, glimpsing her nightgown in a heap on the floor where they had dropped it last night in the full ardor of their passion. She had overslept. What if servants came into the room and found her here?

Hurriedly she slid out of bed, reaching for the nightgown to put it on, and that was when she saw the note. It lay on the bed-side table, neatly folded, waiting for her to open it. Celia stared at it, feeling her body grow cold. Deliberately she put the night-gown over her head and pulled its folds down over her body, postponing the moment when she would have to unfold the note.

But finally she had retied the ribbons of the nightgown and fastened each button. She sat trembling, and at last gathered her courage to open the letter.

Dear Celia.
    What we did last night was wrong. I have left for Lahaina. I am sure you can understand.

That was all—no more than that, a few words, brief and to the point. But those words denied everything that they had felt last night, everything they had shared, the very meaning of the love they had made.

Celia reread the note, tears suddenly blurring her eyes. Her skin felt clammy with the perspiration that had begun to sheen her skin. It hadn't been "love" they had made last night at all. No, Roman didn't love her, he never had. This letter was plain enough proof, if she had needed any. Last night's lovemaking had been a physical act, nothing more. A satisfying of physical tensions.

She'd made a fool of herself by going to Roman's room last night—more than a fool. For he hadn't even invited her, she remembered with a burning face as she jumped off the bed and started toward the bedroom door. *She* had been the aggressor. He had merely lain back and enjoyed himself! Feeling angry and cheated and used, Celia cautiously reached for the doorknob.

She managed to return to her room unseen, and walked through the rest of that day in a daze. Somehow she managed to accomplish ordinary things, to dress, to hug Tina, to smile at her Aunt Hatteras, to speak normally to Leinani and the other servants. She sat on the veranda with her aunt and sipped coffee, only picking at her breakfast. No one must know, no one must suspect that she had gone last night to Roman's bed like any common woman.

Finally, as Hatteras began to talk of her own plans for the day, Celia decided she would go to the schoolhouse and reopen it for the day. The ringing of the bell would summon her pupils, who were probably growing tired of their enforced vacation. Besides, she herself needed the discipline of returning to work. When she was deeply engrossed in teaching, her mind found a sort of peace.

"Celia, oh, Celia!" Tina found her as she was packing up her school satchel. "What are you going to wear for your wedding to my brother?"

It was the same question that Melanie Cousineau had asked. Celia explained about the satin gown, and showed it to Tina, allowing the little girl to finger the expensive seed embroidery that had taken weeks of hand work to apply. Finally, when the little girl had had her fill of admiring, Celia told Tina that there would be school soon, and fled to the schoolhouse.

She forced herself through the rest of the schoolday, almost enjoying the high-jinks of the children, who were restless after the stress of the funeral, again testing Celia's determination with them. She met their challenge, deliberately keeping her thoughts away from Roman and Kinau. She would not try to picture to herself what it would be like, for the two of them, settling themselves into Roman's quarters, laughing together, making love.

No, the feelings she had had for Roman were finished. Over with, at long last. He would make a fool of her no more.

Let him come to the wedding, she told herself grimly. Let him see her marry Beau with a smile on her face. Let him see her *happy*.

That night as she left the school, Beau himself was waiting for her. His eyes raked over her body, his look sexually possessive. Celia shivered under his scrutiny.

"Well, Celia, the funeral guests have all departed. I tried to find you this afternoon, but you were nowhere in sight. Then your aunt told me you were at the school. Why on earth have you come here, when there is so much to do to plan our wedding?"

Celia looked at Beau, seeing the thin, good-looking features, the spoiled mouth, the amber eyes that gazed at her so intensely. Beau always looked intense. Her husband-to-be.

"Beau, your father has been dead only a few short days and surely it is in poor taste to plan a wedding before he is even cold in his grave."

Beau had the grace to flush. "I don't know . . . I just wanted to talk about our plans, that's all. A big feast lasting two or three days. Lots of people, filling up the whole house, all those who attended my father's funeral and more. I want to invite people from Hololulu and the other islands as well. I want everyone to see the bride I am getting. And to know that *I'm* master here at Mountain View now, I'm the one running it, the one in control."

Celia walked a few steps in silence, feeling a chill. To show everyone who was master now at Mountain View; to marry the woman that John Burnside once had reserved for himself—were those the real reasons for Beau's wishing to marry her?

She spoke slowly. "We will need at least three or four weeks to make plans for a big celebration such as you describe. It takes time to send invitations to the other islands and to receive replies. And of course you will need to provide a list of those you wish to invite."

Beau scowled. "I know whom I *don't* wish to include."

"And who is that?"

"Why, Roman, of course."

Something cold hardened in Celia as she drew a deep breath. "If he does not come to our wedding, then I won't be there either."

Beau stopped his lanky strides and turned to stare at her. "Whatever do you mean?"

"I mean that if I'm going to be mistress of Mountain View, then I have certain rights too. One of them is to be able to invite whomever I choose to my own wedding."

Beau glared at her, and Celia felt her chest tighten. But Roman had to attend the wedding, she told herself feverishly—he had to see her being married to Beau, he had to see her looking blissfully happy.

It was a matter of her pride.

"But you can't—"

"I can do anything I wish," she told him flatly. "In spite of the announcement you made to all the guests forcing the issue, I don't have to marry you. And even after I do marry you, I don't have to stay here at Mountain View." She eyed him, sensing she must win this argument if she were to get along with Beau later at all. "What would all of your planter friends say if I were to leave you after you married me? Wouldn't they make you into a laughingstock? Say that you were not the equal of your father, that you could not—"

But she had gone too far. Beau suddenly whirled on her, gripping her upper arms with a strength she had not believed possible. "Stop that. Don't toy with me, Celia," he warned.

"Beau . . . please let go."

"I am not my father. I am a better man than he was—and I'm going to prove it." Slowly Beau released her arm. "Just cooperate with me, Celia, just show the world that you are submissive to me, and I'll let you do anything else you want. I'll be a good husband to you, I swear it, I'll do everything I can for you. And I insist that our wedding take place soon.''

It was an eerie echo of what John had once said.

However, despite Beau's wishes, the wedding had to be delayed. Before it could take place, Tina came down with measles and had to be strictly isolated in her bedroom until all danger of infection was past. Roman, who had been summoned to her bedside against Beau's objections, explained that measles, for white children, was an ordinary childhood disease, easily weathered. But Hawaiians had no natural immunity to the illness. Measles had killed thousands of the native Hawaiians, dropping them like flies, contributing to the huge and tragic decrease in their numbers.

"It's deadly serious, Celia, especially when many of the wedding guests would bring their children. We simply can't take the chance of spreading this to the islanders. Tina must be attended only by those who have already had measles, and under no circumstances are you to allow any of the Hawaiians to go near her.''

Celia nodded. "I had measles when I was ten. So I can take care of her, thank heaven.''

"Remember," Roman warned. "Don't allow her among the Hawaiians until she is totally well. And I would advise you to close your school to stop any possible epidemic.''

Roman had spoken to Celia as if she were a stranger, just anyone to whom he would impart such unpleasant news. Celia responded impersonally too, hiding the emotions that flooded her at the sight of him. She was actually relieved when he left again, saying that he had patients to see. Was Kinau waiting for him in his surgery in Lahaina? Did she assist him at his work? And again Celia forced away the tormenting questions. What use was there in torturing herself? Roman Burnside wasn't hers. He never would be. She had her own life to live.

The weeks of Tina's recuperation passed slowly. Tina lay at first listlessly in a darkened room, then slowly recovered. Finally she grew lively again, chafing at her solitary confinement, begging to be read aloud to and for special treats, while Celia was hard pressed to amuse her.

One day, during a game of dominoes with Tina, Celia realized with dull shock that she had not had her menstrual period. She had not thought about her monthly flow in weeks, and now she sat feverishly counting dates, trying to remember.

"Celia!" Tina was in an autocratic mood today, seated cross-legged on her bed in a cambric nightgown stained with spilled cocoa. She bounced up and down on the feather mattress. "Celia, I want you to read to me now. I am getting so bored, I hate all the books we've got, and I want you to order me some new ones!"

"I . . . Yes, darling, of course." Celia managed to say the first words that came into her head, her heart pounding thickly. Weeks, she thought. It had been weeks. Which meant . . . No. Oh, no. . . .

Shock rocked her. She was perspiring, her skin clammy.

"Celia!" Dazed, she felt Ting tug at her arm. "Celia, you aren't listening to a word I say! You don't pay any attention to me at all, and here I've been so sick—"

"The way you jump around, you are getting better each day and soon will be out of your sickbed." Celia's throat felt so thickened that she didn't know how she was able to talk at all. She managed to walk out of Tina's room, to close the door behind her. She walked down the corridor to her own room and went inside.

She lay down on her bed, her movements stiff. She wanted to laugh, to cry wildly. Pregnant. What sort of devilish joke had fate played on her? For her child had to be Roman's, but Beau would surely think it his, for he thought he had made love to her. . . .

Feverishly she recounted, as if she might have made a mistake, knowing all the while that she hadn't. Finally she lay breathing shallowly, trying to calm herself. If she had had any notions of backing out of her marriage to Beau, she knew with a twist of her heart that that hope was gone now. She was expecting a child. It must be legitimized. Beau had announced their marriage, was waiting now only for Tina's quarantine to be over so that the nuptials could take place.

She had no choice but to go ahead.

Later that evening, Celia tried on her wedding dress, turning woodenly in front of the long mirror in her aunt's bedroom.

Hatteras, with her usual burst of energy, had announced that Tina was well and it was time to begin wedding plans, insisting that Celia put on the dress to see if it needed alterations.

While Hatteras supervised from the chaise, Celia smoothed her hands down the lush, expensive satin. A graceful neckline revealed creamy skin. Delicate folds and loops of lace puffed the sleeves above the elbow, giving a flowerlike effect, and the seed pearls were thickly encrusted, opulent. It was a Boston dress, designed for a society that delighted in display.

"Beautiful," Hatteras murmured in satisfaction.

"Yes." But Celia was not thinking about the dress. "Aunt, I am wondering . . . is it possible to be . . . well, happy . . . married to a man with whom you are not in love?"

Hatteras looked up. Her sharp blue eyes bored into Celia's. "You aren't in love with Beau?"

Celia said nothing.

"I didn't think you were."

Shamefacedly Celia stared downward at her aunt's dressing table, where a silver-backed hairbrush and small hand mirror seemed suddenly to draw all of her attention. No, she wasn't in love with Beau. Far from it. She didn't even know if she liked him. Perhaps she felt sorry for him—maybe that was the strongest emotion she felt for Beau. Was that enough to base a marriage on? My God, Celia thought dully. It was like weaving a mistake into a sweater that you were crocheting. First you made a tiny mistake, altering a stitch or two. That mistake grew bigger and bigger, throwing off more and more stitches, until finally the whole shape of the sweater was changed.

She had done that to her life.

She stared at the gleaming surface of the hand mirror and felt her heart pound thickly.

Hatteras cleared her throat. "I am not sure how to say this, and I hope you won't find it amiss if I speak to you frankly. I have an idea that you believe in love—in some high-flown, romantic fantasy, some magical chemistry, that happens between a man and a woman."

Celia looked at her aunt, stricken. She did believe that. Hatteras seemed to be looking into her mind, reading every thought.

"Isn't that how it's supposed to be?"

"Celia. Oh, Celia. Do you really think that I felt that kind of grand emotion when I married my husband forty-odd years ago? I didn't. I had met Jud exactly six times before the wedding ceremony. The marriage was arranged for us by our parents, who believed that we were temperamentally very well suited for each other. As it turned out, they were right. We did match. And our love grew, little by little, day by day, year by year."

Celia touched the encrusted seed pearls, feeling their hard texture beneath her fingertips. "Do you mean that you didn't . . . When you married him . . ."

"No, Celia. Few women of my generation did. *Love* hasn't always been considered a requirement for lasting happiness, you know. Now, personally, I would have preferred that your husband be John Burnside. He was a mature man, well able to provide for you. Beau is more of an untried element, and he seems moodier, less predictable.

"But as master of this big plantation, he is extremely eligible. There is no doubt about that. And he certainly does seem to have a fever for you. Once his first flush of passion is spent, I am sure your married life will smooth out and become very tolerable. And there will be many compensations."

Tolerable. Compensations. What an odd way to talk of a marriage. Celia turned back to the mirror and began to fumble behind her for the tiny satin-covered buttons that fastened the wedding dress.

"Here," Hatteras ordered. "Stoop down, here, by the chaise, so I can undo those for you."

Obediently Celia allowed Hatteras to unbutton the gown. As she did so, her mind repeated the word over and over. Compensations! But Hatteras was right, she knew. There would certainly be compensations for marrying Beau. She'd have Tina to love, who had become like a daughter to her, or a beloved younger sister. She couldn't imagine coldly leaving Tina, never to see her again. It was unthinkable.

And she'd have her children, her eager, lively, amusing, bright, and incorrigible pupils. Her adult students, too, and the knowledge that she was making a tremendous difference in their lives, giving them something precious and permanent.

And in about seven months she'd have her own child. Her

very own baby to hold and caress and pour out her love for, to fill up her life with happiness.

Weren't those wonderful compensations?

But there would be more. Wealth, ease, position. She'd be mistress of Mountain View, which she already loved. There would be a home here for Aunt Hatteras as long as her aunt lived. Last, she would be fulfilling the destiny her family had planned for her. . . .

She slipped out of the wedding dress. Lifting the heavy fabric, she repositioned it on its satin-lined hanger and hung it on a door hook. Hung, the dress looked stiff and uncomfortable, its shape unyielding.

"We'll air that," Hatteras remarked. "Give it some good sweet Maui sunshine. In a year or so, you can visit Boston," she went on cheerfully. "Show off your new husband, see your mother and sisters again. Wouldn't you like that, Celia?"

Celia wondered what her sisters would think of the handsome, mercurial, moody Beau, what her mother would say. A year. She'd have a baby by then.

It all seemed very far away. She could scarcely imagine it.

Six days later Celia again took the wedding dress from its hanger, holding it up to smell the fresh odor of island sunshine. Today . . . today she would at last wear the gown to become Beau's wife.

She stood in petticoats and corset cover, remembering the hectic past week. Cousin Rebecca had insisted on attending the nuptials, and had arrived on the *Kilauea*, this time leaving her missionary husband behind in Waimea. Rebecca's pregnancy had caused some depression, and her husband thought a change of scenery would help her. Celia's cousin looked pale, but other than that she seemed the same old Rebecca. Now Rebecca had ensconced herself at Mountain View, insisting on helping with the wedding. Imperiously she issued orders to the servants, made lists of organ music to be played by Chang Liu's daughter, and argued with Hatteras.

"I hate to say this, Celia, but you need my help," Rebecca had insisted. "Your aunt means well, but she is . . . well, I would not say *crippled*, but certainly indisposed, and—"

"There is nothing wrong with Aunt Hatteras," Celia had retorted, losing patience with her officious cousin.

"Nothing wrong with her? Why, Celia, where are you eyes? She is becoming as plump as a pillow from lying about, she has to be carried everywhere by two servants, and if she keeps on getting fatter, it will have to be three. I'm sure you are very noble to put up with her as you do."

Celia had faced Rebecca furiously. "Becky, Aunt Hatteras is a wonderful person, a very special person, she would make ten of any of the rest of us. Without her this house couldn't even run. It's *she* who has been doing it all—not me. If she ever decides to go on her travels, to answer those ads she put in the San Francisco papers, I don't know what we would ever do without her."

"What ads?" Rebecca had sniffed. "Whatever are you talking about, Celia?"

"Why, Hatteras has advertised saying that she will be a companion for any wealthy young women who need a respectable female escort on a Grand Tour, and she has even had a response—"

Celia was interrupted by Rebecca's high, pealing laugh. "Nonsense, what silliness! How could she do that when she can't even get about unless she is carried?"

"But Roman is going to cure her," Celia said stubbornly.

"Oh? How? I have never heard of a broken hip being cured. You are a dreamer, Celia, that's your trouble. And now, about this wedding. Despite what Hatteras says, I have decided that we should have the reception out-of-doors, under a tent, so that the trade winds can cool us as we eat. You know how hot it gets indoors during the heat of the afternoon— it's one of the curses of this tropical climate."

Rebecca was off again, managing the wedding. Celia had smiled to herself wryly, imagining the confrontation that would take place between Rebecca and Hatteras, who wanted the reception to be held on the veranda.

And now, she thought as she slid the dress off its hanger, it was the actual day of her wedding. Plans had been discussed, argued over, and settled, for better or for ill, and Hatteras and Rebecca had reached a wary truce. It would be the veranda. More than one hundred fifty guests, most of whom had also attended John's harvest party, filled the house and several outbuildings to overflowing. Baldwin, Makee, Dole, Wilcox, Rice, McNally, Castle, Cousineau—their names were a litany of island leaders. Even the Roger Whitts had come from Honolulu, Kathryn stunning in pale lemon watered silk, her every glance accusing Celia, as if she held her personally to blame for John's death.

Pounds of food had been cooked, under Hatteras' direction. Cakes, pies, tarts, fruit candies, and French pastries. There would be four kinds of punch, a dozen roast pigs, and rare island beef, roasted to perfection. A special wedding cake had been baked with egg whites and cream, its icing delicately tinted and adorned with candied violets.

Only Roman had not yet arrived, but he had sent an acceptance to Celia's invitation and presumably would arrive later today before the ceremony.

"Do you need help with that?" Rebecca bustled into Celia's bedroom without invitation, clad in bottle-blue silk tightly corseted to conceal her burgeoning pregnancy, with a matching mantelet designed for the same purpose.

"Thank you, but Tina said that she wanted to come in and help me dress," Celia told her. "She's been looking forward to it."

"A child, helping you to dress? Don't be silly. She would be as bad as one of those Hawaiians. Why, she probably will crush the folds and get the buttons fastened all wrong. And the train needs careful straightening out, or it won't hang right."

But Celia had had enough of Rebecca and her managing. Her stomach felt as if a dozen Japanese carp were swimming in it, and she wanted someone around her who loved her uncritically.

"I am sorry, Rebecca, but I did promise Tina. And Aunt Hatteras will supervise."

"Oh, very well," her cousin huffed. "If that's the way you want it, Celia. You always were stubborn, weren't you? I must confess, I'm surprised that you let this wedding progress as far as it has. At any minute I expected you to back out of it. That's really why I wanted to dress you—in case you got any funny ideas at the last minute."

Celia looked at her cousin, feeling a twist in her midsection. "So you expect me to jilt Beau?"

"Haven't you jilted two others, don't you have a reputation for it? I'm here as a representative of your family, Celia,

to see that such a thing doesn't happen again. That's why I
came to Maui in my delicate condition, to see this through.''

Pushing back her anger, Celia stepped forward and opened
her bedroom door, holding it pointedly wide. "I don't mean
to disappoint you, Rebecca," she drawled, "but I do intend
to show up at the church.''

After her cousin had left, Celia sank into a chair, feeling
her body shake with half-hysterical laughter. Rebecca thought
that she would back out of her marriage to Beau! But Becky
didn't know about the baby. What if she did—what would
she say about shame then? Tears sprang to Celia's eyes, but
violently she dashed them away. This was what she had come
to Hawaii to do. Well, wasn't it? *Compensations,* as Aunt
Hatteras said.

She must remember that today.

"Celia, Celia, oh, Celia!" Tina bounced into the room,
curls flying, her cheeks flushed. Energy spun from her. "I'm
going to help you put on your gown and do up your hair, and
Aunt Hatteras said we could weave white plumeria into your
braids. I know how to do braids, I can braid hair! Oh, you are
going to look so beautiful!''

Celia hugged the vibrant little girl, feeling cheered in spite
of herself. "Braiding hair? Is that a new accomplishment of
yours, Tina?"

"Aunt Hatteras taught me, this week. As a surprise. We
looked in *Godey's* for a very elegant coiffure and I practiced
it on Aunt.''

At the picture this brought to mind, Celia couldn't help it;
she threw back her head and laughed. "Well, then, I'm sure
I'll be gorgeous. Shall we get started, then?"

"Yes . . . Oh! I forgot the flowers!" Tina darted out of the
room and returned lugging a basket of dew-fresh blossoms,
white and thick with fragrance. "I picked these myself,
Celia. Aren't they pretty? And I have a needle and thread.
We'll weave them lovely, just lovely.''

In the face of Tina's joyous enthusiasm, what was there to
do but smile? So Celia did. And perhaps, she assured herself
as she sat down before the mirror, perhaps it would all come
out all right.

Beau would make her a good husband. Hadn't he sworn
that he would?

19

"Oh, Celia!" Tina said it in an awed-little-girl voice. "Oh, you look wonderful, so pretty, so . . . pretty," she finished.

Trembling, Celia gave herself a last inspection in the mirror, while Tina craned for a look and Hatteras supervised from her chaise. Leinani and Malia, another maid, stood by to hold her train so that it would not drag in the red Maui dust as she walked to the church.

She leaned forward to stare at herself. In the glass, she saw a beautiful stranger swathed in lace and satin. Her hair had been swept into a crown of braids threaded through with waxy white plumeria. Tina had done it all, under Hatteras' supervision.

"*Oh*," the little girl sighed rapturously. "I want to look just like you, Celia, when I grow up and get married. Do you think I will?"

"Of course you will, child," Hatteras put in. "But today is Celia's day. And I don't think Mountain View has ever seen a prettier bride."

Celia gazed at herself, feeling an odd, surprising pleasure. Like Tina, she too had always imagined herself as a bride. And yet her pleasure swiftly evaporated as she remembered the circumstances of this wedding.

"If only your mother could be here," Hatteras continued. "I'm sure that Lydia would be vastly relieved to see you wed so well." She pulled out the chatelaine watch she wore on a loop of velvet around her neck. "But for now . . . Come,

Celia. I think it's time we went to the church. Beau and the guests will be waiting.''

Fifteen minutes later, they were on their way to the church, forming a straggling train consisting of Celia; Tina; Hatteras in her litter; Cousin Rebecca, who would be the matron of honor; and three or four giggling servant girls, everyone draped in flower *leis* for the occasion.

Relaxed now that the moment was at hand, Rebecca chatted to Hatteras, full of tales of other weddings she had attended. Tina, too, talked nonstop, her excitement at a high peak. Only Celia fell silent, walking slowly in order that the two Hawaiian girls should not drop the heavy pearl-embroidered train in the dust. Overhead the sky was very blue, scattered with filmy white clouds that gathered in huge masses over the mountains. There was a feeling in the air of moisture and storm, Celia decided. In fact, the whole day reminded her of one of Beau's paintings, everything depicted in lowering clouds and harsh, angular lines.

Stop it! she told herself fiercely. It won't storm. It's a perfectly ordinary day, and inside an hour you are going to be a married woman, mistress of Mountain View.

Had Roman arrived yet? No one had mentioned his name, and Celia dared not ask as they walked down the path toward the little Mountain View church that rested in a hollow of the sloping land in a tangle of bushes, vines, and bougainvillea.

She caught her breath, feeling as if swarms of swooping moths battled in her throat. She almost wished she hadn't sent him an invitation. What if she saw him and started to tremble, or to weep?

No. She was stronger than that. She wanted him to see her triumph. She *wouldn't* react to his presence, she'd keep a smile on her face, the most beautiful and brilliant smile of her life. For a few minutes she'd be an actress, she'd play the part of the ecstatic bride, and *damn* Roman, she thought, damn him anyway!

They came to the church. From the windows, open in the late-morning heat, came the discreet murmur of the wedding guests. A group of servants wearing a colorful assortment of bright *holokus*, gaudy shirts, and Mexican bandannas clustered outside the door, plainly prepared to enjoy every second of the spectacle.

"Look at them, you'd think this was a circus," Rebecca remarked tartly. "Oh . . . look, Celia, there's Beau, there's your bridegroom now."

Celia felt a clenching of her insides. Beau wore an elegantly tailored formal suit with clawhammer tails that tapered down the lithe, narrow lines of his body, giving him a sophisticated elegance. His collar was high, his cravat made of silk, his bearing stiffly erect. The hot Maui sun gleamed on his mass of curls and caused his eyes to glitter, so that Celia could not read their expression.

With him were Ruark Cousineau and Kilohana Gregory, the pastor of the little church.

"Well, so it's my fetching bride-to-be," Beau said as the men approached. His eyes admired Celia, taking in every detail of her appearance. Faintly she could smell *okolehao*, the Hawaiian liquor, on his breath. "You should be painted, Celia, just as you are. In that breathtaking dress of pearls and satin."

"Thank you."

"Mr. Burnside . . . Miss Griffin . . . really, this isn't quite etiquette for you to be standing here like this talking. We have a ceremony . . ." Nervously the pastor separated them, issuing instructions for their entrance into the church.

"Are you sure that you don't want to back out, Celia?" Beau whispered to her in the confusion.

"Why, of course I don't." Even as she protested, Celia's heart began to pound thickly. She did want to back out. Suddenly she wanted it very much; she was filled with a flooding, horrid panic. Oh, God, what had she done? She'd been a fool! An utter fool to say she would marry Beau.

The words of refusal actually hovered on her lips, and for a moment she thought she had said them. But then she realized that she hadn't, that Beau was smiling.

"You do love me, don't you?" He leaned toward her. "I knew it, I always knew you did. Oh, God, Celia . . ." Then, for one moment, she saw the naked emotion in his eyes. A fierce longing.

She felt her cheeks flush dark red. So Beau did have feelings for her. Maybe not love, but . . . something. And there was her pregnancy, there was Tina.

Reverend Gregory was motioning to her, indicating she

should enter the church. Organ music had already begun, rolling out rich and loud in the clear Hawaiian air. Wedding music. Celia moistened her lips nervously.

"Miss Griffin, haven't you been listening? We're ready."

"I . . . Very well."

It had begun. After having jilted two other men, and almost a third, she was to be married at last.

Inside the church, it was hot with the press of many human bodies jammed together on the narrow wooden benches. Celia stood beside Beau, shaking. She had glimpsed Roman, standing at the end of one of the aisles, tall, dark, somber in his formal apparel. His eyes were focused on her with single-minded intensity.

For one heart-stopping instant it had been as if the two of them were alone in the church, Roman's eyes boring into her own. Then with an effort she had averted her eyes. From somewhere she summoned a smile, a brilliant and gloriously happy smile. Somehow she had managed to complete her walk down the aisle, and now she stood beside Beau, feeling as if she would faint.

Do you take this woman . . . ? The words of the ceremony washed over her, as disconnected as the chattering syllables of the plantation's mynah birds. Celia was aware of the heavy weight of the dress she wore, the smell of the plumeria with which her hair was adorned, the almost sickeningly sweet smell of the gardenias and other flowers with which the church was decorated.

Beau squeezed her arm tightly and then pulled her to him, crushing her mouth against his. The wedding kiss. She was now his wife.

Celia never knew how she got through the rest of that interminable day, the endless feasting and celebration through which she moved like a smiling puppet on Beau's arm.

"Celia, I wish you happiness." Hatteras reached out both arms to Celia, who bent to receive her aunt's embrace. "You are such a beautiful bride, and Beau is a handsome bridegroom. It all went very well, don't you think?"

Hatteras wore a look of smiling satisfaction, as if she had accomplished some task well. In spite of the tropical heat, a little chill rippled through Celia. Was that what this wedding meant to her aunt, a duty accomplished? And "love" would come later, a natural outgrowth of marriage?

The day wore on. Celia changed out of her wedding dress into a soft russet silk, and circulated among the guests. She paid attention to an excited Tina, and talked with Melanie Cousineau and the other planters' wives. The sugar boiler, McRory, had drunk far too much punch and stood swaying in a corner of the veranda, looking as if he might topple over at any moment. And always there was Beau, never very far from her, his touch on her arm insistent, possessive.

Several times, at the fringe of a conversation group, Celia overheard whispers. Many of the planters thought it shocking that Beau should have married his father's fiancée only brief weeks after John's death.

"He's a young puppy," Rafe Cook remarked. Red-faced from drink, the cattle rancher spoke too loudly. "Bold as nails. He thinks he can do anything he wishes now. But you can't deny she is pretty. Ah, but she looks a handful, that one." The rancher, who owned several thousand acres on the slopes of Haleakala, nudged his companions, and they all laughed loudly.

When Celia went to freshen up, she passed a cluster of women in the upstairs corridor, who were so busy talking that they did not notice her. "Personally," Melanie Cousineau was saying, "I think Beau is far more handsome than his father, don't you agree?"

The other wives, all young, giggled.

"And he seems so enamored of Celia." Again the women tittered.

"All she wanted was a Burnside," another woman hissed. "And she didn't care which one. Some say she would have taken Roman, too—any of them, any of the three."

Then, as Celia pressed herself back into a doorway so that she wouldn't be seen, the women brushed on past her, trailing after them the scent of perfume.

The late-afternoon sun glittered on the far-off Pacific. As they strolled on the lawn together, Beau leaned close to Celia, and she could smell, stronger than before, the odor of *okolehao* on his breath.

"I wish these people would leave—all go to their rooms or something and leave us alone," Beau whispered in her ear.

He gestured toward the wedding guests, who wandered on the broad parklike lawn with its view of the sea or gathered in knots on the veranda.

She looked at her new husband. His face was flushed, and his eyes glowed at her, full of desire.

"We've invited all these people, we have offered them the hospitality of our home." She had said *our* home, Celia realized in dull surprise. "Surely we can't simply desert them to . . . at this early hour . . ."

She stopped, flushing scarlet.

"But we can if we wish." Beau had taken her meaning, and looked down at her, grinning. "We're married now, it's all legal, we can do anything we want to do. I can possess you and the whole world can know about it!"

"But—"

"Come, my darling wife." He pulled her along to the veranda, where Cousin Rebecca was telling a group about the inconveniences of living on Kauai. "Come, we will make our farewells to our guests before we go to our room."

Celia, flushing, realized that he intended to flaunt her before these people, these strangers. She belonged to Beau now, and he would take her to the marriage bed in the late afternoon, announcing to the world that she was his, not his father's, that *he*, not John Burnside, was now master of Mountain View.

Shutting out the sunlight, Celia pulled the draperies closed in the room that she had once occupied alone and now would share with Beau. Hatteras had moved out of the small adjoining bedroom and it had been converted into a sitting room. Celia planned to decorate it with wallpaper that she had ordered from New York, in a delicate pattern of leaves, ferns, and flowers. She intended to have an island seamstress upholster two slipper chairs in pale green silk, to match the greens and golds of the Aubusson rug already there.

But those changes had not been made yet. For now, the room was the same as always, filled with the usual scented masses of island flowers, and it seemed strange to have a man in it, pacing about restlessly.

"Well? Aren't you going to go and change into something else?" Beau looked at her quickly, and then away. Now that he was alone with her, he seemed less confident of himself. In fact, she decided, he seemed definitely nervous.

"All right." She took out a nightgown and went into the adjoining room to put it on, feeling its folds settle over her skin. She wondered what the wedding guests were whispering now. They'd know what she and Beau were doing in these rooms . . . were about to do. . . . She swallowed back a sick nervousness as she fastened the silk ribbon ties of the nightgown.

When she returned to the bedroom, Beau was already in bed. "Celia. . . ." He reached for her almost before she had slid onto the soft feather mattress. "Celia . . . my God, you're so beautiful, and you belong to me now. To me. . . ."

He reached for her, began kissing her, his kisses hard, tense, his whole body trembling violently. She could feel perspiration damp on his skin, sticking to both of them. Why he was as afraid as she was, she realized. He was terrified.

"Celia . . ." he groaned.

He fumbled for the ribbons of her nightgown and pulled them untied, nearly breaking one. "Celia, you must . . . I can't . . . sometimes I'm not able to . . ."

"What do you mean? Beau?" she whispered. "What's wrong?"

He flung back the bedcovers to jump out of bed, pacing the floor almost violently, his eyes dark pools in the shadowed room. "I have problems sometimes," he told her in a thick, choked, shamed voice. "But I did make love to you once. That night in the library . . . it was a good sign. It means we can be together. I can be a man with you, Celia. In time . . ."

She listened, appalled, barely able to understand much of what he muttered to her that night, strange talk of women and rejection, anger and desire. She was aware only that she must never tell Beau that he had never penetrated her body.

Finally, toward dawn, the storm that had been brooding all day broke loose, wind lashing at the shutters of the house and whistling eerily in the jalousies. Beau crawled back in bed. He pulled Celia close to him and finally they lay together under the sheets, their skin just barely touching.

* * *

Celia sat on the veranda nursing a cup of coffee and staring out at the Pacific, where the islands of Molokai and Lanai floated on the shimmering blue like mirages, looking close enough to touch.

It was two months later.

Each day had merged into the other as easily as the surging combers of the sea, until it seemed as if she had been married to Beau forever, a wife whose marriage had never been consummated, whose husband seldom even embraced her, often leaving their bedroom to return to his old quarters in the far wing.

"Don't tell," Beau begged her. "Don't tell anyone that I can't—for I *did* make love to you, Celia. I did give you a child. In time, I'll get over this. We'll just have to wait, that's all."

She continued to teach at the tiny grass-thatched school, still coping with her irrepressible pupils, still teaching a small class of adults, although Beau had tried to stop her.

"It isn't proper, Celia, for a woman in your position."

"A woman in what position?" she had retorted sharply.

"Why . . . mistress of Mountain View, and my wife." Beau looked at her, knitting his brows together in a frown. "What are people going to think, that I put you to work like some sort of a slave? I told you, Celia, before I married you, that I was going to take care of you, that you weren't going to have to lift a finger."

"But what if I want to 'lift a finger,' as you put it? Beau, I like to teach. It makes me feel . . ." She searched for words. "Valuable, important, needed. This isn't Boston, where teachers can be found easily. If I weren't here, those youngsters would probably grow up illiterate, there wouldn't even *be* a school."

"I'd get someone else," Beau said a trifle sullenly.

"Would you? Oh, perhaps for Tina. I am sure you wouldn't let her grow up entirely wild. But Aiko, Kaweo, the McRory boys? It would be so easy to let their education go. After all, they don't need reading and writing to cut sugarcane, do they?"

Beau had the grace to redden. He gave her a mocking half-grin. "Oh, all right. But it's going to have to stop when the baby comes. Or do you plan to carry him down to the schoolhouse in a basket?''

Celia smiled impishly. ''That's a wonderful idea, Beau. I'm so glad you thought of it.''

When they had been married a month, Roman came to Mountain View to examine Hatteras' hip, the occasion one of nervous anticipation for Celia. She dressed her hair in three different coiffures and tried on four dresses, dissatisfied with her appearance.

What was wrong with her? she asked herself impatiently as she at last smoothed on an airy cambric dress trimmed with torchon lace. She had not expended this much effort to dress for her husband since their wedding day. Now she had spent nearly two hours trying on gowns, all for the sake of a man who had rejected her, who kept another mistress.

She went to the mirror and examined her reflection. Did she look happy enough, the blissful bride? She tested a smile, gazing at the high color of her cheeks, the delicate apricot flush that came and went. Then she turned away. She was letting Roman affect her entirely too much. When he arrived, she would be cool and distant. In no way would she let him know her true feelings.

An hour later, Leinani came running to Celia with the news that a rider had been seen on the Lahaina road and was now turning into the plantation drive. Roman. Celia thanked the Hawaiian girl, fighting the waves of excitement that began to pour over her like high tide. She closed her eyes, forcing calm upon herself.

She would not let him affect her. She would not.

''Celia, you're looking well.'' Roman entered the large foyer, a burst of wind swirling into the house with him, for the trade winds were strong today, bringing with them the scents of sea, flowers, and sugar.

''I . . . Thank you.'' She fought for composure. He seemed taller than she remembered, almost filling the hallway with his presence, his energy. Today he wore riding dress, dark gray broadcloth tailored over the hard, muscular lines of his body. His craggy face was sun-darkened, his jawline squarer than she remembered it, his gray eyes pale. She struggled against the desire to reach out and touch him, to throw herself into his arms.

"Well, where is our patient?" Roman said it briskly.

"Hatteras is waiting for you on the side veranda, and I believe McRory said there are several workers who also need your attention. Genzo cut his foot on a piece of metal, and one of the other men has had fainting spells."

"Ah. Well, Hatteras first, and then the others. Then I must confer with your husband."

"With my . . .? Oh, yes, with Beau." Celia flushed beet red, staring down at the elegantly parqueted floor.

When she looked up, Roman was grinning at her, his teeth very white against his dark suntan. "Did you forget, Celia, that you have a husband? I certainly haven't."

In confusion she led him to the veranda, where her aunt waited, lying on the chaise where she had been placed that morning by servants.

"Do you mean . . . I'm to be freed?" Hatteras looked at Roman with a wide grin spreading over her features.

"Indeed! You are going to be weak for a time, Hatteras, and you may have to walk with a cane, or even two canes. But you will walk. I guarantee it."

"Oh . . . oh . . . it's *wonderful* . . ." Hatteras was at a momentary loss for words, and Celia, too, felt touched. Hatteras had been uncomplaining about her situation, behaving as if it were only an inconvenience to have to be carried about on a litter like an invalid. Now Celia saw that her helplessness had disturbed Hatteras far more than she had revealed.

Roman bent down to take both of Hatteras' hands in his own. "Hatteras, I won't lie to you and tell you that it will be easy. It won't. As soon as you begin to place weight on your legs, your limbs are going to swell up painfully with fluid. You'll be weak, and it may take months before you are really walking well. But you will walk."

Unashamedly, Hatteras brushed away tears. "Good," she said. "And without canes, I hope. I have traveling to do. I am in correspondence with a gentleman in California who needs a chaperon for his granddaughters, and I intend to be ready to go when the time comes."

Roman nodded, for Celia had told him of her aunt's advertisements, and desire to travel. "I personally will be on the wharf at Lahaina to see you off. All I ask is that you take it one step at a time. Literally. Put a little weight on your legs today—five minutes, no more. Tomorrow ten minutes. You'll work up gradually.''

"I . . . I see.'' Hatteras hid her disappointment.

"The time will go quickly,'' Celia put in. ''As soon as you're able, I'll walk with you, and one day soon we'll go up the mountainside to Pele's . . .'' She stopped. She had almost said ''Pele's Pool.'' She was aware of Roman's look, and heat flooded her face.

When he was finished talking with Hatteras, Celia walked with him back through the house, again burningly aware of his physical presence, the bigness of him, the maleness. She had lain naked next to that compelling body, she thought with a rapid, shivering intake of breath. Had felt him move deep within her . . .

She shoved away the thought violently.

"You will be staying overnight here, I assume?'' she asked, retreating behind her role as hostess.

"No. I think not. There are patients awaiting me in Lahaina, and other business as well.''

Business? Like Kinau, his beautiful Hawaiian mistress with the lithe body that could dance so fetchingly? Celia felt her composure slip. Stiffly she managed to conclude the conversation, to escort Roman to the door. As she watched him disappear behind the avenue of trees, she thought she would be ill with the spasm of jealousy that swept over her, as irresistible as a *kona* storm.

But if school was the same, and Hatteras, there were also many differences in Celia's life now, and most of them had to do with being married.

She was a wife. Although Beau had not possessed her physically, he seemed to wish to compensate by owning her in every other way. In a dozen ways, throughout each day, he let Celia know that she was *his*, that he wished to control the way she dressed, the manner in which she did her hair, the hours she worked at the school, and even what she did with her free time.

He gloated over her pregnancy, talking constantly of the heir she would produce, the son to inherit his share of Mountain View, refusing to admit the idea that the infant might be a girl.

"Mountain View needs boys, Celia—a male heir for me!"

At night Celia tossed and turned, immersed in confusing dreams in which she was rocking a cradle over which bent both Beau and Roman, each of them arguing that the child was his.

"I want to paint a portrait of you," Beau announced one morning as they sat on the veranda with their breakfast. Tina had already bolted her food and run outside to the lawn to play with Hili, while Hatteras, who had now worked up to an hour a day with her canes, and was beginning to lose the weight she had gained during her inactivity, had gone for a walk.

Celia looked at her husband. He seemed thin and distracted, his facial muscles tense. "Beau . . . I really don't think . . ."

"I asked you when you first came here if you would sit for me, but you very haughtily refused. Now you can't deny me, you're my wife."

He smiled at her, but she saw in his eyes that he meant what he said. "I have several portraits in mind. One of them will be formal, of you in your wedding dress, to hang in the drawing room over the fireplace. And the other . . ." Something flickered in her husband's eyes. "The other will be just for me. To hang in my quarters so I can look at it whenever I choose."

Beau had still kept his bachelor apartment in the far wing of the house, insisting that he needed a place where he could paint and where he could retreat whenever the pressures of running the plantation proved to be too much. He often used it, allowing no one but Chang Liu to bring him food or linens. None of the servants seemed to consider this unusual, for Beau had always been moody, Leinani told Celia, giggling. He still was. Why should anyone be concerned?

Celia looked at him now. "But, Beau . . . two portraits? How much time will it take to sit for them? I am very busy, I have my students, my school, my—"

"You are my wife, Celia, and soon to be the mother of my child. Those obligations override any others you may have."

What else was there for her to say? If Beau wanted to paint her, she told herself, that was harmless, and she ought to be generous enough to give him the time.

The next day she sat for the preliminary sketches, posing in a russet chair by the big fireplace in the drawing room, the satin wedding dress flowing about her gracefully. She held the pose for twenty minutes, then took a five-minute rest before posing again. Beau puttered with his paints, totally absorbed in his work, and Celia tried her best to sit quietly.

Her mind drifted, going over the next day's lessons, pondering the problem of what to do with Kaweo. The Hawaiian boy read many letters reversed, and seemed restless and unhappy at the confinement of school. Celia fretted over him, wondering what would happen to him in later life.

Then, too, there were her persistent thoughts of Roman. When would he next come to Mountain View? Did he ever think about her, as she thought of him?

With a start, she realized that the sitting was over. Beau was motioning to her to come and look at the work he had done.

Celia stared at the canvas. Beau had laid down a base coat in a dark flesh tone, and on it had sketched a woman sitting in a chair. Even in rough form, the resemblance to Celia was unmistakable. Yet the drawing looked harsh. The lines, Celia saw, were too abrupt, too angular.

"Well, what do you think?"

She hesitated. "Beau, you make me look different than I really am. Hard, cold. Is that the way you really see me?"

He shrugged impatiently. "Of course not. Whatever made you think that? I'm going to paint you as you are. Beautiful, regal, the mistress of Mountain View."

On the following evening, Beau again requested that she sit for him, and Celia put on the wedding gown, sweeping downstairs holding up its train, so that she would not trip on the long length of pearl-encrusted satin.

"What have you got that on for?"

"Why, you wanted to paint me. I thought . . ."

"Tonight we are going to work on the other portrait. I have your costume all prepared for you, and we are going to do it in my quarters, where we can lock the doors and not be disturbed."

"I . . . I see."

"Come along, Celia. Come with me. I am going to make

you look beautiful as you have never looked before. When
you see the way I do this portrait, I know you're going to be
thrilled.''

There was a glassed-in shelf filled with books, a little
alcove stacked with what appeared to be hundreds of stretched
canvases. A second room was being used as a studio, and
contained more paintings, some hung on the walls, others
arranged in disorderly piles.

Celia walked into the studio, wrinkling her nose at the
pungent odor of turpentine and paint. Was this the odor that
Tina had said she smelled? If so, she thought, it didn't smell
anything like flowers. The child must have been mistaken.

While Beau rummaged on a shelf, Celia paced about,
looking at some of the paintings. Here were more Hawaiian
landscapes, and some done in California, in the mining camps.
More dark, lowering clouds and angular lines. But there were
also paintings of women, Celia saw, sucking in her breath
with surprise. Half-naked women with dark, sensuous eyes,
carelessly draped in heavy, ornate cloths that revealed bare
flesh.

''What do you think of my work?'' Beau's voice came
from behind her.

She turned. ''Why, you know what I think of your work,''
she hedged. ''You are a very gifted and talented artist.''

But she could not stop staring at the sensuous portraits of
women. The subjects did not look Hawaiian; had Beau done
these paintings in California? No decent woman would pose
half-naked. . . .

''Why don't you stop gawking at those pictures''—Beau's
voice came tartly—''and put on the costume I've prepared for
you?''

''Costume . . . ?'' With a horrid spurt of realization, Celia
knew two things simultaneously. The women in the paintings
on Beau's wall were *not* decent; they were probably prostitutes;
and Beau wanted her, his wife, to pose in similar dress—or
undress. Why?

''Why, yes, Celia. . . . Oh, I promise you no one will see
the picture of you, if that's what you're worried about.''
Beau gestured toward the array of canvases. ''No one but

Chang Liu has seen these, and he doesn't count—he's Chinese.''

She stared at her husband, who was holding out to her a length of silk brocade, the threads picked out in gold. It was as if the fragile facade that was her marriage had split apart, revealing something dark.

"Beau, I can't believe you would ask me to do such a thing. I'm your *wife*, not a . . . one of those women.''

"I need you to pose like this, Celia. As an odalisque, a slave in a harem, a . . . a whore. With whores I can . . . I'm a man.''

He stopped, but he did not need to go on, for Celia had caught his meaning. She felt chilled. He could perform sexually only with prostitutes. He wanted her to pretend she was one, so that he could make love to her. That was the real reason he had brought her to his quarters.

"Go and change into the costume. I insist on it.'' Beau's voice rose.

"*No.*'' They faced each other. "I won't masquerade as a prostitute.''

"Why not? Are you too proud, too haughty, to please your husband, Celia? I have done everything for you—provided you with a luxurious home to live in, the best house on Maui, and indeed in the Sandwich Islands. There is plenty of money for anything you want, I've given you a child, I've even humored you by allowing you to continue to teach in that school of yours. And now you deny me this?''

"But why, Beau? Why do you want to force me to do such a humiliating thing?'' Her voice shook. She thought she would be sick. After the wonderful love she'd shared with Roman . . . No, no, she couldn't perform this travesty of sex with Beau. The very idea filled her with revulsion.

Beau looked at her. "I don't want to *force* you, Celia. I . . .'' Then, as she shook her head, he said sharply, "Never mind. I see that you're not going to oblige me. I didn't expect that you would—not really. Well, then, you might as well leave here, Celia. Leave my rooms right now. I don't want you in them.'' Beau's voice rose. "Go, I said. Go! Right now!''

She had never seen him like this, so petulant and angry. "I'm sure after you calm down, you'll see—''

"I won't! I won't see anything! I want you to leave, Celia, and I want you to send Chang to me. I want to see him, I need him now. Send him."

"Why?" she dared to ask.

"Because I need him!" Beau shouted. Celia backed out of the room, closing the door behind her. She knew instinctively that Beau was about to retreat into his room again, in one of his well-known moods. Shaking, she went to the kitchen and summoned the Chinese cook.

"I go to him, missy."

She hesitated, looking at the cook with his bland, closed expression and bright eyes. She didn't like Chang Liu, she realized. She never had. She didn't like the idea that Chang was Beau's only real confidant, the one he called for when he was angry.

What did Beau *do* in his rooms all day when he withdrew there? But then she answered her own question. Beau painted. He read books, and probably gazed out of the window at the view of mountains and hills. Maybe he brooded, or paced. Anyway, what concern was it of hers? If today had been any example of his mood, she was probably lucky he had decided to hole up in his rooms.

Beau stayed in his quarters for six days, refusing to respond to messages sent in to him, served only by Chang Liu.

McRory, the sugar boiler, came persistently to the house, each time demanding to talk to Beau. He acted annoyed when Celia told him that her husband could not be disturbed.

"Well, he'd just better disturb himself," the sugar boiler burst out on his fourth visit, glaring at Celia as if this were all her fault. "Who does he think he is, some little king who can sit up in his castle and watch the kingdom run itself?"

"Why, no, I'm sure he—"

"What do you know about it, missy? If you'll pardon me sayin' it, you're sweet and pretty, but you don't know anything about sugar, and neither does that fine husband of yours, either. Mountain View is going to hell in a hand basket."

"What do you mean?"

McRory rubbed a broad, perspiring face where freckles had merged together to form a splotchy suntan. "I mean that the workers are chafing. They're angry about the new *luna* Beau has hired. They don't like the high-handed way this new man treats 'em, and they've grown surly.''

"I see," Celia said.

"No, you don't see. Them Japanee men make good workers, but they can be angry bastards, too, pardoning my language, missy. John Burnside knew that. He ran this place strict, but he was fair, too, he knew what was what. Beau, now. He isn't running Mountain View at all.''

Celia drew a deep breath. Beau had been going into the office several times a week and had talked importantly about changes he was making in the plantation's operation. "I'll go in myself and talk to my husband, then, Mr. McRory. I'm sure we'll be able to straighten out this matter at once.''

But when she sent a note in with Chang, Beau returned it to her unread.

"Chang." She confronted the Oriental. "Why won't Beau answer my note? Is he ill, is there something wrong that he won't come out of seclusion? This was about the plantation. An important business matter.''

"Master Beau, he not talk to anyone," Chang said.

"But he has to talk to someone—he can't just bury himself in those rooms of his and paint all day!''

The cook's hooded eyes revealed nothing. "He say he not want to talk to woman. Not to McRory, not to anyone. You must abide by that, missy.''

"But it's a matter of Mountain View, of the sugar plantation!'' she repeated helplessly.

Chang grinned, his teeth very white and perfect in his oval face. "Sugar," he repeated. "Master Beau, he hate sugar.''

She stared. "But he loves Mountain View! He has longed for nothing more than to be its master.''

Chang's eyes darted away. "Master Beau, he hate sugar," was all that he would say.

Later that day, she went to McRory's office in the sugar mill with the puzzling news that Beau would not leave his quarters even for mill problems.

McRory shrugged angrily. "I expected that. Beau is nothing but a walkabout, a wastrel. John was right to be wary of him. He has no more ability to run a plantation and mill than . . . than that *poi* dog, Hili.''

That night, after a quiet supper with Hatteras and Tina, Celia went to bed early, curling up with a novel under the soft glow of an oil lamp. Tiny midges circled in front of the light, landing on her pages. She frowned, waving them away absentmindedly. Hadn't her husband longed desperately to be master of Mountain View? And now Beau had achieved that goal. He had taken his father's place, marrying the woman John had wanted, occupying his father's mill office, and issuing orders to his father's sugar boiler.

Unwillingly she remembered what Roman had told her— that Beau would run the mill into the ground within six months.

Was that true? Everyone here, from the lowliest servant girl to the hundreds of mill workers, depended on Beau to keep Mountain View running. There were even several other island planters who shipped their cane to the mill to be crushed.

Now Beau had lost interest in the mill. Why?

It was hard for Celia to concentrate on her novel that night. Twice she actually closed her book and started down the corridor toward the west wing, thinking to confront Beau, to have this out with him.

But something stopped her, some unease that prickled at her and left her feeling restless and uneasy. Something was wrong at Mountain View. Something that centered around Beau. She no longer could deny the feeling.

The following morning, Celia rose early. To her surprise, she encountered Beau on the veranda, frowning at a cup of coffee. An untouched plate of eggs and sausages sat in front of him.

"Why, Beau! You're here, you're up and about! Are you going to the plantation office today?"

"I thought I would," he said sullenly.

Mynah birds chattered raucously in the vines that grew near the house, and a tiny tan gecko scurried across the *lauhala* matting and up one of the support posts.

"I'm sure Mr. McRory will be very glad to see you," she began. "He's been trying to get in touch with you for several days now, about some problem with the workers. He said—"

"Enough nagging, Celia. I'm up, aren't I?" Beau gave an

angry shove at his plateful of food. His skin seemed stretched tight over his cheekbones, creating hollows of new shadow. He was thin, Celia realized. And his eyes held a disconcertingly blank, flat look, focused on some point in the distance, as if he didn't see her at all. "Isn't that enough for you? That I came downstairs, that I'm eating breakfast with you? What more do you want from me?"

"Eating? You haven't touched a bite of food." She looked at her husband. "I want you to be civil, Beau. That's what I want from you."

The day passed slowly, and even the children seemed edgy and too hilarious, jumping about on the wooden benches as they had done on her first day of teaching, tossing small pieces of sweet sugarcane at each other. Celia was forced to speak to them sternly. She requested that Kaweo, the ringleader, stand outside the schoolhouse door until he felt calm enough to do his reading and sums.

"I no have to do what you say," the Hawaiian boy told her in defiant pidgen, lifting his chin. "I can quit quick-quick and get job in the mill—Mr. Griggs say it."

"Who is Mr. Griggs?"

"He the *haole nui,* the new *luna.* He say I will be a good ox boy. And I will!"

Celia could not hide her disappointment. "And that's all you'll *ever* be, too, Kaweo, if you don't learn to read better than you have been."

The boy gazed at her, stricken. Sudden tears welled to his eyes.

"Oh, Kaweo . . . I'm sorry." Celia put her arms around him, pulling the youth to her.

"I can't," he whispered into her shoulder. "I no see the letters right, missy. They keep coming backward."

Her heart ached for him. "Then we'll just take it slower, Kaweo. We'll work harder than ever, until you learn it. Would you like to stay after school for an hour or so tonight? Just to work privately, the two of us?"

He brightened. "Yes. Oh, yes, missy."

On her way home from the school that afternoon, Celia took a branch of the path that wound toward the mill. The mill today was its usual picture of activity. Ox wagons laden with corn stalks lumbered across a dusty square toward the main entrance, their drivers shouting at the cattle and cracking long leather whips in the air only inches away from the animals' backs. A worker galloped past on horseback, while a dozen Japanese loaded barrels of molasses onto another wagon. However, today the setting seemed less peaceful than usual. Celia saw that some of the workers milled around in a tight, angry knot. Shouts drifted toward her on the clear air.

Remembering what McRory had said about rebellious workers, Celia approached the group cautiously.

"No one touches me, no man, not even a *haole!*" The furious cry came from the center of the excited cluster of men. When several workers shifted, Celia saw two men facing each other angrily. One was Griggs, the new *luna,* or foreman, the other was Genzo, the small Japanese to whom Celia had been teaching English.

"You little yellow devil-worshiping bastard!" Griggs advanced on the small Japanese, his sunburned face twisted into an ugly expression. He was a big, beefy man, his accent that of the Southern United States. "When I tell you to work, I mean work, I don't mean bow down to your heathen idols!"

"You are mistaken." Genzo faced the *luna,* his English perfect. "I was merely saying a prayer to—"

"I don't care *who* you were saying a prayer to. I won't tolerate laziness in my workers. You'll go on half-rations."

"I work as hard as any man."

"Yeah?" Griggs lifted the leather whip he had been holding and flicked it toward Genzo. The tip bit into the skin of the worker's forearm, drawing a red spurt of blood. "You, a man? Why, you aren't a man at all, you're a skinny, scrawny toad. Yes, a little yellow . . ."

The workers stirred uneasily.

"Griggs." Celia said it in a low, firm, furious voice that caused the Southerner to turn, startled. "Leave Genzo alone."

The *luna* scowled. "I'm only doing my job, Mrs. Burnside."

"Doing your job! Does that mean whipping the men?" Celia did not know when she had ever been so furious. She had taught Genzo to read and speak English, she knew him for a mild-mannered, dogged, scrupulously polite man. How dare Griggs insult him, whip him? It was Beau, she thought feverishly, who had hired this awful man. Whatever John

Burnside's flaws had been, he had never mistreated his employees, or allowed anyone else to do so.

"A woman can't know what's going on, Mrs. Burnside, if you'll pardon me saying so." Moving away from the workers, Griggs lowered the whip and grinned at Celia. "The mill is a matter for your husband, and he has given me full orders to do what is necessary."

"Mistreating our people? I don't think that's necessary," Celia snapped. "If I ever see such an incident again, I promise you I'll take action—I'll have you fired!"

But Griggs only laughed at her, and turned away, his shoulders thrown back cockily. The workers dispersed into the mill, their heads down. Genzo walked apart from them, his spine held straight.

Angrily Celia hurried to the mill office.

The office was set apart from the mill itself, a small clapboard building with a tiny veranda and windows open to admit the warm tropical air. When Celia stepped on the wooden porch, the boards creaked, making her think of John. This had once been John's domain, and before him, Amos Burnside, the seat of power here at Mountain View.

She pulled open the door without knocking and stepped inside.

Beau looked up from a desk, thin, handsome, his cheekbones prominent, his eyes holding that now familiar staring look. "What are you doing here?"

"I have to talk to you, Beau."

His face twisted. "What about? Can't you see I'm busy?"

Celia looked around her. The mill office was divided into two rooms, one used mostly for storage. The main room, where John had kept his desk, was also stacked high with ledgers. Overhead, a tropical fan whirred. But always, Celia remembered, the office had been clean.

Now she saw papers strewn everywhere, ledgers lying about, some of their pages stained with coffee. More scraps of paper lay crumpled on the floor, many filled with charcoal sketches, as if Beau had grown bored with plantation business and had turned, instead, to his art. A film of reddish Maui dust lay over everything.

Beau might have been coming here often, Celia realized in dismay, but if so, he had not been working.

"Busy!" She had lost her patience. "Doing what, may I ask? More sketches for a half-naked painting? Don't you know that your workers are upset, that you have hired an overseer who whips and insults them? What are we to do if our people quit Mountain View? They could, you know. I'm sure James Makee would be very happy to have them at Ulupalakua, and he would not . . ."

"He wouldn't what, Celia?" Beau asked dangerously. Outside, another ox wagon rumbled past, an animal bellowing loudly.

"He would not risk alienating his men, as you are doing, Beau."

Beau rose from the untidy desk. For the first time, she smelled the *okolehao* on his breath. "No woman," he emphasized, "is going to tell me what to do with Mountain View. And no man, either. Not my father, not Roman Burnside, not anyone. Do you hear me?"

"I hear you, Beau," she said quietly. "But Genzo is my pupil and my friend. I must insist that—"

"You'll insist on nothing, Celia. *I* am master here at Mountain View, do you hear me? *I run Mountain View, I and no one else, no one!*"

She advanced a step forward, anger giving her courage. The welfare of everyone at Mountain View depended on what she did and said now. If Beau was allowed to run his course unchecked, he *would* ruin Mountain View, just as Roman had predicted. Tina, Hatteras, Celia's unborn infant, hundreds of Hawaiian and Japanese workers, a pastor, an entire village— all depended on the sugar plantation for livelihood. If it failed, as other plantations had failed . . .

She spoke clearly. "Beau, *is* Mountain View yours? Doesn't Roman own a half-share of the mill and plantation? You have refused to recognize that, you and your father both. You have acted as if you own Mountain View alone. But Roman does possess a full fifty-percent share. He, too, has a say in what goes on here, and that's one of the things that eats at you, isn't it?"

"Celia—"

"Our child can only inherit *half* of Mountain View, your half. Roman Burnside owns the other half, and if I ever see another worker whipped, I am going to go to Lahaina and get

Roman. Then we'll see just who is really running Mountain View!"

Beau seemed visibly to pale. "Celia, you wouldn't . . . You don't know . . . He is a murderer."

"Is he? I was present when your father died. I heard John confess that he provoked Roman to attack him. He himself was the aggressor all those years ago, not Roman. Roman was only trying to defend himself."

"You lie."

"I *don't*. Genzo was a witness, if you need one, Beau, if you dare to ask him to corroborate what I've said."

They stared at each other, and finally Beau lowered his eyes, to look at the desk, where a few sketches still lay. She had won, Celia knew. Why didn't she feel better about it, why did she feel as if she had trampled on some painful and vulnerable area in Beau in order to achieve her ends?

Beau was staring at the crumpled papers as if he had completely forgotten about her presence.

"Please speak to Griggs," she finally said. "Tell him he's no longer to beat or whip the workers."

"As you wish."

"Yes, I do wish it, Beau. And I also wish . . ." But she forced back the cry. What point in saying it? Her marriage was an empty facade, a travesty, a poor bargain suffered by both of them. They didn't understand each other, they never would.

She turned and pushed her way out of the mill office, starting blindly out into the sunlight. Somewhere a wagon rumbled, but she did not hear it, so preoccupied was she with her thoughts.

Celia descended the stairs and stepped into the square.

"*Missy* . . ." The warning shout reached her, enveloped in the rumble of iron wheels. Then it all seemed to happen at once. An ox's bellow, the crash of heavy wheels, as the lead ox slammed into her with its massive shoulder, pushing her violently backward and then down into the dust.

20

Pain. Surging pain that pounded at her, lifting her up like a chip of balsa wood in a torrent. Vaguely Celia was aware of arms dragging her away from the oxen. Someone slapped her face, calling out her name.

Her eyes fluttered open and shut. Beau's anxious face floated above her.

"Celia! My God . . ." He said more words, things she couldn't catch, his voice full of fear. Then time seemed to telescope and suddenly she was in her room at Mountain View, lying on top of the quilt. Someone was moaning.

Time passed. People came and went, saying words like "doctor," changing linens, talking about Celia in low voices. Hatteras, Leinani, talking anxiously. Were they going to fetch Roman? He was a doctor. He loved her. She loved him. Celia felt fuzzy, the pain swirling her thoughts raggedly, mixing them like pudding. Her belly felt as if it were on fire, and she arched her back and groaned. "Roman . . ."

"He isn't here, child, not yet. He must ride all the way from Lahaina, and you know how long that takes, especially if he has been with a patient and has been hard to reach." Someone smoothed her forehead with a damp cloth. She smelled Aunt Hatteras' heliotrope scent. "Celia, poor girl, you're lucky to be alive. Thank God that you are."

She stirred, fighting the pain that seemed to center both in her right calf and in her groin. "What . . . what happened?"

"Why, child, you were nearly trampled by an ox wagon.

The lead animal shouldered you down and tried to walk over you. If the driver hadn't seen it . . . if Beau hadn't heard his shouts and come running . . ."

"Beau?" She shook her head groggily.

"Beau and the driver rescued you, my darling. And now your husband is waiting outside to see you. He's been very anxious."

Beau, anxious? Celia struggled to comprehend. "But what . . . what happened to me? My leg . . ."

Did Hatteras seem briefly to hesitate? "You are badly bruised, and your leg was lacerated in several places. You have a bad sprain, but I don't think anything is broken. Roman will have to tell us that for a certainty." Hatteras closed her mouth, as if there were more she would like to say, but had changed her mind.

Celia sank back on the pillows and closed her eyes.

Then Beau was bending over her, his hand clutching at hers with a strength that seemed too much for Celia to bear. His voice was thick with emotion, his eyes wild. "Celia! You stepped right in front of that ox wagon. What was the matter with you, didn't you see it?"

He clutched her hand harder, and she realized that he was crying. "Don't," she managed to whisper.

"I don't see why you stepped in front of that wagon. It was foolish and dangerous. And now . . . now you've lost it."

"Lost?" she whispered.

"Why, yes, Celia. Didn't Hatteras tell you? You've lost the baby—my baby boy, my son. You've lost him! And it's all through your carelessness, your selfishness . . ."

Lost her baby. Celia stared up at Beau, shocked.

"You're upsetting her." Hatteras' sharp words came from a long distance away.

"I don't care, she—"

"I won't have her upset. Please leave, Beau, and come back when you can be calmer."

Reluctantly Beau left, and Celia lay pressed against the goose-down mattress, feeling as if the canopy of the bed had lowered itself upon her body, crushing her with its weight. Her baby, dead. Tears blurred her vision. "Aunt Hatteras

. . .'' She could barely get the words out. "Is . . . is it true?''

Hatteras sighed. "Yes, Celia, I am terribly afraid that it is. The accident caused you to have a miscarriage. Leinani and I did the best we could to help you.''

"*Oh* . . .'' Still, she could not seem to take it in. She felt numbed, stunned, confused. Her baby! It was dead, it would never be born.

"It's a terrible blow, Celia, but there will be other children.''

Celia mumbled something. The Burnside curse, she was thinking, the tales of death in childbed that Kathryn Whitt had whispered to her months ago in Honolulu. She was a Burnside wife now.

A sudden shiver convulsed her and she reached out blindly for Hatteras' hand. No. It couldn't happen to her. It wasn't going to—how could it, when she had plainly survived the miscarriage and was fine? Celia shook her head, trying to clear it. She *was* fine; she had only injured her leg slightly. Roman would come and bind it up with bandages, tell her to hobble about with a cane for a while. . . .

Somehow she had sunk into drowsiness again.

"Rest, Celia,'' Hatteras whispered. "Roman should be here in a few hours, and he'll know what to do about that leg of yours. As for the other—that's finished. All you need to do now is to get better.''

It was evening and the lamps had been lighted in Celia's room, flickering fitfully. Leinani had brought a tray of bouillon and biscuits and some fresh mango juice that Celia had barely been able to touch. Midges danced again around the lights, and light reflected on Roman's face, bringing his high carved cheekbones into relief. He looked anxious and angry.

"Celia, dear God. Why didn't you tell me you were pregnant?''

She stared at him, trying to rouse herself from the lethargy of pain that still consumed her, although she had thought it would be over by now. Her skin felt hot and feverish, even her eyes hurt, and her sprained ankle throbbed agonizingly. "Why should I have told *you*?'' she retorted. "I had not yet announced it officially.''

"Do you think that I'm a person to whom things should be announced 'officially'?'' She had never seen Roman look so furious, as, harshly, he rolled up the gauze that remained from her ankle bandage.

Celia struggled with the pain. Not for anything, even as terrible as she felt, would she admit to Roman that the baby she had lost was his. "It was a matter to tell my husband," she managed to say.

"Your husband!" Roman punched at the ball of gauze and then hurled it into his medical bag. "That arrogant young puppy. Celia, *Celia* . . ." His voice broke huskily. "And now you have lost your baby. A child I didn't even know about until it was too late."

"And what would you have done if you had known? Offered me congratulations?" From somewhere she found the strength to glare at him.

"I would have . . ." Roman's hands gripped Celia's face, his expression savage. Then slowly he dropped his hands. "I'm sorry," he whispered. "I could have done nothing, Celia, since you are married to another man."

Celia gazed into Roman's clear gray eyes, trying to find the truth there. Was it love she saw in his intent gaze? Or merely anger?

She tried to formulate a reply to him, but words would not emerge. Nothing would. The fuzziness in her brain seemed to intensify, to grow darker and darker. Or was it the room suddenly growing black? Her skin felt very, very hot.

Her eyes fluttered shut.

After that, everything became a hot, painful blur. She twisted and turned, fighting the sheets that someone kept pulling over her, battling the hands that held a cold poultice against her forehead. She was sick. Very sick. Dimly she was aware of this fact, but somehow it didn't seem to matter; it belonged to a part of the world over which she had no control.

Occasionally she heard voices, discussing her over the bedside. "Puerperal fever," someone said. Was it Roman? "It's serious, very serious, Hatteras."

Time, passing in spurts, unclear. Fever burned her like the fire that glowed under the sugar kettles, searing her skin. She tossed and struggled, crying out.

"Celia, I want you to get well. I *order* you to get well! I don't like this, your being sick. I haven't even finished my painting of you.'' That was Beau, his voice sounding petulant and anxious all at once. She felt his hands grip hers, the touch painful. ''I . . . I'm sorry for anything I did to you, Celia. I am. Really I am. I wanted our son, but there can be other sons. You will still give me an heir, won't you? You're the only one I can . . . I need you, Celia.''

Celia muttered something and closed her eyes. It hurt to see, hurt to think.

Then someone was bathing her. It was agony, icy water on hot skin. She fought savagely, kicking out, rearing up from the bed to flail out wildly at restraining hands.

''Celia! For Christ's sake, stop struggling. I'm trying to help you,'' Roman said.

''No! It hurts, stop it. Leave me alone.''

''Dammit, no, I won't leave you alone. I'll bring the fever down if it's the last thing I do. Stop fighting me.''

She felt his arms grip around her and push her gently to the mattress again. ''No! Don't touch me!'' she screamed, struggling up again. ''I want you to leave. Go, Roman, go back to Lahaina! Go back to your damned mistress!''

Roman gave a hard, bitter laugh. His face looked ravaged and tired, as if he had not slept in several nights. A stubbly dark bristle of beard showed on his skin. ''Not until you are better, my little tigress. Then I'll leave if you wish it. I'll go far away from you. Ah, would that please you, Celia?''

Why was Roman's voice so brusque, why did his eyes glitter with tears? But Celia felt too ill, she did not have the energy to figure out these things. The fever swirled about her again, as hot as the steam in the boiling room.

Hours. Days. It seemed she had lain here forever, drugged with fever beyond thought, beyond caring. She was sugar, she thought wildly, simmering in a pot to the strike point. Soon she'd split apart into a million sweet white crystals. . . .

Several times Beau came and shouted at Roman, and Roman shouted back. Some disagreement about her treatment, the medicines that Roman had given her, some of which he had picked in the rain forests of Kipahulu and the Iao Valley.

Once she felt soft arms go around her. Tina's pinched, worried face was only inches away from hers. ''Don't die,

Celia," the little girl whispered. "They are all saying you might, they said it's bad, this fever you have. You have to be strong or you won't conquer it."

"Tina." Celia forced out the whisper. She squeezed the little girl's hand.

"Oh, Celia! They are all arguing and fighting. Beau wants to get rid of Roman, he says his baths and medicines are not making you better, but worse. And Roman refuses to go. He threatened to whip Beau if he dared to oust him from your bedroom. They nearly came to blows, and Beau even produced a pistol. But Roman knocked it away from him."

Through the daze of fever, Celia struggled to make sense of it. Beau and Roman fighting over her? Shouting at each other? It didn't seem real. Nothing did.

"Kaweo and Aiko and all the children," Tina persisted. "They have made *leis* for you, they want you to get better."

"Yes . . ."

Tina's voice grew high, frightened. "You will get better, won't you?"

"Child, whatever are you doing here talking to Celia like this?" Hatteras' voice interrupted. "She must be allowed to rest."

"I wanted to talk to her, to tell her—"

"You'll have plenty of time to talk to her later, I promise." Celia heard the tap of a cane on the floor, the rustle of petticoats. "Go, child, and find Hili, or play with Aiko. I'll call you when Celia is well enough to see you, you may depend on it."

"But—"

"Run, Tina. Do as you are told."

Dreams. They swirled in her mind like brightly colored clouds. Sometimes she was aboard the *Fair Wind*, gazing out at a vista of rolling, undulating combers capped with jeweled foam. At other times she was walking up the long avenue of *koas* toward Mountain View, seeing the plantation house set at the end, a gracious Georgian mansion draped with wisteria, bougainvillea, and other tropical shrubs.

She floated in the waters of Pele's Pool, her companion a beautiful naked woman whose black hair floated behind her like jet silk: Pele herself, the beautiful, vengeful goddess of the volcano.

The goddess's lustrous dark eyes gleamed with triumph. *Roman is my man,* she murmured, her voice blending with the musical lappings of water against rock. *How could you ever have thought he loved you? I am the one he wants, he has always wanted me. You were a fool to think otherwise.*

Celia tossed and moaned, her body pouring with sweat. She yanked at the sheets that seemed to tie her down like a shroud. Then somehow she was at Olowalu beach, where dozens of Hawaiians had been massacred. Their faces floated in the air above the sand, frightened, distorted in terror. . . .

"Celia, take this medicine." Something touched her lips.

Celia resisted, hitting out wildly.

"Help me, Leinani, help me to hold her," a voice ordered. "She's delirious . . . it's the crisis. If she doesn't get through tonight . . ."

More dreams, coming in frightening succession. Celia walked through the Burnside cemetery past rows of open graves. In each coffin lay a Burnside wife, a beautiful icy statue. Susan. Ariadne. Hope. Their eyes followed Celia accusingly.

You toyed with the Burnside men. First John, then Beau, and even Roman. You hurt them, all of them. Now you'll be punished . . . cursed, as we were. . . .

"No!" she screamed, grappling with the sheets that seemed bound around her body, tying her down. "I didn't mean it, I didn't!"

"Roman. My God, how long is this crisis going to last?" Hatteras' voice echoed fuzzily, seeming to be a part of some other, simultaneous dream.

"I don't know. It can't go on much longer or it will kill her. She's burning up. I have given her everything I know, every fever-breaker, every fighter of infection. I don't know what else I can do now, Hatteras."

"Except pray."

"Yes. God . . . Did *I* have a part in this, Hatteras? Did I?"

"You?"

Roman groaned. "I cannot tell you . . ." And then, distinctly, Celia heard the harsh, racked sounds of a man's sobs.

She wanted to reach out, to touch him, to tell him it was going to be all right. But now the bad dreams were coming again, and the corpses of the Burnside wives sat up in the coffins, their heads turning all the way around on their necks so they could stare at Celia.

A coquette, that's what you are. You'll die of the curse, just like us.

"No!" Celia gagged on her terror, twisting from side to side, sweat pouring down her body. "No, I won't, I won't— you can't make it happen! You can't! I didn't . . . I'm not a coquette, I'm not!"

The voices in the bedroom continued, forming a pattern, a counterpoint to pain. She heard words, but not their meaning.

"What is she babbling about?" Hatteras said.

"It is . . . something I said to her. Something I didn't mean, something spoken only from pain and a desire to hurt."

A hesitation. "You love her, don't you, Roman?"

"Yes. God help me, I do."

"Then why didn't you marry her?"

"Because she didn't give me a chance. She married Beau. It was a deliberate thing, Hatteras, she did it to spite me, I'm sure of it. And now this has happened. A miscarriage, my God . . . Celia, poor Celia . . . if only she can stay alive a few more hours! I'll make it up to her, Hatteras, I swear it. I swear it with every bone in my body, every cell of my blood and heart."

"How?" Hatteras demanded. "How are you going to make it up to her now? It's too late. She already has a husband, she has taken vows in the sight of God and the world. What can be done now?"

"I don't know." Roman's voice was hoarse, agonized. "I just want her to live, and I'm not sure she's going to."

She was walking through a long dark lava tube overgrown with vines and ferns that had thick, unyielding stems. She had to push them aside if she wanted to pass. At the far end of the tunnel were the voices, and she wanted to go to them. But vines were in her way, blocking her passage.

She stirred and moaned, slapping at them.

"Celia . . . darling . . . you must fight. Please. Try to fight this. Don't give up. I'm going to bring you through this."

Voices. Without meaning, yet with a curious urgency t[...] them, as if something very important were at stake. He[...] struggle in the lava tunnel grew harder, more difficult an[...] intense. She gasped and sobbed with effort. The stems of th[...] vines were heavy—she could not push them aside, she di[...] not have a knife to cut them. . . .

"Live, Celia. Live! You must, my girl, you must come ou[...] of this. I'll do anything, give anything. . . . Oh, God . . ."

Strange; the vines that blocked the tunnel seemed to shrink. At last, by clawing at them until her fingers bled and he[...] arms agonized with pain, Celia was able to shove some o[...] them aside, creating a place for herself to squeeze past. The voices grew louder. They came from the area beyond the entrance to the tunnel, a place where there was blindingly bright light.

"She seems better now, don't you think, Roman? Her color . . . Or could it just be my imagination?"

"No, it's not your imagination. The fever is subsiding. She's shivering, Hatteras—blankets, more blankets, quickly. I don't want her to convulse."

Celia dreamed that she crept out of the tunnel, squeezing her eyes shut against the terrible glare that cut like knifes into her eyes. She moaned, her hands spread in front of her face to keep away the worst of the light.

"Celia," someone said gently. "Here . . . drink this."

She smelled something like moldy plants, a thick, fetid odor that turned her stomach. She retched, and tried to push it away.

"Drink, Celia. It's a medicinal tea, I brewed it myself, it will help you feel better." Roman's voice. "And open your eyes, it's a beautiful day. There are whitecaps this morning, the winds are high. Can you hear the wind whistling around the corners of the house?"

Celia lay very still. Yes, she could hear the wind. It sounded wonderful, a familiar sound that pulled her back to normality, to life. And there were whitecaps today. Yes. She felt as if she had returned from a very far journey. But she did not want to drink the noxious herb tea; the very smell made her gag.

She pushed at the proffered cup. "Ugh!"

Roman chuckled, the sound low, rich. "Well, I see that you've recuperated enough to be contrary. That's a good sign. From now on your recovery should be steady. If you take your medicine, that is. Come on, swallow."

Celia opened her mouth and managed to choke down a mouthful of the bitter concoction.

"It's an old Hawaiian remedy," he told her, smiling. I picked it myself at Kipahulu. I hope you appreciate the effort I went to on your behalf." He grinned down at her, his gray eyes tired, his face a mask of weariness. He had not shaved in days; his beard had grown several inches, giving him a shaggy look. But his eyes held hers with a warm look, and his hand pressed hers tightly.

Celia gripped his hand, wishing she never had to let it go. "Don't leave me yet," she whispered.

"Leave you? After all the work I've done on you? You're the best advertisement I have for my services, Celia Burnside, and I have no intention of leaving Mountain View until I'm absolutely sure that you've mended." Roman gave her another slow smile whose sweetness twisted at her heart. "Meanwhile, you're stuck with this."

Again he thrust the cupful of vile-smelling tea toward her. "Drink, Celia. Every last drop. I insist on it."

"You owe a great deal to that man, to Roman Burnside." Hatteras stirred a bowlful of chicken soup before pronouncing it ready to serve to her patient. "He stayed at your bedside for five nights, Celia, barely snatching a wink of sleep."

"He did?" Celia stretched and blinked, feeling kitten-weak, as if the past days had been a dream, barely real—Roman's face bent over hers, the sounds of his weeping, the tender way he had held her.

"What's more, he nearly precipitated a battle royal with your husband, who disagreed with his method of treatment. For a moment I thought they were going to kill each other over you, Celia. Fortunately, Roman won out." Hatteras shuddered delicately. "I must confess that I, too, was terribly worried about you. I have no desire to outlive you, my dear."

Within a few days Celia was sitting up in bed. Beau visited her several times, making it clear that he blamed her for the loss of the baby. Her husband looked thinner than ever, fine lines etched around his mouth and on his forehead. Dots of perspiration beaded his skin, and he talked wildly of manhood and loss.

In spite of her weakness, Celia felt a surge of anger. "This has nothing to do with *your* manhood! It was an accident. Do you think that I would deliberately step into the path of an ox wagon?"

Beau shrugged, pacing the sickroom restlessly. "Who knows what you would do, Celia? You are utterly unpredictable. As for Roman, how dare he strut about here like an arrogant cock, merely because he saved your life?"

Celia looked at her husband, biting back a quick reply. Beau was jealous, of course. And she could not blame him. If he knew . . . if he even suspected that the child she had lost was Roman's, it would devastate him.

But there was no way for Beau to know that, and she certainly had no intention of telling him.

That evening Roman came to Celia's rooms to take her temperature and listen to her chest.

They talked lightly of plantation matters, of other patients that Roman had treated, the school. Tonight Roman looked rested, and he was clean-shaven again, the lines in his face relaxed. Celia could smell fragrant shaving soap. His mane of black hair, freshly washed, fell silkily over his forehead. She longed to touch it, to smooth it back. How beautiful he was, if a man could be said to be beautiful. He might have been an ancient statue, his features proudly chiseled, his mouth arrogant yet tender.

Several times as they talked, their hands brushed accidentally, and each time Celia felt a thrill shiver through her. She swallowed thickly. Even now, weak as she still was, she responded to him physically. She was like a flower responding helplessly to the sun, forced to turn its leaves in the direction of the heat that drew it.

In a few days Roman would leave again, to return to his practice in Lahaina. But Celia pushed back the thought of that bleak prospect. He was here with her now, wasn't he? Desperately she grabbed at the thought of the few hours she could share with him. She'd try to enjoy them and not think about the long, lonely times when he would not be here.

They talked quietly. Celia confessed to Roman her worry, early in her illness, that she might be suffering from the Burnside curse.

Roman frowned. "What do you know about that?"

"Why, only what I've heard others say. About the wives who've died in childbirth. Their graves are down in the Burnside plot—surely it's not any secret." Celia looked at him. "Your wife, Hope, died in childbirth too," she dared to add.

Roman was silent, his mouth tightening. His eyes looked pale, like stones washed under clear water. Finally he spoke, his voice deeper than usual. "We talked about that before. There are times, Celia, when I've tormented myself with questions that have no answers. Is there such a thing as a family curse, transmitted from generation to generation? Did I destroy Hope by loving her?"

"By . . . No, of course you couldn't have!"

"Are you so sure? Other diseases are passed down in families—bleeding, mental illnesses, malformations. What if there is some congenital predisposition in the Burnside blood to create miscarriage or stillbirth in the female? Some family taint carried by the males and transmitted to females?"

Fiercely Roman went on. "I don't want to hurt any woman. *Ever.* My own mother died in childbirth, you know."

They looked at each other, and Celia read in Roman's eyes that he knew her child could have been his. Of course, she told herself raggedly, Roman knew. Her heart pounded in slow, hard thumps as she faced his scrutiny.

"I never meant to subject you to risk," he told her after a moment.

"I . . . I didn't care about the risk."

Something naked hung between them. *"I did. Celia, it never should have happened between us. Dammit, girl, can't you see? I could have been the one who brought death to you."*

She moistened her lips, suppressing a shiver. "But you didn't. I didn't die."

"What if you had?" Roman's expression was agonized. "Do you think I could ever have forgiven myself? I would have carried that guilt with me to the grave. I killed Hope,

Celia. I killed my wife, for I was the one who impregnated
her. If it were not for the fact that Kinau is barren—''

"Kinau is . . . is barren?"

"Yes, she is."

Realization swept through Celia, flooding her. Roman didn't
want to "curse" any woman, to cause her death as Hope and
the other Burnside women had died. That was why he'd
selected Kinau as his mistress—not for her beauty, but because *she could not have a baby.*

She was shaking, her skin alternately flushing hot and
cold. Maybe . . . maybe he didn't love Kinau after all.
Maybe he had only chosen her because he was male and
required someone, needed a woman to satisfy his needs. . . .

She forced out a whispered question. "Do you love Kinau?"

Roman's eyes dilated, their color washing out to pale
silver. His brows knotted together, forming a dark frown line.
"No," he said heavily. "I don't."

Relief swept through her as she heard him go on. "I enjoy
Kinau, I am fond of her . . . yes, more than fond. I admire
her intelligence, her help in my office, and she meets my
physical needs." A muscle tightened at the corner of Roman's
mouth, the muscle that always flickered when he was under
stress. "During the hours that I sat by your bedside, Celia, I
thought long and hard about Kinau. Am I being fair to her to
keep her as my mistress when I cannot feel for her what I feel
for . . .?"

For you. She was almost sure he had been going to say
that, but he chopped off the words as if they had been snakes.

"I am going to ask Kinau to leave my quarters, Celia. I
will be responsible for her financially, of course. But it will
end between us."

Celia felt her heart twist. She looked at Roman, feeling
confused. She had dreamed so often of hearing those very
words. She couldn't understand why she didn't feel more
joyous now. Roman was going to give up Kinau, her beautiful rival. She should be happy. But she wasn't. She felt only
dread, a horrid foreboding that something terrible was going
to happen.

She heard Roman go on. "I wronged both of you, Celia. I
see it clearly now. I took up several good years of Kinau's
life, years when she could have been finding some other man

to make her happy, even if she could not give him children.
As for you, I created feelings in you, in both of us, that
should have been left alone."

"No," she whispered in agony. "Don't say that! I'm glad
we had those feelings. I . . . I love you, Roman. I always
have. I—"

"Hush." He put a finger firmly to her lips, sealing off her
declaration of love. His eyes were bleak. "You're married. It
can't be. I must return to Lahaina and do what I can to set my
life straight again. And after that . . ."

Celia felt a twist of fear. "After that, what?"

"Perhaps it is time for me to leave Maui." Roman said it
heavily. "Permanently."

21

The next day Roman went back to Lahaina and Celia forced herself to get out of bed, to go about her life. Roman had gone, and it hurt in a searing way she had never dreamed possible. Yet from somewhere she gathered the courage to go on. What purpose, she asked herself, was there in lying in bed feeling sorry for herself? She was alive, and Mountain View, with its sweeping vistas of sea and mountains, was seductively beautiful. The air shimmered with the fragrance of flowers, and even the ever-present odor of sugar seemed energetic, full of promise.

Beau, however, did not seem to share her hope. Apparently despondent over the loss of his "heir," he had retreated to his quarters again in the pattern that Celia now knew so well—the increased agitation, the withdrawal, the long days when he refused to see anyone but Chang Liu.

She sent repeated messages to her husband, asking him if he were all right, if he needed anything, if he would please appear at the dinner table with the rest of them. "Leave me be," came back one scribbled message, its handwriting nearly illegible.

A week later a visiting planter brought news of Roman. He had, indeed, sent Kinau away from him. His former mistress was now working at the Seamen's Hospital. Their visitor said, too, that Roman had made inquiries at a steamship company about passage to Europe.

Vienna. Celia's heart shrank. Roman had talked of wanting

to study there under a famous physician. Europe seemed a world away from blue Pacific skies and cobalt sea, and painfully Celia realized that if Roman went there, he would never come back to her. She would never see him again.

She fought the temptation to go to Lahaina and beg him to reconsider. To tell him of her love for him, plead with him not to go. During long, sleepless nights she fantasized the moment when Roman would pull her into his arms, crush his mouth down on hers, tell her he would never leave her. . . .

They'd run away together. To . . . Yes, to Kauai, perhaps, or the Kona coast of Hawaii, which was said to be heartbreakingly lovely. Or to one of the other Pacific islands, or even to San Francisco. They'd mine for gold. . . .

Then, with enormous effort, Celia wrenched herself out of the fantasy. This was real life, not a dream. She was too proud to beg. Further, she had a husband, plus other responsibilities she could not just casually abandon.

As the slow island days passed, the reins of Mountain View gradually fell into Celia's hands. Gladly she buried herself in the hard work the plantation required, finding solace in it. She went from school to mill office, trying to solve problems. Should new crushers be ordered? Should new ditches be dug to bring water from the mountains to the fields? What of the two workers who were sick with dysentery? Should Kaweo be allowed to drop out of class to work as an ox driver?

With Beau locked in his rooms, Celia seized the opportunity to fire Griggs, the Southern *luna* who had beaten Genzo. Griggs muttered angrily, but finally boarded an ox wagon for Lahaina.

"You'll fail here," were his parting words to Celia as he tossed a worn leather suitcase into the back of the cart. "A woman, running a place like this, with an owner who doesn't even bother to see what's happening with the men? *You* don't know a damn thing about sugar."

Celia drew herself up. "I am learning fast. I'm the mistress of this plantation, and I'll thank you to leave now, Mr. Griggs, before I call the servants and have you forcibly ejected."

To her relief, Griggs swung himself into the wagon and signaled the driver. The wagon rumbled off down the drive, churning up the usual reddish cloud of Maui dust. Celia watched the cloud gradually get smaller. She had told Griggs that she was mistress here—and, God help her, she was. This was the second week now that Beau had kept to his rooms, the longest period thus far that he had incarcerated himself.

"He fine, missy," Chang Liu said when Celia went to the kitchen to question the cook, who took Beau two meals a day on a tray.

"But he can't be. . . . What does he do all day, Chang?"

Chang shrugged, his dark eyes opaque. "He read. He look at paintings on wall. He sleep."

"Sleep?" She was puzzled. "But doesn't he paint, Chang?"

"No."

"But he has always painted. . . . I don't like it. I want to know what's wrong with him. Is he sick? Should I summon Dr. Burnside to come and look at him?"

She thought Chang looked alarmed. "He not sick," he insisted. "He rest now, missy. He come out soon. Then all be well, you see."

Celia left, more worried than ever, deciding that no matter what sort of notes Beau sent out, or what Chang said, she must find out for herself.

"Beau!" Repeatedly she knocked on the door of Beau's quarters, located at the end of the west wing, along a corridor hung with a collection of Beau's paintings, most of them Maui landscapes. "Beau, are you in there? I need to talk to you!"

She jiggled the knob. This was not the first time she had tried to gain entrance to Beau's rooms, only to be frustrated by the drawn bolt, the stubborn silence from the other side of the door. But this time she had come prepared. She had brought Genzo with her, equipped with a hammer and crowbar. If Beau did not open his door, she planned to break into his rooms.

"He refuses to answer, missy," the Japanese said.

She nodded. "Do you smell anything strange, Genzo?"

The mill worker sniffed the air. "I think it is flowers, perhaps. Or maybe not. Maybe it is . . ." He suddenly closed his mouth.

"Well, whatever it is, we'll soon find out, won't we?"

Celia gestured toward the tools they had brought. "I'm afraid we don't have any other choice, Genzo. We'll have to break in."

"Very well. I will start."

The Japanese was wiry from years of handling heavy equipment and cane knives, and he swung the crowbar easily. It smashed into the oak door with a crash that seemed to Celia to shatter the air. Soon the door split into jagged splinters, and Genzo reached through the aperture to release the bolt. Still there was no response from inside.

Celia waited while Genzo swung the broken door open; then she stepped inside, the Japanese following behind her.

The odor of flowers—*burned* flowers—grew stronger with every step into the darkened room. What could it be? Some kind of incense? She had never smelled anything like it, the odor thick, heavy, sweetish, strong with an aura of brackish decay.

She looked around in dismay. The scene was eerie. Beau's draperies were drawn, shielding the rooms from light and giving a cavelike effect, in which the collected paintings glimmered darkly. Beau himself lay on the bedcovers, and Chang Liu bent near him, doing something to a small oil lamp.

"Beau?" She stared at her husband in growing alarm.

He lay on the bed on his side, his left leg propped up negligently. In his hands he cradled a long silver-chased pipe on which he sucked deep breaths. A sickening sweet-decayed odor rose from the pipe smoke.

Before, Beau had been thin, his good looks drawn into fine relief. But now it was as if Beau had undergone some profound change from the wiry but vital man she had first met at Mountain View. For his loss of weight must now be more than thirty pounds, she realized in horror. His cheekbones dominated his features, creating caves and hollows of shadow from which his eyes stared out like empty holes, fixed into the distance on God knew what.

Celia's mind spun. It had been so gradual—each of Beau's disappearances had drained him a little more, removing him even further from the world. Something was terribly wrong. And she—she had been so involved in the loss of her baby, in the running of the plantation, her obsessive thoughts of Roman, that she'd let it happen.

"My God," she whispered, heartsick. "Oh, Beau . . ."

Now, for the first time, she saw in detail what Chang was doing. The cook was spearing a little ball of some sticky brown substance on the end of a long needle. Carefully he heated the ball against the flame of the oil lamp, pressing it against the glass funnel to produce an oblong shape. As soon as the paste was soft, he transferred it to the bowl of a second pipe, where it swelled and bubbled, giving off perfumed vapors.

Celia stared at the bizarre scene. Her thin, silent, staring-eyed husband attended by the plump servant. The sweet, horrible smoke. Every instinct told her that something was terribly amiss.

"Chang! What is happening here?"

Chang Liu touched his queue nervously.

"Opium, missy," Genzo muttered behind Celia. Celia jumped and turned; she had totally forgotten about the Japanese.

"*Opium?* Oh . . . oh, my God." Shocked realization flooded her. Of course. Why hadn't she realized? How could she have been so stupid? Hatteras had talked about the drug imported from China that had created many addicts in the Chinatown sector of Honolulu. Opium dens, rooms filled with couches on which men lay smoking pipes of sweet smoke. Celia had thought it only one more fascinatingly strange aspect of the islands, like the *awa* and the *okolehao* to which many Hawaiians were addicted. Now that exotic vice had penetrated into her very home. Now her husband was involved.

Her mind struggled to make sense of it. Chang. . . . The cook must be supplying Beau with the opium—he ran a small store for the workers that sold imports from China; how else could Beau get the stuff? That was why Beau allowed only Chang into his rooms. . . .

Her shock began to change to anger.

"Beau, you must stop this. . . . Beau, you're sick, you've lost pounds and pounds." She grasped her husband's shoulder and shook him, stunned to realize that the skin of his arms was soft and loose, hanging from his bones.

But Beau acted as if she were not there, as if she were of less importance than the bluebottle fly buzzing near the ceiling of the room. He drew deeply on the sweet smoke, gesturing to the servant, who hurried forward with the second pipe.

"No!" Celia flung herself forward, snatching the pipe away from Chang Liu. "Don't give it to him!"

"I must." The cook gave her a pitying look. "It no use, missy."

"What . . . what do you mean?"

"He need *chandoo*."

"Needs it? What are you talking about?"

"He must have, missy, must have it."

But before she could argue further, Celia felt a hand on her arm, pulling her away from the bed where Beau lay. "Come away now, missy, into the corridor. It is best that we talk."

"But, Genzo—"

"Chang is right, it is no use, you must come away now, and I will tell you about opium."

Blindly Celia allowed herself to be led from Beau's quarters, from the darkened rooms that smelled of burning flowers and had been turned into an opium den. Tears of horror burned her eyes. Were they for Beau, who had somehow disappeared, to be replaced by the shell of a man with unfocused, staring eyes? Or were they for herself, who was now married to such a man?

She did not know.

Summer came, bleak, hot months in keeping with Celia's mood of despair. This was a dry year that left the fields of cane limp, their blades hanging down listlessly, coated with dust and bits of lava that had been blown there by the winds. Planters talked gloomily of crop failures, of plantations that had gone bankrupt.

Celia tried not to listen to their pessimism. She coped with water ditches that were blocked up with rocks and debris and would not flow, with the hiring of a new *luna* to replace Griggs. She rose at six in the morning in order to spend as much time at the mill as she could before school. After class, again she went to the mill office, seating herself in the large leather chair once occupied by John Burnside, to struggle with accounts.

But always haunting her mind was the conversation she had had with Genzo. Opium, he had told her, was the curse of China, enslaving thousands, who inhaled the fragrant smoke, calling this act "chasing the dragon." For the sweetish smoke looked like a dragon's tail, and the dragon itself was care and hardship.

"The man who smokes *chandoo* cannot stop. He cannot turn away the drug and say that he does not need it, for that would be an untruth. He does need it. He cannot live without it now, and in fact would suffer terribly and perhaps die."

Fear convulsed her belly into a hard knot. "Oh, Genzo."

The Japanese looked troubled. "You must not stop Beau from his dragon smoke. It is too late for that."

So Chang Liu continued to visit Beau's quarters daily, bringing him meals on trays and opium. In due course the trays were returned to the kitchen, sometimes full, more often empty. Chang himself ate the food, Celia concluded. Beau certainly did not.

"Beau, oh, Beau!" She caught her husband in one of his lucid moments. His amber eyes had tiny pupils and his complexion seemed waxen and sallow. Light perspiration sheened his skin. "What are you doing to yourself, my husband? You're wasting away before our very eyes."

Beau's movements were slow, languid. "I'm happy." He shrugged.

"Are you? I wonder! You've run away from everything, haven't you? Mountain View needs someone to run it, not a man who hides in his room all day, losing himself in . . . in dragon smoke!"

Beau's smile was a travesty of what it once had been, and yet it held a mingled sadness and anger that tore at Celia's heart. "*You* run Mountain View, then. Since you seem to want to so much."

"What are you talking about? Who ever said I wanted to run your plantation for you? Oh, Beau—"

"Go away, Celia. Go to my father's office and sit in his chair. I could never fill it anyway. I could not even provide an heir."

Later, Celia wrestled with her troubled thoughts, her agony and guilt. She had, of course, made a terrible mistake in marrying Beau. Now she herself was running Mountain View far better than he had, and even in this drought, its profits had climbed. If she were to be honest with herself, she didn't need Beau now.

But he needed her.

Without Chang, without his supply of opium, he would be lost. And she was the one who kept Chang on the payroll, who, in an indirect way, subsidized her husband's addiction.

At night, fear clutched at her. How, she wondered sometimes in her deepest nights of despair, could it all have happened this way, and where was it going to end? Surely Beau could not live long, wasted away as he was.

During this time, Hatteras was Celia's confidant and cheerful companion. Hatteras was walking well now with the aid of one cane, and had again plunged into her gardening, the management of the big house, and a burgeoning correspondence with the widower in San Francisco who had replied to her advertisement.

"Oh, Aunt Hatteras, what am I going to do?" Celia burst out one morning as her aunt walked with her down the path toward school. Hatteras wore a gardening hat and gloves, and once more her complexion had begun to take on a deep Hawaiian suntan. "I'd like to get rid of Chang Liu—fire him, tell him to leave Mountain View and never darken its doors again. But how can I, when he is Beau's only source of that terrible drug? Beau will suffer horribly if he doesn't get it. Genzo told me, and Chang verified it."

She shivered, thinking of what Genzo had said. Typically, an addict grew thinner and more emaciated as he lost all interest in food, smoking as many as twelve pipes a day. If opium was withdrawn, there was a restless, tossing sleep called the "yen," violent vomiting, convulsions, and sometimes even death.

Now Hatteras frowned, bending forward to examine some hibiscus, bright red splashes of color in the clear Hawaiian morning. "Things may change. Perhaps God will be merciful."

Celia squared her shoulders, surprised at the deep bitterness she felt. "God might be merciful, aunt, but opium is not. I can't stand back and watch this happen to Beau. No matter what his weaknesses are, or what he's done, no one deserves to have this happen to him."

"Then you are going to have to do something, girl."

"But what?"

"That is up to your own judgment, but I suggest that you try to get medical help for your husband."

So that was how Celia at last found herself journeying into Lahaina to ask Roman's help.

Riding into the whaling town, dust spattered on her riding skirt, she paused in the shade of a grove of palms to brush her hair and freshen her face. Today she wore a dove-gray faille with piped trimming. Perhaps it was too warm for the climate, but its tailored seams clung to the curves of her breasts and waist. She smoothed her hands along its seams, wondering if it would attract Roman's eye.

Then swiftly she dashed away the thought. This wasn't a personal errand. She was here on behalf of Beau, to try to help him if she could.

Finally, nervously, she spurred on her mount. She rode through town, past the Seamen's Hospital where Kinau now worked, the royal *taro* patch and missionary compound, the grass dwellings of vacationing Hawaiian royalty, the rows of grog shops, brothels, and saloons that served the sailors.

When she reached Roman's surgery, she dismounted and tethered her horse. A scrawled note was tacked to the door, penned in Roman's bold, looped handwriting. "At beach" was the terse message.

Celia stared at it, swallowing as she remembered the time she had encountered Roman near Diamond Head, the wild excitement of being held in his arms. . . . Leaving her horse, she started toward Front Street.

She walked onto the coarse yellow sand, feeling it give beneath her feet. Overhead, the tropical sun blazed, creating a sensuous heat on her shoulders. She gazed outward, where whitecaps broke on an offshore reef. Brown men were balancing on long wooden boards, riding the waves with exquisite skill, their bare muscular bodies gleaming. One of the surfers drew Celia's eye. He rode his board with the stance of a king, his body larger and wider than the others', naked except for a brief *malo*.

She shaded her eyes against the bright glare. It was Roman, of course—a rakish and playful Roman she had never seen before, laughing as a large comber rolled in and he skimmed his board dangerously close to its powerful, sweeping crest. How gorgeous he was, she thought with an indrawn breath. Like some ancient Hawaiian god, lithe, rippling with bronze muscle, perfectly at home in the crashing waves, master of them.

It seemed hours that she stood there caught up in the display of skill and daring. The men sported and played, Roman always in their lead, but at last she saw him paddle his board in through the breaking surf to shore.

"Celia! It's you. I thought I saw you silhouetted against the sun, but I assured myself it was only a mirage, my imagination conjuring up beauty."

His smile teased her. Droplets of water clung to his bronzed skin, sheening the ripples of his magnificent body, almost completely bared to her gaze. As always, Celia felt a physical response to him that was utterly impossible to stop. If he were to reach out and touch her now, to pull her to him, she'd go. She'd do anything, anything at all that he asked of her.

But Roman did not ask anything of her, other than for her to accompany him to his clothing, which he had left in a pile in the shade of a palm. Quickly he pulled on pants and a loose shirt, adding a Mexican straw hat that tilted rakishly low over his forehead.

"Come on," he urged, his smile making her heart skip. "Back to my quarters, where my manservant has lunch waiting. Lobster salad. Does that appeal to you, Celia? I speared them myself."

"I was surprised to find you surfing," she said as they started through town again, Roman being greeted often by passing sailors or Hawaiians.

He nodded. "By some miracle, Lahaina seems to be quiet today—no stabbings, fires, accidents, birthings, or pestilence. A free day doesn't come along that often, and when it does, I take full advantage of it."

He seemed boyish, more carefree than she remembered, and as Celia walked with him back to his surgery, she felt a strange, hurtful pang. Was he so happy because he had finally made up his mind to leave?

Finally she dared to ask him of his plans.

Roman hesitated. "I've made arrangements for passage
Vienna, Celia. I hope to study under a pupil of Semmelwei
He is studying infection, and there is much he can teac
me."

"But . . . how long will you be there?"

Roman glanced at her sharply. "I have no idea. Perhap
years."

Years. Her mouth went dry as she fought to sound calm
"But what of your patients here? Of your responsibilities
Mountain View?"

"I'll bring back better knowledge for my Hawaiian patient
. . . *if* I return," he told her. "As for the plantation,
understand you are running it superbly, Celia. I trust you
business acumen."

"But . . ." Her eyes ached with unshed tears. "But how
will you know . . . I mean, how I'm doing at running it?
you are so far away—"

"Once a year you can send me a report on how Mountain
View is faring, and a bank draft for my share of the profits
Now, let's drop the topic, if you don't mind."

As they sat over lobster salad and Lanai pineapple, drip
ping with juice and incredibly sweet, Celia told Roma
everything. Of the night in the study, Beau's belief that h
had made love to her, had fathered her child. Then Beau'
impotence, the loss of the baby that seemed to take awa
what remained of Beau's manhood. She told him of Beau'
withdrawals to his quarters, each time for a longer period, hi
loss of weight, the smell of burning flowers in his room. Sh
concluded with the story of her breaking into Beau's rooms t
find him smoking opium.

"He is addicted to it, Roman," she said miserably. "It i
wrecking him. He isn't even the same person any more—it'
frightening to see."

Roman's expression had turned grim. "Celia, if you have
come to me for hope, I'm not sure I can give you any. Ther
is an old Cantonese man here in Lahaina who once ran one o
the seamen's brothels. Now he lies in an upstairs room, a
emaciated skeleton of a man, lost in opium dreams. And
misspoke myself when I referred to him as an old man. He
only looks ancient. He is actually less than thirty years old."

Celia shivered violently. "Thirty!"

"Worst of all, Celia, the poor soul won't live very long. He'll waste away, getting thinner and thinner, and finally death will come—from actual malnutrition or just from an overdose someday. It's pitiful."

"I'm frightened, Roman." Celia tried to warm herself with her hands. "Beau is . . . he doesn't deserve such a fate. No human being does."

Roman hesitated. "The Chinese say there is one cure for addiction, but it is terribly risky, so dangerous that only the strong in body and will can possibly survive it."

Celia grasped at the straw of hope. "But some do survive?"

"Yes. Indeed, some do. But the cost, Celia, is—"

"I don't care about the cost! Beau is dying, Roman, don't you understand that? Right before my eyes! You have to help him, before it's too late."

Roman put down his lobster fork and gazed deeply into Celia's eyes, scrutinizing her minutely. His eyes were as pale as water, as cold. "Celia. Tell me, I want only the truth from you. Wouldn't it be better for you if Beau did die?"

"What?"

"Be realistic. If he died, you would inherit his holdings and investments. They are not worth as much as his share of Mountain View, of course, but still, they amount to quite a nice nest egg. Enough to keep you comfortably for life."

She felt the hot, angry blood pound to her face. "Do you mean that I should just let Beau *die* . . . so I can inherit his money? Cold-bloodedly, callously . . . I'm not a fortune hunter, Roman Burnside, and I deeply resent your insult! I came here in good faith to ask you to help my husband."

Furiously she shoved back her chair, preparing to leave. It had been foolish to come here! Roman was arrogant and impossible, insulting her for her very efforts.

But then, even as she turned and started toward the door, something stopped her. Roman *had* said there was a cure. She forced herself to turn back. "Tell me. I want to know what will help my husband."

"Ah? Do you?" His laugh was bitter, rich, mocking.

"Yes, damn you!" She whirled on him, longing to smack his handsome sun-bronzed face. But before she could do so, he scooped both of her hands into his own, trapping her.

"And damn you, Celia, for the treacherously beautiful

woman you are—coming to me like this, when you know I've wanted to see you . . . have thought about you constantly . . .''

She was stunned to feel his mouth crush down on hers.

"No . . .'' Weakly she struggled to pull away. His kisses forced open her lips, plundering her, robbing her of all rational thought. The feel of him, the strength, the hard maleness of him—she thought she would faint with the sheer sensuous shock of contact with him.

They staggered away from the table to a nearby couch, where, after barring the door, Roman tore feverishly at her riding habit, ripping its seams in his haste to have her unclothed.

"Oh, God, my darling . . .''

"Roman!''

This was wild, crazy, totally unplanned. Yet she could not stop . . . neither of them could. They plunged together, fierce in their desire for each other. What they did was forbidden. A thin, suffering Beau waited for her back at Mountain View, and still Celia could not stop this thing she did with Roman, this wild, terrible love.

They embraced, skin against naked skin. They tore at each other, Celia's desire as fervent as Roman's own, as incendiary. She explored his body with growing passion, kissing the sweet muscles of his chest and belly and groin, tasting him, the hard throbbing swell of his maleness.

When Roman at last pulled her to him, she was moistly ready, arching her hips, her legs spread wide to receive him. He groaned aloud as he entered her, and she clung to him, totally giving herself to him.

He moved within her with sure strokes, slowly and deeply, penetrating deep inside her to a core of pleasure she'd never known, never imagined before. He rode her hard, and she gave herself up to his mastery, meeting it with her own femininity.

They were joined, rocking in love, they were one, one. . . .

The pleasure built slowly, with trembling intensity, until it passed pleasure and became a wild, flowing sweetness. Celia arched and convulsed with the wonderful violence of her orgasm and felt Roman shudder within her, heard his hoarse cry of fulfillment.

Later they lay wrapped in each other's arms. The scent of

their lovemaking rose around them like the most powerful of aphrodisiacs. Roman's satiny skin was sheened with a light, salty coating of perspiration. Celia stroked him, savoring the texture of his skin, the hard structure of muscles beneath, enjoying the feel of him. How male he was, to her femaleness.

She stirred, stretching, feeling as lazy and satisfied as a cat. She wanted to lie here forever in Roman's arms, she wanted to grow old with him, to curl naked against him every single night for the rest of her life.

Then a wave of sadness overtook her. For that was impossible.

There was still Beau. For a brief, joyous interlude, Celia had managed to forget that she was married. Now she remembered, and it was as if a leaden cloud settled over them, as gray as the rain that hung over the mountains.

"Roman . . ." she whispered. "Roman, what is this cure you spoke of? Does it really exist?"

Roman sat up, pulling a light quilt over them both. "It does. It is simply this, Celia—total withdrawal from opium. Many do not survive such harsh treatment, however, and he will be in great—"

But Celia, her mood brought low by the reminder of her obligations, interrupted him. "But some do survive."

"Yes. Some."

"Then you must help Beau, of course! Come to Mountain View, see him, start us on the cure."

Roman frowned. "It isn't that easy. Beau will be risking his life. And he won't want to be helped. Not once the treatment begins. He'll fight us, rage, scream, curse his keepers. He'll do anything, anything to have his opium back again."

"I'll get his permission somehow," Celia assured Roman. "If you'll only help, I'll manage everything else."

"Pray God you can. Pray long and hard, Celia, for we'll be taking much into our hands, and the responsibility may prove far more painful than we wish."

22

The stench of stale opium smoke pervaded Beau's rooms, lending them the sweetish musty odor of rotting flowers. On the walls, the half-naked odalisques looked down, their eyes soft and mocking.

"Beau?" Celia wrinkled her nose as she entered Beau's quarters. Her husband was lying on the bedcovers, one of the silver-chased opium pipes on the table beside him. As always, the sight of him chilled her. This was a far different Beau from the slim, arrogant young man she had first met on coming to Mountain View.

This Beau had a sallow face, the cheekbones sharply prominent. His eyes were dark, staring pools. He had secluded himself in these stale rooms for more than a month now, sleeping, nodding away his time. Growing thinner and thinner, withdrawing further each day from the world.

"What do you want, Celia?" he asked her fretfully.

"I want to talk to you."

"Then talk. But if it's about Mountain View . . . if you're going to nag at me about my not going to the mill office, then I won't listen."

She felt a surge of fury. "You're going to listen, Beau, you have to! Don't you realize what you've become? You're a . . . a vegetable! Nothing matters to you anymore, not your painting, not your own wife, not even Mountain View. It's only these dreadful pipes!" She snatched up the silver pipe with its exotic Oriental engraving and hurled it to the floor. It rolled across the Aubusson rug and came to a stop against a chair leg.

"Don't," Beau said. "Don't do that."

"What *should* I do, then?" She advanced on him. "Praise you? How many pipes do you smoke a day? Is it ten, twelve, fifteen? Do you want me to polish them up for you, dismiss Chang Liu and fill them myself? Well, I won't. And I don't believe that your father would have allowed you to do this to yourself, either. You've turned into a wreck! You're *dying*, Beau!"

Beau's mouth had tightened, his sallow skin turning chalky. Celia pressed her advantage. "What kind of coward are you? Are you afraid that you can't measure up to him? Is that what's really eating at you, Beau—is that why you smoke opium, to try to forget that you're less of a man than *he* was?"

With each word, Beau seemed to go more rigid. "It isn't like that," he muttered. "Celia . . . pick up that pipe off the floor, and call Chang Liu. I want him to prepare it for me."

"No."

"Celia . . ." he whined.

"I said *no*. I won't pick up your pipe and I won't call your servant. Your *father* never would have allowed himself to sink into this terrible state. *He* would not have . . ."

As she spoke, Beau twisted uncomfortably, and Celia felt a spasm of pity for him. It was cruel for her to say these things; the truth could be lacerating. Yet what other choice did she have? Beau could not be allowed to go on like this, to destroy himself. No matter that she didn't love him, he was a human being. She had to do what she could for him.

"Stop, Celia," he begged. "Please, you know that I . . . that my father—"

"Your father would laugh to see you like this," she taunted, wondering if it were true. "He'd say you were a coward, not worthy to be master of Mountain View, a poor weakling who cannot stop smoking opium."

Something flared behind Beau's eyes, intense, smoky.

"You can stop, Beau," she said earnestly. "I know you can. It will be difficult, harder than you could ever have imagined or dreamed, but it is possible."

"Do you really think I could?"

Startled, she looked at him, struck by the pathetic pleading in his voice. Had he no strength of his own? Pity stirred in her. "Yes, Beau. I think you can. But I think you should know it could be very dangerous. Only the strong can survive a cure."

She moistened her lips, dreading what she must say next. "But if you don't try to help yourself, Beau, you will die anyway. Roman has sworn to me that this is so. You'll waste away and eventually starve to death. Or you'll take an overdose of opium . . ."

"I see." Beau gave a brief grin, and for a moment he seemed the old Beau, lucid, sardonic, bitter. "I do want to live, Celia. I hate myself as I am."

"Oh, Beau. Beau!" Impulsively she threw herself into his arms, pulling him to her, cradling his painfully thin body. "Do it. Please do it, please stop the opium. For me. For your father. For all of us."

He hesitated, clinging to her, his hands clutching at her arms. For several minutes they held each other, and Celia felt her husband drawing from her strength. She the giver, he the one in need. Oddly, it was the closest they had ever been in their months of marriage.

Then she pulled away, knowing that she had to seize this chance, for at any time Beau could sink back into the forgetfulness of the "dragon smoke."

"Beau, will you do it?"

"I . . . Celia . . . I don't know if I can."

"I'll help you to be strong," she promised. "Roman and I are going to help you."

It seemed forever before Beau finally said, "Very well, then. I'll try."

Had she seen a flash of anger and fear in his eyes at the mention of Roman's name? But if she had, it was quickly gone, and Celia busied herself adjusting the covers of her husband's bed, feeling only a vast relief that he had consented to be helped.

"What?" An hour later, she stared at Roman, unable to believe what she was hearing. "Do you mean that we must *tie* him to his bed?"

"Yes." Roman looked unhappy. "I'm afraid so."

"But that's barbaric and cruel! I can't imagine that you

would really suggest such a terrible thing, trussing Beau up like a lunatic.''

"That's exactly what he's going to be, Celia. A lunatic. You couldn't have used a better word. Do you think it's going to be easy to give up opium? There will be vomiting, violent convulsions, perhaps even respiratory failure. He'll fight, he'll struggle and curse and abuse us. He may even wish to die. Once treatment starts, he'll do literally anything to get his drug back. I told you, only the strong can survive such profound physical torture.''

She fought her dismay. "But Beau has no idea——"

"Then we must tell him the truth.''

"But if we do, then he'll refuse treatment. Anyone would!'' Angry tears filled her eyes. "I can't believe there isn't some medicine you could give him, something to ease him from this dependence . . .''

Roman threw up his hands angrily. "There *is* no medicine. Not for this, and perhaps there never will be. Don't you think that the Chinese have tried? All I can do is try to treat his symptoms as they occur.'' He rose from his chair on the veranda, where they had been sitting over coffee. "I'm going to talk to him, Celia.''

Celia waited tensely for Roman to return, her mind in turmoil. Half an hour later he was back, his face a grim mask.

"Well?''

"He has consented. But it is only because you shamed him into it, Celia. He is afraid—desperately so.''

Celia nodded. "Maybe when he is cured and is himself again, he'll be grateful to you for helping him.''

"Perhaps. If a physician had to live on gratitude, though, he'd starve to death. Meanwhile, there are preparations we must make. I want six strong male servants at my disposal, so I can have people with him around the clock. There must be clean linens and bedding . . .''

"I'll see that you get everything you need,'' Celia said. "Aunt Hatteras will help, too. Everything at Mountain View is at your disposal if you need it.''

"Celia.'' He touched her arm. "Are you sure—*very* sure—that you want to do this?''

"I want to save my husband,'' she told him steadily.

* * *

Even though Celia had thought she was prepared for Beau's withdrawal from opium, the reality was far worse than anything she could have imagined. It began calmly enough. On Roman's orders, Celia dismissed Chang Liu, paying the cook several months' severance pay. He and his family were never to return to Mountain View, she warned the Chinese. If she ever learned that he had given Beau more opium, she would see that he was sent back to China. She did not know how she could carry out this threat, but she put determination into her expression, and was relieved when the cook finally departed for Lahaina, his belongings and his family crammed into an ox cart.

At first Beau did not need restraints. He sat in his rooms with Roman and Maka, the burliest of the Hawaiian servants, who had already been warned against accepting bribes. To prevent Beau's using the servants for his own ends, Roman himself planned to stay in Beau's rooms twenty-four hours a day.

Celia sat with them too, trying to distract her husband with jokes and conversation. However, Beau was surly and spent the time immersed in scowling silence.

"I want my pipe," he complained after only a few hours of withdrawal. "I need it, Celia."

Roman had warned her about this.

"I'm sorry, but you can't have it," she said, feeling a pang.

"I want it. My eyes are already beginning to tear, Celia. See? See how I have to wipe them?"

Celia saw. Beau's nose had begun to run, and he was beginning to be plagued by constant yawning and restlessness, his skin coated with clammy perspiration. He stirred agitatedly, as if he could not get comfortable.

Roman had brought a deck of cards and a cribbage board, and now he pulled up a table and began shuffling the deck and dealing out cards. "Come, Beau. I'll challenge you."

"No, I don't wish to."

Roman's eyes met Beau's with steely intensity. "Are you afraid you can't beat me?"

Beau scowled, leaning over to take the cards. "I'll play

with you, Roman—damn you. But later . . . later, when I am feeling better, things will be different. Then I may not be so polite."

Slowly the hours passed. Celia, Roman, Tina, and Hatteras sat with Beau, always accompanied by a heavyset Hawaiian servant or mill worker. The games of cribbage stretched into boredom. Tina read aloud to Beau from *David Copperfield*, struggling over the hard words. When she grew hoarse, Hatteras took over, then Celia.

On into the next day they read, to a Beau with dilated pupils and sallow, perspiring skin, a Beau who tossed and turned, dropping in and out of uneasy sleep.

He awoke from one of these sleeps paler than before. Hatteras and Tina had gone for a walk, but Celia and Roman remained, along with Maka, the servant. Beau yawned so violently that he groaned with pain.

Roman, who had been pacing the floor, looked at his patient sharply. "Is it getting difficult?"

"Difficult! Yes, goddammit . . ." And Beau launched into a string of gutter epithets, in which he cursed Roman, the servants, Celia, even his father, for his physical misery. Celia sat rigidly, appalled by the violence in his outburst.

"I'm sorry you're suffering, Beau," Roman began, "but I warned you—this is only the beginning. It's going to require all the fortitude you have to survive this."

"I want to stop," Beau moaned. "Now. Please. Bring me my pipe."

"That's not possible. Chang has been dismissed, and you have no source here at Mountain View any longer. He and his family have left for Lahaina, and I assume they'll take passage for Honolulu."

Beau let out a frightening roar of anger.

Roman's eyes met those of Maka, and both men nodded. Then quickly Roman came to Celia and took her arm, pulling her up from her chair. "It's time you left these rooms."

"But—"

"I don't want you here. Beau is angry and struggling, and it's going to get worse. Keep Hatteras and Tina away, too."

As Beau's shouts rose, terrifying in their fury, Celia had to raise her voice to be heard above the din. "But I'll want to know how he is."

"I'll send out reports on his progress. But stay away, Celia. *I don't want you here.*"

So Celia had no choice but to leave. To ease her distress, she walked out to the garden, where she found Hatteras and Tina pulling the hardy weeds that had sprouted between the bougainvillea that Hatteras had recently transplanted.

Celia threw herself into the work, welcoming the heat of the sun on her face, the gritty feel of the dirt. She jerked up a weed with unnecessary violence, wondering what was going on in that room now. She felt sure that Roman had tied Beau to the bed, as he had warned her he would have to do. She shuddered at the thought.

When Tina dropped her spade to chase across the lawn after Hili, Celia voiced her fears to her aunt.

Hatteras sighed, looking troubled. "It is certainly distressing, Celia, to have to do this to another human being. I've heard stories . . ." She pushed back the rim of her gardening hat, revealing salt-and-pepper hair. "Withdrawal, Celia, is hideous. There is an odd phenomenon that happens . . ." She paused, as if reluctant to speak further.

"What is it?" Celia begged.

"It is something that happens to the body. Male addicts go into . . . How can I say this delicately? I don't think I can. . . . Involuntary ejaculations."

"What?" Celia nearly dropped her gardening spade. She felt a band of nausea tighten across her throat. Opium withdrawal was so violent that a man's body forced him to climax involuntarily. . . .

Somehow that fact brought home Beau's suffering to her as nothing else could.

I do want to live, Beau had said. *I hate myself as I am.* It was only the memory of these words that kept Celia going through the next day, full of a horror that she could not have imagined. Beau's screams filled the entire house, so that the maidservants refused to work, fleeing to the village in panic at the terrible cries, insisting that a *moo,* or lizard god, had cursed Mountain View.

Even the dog, Hili, was uneasy, whining and pacing.

Celia insisted that Tina go to stay in the workers' quarters with Aiko and her family, and she urged that Hatteras take

temporary quarters in the home of McRory, the sugar boiler.
But her aunt refused to go.

"Do you think that I would leave you alone with this
misery, Celia? I might be an old woman, but I am far from
being fragile, and someone is going to have to do the cooking,
since Chang is gone and the maids have deserted us."

"Oh, aunt . . ." Celia hugged Hatteras, grateful for her
courage. "I don't know what I'd ever do without you."

"You would manage excellently, Celia. Perhaps you don't
realize it, but you have changed from the willful young girl
who first came to me in Honolulu. You're a woman now,
Celia. A strong, beautiful, and compassionate one."

That night Celia could not sleep. Finally she got out of bed
and pulled on a dressing gown. Not bothering with slippers,
she padded barefoot down the corridor that led to her husband's
rooms. Even in the hall, she could hear Beau's hoarse voice
shouting out his rage and pain. She had not believed he could
know such vile words, such terrifying epithets.

"Let me die," he begged. "For God's sake!"

Horrified, Celia clapped her hands over her mouth and
fled, doubt cutting her. Were they doing the right thing? It
was cruel to let Beau suffer this way! But later she forced
herself to creep back again, and this time Beau was quiet.

Roman himself appeared at the door. "He is sleeping,
thank God." He looked weary, and deep lines cut from his
nose to his mouth. It was plain that for him, too, this was an
ordeal.

Celia swallowed back the thick lump that clogged her
throat. "I heard his screams. They were terrible. His
curses . . ."

"I thought I told you not to come near this place."

"But I had to see if he was all right."

"He is not all right. He is in the abyss, Celia. Do you
know what that is like? Can you even imagine it? No wonder
he curses. What else is there for him to do?"

As if to bear this out, a voice rose again in the room behind
him, hoarse, unrecognizable as Beau's. "You are filth . . .
vile filth! You are vermin, Roman, you and that slut I'm
married to. I'm going to punish you both. Do you *hear* me?
I'll make you pay!"

Celia shuddered, shrinking away instinctively from the hatred in Beau's cry. It was as if he had been transformed into some demon, some possessed creature, barely human, shrieking out its hatred.

"Roman . . . this is awful. Awful! Isn't there *anything* you can do to ease his suffering?"

Roman laughed harshly. "Yes, give him opium. If I were to do that, you'd see an incredible transformation. It would amaze you."

The screams from Beau's room had subsided again into incoherent groans, sounding exactly like a medieval torture chamber, Celia told herself, feeling sick. She was near tears. "But is there nothing else?"

"No. There isn't." Roman looked at her. "I told you it wouldn't be easy."

She fought her guilt and dismay. She had never dreamed it would be like this, so awful, awful. How could she be responsible for causing another person to suffer so?

She moistened her lips. "Send to Lahaina, Roman. Tell Chang Liu to come back here and to bring some opium with him. This is too terrible for Beau to undergo—he's not strong enough."

"On the contrary," Roman said, his jaw knotting. "He is very strong, far stronger than I had thought. He is tolerating the shock amazingly well. I think it is his anger that is helping him to survive this."

Celia stared incredulously. "Do you mean . . . he may *survive?* He may get well?"

"He has a chance."

Celia wavered. She thought of Beau's sarcastic wit, his paintings that were filled with a dark genius. His hurt at being shunted aside by his father, the way he had clung to her, trusting in her strength. *I don't know if I can,* he had whispered to her. *I'll help you to be strong,* she had recklessly promised.

She squared her shoulders, praying that she was doing the right thing. From somewhere she summoned the courage to speak, knowing that this was the hardest thing she had ever done. "If you think he can do it, then we must go on. Continue the treatment," she told Roman.

"Are you sure?" His eyes bored into hers.

"Yes. We have to save him, Roman, if we can."

Roman expelled a deep breath, touching Celia's hand briefly. The look that he gave her was filled with a deep respect.

Two more days passed, inching by in slow, torturous hours. The servants came and went, whispering of terrible things—of Beau straining at the cords that bound him to the bed, of violent convulsions, of screams, tears. At one point, Maka related, Beau actually stopped breathing, and Roman had to pummel his chest and breathe into his mouth, forcing him back to life again. Four of the six original servants, happy-go-lucky Hawaiians, caved in under the strain and refused to go back into Beau's rooms. Only Maka and Genzo remained with Roman, the three men spelling each other.

Celia taught school as usual, and afterward buried herself in the mill office, struggling with the books and with business correspondence. She was trying to find a new strain of cane more resistant to disease. She worked doggedly until midnight, until her head swam with effort and her entire body shook from exhaustion.

On her way home from the mill, she visited the little stone church where John had been buried and where she and Beau had been married. Was their wedding only a few months ago? She sank down on one of the benches, sitting in darkness lighted by a silver ingot of moonlight, and said a prayer for her husband.

"Dear God," Celia prayed. "Please, in your mercy, ease Beau's sufferings and free him of his addiction. Make him well again, make him not hate me."

She sat for a long time staring at the long shadows the moonlight created on the wooden planking of the church floor before she finally rose and went to her bedroom to try to sleep.

Hatteras saw to it that Roman and the two servants were taken their meals on trays, reporting to Celia that Roman was eating little, and looked worn and exhausted. "He is giving everything he's got to a man who hates him for it," she mused the next evening as she and Celia picked at salads on the veranda, neither of them tasting what they chewed. "I don't see a good end to this, Celia. Even if Beau does survive."

Celia shook herself uneasily. She didn't want to listen to this sort of talk. She had spent two hours praying in the little church last night. Beau's ordeal had affected all of them, and all she wanted was for it to be over.

"But of course," she said, "as soon as Beau is feeling normal again, he'll be grateful to Roman for saving him. Anyone would."

"We must hope so, Celia."

Time dragged on. Two days, four. The entire plantation waited to see what would happen to Beau.

Then one day Celia walked into the school. Stopping, as usual, to ring the big bell, she summoned her pupils. The clear peals rang out, filling the air with the only cheerful noise that Mountain View had heard in days.

Suddenly, as she turned to go into the school, she heard a step on the path. Genzo hurried toward her, a broad grin splitting his face. "Master Burnside is sleeping!"

"He is . . . what?" Celia stared at the Japanese.

"He slept a long time last night, a good sleep, and I believe that he has scared away the dragon for good."

Celia's heart began to pound thickly. Could a miracle have happened? Could Beau be getting *well*? Genzo departed down the path toward the workers' quarters, and Celia could barely restrain herself. Her pupils had begun to stream into the school, among them Tina, her flaming red hair plaited by Aiko's mother into a duplication of the tiny Japanese girl's neat black braids.

Celia rushed toward Tina, feeling as if an enormous burden had been lifted from her. She grabbed the little girl up and whirled her around joyfully. "Beau is better! He's going to get well! Isn't that wonderful news?"

Tina crowed. "Will he be out of his rooms soon? Will we have a school holiday?"

"Yes, to both. We'll take our holiday today." Celia said it extravagantly, knowing that she could be celebrating too soon. But her relief was sweeping her on glad wings. Beau was going to be all right. His addiction was gone, he'd be normal again, her prayers had been answered.

When the children had gone whooping and shouting down the hillside, Celia walked back to the plantation house. As soon as she opened the front door, she could sense the difference in the atmosphere. Warm, yeasty smells of baking came from the kitchen. Giggles pealed from the upper floor, where apparently Leinani and some of the other servant girls were already back at work.

Celia rushed up the stairs to Beau's rooms. Roman pulled open the door and stepped into the corridor to greet her. She had never seen him look so tired, yet there was triumph on his face, a weary joy.

"I think we've saved him. He's sleeping now, but it's a normal sleep. A normal one!"

They looked at each other, and then, as naturally as breathing, Roman held out his arms to her and Celia went into them. They did a mad, whirling little dance in the corridor, while tears rolled down Celia's cheeks and Roman hugged her until her bones hurt.

"We did it, we did it!" he kept saying.

"No . . . you did it. You saved him."

"It was you, Celia. Your courage. I confess there were times when I wanted to quit."

"But I wanted to quit, too. . . ."

They hugged and laughed, knowing that they had, together, won a grueling battle.

A few moments later, when they went into the bedroom, Celia saw Beau lying pale and weak beneath a light coverlet. His face looked drawn, the cheekbones prominent, his eye sockets forming dark hollows. Celia felt her heart lurch with pity as she reached out to take her husband's hand.

"Beau," she whispered. "Thank God you're going to be all right. I'm so happy."

"Are you, Celia?" The whisper was weak, but it was Beau's again, bitter, sardonic. "You nearly killed me, you know."

"But you're well now, you're going to be fine." She squeezed his hand.

Beau's eyes met hers, clearer, more golden than ever, as if his experience had purified him. "Yes. I will. And I'll remember those who saved me."

23

A south wind swirled among the *koas*, lifting their branches and whipping them against each other. Roman stood by his horse, the brisk wind ruffling his hair and causing him to narrow his eyes against its push. Dark clouds were massed over the West Maui Mountains, and a gray-striped area indicated that rain was falling somewhere over the serrated gorges and peaks. Celia wondered if Roman would have to ride through it on his way back to Lahaina.

"Let me know how Beau does," Roman said.

"I will," Celia promised, pressing her hands tightly together. She didn't want him to go, dreaded the thought. She hated this constant series of partings, each one tearing at her heart.

But there was no excuse for Roman to stay longer. Beau was recovered now. Although still weak, he was beginning to leave his room for short walks, and even talked of resuming his painting again. Over and over he had told Roman how grateful he was to him for saving his life.

"You are my benefactor," Beau insisted. "You and Celia, of course. Never think that I'm not aware of it. I think of it constantly. I'll never be able to repay you for what you've done."

"Then you don't resent what we did?" Celia dared to ask.

Beau had looked at her, a thin but still handsome man whose features showed the effects of the torment he had survived. "Resent? Don't think such a word, Celia. No, don't think it."

Now Roman gave her last-minute instructions on Beau's care. "You must be patient with him," he told her. "He seems agitated. Keep Maka nearby, and perhaps Genzo, just in case."

Celia frowned. "But Beau has been so docile and grateful. I'm sure there's nothing to be concerned about." She didn't want to talk of such things now. She wanted to grab on to every little minute that she could see Roman, be near him.

She wanted to beg him never to leave her. But of course this was impossible.

Roman shifted uneasily. "I may not see you again," he said abruptly.

She stifled a cry.

His eyes held hers. "I told you I was going to Vienna. Well, I still am. I've changed my departure time, and now I leave in two weeks."

Two weeks. She struggled to say something, feeling numb. She'd known, of course, that Roman would go back to Lahaina—it was there his practice was. But she'd thought . . . Oh, she'd assumed . . .

Roman swung onto his horse. He looked down at her, tall, wide-shouldered, unbearably handsome. His eyes searched her face, as if imprinting every one of her features on his mind forever. This was good-bye; he really was going. Celia thought her heart would burst.

Feelings hung between them, words that could not be spoken, for her husband stood between them, the man whose life both of them had saved.

"Celia . . ." Roman began hoarsely.

But she could not listen. She turned, unable to bear it, and walked away from him, slowly toward the house.

Celia stumbled toward the house, breathing shallowly, feeling as if her emotions had been flayed raw. She had chosen to cure Beau, and in so doing, she had chosen to live with him, to be married to him.

Well, wasn't it true? Now she had to live with her choice.

Her heart aching, she paused at one of the stone vases that Hatteras had filled with flowers, and stood looking at the plantation house, the gracious Georgian lines, the vines and greenery that reached up to embrace the house, making it one with the tropical landscape. The house had survived transplantation from Connecticut, quarrels, rivalry, dissension, and death. Some of those who had lived here hated it, while others had let Mountain View into their minds and hearts, becoming one with it. But the house had endured it all. As she, too, could endure.

Gradually Celia's breathing returned to normal, the painful knot in her throat seemed to dissipate. She would get along, she decided grimly, without Roman. She'd make a good life here. She would make it up to Beau for the suffering she had caused him. At least she could do that much.

A week passed, as Celia struggled to carry out her resolve. Beau grew stronger each day, taking long walks along the hillsides with his paint box and canvas, much as he had done when she first came to Mountain View. Yet his paintings seemed harsher, their outlines taking on new jagged lines that made Celia uneasy.

"Why do you paint so . . . so angrily?" she asked him one day as he brought in a canvas depicting the grove of *koas*, their trunks drawn in angular, hard brush strokes that made the trees seem like clutching claws. A cloud in the upper left of the canvas seemed to hold a brooding storm.

"Do I?" He gazed at her, his mouth curved in a slight smile.

"Yes, you do." She pointed to the painting. "Look at the way you've slashed on the paint. Something about it makes me shiver."

Beau ran a hand through his mop of curling hair. "Perhaps I wanted you to shiver when you looked at that picture. Anyway, you're just criticizing."

"No, I'm not. I just want to understand you, Beau."

"There's nothing to understand," he told her shortly, turning on his heel to walk away.

The days continued to slip past. Since Beau made no effort to go to the mill office, Celia continued to manage the plantation. If Beau didn't like running Mountain View, she did. She was actually beginning to enjoy the challenge of juggling books, planning crops, supervising workers, investing some of the mill profits in shipping and other commercial ventures as the other planters did. She buried herself in the hard work of it. Work was an anesthetic. When she was thinking about sugarcane, there was no time to think about Roman. . . .

It was beginning to be the season of the *kona* storms, and every day Mountain View, because of its exposed position on the flanks of the mountain, was buffeted by high south winds. They had had to remove the *lauhala* matting from the verandas of the house, for the wind prodded at it mercilessly, nearly blowing it away. Celia set workers to repairing the loose trim on the mill office and outbuildings, battening everything down tightly.

One day the Cousineaus dropped in unexpectedly, Ruark Cousineau explaining that he wished to consult with Beau about a financial matter. They would stay overnight and return to Hana in the morning.

Celia, who had spotted their horses from the window of the mill office and had gone to greet them, stared at the planter in surprise. "But Beau has gone off somewhere with his paints."

Ruark Cousineau frowned. "I thought Beau worked in the mill office. Has he left it to you, then?" His tone implied that Celia was a poor second choice.

"I have been running the office," Celia admitted. "We've been making a very good profit, too," she added proudly.

That night she dressed carefully for dinner, putting on one of her trousseau gowns, a sky-blue silk with a square polonaise trimmed with rows of black velvet ribbon. As she combed her hair into fashionable loops and puffs and debated whether to trim it with a strand of pearls or more velvet ribbon, she thought about Beau. Would her husband be cordial to their unexpected guests?

As he recovered his strength, Beau had grown increasingly moody. He argued with Tina, snapped at Hatteras, and was sarcastic to Celia. To her relief, he had not yet tried to assert the sexual part of their marriage, to remedy the issue of "manhood" that he had hinted at after she had lost her child. It was a fact for which she could not help being grateful. To have to deal with an impotent husband? No, she knew she couldn't possibly make love to Beau when Roman was on her mind and in her heart.

But did Beau sense this? Did he guess at her feelings for the man who had saved his life? In his darkest hours, did he suspect what had really happened that night on the library couch? Sometimes, uneasily, she wondered.

Melanie Cousineau speared delicately at a piece of roast chicken prepared by Jen Ling, the new Cantonese cook that Hatteras had gotten from Honolulu. The young planter's wife wore pink silk and chattered nonstop, mostly about servant problems and the boredom of living near Hana, where nothing ever happened. "And when are you coming Hana-side to visit us? You said you'd visit, but you never have."

"Oh, there has been too much to do here," Celia explained quickly. "Since Beau's illness." They had decided to say that Beau had had a recurrence of tropical malaria, hoping to silence island gossip.

"Much to do! Oh, yes, Celia wears the pants in the family these days. And she doesn't want to relinquish them long enough to pay a call to the far end of the island," Beau remarked sharply.

Celia flushed, ashamed that the Cousineaus should see the way she and Beau snapped at each other these days. "I'd love to pay a visit, of course, just as soon as plantation business will permit it."

"And I say you can visit now." Beau spit the words out, his lips twisting over them. "Do you think that Mountain View can't get along without you, Celia? Do you think that your little mill office is going to curl up and blow away in the first *kona* wind if you aren't there to nail it down?"

Melanie attempted to make peace. "I'm sure we'd love to see both of you, whenever you can travel. And speaking of travel, did I tell you about the new horse I bought? She is a chestnut mare, a full-blooded Arabian. Oh, she's beautiful. Quite unlike the spavined specimens most of the Hawaiians ride. Can you believe the way they treat their horses?"

Conversation moved to safer areas while Beau was forced to sit fuming.

Later that night, when the Cousineaus had gone to their room and Beau and Celia were in the bedroom they again shared, Beau paced the floor restlessly. Outside, the wind banged the shutters.

"Plantation business!" Beau mocked. "You think you're indispensable, don't you? You, the little schoolteacher who came here to wed my father and ended up marrying me instead! Oh, you don't know a damn thing about sugar.''

Celia paused in the act of unfastening the long row of tiny mother-of-pearl buttons on her dress. "I might not have known anything about sugar when I got here, but I certainly do now. I like sugar, Beau, and I like running Mountain View. I only wish that you felt the same way.''

Beau scowled, flinging himself down on the bed so violently that the bedposts shook under his weight. "I hate Mountain View, Celia. Oh, I like *owning* it well enough, that is a satisfaction to me, to have what my father had. But I hate being cooped up in that little office. I always did.''

"What *do* you want, then, Beau?''

For long moments her husband stared at her, his amber eyes darkened through some effect of the lamplight, until he seemed like someone she barely knew. "I want . . . peace,'' he told her at last.

"Peace! Why, Beau . . .'' She gazed at him, stunned that he would say such a thing, that this man who painted such jagged and aggressive paintings, who depicted the grove of *koas* as grasping claws, could want peace and tranquillity.

"Or maybe it's nothingness I want, Celia,'' Beau went on after a moment, scowling. "Yes, maybe that's it. Emptiness, soft, beautiful dreams of blankness.''

Opium dreams, Celia thought suddenly. That was what Beau was really talking about. "Beau. Don't you think that perhaps you should consult Roman again? I believe he has not yet left for Vienna, and there might be a medication he could give that would . . .''

At the mention of Roman's name, Beau paled. A flare of hatred glowed for a second in his eyes; or was that only Celia's imagination? She watched as he rose from the bed and started toward the door. "There is no medication that can help me, Celia. As for Roman . . .'' Beau's pause seemed oddly evil.

"Yes?''

"He can go to hell, Celia. And you too. Yes, I would like to see that, both of you wading about in a river of fire while demons pitchforked at you, stabbing you both through to the guts!''

The words were so vicious that Celia recoiled in shock.

But before she could respond, Beau had already flung the door open, banging it viciously. Leaving the room, he strode off down the corridor toward his old quarters.

Celia turned off the lamp and got into bed, but she could not sleep. She lay staring at the ceiling. Beau hated her and Roman for the torture of withdrawal they had put him through. She could no longer deny this to herself. He had talked of hell, and hadn't he gone through hell himself, had not he been pushed to the limits of human endurance?

Beau refused to run Mountain View, yet resented her because she did run it, because she had usurped his place.

Celia tossed and turned, her thoughts tormenting her. Now Beau said he wanted peace. Peace. What else could he mean but opium, the drifting, flower-scented smoke of forgetfulness? Her husband could not live with the world as it was, could not overcome his hatred and resentments. So he wished to escape it.

The wind had picked up velocity, banging a loose shutter against the house. The noise lacerated Celia's nerves. At last, unable to bear the sound any longer, or her own thoughts, she rose and put on a dressing gown.

"Couldn't you sleep, Celia?" Hatteras was up too, seated at her desk writing a letter. In the warm glow cast by her oil lamp, Hatteras seemed her old, sturdy self, her face once again the deep tan it had been when Celia had first met her.

Gratefully Celia stepped into her room. "I'm afraid not— too many worries," she told her aunt.

"Oh? About what?"

"About Beau, mostly. Aunt Hatteras, I'm afraid for him."

Hatteras wiped her pen with a soft cloth and put the letter away, turning to face Celia with a worried expression. "Celia, I don't wish to alarm you, but perhaps we should think about returning to Honolulu."

Even though Celia was worried herself, it was still alarming to have Hatteras say this. Was she to abandon ship, simply to pack up her things and leave?

"I mean what I say. Perhaps we made a mistake in coming here. Certainly you made a mistake in marrying Beau Burnside. I'll admit that now. He is wealthy, you are mistress of a prosperous plantation, but you have to run it yourself, and he hates you for it. As he hates you for saving his life." Hatteras went on, "And I have the terrible feeling, Celia, that Beau is going to start using opium again. If he hasn't already."

Celia nodded, feeling her heart sink as Hatteras confirmed her worst fears. Outside, the wind had increased in violence, and the loose shutter could still be heard smashing against the house as if trying to get inside at them. She moistened her lips. "But . . . to return to Honolulu, to give up . . ."

"There are times when it is best to admit failure." Hatteras' face, shadowed in the lamplight, was calm. "If it's money you are worried about, Celia, I'm sure we can manage somehow. I still have my house in Honolulu, and we can take in boarders. And you could teach in one of the other schools in Honolulu, or we'll open our own again. Now that I see what a good teacher you are . . ."

But Celia was in no mood for compliments. She felt as if her head were spinning. Too much had happened. They had put Beau through too much, and she couldn't desert him now. Not if he needed her, even a little.

Oddly, she thought again of the plantation house, of the gracious timbers that had lasted so many years, enduring so much. "No," she told her aunt gently. "I can't leave. I'm needed here at Mountain View. I think this is where I belong."

24

That night Celia had tossing, restless dreams in which she was being dragged along on a horse, the bridle cutting painfully at her body as someone shouted a frantic warning.

She awoke at dawn, her heart slamming, the sheets damp with perspiration. The dream had seemed frighteningly real, and there had been an odd roar in its background, a very frightening sound. For a minute she lay still, trying to shake away her feeling of alarm. The wind was still high, unusually so for morning; she could hear it whistling around the corner of the house. It must have been that which she had heard in her sleep, triggering her dream.

She heard someone rap at her door. "Celia!" It was Hatteras. "There's someone here. A messenger. He wants to speak to you."

Celia slid out of bed and found her dressing gown. Hurrying downstairs, she found a tall, muscular Hawaiian youth waiting in the foyer. He looked worn and travel-dusty, and Celia realized that he must have been riding all night. His face looked familiar; he was one of the Hawaiians with whom Roman had been surfing that day in Lahaina, she realized uneasily.

"I have note from Docta Burnside," the youth said in pidgen, handing Celia a folded slip of paper. With shaking hands she took it from him. She stood holding the letter, suddenly afraid to read it.

"Well?" Hatteras demanded. "What does it say? Go ahead

and open it, Celia, since it was important enough to send this poor fellow traveling in the dark of night.''

Celia caught her breath and unfolded the note. ''Dear Celia,'' Roman had written in a hurried scrawl. ''My Hawaiian friends tell me that all signs for a hurricane are present and it should hit us within the next several days. Storms can be very dangerous here, and you must prepare well. I am needed for a difficult birth but will try to come to help if I can. . . .''

The rest of the letter, several paragraphs, had been damaged in traveling and was obliterated by a smear of ink and repeated creasings of the paper.

The messenger was staring at her, and Hatteras looked anxious. ''There is going to be a storm,'' Celia explained. ''We must get ready for it.'' She spoke to the Hawaiian. ''You may go to the kitchen and get something to eat, and then a place will be found for you to sleep in the workers' quarters.''

''Hurricane,'' the Hawaiian said. His grin revealed perfect white teeth. He made a wide gesture to connote heavy winds. ''*Makani-ino*. Big, *big*. Plenty *wili*, plenty *hekili*.''

''What?''

''He is talking about thunder and lightning,'' Hatteras translated, motioning to the man to leave. ''Celia, I've lived through these Hawaiian storms before, and he's right, they can be fierce. Water collects in the mountains and pours down the gorges, sweeping away anything in its path, sometimes even houses. . . . Come, there's much to do to get ready. And the Cousineaus here— Thank God we have a day or so. We're going to need it.''

But Ruark Cousineau and his wife came to bid them a hasty good-bye, insisting they wished to get home before the worst of the storm struck. If caught in the blow, they would shelter with friends in Ulupalakua.

It was odd, but after the Cousineaus left, almost a holiday air seemed to sweep through Mountain View. Celia mobilized the mill workers and servants to prepare for the coming storm. As the wind continued to rise erratically, workers nailed boards over windows and nailed all loose shutters and trim. Shelter had to be found for the plantation's thousand head of oxen and hundreds of horses. The village and the workers' quarters needed to be secured, and there were dozens of other buildings that required attention.

It was a huge, demanding job. Yet the people entered into it with zest, and even Tina raced about, insisting that the schoolhouse, too, had to be battened down. The little girl directed Genzo in the hammering of boards over the schoolhouse windows.

"I didn't know you liked school that much," Celia teased.

"Oh, but it can't blow away, Celia! Not with all of our books in it, and the pictures and maps we've put on the walls!" Tina's eyes danced with excitement. "But maybe we could put the benches outside, maybe the wind will take *them* away. They're much too hard—they hurt my bottom to sit on."

Even Beau paced about, talking of previous storms that the island had endured. High surf that had swept away beaches, tidal waves that had obliterated shoreside grass huts and fish ponds. "I like storms," he said to Celia, his eyes glowing. "I hope this one is big—the biggest of all!"

Celia frowned. Was this any way for the master of a sugar plantation to talk? Some of her holiday spirit began to leave her, for the winds had not abated, but continued to blow with even more lethal force. The sky was filled with huge, sweeping gray clouds that gathered one upon the other. The huge top of Haleakala was obscured behind a gray wall, as were the tops of the West Maui Mountains. Celia thought uneasily of the fact that this *was* an island they lived on, a tiny hump of land set in the midst of a huge expanse of water. If the sea were to roar up, the entire island could be washed away.

But quickly she squelched the thought. The Hawaiian islands had existed for thousands of years, she reminded herself, and surely were not going to wash away in one storm.

She put Hatteras in charge of the house, and went to the mill, where McRory shouted at a dozen Hawaiians who were driving a herd of restless, frightened oxen into the mill. The high wind was whistling in the corrugated iron roof, and the oxen did not like this new, strange sound. They lowed and bellowed uneasily, and several balked, refusing to be moved. Strings of spittle dripped from the mouth of one beast as a driver lashed at it with a whip, attempting to force it through the mill door.

"It isn't going to be easy, miss," McRory shouted above the din. "The beasts feel the change in the air. They aren't going to rest easy until the storm is over." Then the sugar boiler turned, shading his eyes to stare at someone approaching down the path that led from the house. "Well, if it isn't the master of Mountain View, come to save us all."

"What?" Celia turned, startled, to see Beau striding along the path. To her alarm, he had thrust a pistol into his belt. His eyes shone, and his face held a curiously exalted, blank expression as he gazed around at the excitement of the mill yard, the milling oxen.

"Beau . . ." Her heart sank as she hurried toward him. She did not like the sight of that pistol. Why would he carry it? "Beau, what are you doing here? . . . And with a gun! Surely you should be back at the house, making certain that your paintings are safe."

"My paintings!" Beau laughed, his throat working. "Let them blow away—what do I care? Let the whole place blow away."

"That's very well for you to say. Evidently you've forgotten about the hundreds of people and animals we're responsible for here," Celia told him, losing patience.

"Don't tell me what my responsibilities are. I came here to help out. Storms can craze animals. Drive them berserk. An ox might have to be shot."

There was a strange light in Beau's eyes, as if the storm had crazed him, too. Celia felt another spurt of unease. "Very well," she said at last, hoping to placate him. "We can use all the help we can get. But, please, Beau, put the gun in the mill office. I'm sure it won't be necessary."

"I'll do what I need to," he said vaguely, starting toward the mill door. "Aren't I the master here?"

While Beau paced the mill yard, helping to herd the oxen, Celia worked hard, issuing orders for the hundreds of chores that had to be done to secure the plantation and all its outbuildings. The workers were full of excitement, greeting each new rise of the wind with joy.

Gazing at the ocean spread below, Celia saw heavy surf boiling up into huge, crashing swells.

Ordinarily she, too, loved storms, and would have exulted

in this one, giving herself up to the wild force of it, glorying in its growing power.

But that was before, when she had been a girl with no responsibilities. Now there were nearly three hundred people and several thousand animals—horses, oxen, even Hili, the plantation dog—that depended on her for their survival. And she did not like the fact that Beau carried the pistol. Did he really want to help with the animals, or did he just like the idea of having a weapon at hand?

As soon as the plantation was secured, she decided, she would persuade him to put the gun aside.

By late afternoon the wind had increased its velocity. Gray clouds swept in from the south, swirling dervishes of energy. Bits of grass thatch and matting flew through the air, and the sea had turned an ugly gray, capped with lines of thunderous surf. Celia was in the mill office, collapsed in her chair for a few stolen moments of rest, when she heard commotion coming from the mill yard. She went to the door.

"Fire! Fire!" Genzo and several other workers were running toward her office, their faces frantic.

Fire. Celia's heart gave a twist of fear. Even under the best of conditions, in an operation like the mill, fire was an ever-present hazard. But with these high winds . . . She flew out of the door into the mill yard, seeing the dark plume of smoke already rising from the cooper's shed, bent sharply by the wind.

Later she would never be clearly aware of how many hours it took to battle the blaze, evidently started by a spark blown into a barrel of wood shavings. More than a hundred mill workers toiled, hauling buckets of water from the stream that fed the mill, struggling against the winds and the thick smoke.

Flames, fed by the greedy wind, had already leaped to the nearby carpentry shop. Celia ordered teams of oxen to be used to drag away stacks of stored wood, in hopes the flames would not spread to them. Her eyes burning with smoke, Celia hurried back and forth, encouraging the workers.

"The whole mill is going to burn!" Beau lurched past her, lugging two buckets, perspiration soaking his shirt until she could see the thin lines of his rib cage. "You're a fool if you think you can save this place."

His face was twisted with exultation, and she noticed he still carried the pistol thrust into his belt.

"I've sent to the village for more help, and I have every intention of saving it," she shouted back. "Look! The fire is already less. It's mostly smoke now. I think it's controlled."

"Nothing is controlled," Beau shouted back. "Nothing!"

What did he mean? But Celia did not have time to ponder the riddle of her moody and erratic husband, for McRory came running to her with news that a timber had collapsed on two of the workers. They had been dragged safely away from the fire, but both were in need of medical help.

Celia ordered both victims to be carried to the plantation house. One of them was Maka, the burly Hawaiian who had helped Roman to care for Beau. Maka's right leg was broken and lacerated, and searing, smoky air had burned his lungs. Leaving McRory to superintend the final dousing of the fire, Celia sent a worker riding for Roman, then gave her attention to the injured men.

The rains came. Huge, sweeping torrents of gray water swept in from the south in solid sheets, battering at Mountain View with full hurricane force. Rain roared against the house, creating a powerful and frightening din that made all of its occupants feel very small and vulnerably human.

There were eleven people sheltered in the plantation house: Celia, Hatteras, Tina, Beau, three male servants, Leinani and another servant girl, and the two injured men. Hili prowled back and forth, whining anxiously. The remaining human residents of Mountain View were sheltered in the workers' brick dormitory and in McRory's large, solid house.

"Death," Beau said. He walked into the blue guest room where Celia was changing the dressings on Maka's leg and stood staring down at the thick-set Hawaiian who had been part of his opium ordeal. Maka, perspiring with pain, gazed up at him uneasily. "Pain and hellfire and ugly death. You thought it would pass you by, didn't you, Maka? You thought *you* would be lucky."

Beau fingered the handle of the pistol, stroking the metal lovingly.

The Hawaiian gazed at him in fear. "Please . . ."

"I hope you die, Maka," Beau said softly. "I hope it's

nice and slow. Yes, that would be very nice. Gangrene is very ugly, did you know that? Your leg swells up to double its size, and pus comes from it, and there is a terrible stink of corruption . . .''

The injured man twisted on the feather mattress, his dark eyes rolling with terror.

"Beau!" Celia grasped her husband's arm and attempted to drag him out of the sickroom, anger and horror giving her strength. "You can't talk to Maka like that!"

Beau shook her away. "Leave me alone, Celia."

"But you can't talk to Maka of such things. He's hurt, he . . . It's inhuman!"

Beau's amber eyes blazed at her. "Many things are inhuman, aren't they, Celia? But that doesn't stop us from permitting them. I believe there is some justice in this world after all. And now the water is coming down. Perhaps it will wash away sin."

To Celia's relief, Beau left the sickroom, slamming its door behind him. Restlessly he began to pace the house, striding from drawing room to dining room to hallway, to the library and the second, smaller drawing room. Celia watched him in growing dread. The wilder the storm, the more erratic and dangerous Beau seemed to become.

He should be restrained, she knew, calmed somehow. But as long as he continued to carry the pistol, she did not dare order any of the servants to approach him. Two men had already been hurt by the fire; she could not throw away more lives.

"You're going to have to do something about Beau." Hatteras emerged from the library, where she had been reading aloud to Tina, who did not like the sharp, slapping sound of the wind ravaging the shutters of the house.

"I know," Celia admitted. "But what? He is like a caged leopard pacing about. Every time he goes past Maka's room I shudder, wondering what he is going to do. He hates Maka for his part in the cure."

"Cure? Beau was not cured, Celia, he was only rendered more angry. If we had any opium in the house, I would suggest that we give it to him. That, at least, might calm him."

"But we don't have any. And I have given the last of the laudanum to Maka for his leg," Celia said, shivering.

Several hours wore on as the storm continued to batter at the house. As if by common instinct, they all gathered in the library, the servants chattering uneasily among themselves in Hawaiian. The library looked far different now from the gracious book-lined room where once Celia had browsed, looking for a pleasant novel to read.

Now all the shutters had been closed and nailed shut. Two bookshelves had been moved in front of the windows to provide extra protection against flying branches or debris. Celia had ordered the oil lamps lighted, and the flames flickered wildly as fingers of wind thrust through cracks and invaded the room.

Hatteras and Leinani went to the kitchen and came back with sandwiches, and they sat eating, listening to the solid roar of the rain and water outside. Only Beau refused the food, sitting sullenly in a chair near the door. He had donned a dark suit coat that covered the pistol, but from the way his hand occasionally strayed to his belt line, Celia knew it was still there.

"Why is my brother so angry?" Tina whispered to Celia, nudging her when Beau was not looking.

"The storm is stirring up his emotions," Celia said at last. "He'll be all right when it stops, I'm sure."

"But he looks so . . ." Tina struggled to find words. "So . . . horrid," she finished.

Celia soothed the child, thinking privately that Tina was right. Beau did look horrid. He looked tightly strung and brooding and dangerous, and they were stuck here in this beleaguered house with him.

The storm continued, increasing its savagery. Objects smashed against the house, and once, when Celia peered through a crack in the shutters, she saw trees flattened nearly to the ground. A mynah bird hurtled past as if flung by some giant invisible force, its feathers bedraggled, its neck broken.

"I think Pele is very angry," Tina ventured. "Maybe she hates us for planting sugarcane on the slopes of her mountains. Maybe she is taking her revenge on us."

The servants whispered together, and Leinani's eyes widened.

"Nonsense," Hatteras said sharply. "Pele has nothing to do with this."

"But she—"

"A hurricane is an act of nature, Tina, and has nothing to do with gods or goddesses." Hatteras reached for a novel by Edward Eggleston about a Hoosier schoolmaster, and began to read aloud from it, her voice soothing and monotonous.

Celia tried to listen, but her mind kept jumping about. She felt clammy perspiration slide down her sides and trickle between her breasts. She wondered if Roman had gotten her message about the injured men. Was he on his way? He should not come here, she realized with a sick spasm of dread. His presence would only inflame Beau further. If only she hadn't sent for him!

And then there was the storm. What would it do to Mountain View? Water, she knew, collected high along the buttresses of the mountains and poured downward during storms, carving out the huge chasms and gulches that she had often ridden through on sunny days. What if . . . ?

But she swallowed back her fear and went to check on the injured men, returning to listen again to Hatteras' soothing voice. No sense worrying about Mother Nature, she told herself. Not when she had more immediate problems. As long as Beau carried that pistol, he was like a stick of dynamite waiting to be ignited.

Uneasily she glanced at her husband, seeing the tense way he sat, his eyes focused on a point in the distance, as if he were brooding about something. What would trigger him— and when?

Mentally she began going through the cupboards and shelves in the house, wondering what drug or medicine she could give Beau to calm him. Brandy? They had plenty of that in the liquor cabinet, along with the Hawaiian *okolehao* that was so fiery and potent.

But what effect would alcohol have on Beau? Would it serve as a sedative, or would it only fuel his anger, making him twice as dangerous?

A faint banging—barely audible over the shriek of the storm—interrupted her thoughts. Tina, too, heard it, and Hatteras looked up from her reading. But Beau seemed absorbed in his brooding thoughts, unaware of any change. Celia rose and slipped out of the library, going to the front door.

She could hear the sounds of prying on the other side of the door, as their visitor attempted to get into the boarded-up house. There was a crowbar lying on the floor, and Celia picked it up, loosening the boards to let Roman in.

He stepped inside in a wash of water and quickly turned to replace the boards. Water soaked his clothes and plastered his hair to his head. There was a bleeding gash on his cheekbone where he had been cut with debris. He had his medical bag with him, and that, too, was water-streaked.

"Roman!" Celia let out a cry. "Your face—are you all right? Oh, God . . ."

He grinned, his eyes glinting with hard excitement, as if the storm had affected him too, giving him a wild vitality. "It's just a cut. I passed your messenger on the trail—it was foolhardy to send him, Celia. The bridle paths are nearly impassable—they are torrents of water. I sent him on to Lahaina. Is the mill prepared? Are the people safe? And what about the animals?"

Quickly Celia told him all that she had done, and was rewarded by his nod of approval. "And you have two injured men?"

"Yes, they're in the blue guest room. Maka's leg is in bad shape, broken and cut. I did what I could, but he is still in a lot of pain. But, Roman . . ."

Roman had turned, ready to go upstairs, and now looked back at her impatiently. "Yes?"

"It's Beau. The storm has driven his mind over the edge. He's in the library now, but he is terribly dangerous, Roman, he is walking about with a pistol stuck in his belt, and he won't relinquish it. He is so wild-looking, and he talked to Maka in such a frightening way."

Roman frowned, his brows forming a straight black line. "Exactly what did he say, Celia?"

"He said he wanted Maka to suffer. That he hoped he would die, he hoped he got gangrene in his leg."

A muscle flickered in Roman's jaw. "I see."

Feeling a twist of fear, she remembered that Beau had reason to hate Roman, too. Roman had been Beau's physician, had been with him twenty-four hours a day, was, in Beau's mind, the chief instrument of his torment.

Hysteria rose in her. "He hates you, too, Roman. He wants to kill you. I know he does!"

Then, flooded with anxiety, Celia could not help herself. She threw herself into Roman's arms, clinging to his hard male strength. His clothes were wet, but beneath the dampness his body was warm, strong. A sob caught in her throat as she felt a terrible yawning fear for him. Beau's hatred . . . the pistol . . .

She pulled away. "You can't stay here at Mountain View, Roman. You must leave at once. It's too dangerous for you here."

Roman gave her an odd look. "It's dangerous for you, too."

"Beau won't hurt me."

"He will, Celia, he'll hurt anyone, if what you tell me is true." Roman gripped her, pulling her to him again, crushing her against his wide, broad chest as if he would never let her go. "I'm going upstairs and see what I can do for those two poor devils who were hurt in the fire. And then I want you to come with me, Celia. Come away from Mountain View, come to Lahaina with me, and then to Vienna."

"To . . . to Vienna?"

"I love you, darling." Roman's eyes burned at her, filled with emotion. "Didn't you know that? I always have, ever since the first time I saw you aboard the *Fair Wind*. I fought against it, but you ensnared me. . . . Didn't you read my letter?"

"No, I . . . It was water-damaged, and part of it was obliterated." He loved her. Celia felt as if she could barely breathe, as if her heart would pound out of her chest, expanding until it was as large as Mountain View.

"Well, I can't go to Vienna alone. I want you with me, Celia, I need you by my side. And I won't go without you."

Transfixed, she stared at Roman, unaware of the savage pounding of the rain, or the presence of Beau, Hatteras, and the others in the library only a dozen yards away. Roman wanted her. Wanted to take her away with him, wanted her to be his woman.

Joy sang in her, swirling along her veins in an elixir of happiness.

Roman loved her! And she loved him! Every instinct in her cried out to accept his proposal, to go with him wherever he wished. She loved him, she always had, she belonged to him.

And their life together would surely be exciting, would be everything of which she had ever dreamed.

"Celia? Celia, is someone there? Oh, it's you, Roman!" Tina suddenly appeared in the corridor, her flyaway red hair tangled, her face anxious.

"Yes, it's Roman, come to help us." Celia said it with difficulty, her heart suddenly sinking like a stone. Tina. My God, what would happen to the little girl if she left? How could she leave Tina to a crazed Beau? A knot of pain strangled in her throat. She couldn't go. It was impossible.

But she forced out cheerful words. "Go back to the library, darling, and don't tell anyone that Roman is here. He's going to go upstairs and look at Maka and the other man, and then he'll . . . he'll leave again."

She was aware of Roman's start of surprise.

"His being here is our secret, Tina. Can you keep quiet about this, and not let Beau know?"

Tina looked puzzled. "But, Celia, why—?"

"You have to trust me, Tina."

Tina hesitated, then gave one of her impish smiles. "I never had a secret in the middle of a hurricane before." She trotted off, apparently satisfied.

Celia looked at Roman, her body shaking convulsively. She felt as if she were giving up the world, everything wonderful, everything she had ever wanted. She swallowed dryly, forcing out the words in a low voice. "I can't. . . . Roman, I have a responsibility here, for Tina, and for my aunt. I can't just leave them, not with Beau the way he is."

But Roman's lips parted in a grim smile, and his eyes blazed at her. "Then we'll take them with us. But we are going to have to disarm Beau first, Celia, for we can't travel in this storm until it abates. It would be far too dangerous."

Outside, the wind seemed to roar louder, savaging the boards that barred the door. Roman's jaw tightened, but his voice was calm, even. "Go, Celia, and start packing a few essentials for the trail while I make some preparation for dealing with your husband. Thank God I always carry a pistol in my saddlebag. I pray I won't have to use it."

Her throat knotted with dread, Celia hurried to the kitchen, throwing some bread, cold meat, and cakes into a canvas sack, adding a water jug. She finished packing the food and slipped out of the kitchen and up the servants' staircase. Even on the stairs she could hear the howl of the storm. At the top of the staircase there was a window, and she stopped to peer out of a crack. Gray rain smashed down on the house as if sprayed from a giant sluice. How long before the storm was over and they could leave? Or would they leave during the "eye," that calm center about which the hurricane swirled?

Or would they be able to leave at all?—the horrid thought came. What if Roman couldn't disarm Beau? What if . . . ?

But she forced away the fear. Trying not to think of their danger, she hurried to her room. Clothes, she thought feverishly. Warm sweaters and coats, something waterproof against the rain, blankets. And money. They would need all the money they could gather. . . . She began tossing warm clothing into another sack, adding the diamond bracelet that John had once left on her pillow, insisting she keep it.

She held the bracelet up, seeing how the stones glittered in the lamplight. She remembered when John had given it to her, in a frantic effort to win her love. How long ago that seemed! She had been only a girl then, deeply in love with Roman but unsure of herself, manipulating those around her in order to get closer to the man she really loved. She had hurt John Burnside. And she had wronged Beau, too, for her marriage to him should never have happened.

She slid on the bracelet and pushed it far up under the sleeve of her dress, where it would be hidden. She had to stop blaming herself, she told herself firmly. She had done many things wrong, but there was no way to go back and change them now.

She could only go on.

At last she was ready, or, she thought with excitement, as ready as she would ever be. Suddenly her worries slipped away, to be replaced with a soaring confidence. Roman was here now, and he had a pistol. He was strong, calm, in control. In only a few hours they'd be somewhere safe, far away from Mountain View.

She'd go with Roman anywhere, she'd love him forever. . . .

She slipped out of the bedroom and hurried down the hallway to the guest room where she had put the two injured men. Roman, carrying his bag, was just emerging from the room. A slight lump under his jacket indicated the presence of a pistol.

"Roman!"

"I could not leave here without attending to the injured. Kaneohe, the boy, is in pretty good shape. He has only some lacerations and some damage to his lungs from smoke inhalation. You did a good job of dressing his wounds, Celia, and I think, with rest and care, he will survive. I am concerned about Maka, though. That leg could easily turn septic. I washed it with carbolic and cauterized it, and I'll give instructions to the servants for his care."

Roman and Celia looked at each other, and Celia saw the distress in Roman's eyes, that he would not be able to superintend his patient's progress.

"Come." He took her arm, and again she felt his strength flow into her. "You said Beau was in the library. I want you to go downstairs and fetch him. Tell him . . . tell him that you need him to look at the kitchen, that the wind has broken through the windows. Tell him anything, but get him out in the corridor alone."

"*Roman.*" For an instant she clung to him, her courage deserting her.

But Roman put out a forefinger to tilt up her chin so that she was forced to look into his eyes. "Courage, Celia," he whispered huskily. "You have it in abundance, you always have had. You're quite a woman. And you are going to need every bit of bravery you possess tonight."

His kiss was soft on her lips. "Come, darling. Vienna is waiting for us . . . for the two of us."

25

Celia slipped back inside the library, her breathing quickened with fear. The scene was much as she had left it only minutes ago. Hatteras was sitting on a couch, her arm around Tina, and the servants still sat together in a corner, talking to each other in soft Hawaiian. Beau was now pacing the room, his hands clasped behind his back, his features twisted in a frown.

"He has been restless," Hatteras whispered to Celia under her breath. "Staring into the distance, clenching his hands into fists . . . I don't trust him."

"Why are you whispering?" Beau suddenly asked harshly. It was the first he had spoken in several hours. "Do you have secrets?"

Celia swallowed hard, wondering what to say, how to begin. But before she could open her mouth, there was a sudden ear-splitting crack. All the women jumped. Leinani gave a frightened sob, and Tina, too, cried out.

"What . . . what was that?" the child quavered.

The day had been full of such loud, tearing, unexplained noises, caused by trim being ripped off the house or debris blown against the exterior.

"Oh, just the storm," Celia explained as lightly as she could. "Probably something hitting the veranda. I've always wanted to see what a storm is really like, haven't you? It's going to be an adventure!"

Tina nodded, some of her color returning.

But Beau was gazing at Celia suspiciously. His pacing

movements had grown even more erratic. "What's going to be an adventure?"

"Why . . . why, Beau, just seeing the storm." She remembered her instructions from Roman. "Anyway, there is something I think you should look at here in the house—"

"What are you talking about?"

She faltered. "In the kitchen, Beau. The wind has been so strong, it has blown in some of the boards we used to block off the windows, and we need someone to hammer the boards shut again."

"Hammer them yourself."

"Beau—"

"Or is there some reason you want me to come with you, Celia, some reason that you aren't telling me? Your expression looks strange. . . . You've never loved me, have you, Celia? No, not really. I could tell. I could always tell."

Tina and Hatteras were staring, anxiety written on their faces, and the Hawaiians had stopped their talk, bewildered.

"Don't talk nonsense," Celia said at last, as firmly as she could. She forced herself to step forward, to touch Beau's arm in an entreating way. "Please, Beau, we need some help. Come and see what needs to be done in the kitchen."

"Oh, very well, then. But I may rip off all the boards instead of hammering them. Let in the wind, the rain . . . clear the place out."

To Celia's relief, Beau started toward the library door. Tensely she waited as he pulled it open and stepped into the hall. As he started in the direction of the kitchen, she felt her heart begin to slam in huge, swooping beats. But the corridor was empty, with no sign of Roman.

Somewhere in the house the wind again slammed a shutter against wooden siding. Involuntarily Celia jumped and let out a little cry.

"Afraid?" Beau sneered.

"Why, I . . . yes, I suppose I am." She said the first thing that came into her head.

"You deserve to be afraid, Celia. I hope you're frightened out of your skin. I hope you go down to hell crying and weeping and gibbering for your sins, your terrible sins. Lying, torturing bitch, you belong in the flames of hell, where you put *me*."

Beau's talk had gone beyond reason, beyond sense, and she tried to close her ears to it as they took another few paces toward a series of doors that opened onto a drawing room, storage rooms, a buttery, and the kitchen. Where was Roman? When was he going to appear to disarm Beau, and *what if he couldn't?* Beau was dangerously crazed, erratic, no longer making sense.

Suddenly Roman was there, stepping out of the buttery door. Tall, fierce-looking, his hair damp and rumpled, he loomed ahead of them, his face implacable. Never had she seen Roman look so determined, so dangerous.

As Roman had instructed her, Celia took a step away from Beau, to give him space in which to maneuver, but she was not fast enough. Beau's hand snaked out and grasped her arm, its grip incredibly strong.

Her nerves were drawn tight; she could not help screaming. *"Roman!"*

Beau gripped her even more savagely. "Shut up, Celia. Do you think I am stupid enough not to know this was all planned? A broken window in the kitchen, indeed. What sort of fool do you take me for?"

Celia felt the iron talons of Beau's fingers cutting into the flesh of her arm and felt her knees go soft with fear. But she stood as quietly as she could, trying not to cry out with pain.

"Let go of her, Beau. Drop her arm." Roman's voice was calm, soothing, almost hypnotic.

"Why should I?" Beau sneered. "She's my wife, and all *you* are is a murderer, the man who tried to kill my father. . . . And my torturer. Oh, yes, you were that, too, Roman Burnside. Do you think that I ever could forget what you did to me? You and my lovely *wife*, tying me down as if I were a lunatic, putting me through hellfire that beggars description!"

Roman's eyes were as pale as water, as cold. But apparently unarmed, he spoke evenly. "We were trying to save your life, and we had your consent for the treatment. I warned you it would be difficult, I held back none of the truth. Give me the gun, Beau."

"No." Beau's mouth twisted. His free hand moved to his waistband, where Celia could see, partly covered by his jacket, the pearl handle of the pistol. "Why should I, torturer? Physician, heal thyself!" His laugh was high, strained. "What about your oath, Roman? To do no harm, but only good. Hah! Tying me to a bed, forcing me to undergo agonies . . .''

Roman's voice was calm. "I am sorry about the agony you suffered, Beau, believe me. And now I want to make amends. I have opium in my medical bag. Not much, but some, and I'm willing to give it to you if you relinquish the pistol you carry.''

There was a little pause. Beau looked from Roman to Celia, his lower lip thrust out suspiciously. "I don't believe you.''

"It's true. I left my bag upstairs with the injured men, but I'd be willing to take you upstairs and give you the opium that I have. It should be enough to last you for a while, until you can get more.''

Beau's eyes darted to the staircase, then to Roman. However, his painful grip on Celia's arm did not slacken. "I still don't believe you. Why should you do that for me? No, it's all a trick. I have *her* now, and I intend to punish her for what she did—for what you both did!''

With those words, Beau gave Celia a rough jerk, first forward, then back, shaking her like a rag doll. She choked off a cry of fright, struggling to be free of his grip.

"Leave her alone, Beau.'' From inside his jacket Roman produced his own pistol, and for a long, tense moment the two men faced each other. There was a dull sound of the safety catch of Roman's gun being released. "Give me your gun.''

Beau's voice rose hysterically. "I'll give it to you. Oh, I'll give it to you, all right, and to that bitch wife of mine.''

Celia saw it first in Beau's eyes—the infinitesimal change of expression. She screamed a warning.

And then everything seemed to happen at once, a dream, hardly real at all, which she was forced to witness. Roman shouted, and there was a simultaneous crashing explosion, so loud that it seemed to crack apart Celia's eardrums, filling the air with thunder. She smelled acrid smoke, heard her own sob of terror.

A frozen, horrible second passed, and Celia thought she saw horror in Beau's eyes, a brief instant of stark, cold sanity. Then she saw the pistol fall from Roman's hand and a gush of red, red blood.

"Roman!" she screamed. "Roman!"

Fear gave her strength, and she twisted out of Beau's grip, flying toward Roman, who had begun to crumple to his knees, all of it happening slowly, like the ending of the worst nightmare Celia had ever had.

But before she could reach Roman or cry out his name again, Beau had lunged toward her. He dragged her away, his hands digging into her with the ferocious grip of the insane.

"You love him, don't you, Celia? You and Roman—you were going to trick me!"

Was Roman dead? My God, was he? Was the nightmare never going to end? Beau dragged her along as if she were a sack of sugar, yanking viciously at her. Frantically Celia dug her feet into the floor, struggling to use her body weight against him. Desperately she grabbed at a doorjamb, fighting with every ounce of strength she possessed.

But Beau hit her with the pistol handle, and yanked her on again, dragging her toward the back entrance to the kitchen, out of the door into the torrential rains.

Water. It smashed into her mouth and eyes, washing over her, soaking her to the skin instantly. In vain Celia fought the strong, wiry arms that gripped her. Water inundated them both in sheets, making Beau's skin slippery as she fought him, sobbing out her shock and grief and fury.

Roman . . . Oh, Roman . . . my love, my love. . . .

With inhuman strength Beau dragged her to the stables, where frightened horses kicked and whinnied in their stalls. He tied her to a post while he saddled up Premier, a big black gelding that Beau sometimes rode.

Made skittish by the storm, the gelding tossed its head wildly, jumping about and stamping the ground.

Cursing, Beau threw her on top of Premier, quickly wrapping a bridle around her neck to hold her. The wet leather thong cut savagely into her flesh.

"Beau!" she gasped, choking, struggling to loosen it. "Beau, please—"

"Ride, bitch! You're coming with me."

"I won't!" Like a madwoman she fought, clawing at the bridle, while the horse stepped about uneasily. But the thong only tightened.

"If you fight, you'll strangle yourself, Celia," Beau gloated. He mounted behind her, giving her a vicious upward pull so that she lay facedown in front of him across the large Mexican saddle horn.

It was a nightmare ride. They rode up a trail flowing with water, so slippery with mud and rocks that the gelding balked, going on only when Beau whipped him with a small horsewhip or kicked his flanks with the heel of his boot. Once the animal came perilously near to falling, while Celia frantically gripped the leather at her neck, trying to stop herself from being choked. In agony she clung to the saddle as best she could, fighting for every breath of air.

Torrents of floodwater cut across the trail, creating rivers of water and mud. Where were they going? Toward the ramparts of Pele's Pool? As Celia fought to survive on the back of the rocking, struggling animal, at the mercy of a crazed man who hated her, despair gripped her.

Roman was surely dead, and still she hadn't felt the full shock of it yet; she seemed frozen in a well of blackness. A huge knot of tears choked her throat, sobs of horror and unbearable agony. Almost, she wanted to give up. Let Beau kill her, do whatever he wished with her. Without Roman, what was life worth? But something, some instinct of survival, would not let her give up.

They reached Pele's Pool, the place where Celia had swum naked with Kinau and Leinani, where Roman had once made love to her. But the pool was unrecognizable now. Torrents of brown water, flecked with debris, raged downward, overflowing the rocky banks of the little pool. Dirt and broken plants foamed into a whirlpool before rushing viciously downward toward the cliffs. The body of a wild pig bobbed up briefly. It flashed before Celia's eyes, then was gone, mute evidence of the ferocity of this storm.

Beau slowed the horse.

"Beau!" Celia clawed frantically at the bridle that strangled her neck. "Please . . . let me go."

He loomed above her, full of hatred.

But finally Beau did pry away the wet leather thong that bound her neck, and then he gave Celia a shove, pushing her off the horse onto the ground. She felt herself fall, rolling away from Premier's hooves, air rushing into her lungs.

She struggled to her feet again. Only a few yards away was the rushing torrent of floodwater, roaring downward toward the sea. The scene was like one of Beau's paintings, jagged, dark, menacing. Rain swept them both, battering their faces.

Beau dismounted from the gelding, drawing the pistol. "All right, bitch. I told you I would never forget what you did for me—or Roman, either. Well, I paid him back. Now it's your turn."

Celia's blood froze. Beau was going to kill her.

"Don't you think we should . . . talk about it?" She fought her terror. Desperately she tried to keep her voice level, calm. Hadn't she seen, briefly, a look of horror on Beau's face after he had shot Roman? If she could only talk to him, appeal to his sense of reason. Perhaps Beau's sanity was not entirely gone. If she had time . . .

But it seemed that there was no time.

"Talk? What is there to say?" Beau's face was distorted, twisted with a frightening anger. "Go over there, Celia, over by the water. And then turn around. Turn away from me." He prodded at her with the pistol.

Nausea gripped Celia, along with a terrible, debilitating weakness of the knees. Suddenly she had a horribly clear idea of what Beau intended to do with her. He, too, had seen the dead pig swept past in the torrent. He intended to shoot her in the back, so he would not have to watch her die. Then he would throw her body into the water and let it carry her downward. Her body would hurtle over the cliffs and gorges until at last she smashed into rocks or was washed into the sea itself. She'd never be found again. . . .

"*No.*" Proudly, desperately, she drew herself up. "No, I won't do what you ask, Beau. If you intend to kill me, then you are going to have to do it face to face, looking me straight in the eye."

"Celia—"

"No, Beau, I won't make this easy for you. If you want your revenge, you'll take it, and I can't stop you. But it will be face to face."

She let her eyes burn into Beau's. She had no intention of dying like an animal. She'd die like a woman, proudly. As their eyes locked, she wondered if her life, in this moment, was supposed to pass before her eyes in a series of pictures.

But the only picture she saw now was Roman. Not as he had been, lying bloody on the floor of the kitchen, but as she had seen him at Pele's Pool, his eyes glowing with passion for her. Roman. Whom she loved, and always would.

Even if Beau did kill her, her love for Roman wouldn't die.

"Celia!" Beau was fidgeting uneasily under the force of her look. She thought she saw the pistol shake. "Do it, do what I say at once. Or I'll . . . I'll shoot you in the knees first."

Her bravery ebbed; she thought she would vomit from horror. Her heart thumped in her throat like a wild beast as she fought to stand upright. This wasn't Beau anymore; this was some mad, irrational stranger.

"No," she said calmly. "You won't do that. You'll give me the gun, Beau. Hand it to me, handle-first."

He looked at her, and something flickered in his eyes. With relief she realized that he was about to do as she suggested.

"Give it to me now," she urged.

But she must have pushed him too far, for suddenly Beau raised the pistol, his eyes changing again, and Celia knew he intended to pull the trigger. She reacted instantly. She threw herself toward Beau's left, landing hard against his body, knocking the pistol out of his grip.

It all happened in seconds. The impact of her body knocked Beau off balance, and he staggered backward, his hands flying out for suppport. But there was no support, and the ground was rocky, the rocks slippery with mud and rain.

Beau staggered and caught himself, then fell backward into the torrent.

Beau was screaming.

Celia knelt at the edge of the rushing floodwater, attempting to reach him with the length of her petticoat. Over and over she tried to extend it to him, while he screamed and shouted, begging her to hurry before the water swept him over the cliffs.

And frantically Celia tried. Beau was no longer a stranger, a vengeful killer. He was only a frightened human being in danger of drowning, and she was his chance at life.

"Celia!" His pathetic cries tore at her. "For the love of God, help me!"

"I will, Beau, I am. . . ." The wind and rain ripped the words out of her mouth, and she was vaguely aware of movement behind her. A second horse, a man. But there was no time to look. She leaned forward, as far over the current as she dared, giving the petticoat another desperate toss, praying its length would reach far enough.

"Let me help." Someone was behind her. Someone who tossed a saddle rope out onto the savagely swirling water.

Celia's heart wrenched.

"*Roman!* I thought you were . . ."

"Dead?" His teeth showed white in a wild laugh. "I'm not that easy to kill."

He was alive, he wasn't dead, he was here, here. . . . She sobbed with her relief, and then stood back while Roman, one arm and his chest bandaged, awkwardly hurled a rope out into the rushing torrent. Beau scrabbled at it, his arms flailing.

Roman threw the rope again.

But Beau had been carried too far down the white, foaming flood. Celia caught a last glimpse of her husband's terror-stricken face and then he was swept around the bend toward the rocky cataract that waited below.

Celia screamed. She screamed and screamed, and then Roman pulled her to him. She went shaking into his arms and clung sobbing to him, to his strength and love.

Weeks later, moonlight spilled into the large bedroom that Celia and Roman had chosen for their own. Silver light glimmered on their naked bodies as they held each other on their wedding night.

By the clauses of Amos Burnside's will, Roman was now sole master of Mountain View. He and Celia had been married this afternoon in a quiet ceremony in the little stone church. They would honeymoon for six months in Vienna, then return to the plantation, where Roman and Celia would run Mountain View together. They would rear Tina as their daughter, sending her to college in the East when she was eighteen.

Celia sighed with contentment, thinking how well everything had worked out. Hatteras planned to leave the following week for California, where—her dream finally realized—she would take the two granddaughters of the gold magnate with whom she had been corresponding on their "Grand Tour" of Europe. But Celia suspected that something else would happen. That Hatteras and the widower would discover the sparks of love fanning between them, that perhaps it might be four people discovering Europe, rather than three. . . .

"Darling," Roman whispered, holding her close. "To think that I almost lost you."

"And to think that I almost lost *you*." Celia felt a shudder ripple through her, thinking of it. Almost. . . .

But thank God, that wild night of Beau's death was now only a memory. Roman had received only a glancing flesh wound in the shoulder, which had produced a frightening amount of blood but had not been serious. After Beau had dragged Celia away, Roman managed to get to his feet. Bandaging himself with a kitchen towel, he had then struggled out into the storm. He had gone to the stable, saddled up one of the frightened horses, and followed the hoofmarks in the mud.

"Nothing could have saved Beau," Roman assured Celia later, holding her until her sobs quietened. "The force of the water was too strong and, frankly, Celia, I don't think he wished to live. Not really. If he had, he would not have gone to the pool as he did. In fact, I suspect that after he killed you he intended to throw himself in."

"*No*," she had whispered in horror.

"Yes, darling, I am afraid it's true. Some of the things that Beau shouted in his madness during the opium cure . . . He was a tormented man, Celia. Now he is at rest."

Celia remembered what Beau had said once. How he wanted peace, nothingness. . . . Well, he had it now, for all eternity.

Now she snuggled into the warm, safe shelter of Roman's arms, glad that all the horror was behind them, and only joy lay ahead.

"Happy?" Gently, smiling, Roman touched her nose with his forefinger.

She looked at him, at his beloved face, the lineament of which she knew so well. She had seen him grim and angry, suffused with passion, intense, playful, loving. There was not a part of him that she had not kissed, caressed, loved. And he, too, knew every part of her intimately.

Then she, too, smiled. *"Happy?* Oh, Roman . . . I'm so much more than that, I don't think there is even any word for the way I feel. It's as if . . . as if my whole life has just exploded into wonderful joy. I have you . . . Tina . . . Mountain View. What more can I want?"

He pulled her to him. His mouth was tender. "A child someday, Celia. A baby not tarnished by the Burnside curse. I'll give one to you. I plan to study in Vienna until I discover the secrets of childbirth infection and know as much as I can about obstetrics. Then we will come home to Mountain View to start making heirs."

"Heirs?" she teased. "Do you mean in the plural?"

"Naturally! Two boys and two girls. Or do you want more? There is room here at Mountain View for a whole crew. Oh, my darling, I love you so much. When I first saw you on the *Fair Wind*, I fell helplessly in love with a girl. A fascinating, willful, lovely witch who twisted men's hearts about her little finger and bent them to her wishes. I drew back from that girl, Celia, I was wary of her."

Celia made a wry face. "I know. But I surprised you, didn't I? I grew up."

"Witch. You certainly did." His hands caressed her, smoothing over her satiny skin, drawing up the sweet fire from her nipples, all the curves of her. "Beyond my imagining, beyond my wildest expectations. When my brother, John, was injured, you nursed him bravely, and you stuck by Beau when any other woman would have quailed, seeing him through the torment of opium withdrawal. You were warm and loving to Tina, you accepted her as your own, and would not leave her.

"But when I saw you trying to pull Beau out of the water, the man who had just tried to kill you—then I knew how truly lucky I am." Roman drew in his breath softly. "You're quite a woman, Celia. And I mean *woman*. You're compassionate, warm and loving, and brave—you're everything I've ever wanted. And now that I have you, I'm never going to let you go."

Moonlight filled the room with its silver, burnished glow, and the scent of flowers was sweet, sweet. Roman whispered to her, murmuring more soft and wonderful things endlessly throughout that night.

Celia gave herself up to the joy of his lovemaking. As they loved each other until dawn and beyond, she knew that she had found what she'd been looking for. Everything she ever wanted was right here in the tender circle of Roman's arms, the enchantment of his love.

About the Author

Julia Grice grew up in Michigan and has lived in Florida and Hawaii. She has worked as a newspaper reporter, social worker, librarian, and cookie packer, but for the past eight years, she has devoted all her energy to writing. The mother of two teenage sons, Julia Grice now lives in Michigan, where she loves to swim, paint, play racquetball, and do original needlepoint. Her two previous novels, KIMBERLEY FLAME and SEASON OF DESIRE, are available in Signet editions.

JOIN THE REGENCY READERS' PANEL

Help us bring you more of the books you like by filling out this survey and mailing it in today.

1. Book title:_____

   Book #:_____

2. Using the scale below how would you rate this book on the following features.

Poor		Not so Good			O.K.			Good		Excellent
0	1	2	3	4	5	6	7	8	9	10

Rating

Overall opinion of book. . . . . _____
Plot/Story . . . . _____
Setting/Location . . . . _____
Writing Style . . . . _____
Character Development . . . . _____
Conclusion/Ending . . . . _____
Scene on Front Cover . . . . _____

3. On average about how many romance books do you buy for

   yourself each month?_____

4. How would you classify yourself as a reader of Regency romances?
   I am a ( ) light ( ) medium ( ) heavy reader.

5. What is your education?
   ( ) High School (or less)   ( ) 4 yrs. college
   ( ) 2 yrs. college   ( ) Post Graduate

6. Age_____   7. Sex: ( ) Male ( ) Female

Please Print Name_____

Address_____

City_____State_____Zip_____

Phone # (   )_____

Thank you. Please send to New American Library, Research Dept, 1633 Broadway, New York, NY 10019.